TALES OF MYSTERY & THE SUPERNATURAL

TERROR BY NIGHT
Classic Ghost and Horror Stories

TERROR BY NIGHT

Classic Ghost and Horror Stories

Ambrose Bierce

with an Introduction by
DAVID STUART DAVIES

WORDSWORTH EDITIONS

In loving memory of
MICHAEL TRAYLER
the founder of Wordsworth Editions

2

Readers who are interested in other titles from
Wordsworth Editions are invited to visit our website at
www.wordsworth-editions.com

For our latest list and a full mail-order service contact
Bibliophile Books, 5 Thomas Road, London E14 7BN
Tel: +44 0207 515 9222 Fax: +44 0207 538 4115
e-mail: orders@bibliophilebooks.com

This edition published 2006 by
Wordsworth Editions Limited
8B East Street, Ware, Hertfordshire SG12 9HJ

ISBN 978-1-84022-534-1

© Wordsworth Editions Limited 2006

Wordsworth® is a registered trademark of
Wordsworth Editions Limited

All rights reserved. This publication may not be
reproduced, stored in a retrieval system or
transmitted in any form or by any means, electronic,
mechanical, photocopying, recording or otherwise,
without the prior permission of the publishers.

Typeset in Great Britain by Antony Gray
Printed by Clays Ltd, St Ives plc

CONTENTS

INTRODUCTION

'Nothing is so improbable as what is true.'

Of all the writers of ghost and horror stories, Ambrose Bierce is perhaps the most colourful. He was a dark, cynical and pessimistic soul who had a grim vision of fate and the unfairness of life which he channelled into his fiction. And in his death, or rather his disappearance, he created a mystery as strange and unresolved as any that he penned himself. But more of that later.

Ambrose Gwinett Bierce was born in a log cabin on 21 June 1842, in Horse Creek, Meigs County, Ohio, USA. He was the tenth of thirteen children, ten of whom survived infancy. His father, an unsuccessful farmer with an unseemly love of literature, had a given all the Bierce children first names beginning with A. There was Abigail, the eldest; then Amelia, Ann, Addison, Aurelius, etc. So oddness was a part of Bierce's life from the beginning.

Poverty and religion of the extreme variety were the two chief influences on young Ambrose's childhood. He not only hated this period of his life, he also developed a deep hatred for his family and this is reflected in some of his stories which depict families preying on and murdering one another. For example, the unforgettable opening sentence of 'An Imperfect Conflagration' seems to sum up his bitter attitude: 'Early in 1872 I murdered my father – an act that made a deep impression on me at the time.' These strong feelings against his family helped to develop his mordant wit and brutal irony – and, some would say, made him a difficult and unpleasant fellow to know.

These aspects of his character were further amplified by his involvement in the American Civil War when brother did in fact kill brother and families were divided against themselves. Bierce served in the war on the Union side. The horrible accidents and cruel twists of fate that he encountered during the conflict stimulated his imagination into creating what was regarded as a new genre – the short story that begins as a war story but then subtly changes into a psychological tale of terror. The most famous of Bierce's tales, 'An

Occurrence at Owl Creek', is a fine example. The story concerns a soldier caught by the enemy who is sentenced to be hanged. And then, miraculously, he believes that he has escaped the gallows. Bierce's ability to play with the notion of time and the reader's preconceptions is brilliantly handled in this narrative. At least three films have been made of the story. There was a silent version in the 1920s. A French version, called *La Rivière du Hibou* and directed by Robert Enrico, was made in black and white in 1962, faithfully recounting the original narrative using voice-over. A third version, directed by Brian James Egan, was released in 2005. The 1962 film was used for an episode of the television series 'The Twilight Zone'. This story typifies most of Bierce's other work in that it is bleak, with a cruel twist at the end. But that was how this writer saw life. He once observed, 'Death is not the end. There remains the litigation over the estate.' For such thoughts one critic gave him the nickname 'Bitter Bierce'.

He was a good soldier, achieving the rank of major for 'his distinguished services', and was given permission to resign his commission shortly before the Civil War ended. Having entered the conflict as a lowly farm lad, he was now a gentleman. He had escaped the shackles of his claustrophobic and impoverished upbringing. He landed in San Francisco in 1867, and there decided on a career in journalism. Self-taught, he eventually attained a regular job on the *San Francisco News Letter*. Very soon Ambrose Bierce became one of the city's great literary figures, being numbered with the likes of Mark Twain and Bret Harte.

In 1871, he courted and wed Mary Ellen ('Mollie') Day, a San Franciscan socialite from one of the best families of the city. The same year his first published story, 'The Haunted Valley', appeared. This strange and engrossing tale has none of the stylistic immaturities of a writer's early work. It is assured and confident in tone and quite complex. This short story has many of the qualities and structural features found in most of Bierce's work, including the rather shocking surprise ending which makes you want to read it again in order to reassure yourself that some important detail did not escape your notice. Certainly, the casual reader will miss many of the subtleties, clues if you like, which support and illuminate the dénouement. But Bierce is not for the casual reader.

He remained in San Francisco for many years, eventually becoming famous as a contributor to, and/or editor of, a number of local newspapers and periodicals, including *The San Francisco News Letter*, the

Argonaut, and the *Wasp*. He continued to write short stories as well as penning controversial columns full of wit and criticism, the most famous of which was called Prattle. He lived and wrote in England from 1872 to 1875. Returning to the United States, he took up residence in San Francisco once more.

It was during this later period that he began work on his most famous book, *The Devil's Dictionary* (originally called *The Cynic's Work Book*), a collection of definitions editorially tinged with bitterness, scepticism, pessimism and social comment. Above all, they are very funny, demonstating there was a dark vein of humour present in the apparently gloomy and troubled persona of the author. Here are a few examples of entries in this notorious volume:

Cat: a soft, indestructible automaton provided by Nature to be kicked when things go wrong in the domestic circle.

Idiot: member of a large and powerful tribe whose influence in human affairs has always been dominant and controlling.

Justice: a commodity which in a more or less adulterated condition the State sells to the citizen as a reward for his allegiance, taxes and personal service.

Love: a temporary insanity curable by marriage.

Patience: a minor form of despair, disguised as a virtue.

Philosophy: a route of many roads leading from nowhere to nothing.

Religion: a daughter of Hope and Fear, explaining to Ignorance the nature of the Unknowable.

Vote: the instrument and symbol of a free man's power to make a fool of himself and a wreck of his country.

Zeal: a certain nervous disorder afflicting the young and inexperienced.

In 1887, Bierce became one of the first regular columnists and editorialists to be employed on William Randolph Hearst's newspaper the *San Francisco Examiner*, eventually becoming one of the most prominent and influential among the writers and journalists of the West Coast. In December 1899 he moved to Washington DC, but continued his association with the Hearst newspapers until 1906.

At the turn of the century, Bierce's personal life began to crumble. His son Leigh died of pneumonia related to alcoholism. In 1904, his wife Mollie filed for divorce on the grounds of 'abandonment', but she died before the proceedings were finalised. Bierce continued writing through this period, but became less and less involved in the world around him.

Ironically, the greatest fame that Ambrose Bierce achieved was by simply vanishing from life. In 1912, after three years of fitful retirement from literary endeavours, he journeyed to Mexico with no apparent object in view. The last word that was ever heard from him came in a letter he posted in Chihuahua, Mexico in 1913: 'If you hear of my being stood up against a Mexican wall and shot to rags, please know that I think it's a pretty good way to depart this life. It beats old age, disease, or falling down the cellar stairs. To be a Gringo in Mexico – ah, that is euthanasia.' He was never heard of again. His death has not been recorded and no body has ever been found. What really happened to Ambrose Bierce is still a mystery and is likely to remain so. In many ways it is fitting for a man who created so many dark and surprising scenarios in his fiction to end his life with a question mark – his own personal, autobiographical twist in the tail.

Ambrose Bierce wrote ninety or so stories during his lifetime, but never turned his hand to writing a novel. In fact, he derided the novels of his time because he believed they were constructed in a manner that became predictable and slavish to the demands of probability. He defined the novel as 'a short story padded'. His short stories were the polar opposite of such an approach. He was the master of improbability. Stating his philosphy on this matter, he wrote: 'Nothing is so improbable as what is true. It is the unexpected that occurs; but that is not saying enough; it is also the unlikely – one might almost say the impossible.' He certainly applied this theory to his own fiction. He believed that the short shory was a superior form of creative expression because it was limited only to truths of the psyche rather than being committed to the realistic creation of social events and interaction. He was more interested in the unexpected, the strange incidents of fate and accident: improbable truths – and, indeed, sometimes apparently impossible truths. But the reader who has read his words will always be prepared to believe in these truths.

His stories invariably turn on these strange and often heart-stopping twists of fate – twists that are calculated to shock and shake the reader out of a comfortable complacency to reevaluate the events in the story and indeed in reality itself.

Bierce scholar Professor E. J. Hopkins divided the author's output into three categories: the Tales of Horror, the World of War and the World of Tall Stories. However, many of the stories seem to fit more than one heading. 'An Occurrence at Owl Creek' is a case in point. Because of its American Civil War background, Hopkins places this in the World of War section, but it remains one of Bierce's most chilling and unnerving tales. Certainly for this collection we have scooped up all of the Tales of Horror but we have also dipped into the other two categories for suitable tales to add to our dark brew.

It would be inappropriate and a rather a demanding task to talk about all the stories in this volume before you, the reader, are let loose on them. However, certain stories are worthy of comment if only to alert you to the kind of experiences which await you when you start to devour them.

One of the most anthologised of Bierce's tales is 'The Eyes of the Panther'. The story is created like a jigsaw with four pieces that the reader needs to fit together in order to see the whole picture. However, this is not easy as incidents are presented to us wreathed in the diverting mist of words that Bierce typically uses to entice the reader, while at the same time not quite providing a clear view of events. The story, short though it is, is split into four parts, entitled in a bleakly humorous way: One Does Not Always Marry When Insane; A Room May Be Too Narrow for Three, Though One is Outside; The Theory of Defence; An Appeal to the Conscience of God. On reaching the chilling end, you are still not sure you have quite grasped the truth of the matter or, if you have, it is really too horrible to contemplate. This story exemplifies the format that Bierce returned to time and time again: the factual, objective style; the often puzzling delivery of the narrative; the touches of dark, some might say misplaced humour; and the final surprise twist. The story also demonstrates that Bierce is not an easy read. I hesitate to use the phrase 'an acquired taste', but we are certainly in that area. However, those who do not find a natural affinity with his prose but who persevere are richly rewarded.

His classic 'The Moonlit Road' tells a ghost story from three perspectives, including that of the dead victim. It slowly unravels a tragedy which even when it is fully exposed is not really fully explained. And this element of uncertainty is what lifts this story to make it a great one. There is also, in the telling, a great sadness which perhaps reflects Bierce's own miserable view of existence. In the story, the narrators – the son, the murderer, the dead woman – all convey a sense of despair with life. The story opens with a typically bitter, ironical observation from the son:

'I am the most unfortunate of men. Rich, respected, fairly well educated and of sound health – with many other advantages usually valued by those having them and coveted by those who have them not – I sometimes think that I should be less unhappy if they had been denied me, for then the contrast between my outer and inner life would not be continually demanding a painful attention.'

It is a case of you can't win. Even with all the advantages he has, fate decrees that the son cannot enjoy them because his inner life has been damaged by events. While we may have some control over our outer life, Bierce observes, we have none over the inner life.

One final example of Bierce's work is 'The Middle Toe of the Right Foot'. Again we are challenged to piece together a complex ghost story which is presented to us in three sections. Again comes the surprise ending and the strange sense that we are not being given all the information we need to create a full and comprehensive narrative. There remains, yet again, a shady corner which can only be illuminated by the reader's individual imagination.

Although Bierce's stories are short – bite-sized, you might say – they are not quickly or easily digested. To continue the food analogy, they are like rich puddings, thick of texture and laced with some unkown intoxicant. Devour them slowly; savour them and digest at leisure. They are an indulgence well worth giving way to.

DAVID STUART DAVIES

An Occurrence at Owl Creek Bridge

I

A man stood upon a railroad bridge in northern Alabama, looking
down into the swift water twenty feet below. The man's hands were
behind his back, the wrists bound with a cord. A rope closely
encircled his neck. It was attached to a stout cross-timber above his
head and the slack fell to the level of his knees. Some loose boards
laid upon the ties supporting the rails of the railway supplied a
footing for him and his executioners – two private soldiers of the
Federal army, directed by a sergeant who in civil life may have
been a deputy sheriff. At a short remove upon the same temporary
platform was an officer in the uniform of his rank, armed. He was
a captain. A sentinel at each end of the bridge stood with his rifle
in the position known as 'support', that is to say, vertical in front
of the left shoulder, the hammer resting on the forearm thrown
straight across the chest – a formal and unnatural position, enforcing an erect carriage of the body. It did not appear to be the
duty of these two men to know what was occurring at the centre of
the bridge; they merely blockaded the two ends of the foot planking
that traversed it.

Beyond one of the sentinels nobody was in sight; the railroad ran
straight away into a forest for a hundred yards, then, curving, was
lost to view. Doubtless there was an outpost farther along. The other
bank of the stream was open ground – a gentle slope topped with a
stockade of vertical tree trunks, loopholed for rifles, with a single
embrasure through which protruded the muzzle of a brass cannon
commanding the bridge. Midway up the slope between the bridge
and fort were the spectators – a single company of infantry in line, at
'parade rest', the butts of their rifles on the ground, the barrels
inclining slightly backward against the right shoulder, the hands
crossed upon the stock. A lieutenant stood at the right of the line, the
point of his sword upon the ground, his left hand resting upon his
right. Excepting the group of four at the centre of the bridge, not a

man moved. The company faced the bridge, staring stonily, motionless. The sentinels, facing the banks of the stream, might have been
statues to adorn the bridge. The captain stood with folded arms,
silent, observing the work of his subordinates, but making no sign.
Death is a dignitary who when he comes announced is to be received
with formal manifestations of respect, even by those most familiar
with him. In the code of military etiquette silence and fixity are
forms of deference.

The man who was engaged in being hanged was apparently about
thirty-five years of age. He was a civilian, if one might judge from his
habit, which was that of a planter. His features were good – a straight
nose, firm mouth, broad forehead, from which his long, dark hair
was combed straight back, falling behind his ears to the collar of his
well-fitting frock coat. He wore a moustache and pointed beard, but
no whiskers; his eyes were large and dark grey, and had a kindly
expression which one would hardly have expected in one whose neck
was in the hemp. Evidently this was no vulgar assassin. The liberal
military code makes provision for hanging many kinds of persons,
and gentlemen are not excluded.

The preparations being complete, the two private soldiers stepped
aside and each drew away the plank upon which he had been standing. The sergeant turned to the captain, saluted and placed himself
immediately behind that officer, who in turn moved apart one
pace. These movements left the condemned man and the sergeant
standing on the two ends of the same plank, which spanned three of
the cross-ties of the bridge. The end upon which the civilian stood
almost, but not quite, reached a fourth. This plank had been held in
place by the weight of the captain; it was now held by that of the
sergeant. At a signal from the former the latter would step aside, the
plank would tilt and the condemned man go down between two ties.
The arrangement commended itself to his judgement as simple
and effective. His face had not been covered nor his eyes bandaged.
He looked a moment at his 'unsteadfast footing', then let his gaze
wander to the swirling water of the stream racing madly beneath his
feet. A piece of dancing driftwood caught his attention and his eyes
followed it down the current. How slowly it appeared to move! What
a sluggish stream!

He closed his eyes in order to fix his last thoughts upon his
wife and children. The water, touched to gold by the early sun, the
brooding mists under the banks at some distance down the stream,
the fort, the soldiers, the piece of drift – all had distracted him. And

now he became conscious of a new disturbance. Striking through the thought of his dear ones was a sound which he could neither ignore nor understand, a sharp, distinct, metallic percussion like the stroke of a blacksmith's hammer upon the anvil; it had the same ringing quality. He wondered what it was, and whether immeasurably distant or nearby – it seemed both. Its recurrence was regular, but as slow as the tolling of a death knell. He awaited each new stroke with impatience and – he knew not why – apprehension. The intervals of silence grew progressively longer; the delays became maddening. With their greater infrequency the sounds increased in strength and sharpness. They hurt his ear like the trust of a knife; he feared he would shriek. What he heard was the ticking of his watch.

He unclosed his eyes and saw again the water below him. 'If I could free my hands,' he thought, 'I might throw off the noose and spring into the stream. By diving I could evade the bullets and, swimming vigorously, reach the bank, take to the woods and get away home. My home, thank God, is as yet outside their lines; my wife and little ones are still beyond the invader's farthest advance.'

As these thoughts, which have here to be set down in words, were flashed into the doomed man's brain rather than evolved from it the captain nodded to the sergeant. The sergeant stepped aside.

2

Peyton Farquhar was a well-to-do planter, of an old and highly respected Alabama family. Being a slave-owner and like other slave-owners a politician, he was naturally an original secessionist and ardently devoted to the Southern cause. Circumstances of an imperious nature, which it is unnecessary to relate here, had prevented him from taking service with that gallant army which had fought the disastrous campaigns ending with the fall of Corinth, and he chafed under the inglorious restraint, longing for the release of his energies, the larger life of the soldier, the opportunity for distinction. That opportunity, he felt, would come, as it comes to all in wartime. Meanwhile he did what he could. No service was too humble for him to perform in the aid of the South, no adventure too perilous for him to undertake if consistent with the character of a civilian who was at heart a soldier, and who in good faith and without too much qualification assented to at least a part of the frankly villainous dictum that all is fair in love and war.

One evening while Farquhar and his wife were sitting on a rustic bench near the entrance to his grounds, a grey-clad soldier rode up to the gate and asked for a drink of water. Mrs Farquhar was only too happy to serve him with her own white hands. While she was fetching the water her husband approached the dusty horseman and enquired eagerly for news from the front.

'The Yanks are repairing the railroads,' said the man, 'and are getting ready for another advance. They have reached the Owl Creek bridge, put it in order and built a stockade on the north bank. The commandant has issued an order, which is posted everywhere, declaring that any civilian caught interfering with the railroad, its bridges, tunnels, or trains will be summarily hanged. I saw the order.'

'How far is it to the Owl Creek bridge?' Farquhar asked.

'About thirty miles.'

'Is there no force on this side of the creek?'

'Only a picket post half a mile out, on the railroad, and a single sentinel at this end of the bridge.'

'Suppose a man – a civilian and student of hanging – should elude the picket post and perhaps get the better of the sentinel,' said Farquhar, smiling, 'what could he accomplish?'

The soldier reflected. 'I was there a month ago,' he replied. 'I observed that the flood of last winter had lodged a great quantity of driftwood against the wooden pier at this end of the bridge. It is now dry and would burn like tinder.'

The lady had now brought the water, which the soldier drank. He thanked her ceremoniously, bowed to her husband and rode away. An hour later, after nightfall, he repassed the plantation, going northward in the direction from which he had come. He was a Federal scout.

3

As Peyton Farquhar fell straight downward through the bridge he lost consciousness and was as one already dead. From this state he was awakened – ages later, it seemed to him – by the pain of a sharp pressure upon his throat, followed by a sense of suffocation. Keen, poignant agonies seemed to shoot from his neck downward through every fibre of his body and limbs. These pains appeared to flash along well-defined lines of ramification and to beat with an inconceivably rapid periodicity. They seemed like streams of pulsating fire heating him to an intolerable temperature. As to his head, he was conscious of nothing but a feeling of fullness – of congestion. These sensations were unaccompanied by thought. The intellectual part of his nature was already effaced; he had power only to feel, and feeling was torment. He was conscious of motion. Encompassed in a luminous cloud, of which he was now merely the fiery heart, without material substance, he swung through unthinkable arcs of oscillation, like a vast pendulum. Then all at once, with terrible suddenness, the light about him shot upward with the noise of a loud splash; a frightful roaring was in his ears, and all was cold and dark. The power of thought was restored; he knew that the rope had broken and he had fallen into the stream. There was no additional strangulation; the noose about his neck was already suffocating him and kept the water from his lungs. To die of hanging at the bottom of a river! – the idea seemed to him ludicrous. He opened his eyes in the darkness and saw above him a gleam of light, but how distant, how inaccessible! He was still sinking, for the light became fainter and fainter until it was a mere glimmer. Then it began to grow and brighten, and he knew that he was rising toward the surface – knew it with reluctance, for he was now very comfortable. 'To be hanged and drowned,' he thought, 'that is not so bad; but I do not wish to be shot. No, I will not be shot; that is not fair.'

He was not conscious of an effort, but a sharp pain in his wrist apprised him that he was trying to free his hands. He gave the struggle his attention, as an idler might observe the feat of a juggler, without interest in the outcome. What splendid effort! What magnificent, what superhuman strength! Ah, that was a fine endeavour! Bravo! The cord fell away; his arms parted and floated upward, the hands dimly seen on each side in the growing light. He watched them with a new interest as first one and then the other pounced upon the noose at his neck. They tore it away and thrust it fiercely aside, its undulations resembling those of a water snake. 'Put it back, put it back!' He thought he shouted these words to his hands, for the undoing of the noose had been succeeded by the direst pang that he had yet experienced. His neck ached horribly; his brain was on fire, his heart, which had been fluttering faintly, gave a great leap, trying to force itself out at his mouth. His whole body was racked and wrenched with an insupportable anguish! But his disobedient hands gave no heed to the command. They beat the water vigorously with quick, downward strokes, forcing him to the surface. He felt his head emerge; his eyes were blinded by the sunlight; his chest expanded convulsively, and with a supreme and crowning agony his lungs engulfed a great draught of air, which instantly he expelled in a shriek!

He was now in full possession of his physical senses. They were, indeed, preternaturally keen and alert. Something in the awful disturbance of his organic system had so exalted and refined them that they made record of things never before perceived. He felt the ripples upon his face and heard their separate sounds as they struck. He looked at the forest on the bank of the stream, saw the individual trees, the leaves and the veining of each leaf – he saw the very insects upon them: the locusts, the brilliant-bodied flies, the grey spiders stretching their webs from twig to twig. He noted the prismatic colours in all the dewdrops upon a million blades of grass. The humming of the gnats that danced above the eddies of the stream, the beating of the dragonflies' wings, the strokes of the water-spiders' legs, like oars which had lifted their boat – all these made audible music. A fish slid along beneath his eyes and he heard the rush of its body parting the water.

He had come to the surface facing down the stream; in a moment the visible world seemed to wheel slowly round, himself the pivotal point, and he saw the bridge, the fort, the soldiers upon the bridge, the captain, the sergeant, the two privates, his executioners. They were in silhouette against the blue sky. They shouted and gesticulated, pointing at him. The captain had drawn his pistol, but did not fire; the others were unarmed. Their movements were grotesque and horrible, their forms gigantic.

Suddenly he heard a sharp report and something struck the water smartly within a few inches of his head, spattering his face with spray. He heard a second report, and saw one of the sentinels with his rifle at his shoulder, a light cloud of blue smoke rising from the muzzle. The man in the water saw the eye of the man on the bridge gazing into his own through the sights of the rifle. He observed that it was a grey eye and remembered having read that grey eyes were keenest, and that all famous marksmen had them. Nevertheless, this one had missed.

A counter-swirl had caught Farquhar and turned him half round; he was again looking at the forest on the bank opposite the fort. The sound of a clear, high voice in a monotonous singsong now rang out behind him and came across the water with a distinctness that pierced and subdued all other sounds, even the beating of the ripples in his ears. Although no soldier, he had frequented camps enough to know the dread significance of that deliberate, drawling, aspirated chant; the lieutenant on shore was taking a part in the morning's work. How coldly and pitilessly – with what an even, calm intonation, presaging and enforcing tranquillity in the men – with what accurately measured interval fell those cruel words: 'Company! . . . Attention! . . . Shoulder arms! . . . Ready!. . . Aim! . . . Fire!'

Farquhar dived – dived as deeply as he could. The water roared in his ears like the voice of Niagara, yet he heard the dull thunder of the volley and, rising again toward the surface, met shining bits of metal, singularly flattened, oscillating slowly downward. Some of them touched him on the face and hands, then fell away, continuing their descent. One lodged between his collar and neck; it was uncomfortably warm and he snatched it out.

As he rose to the surface, gasping for breath, he saw that he had been a long time under water; he was perceptibly farther downstream – nearer to safety. The soldiers had almost finished reloading; the metal ramrods flashed all at once in the sunshine as they were drawn from the barrels, turned in the air, and thrust into their sockets. The two sentinels fired again, independently and ineffectually.

The hunted man saw all this over his shoulder; he was now swimming vigorously with the current. His brain was as energetic as his arms and legs; he thought with the rapidity of lightning.

'The officer,' he reasoned, 'will not make that martinet's error a second time. It is as easy to dodge a volley as a single shot. He has probably already given the command to fire at will. God help me, I cannot dodge them all!'

An appalling splash within two yards of him was followed by a loud, rushing sound, *diminuendo*, which seemed to travel back through the air to the fort and died in an explosion which stirred the very river to its deeps! A rising sheet of water curved over him, fell down upon him, blinded him, strangled him! The cannon had taken a hand in the game. As he shook his head free from the commotion of the smitten water he heard the deflected shot humming through the air ahead, and in an instant it was cracking and smashing the branches in the forest beyond.

'They will not do that again,' he thought; 'the next time they will use a charge of grape. I must keep my eye upon the gun; the smoke will apprise me – the report arrives too late; it lags behind the missile. That is a good gun.'

Suddenly he felt himself whirled round and round – spinning like a top. The water, the banks, the forests, the now distant bridge, fort and men, all were commingled and blurred. Objects were represented by their colours only; circular horizontal streaks of colour – that was all he saw. He had been caught in a vortex and was being whirled on with a velocity of advance and gyration that made him giddy and sick. In few moments he was flung upon the gravel at the foot of the left bank of the stream – the southern bank – and behind a projecting point which concealed him from his enemies. The sudden arrest of his motion, the abrasion of one of his hands on the gravel, restored him, and he wept with delight. He dug his fingers into the sand, threw it over himself in handfuls and audibly blessed it. It looked like diamonds, rubies, emeralds; he could think of nothing beautiful which it did not resemble. The trees upon the bank were giant garden plants; he noted a definite order in their arrangement, inhaled the fragrance of their blooms. A strange roseate light shone through the spaces among their trunks and the wind made in their branches the music of Aeolian harps. He had no wish to perfect his escape – he was content to remain in that enchanting spot until retaken.

A whiz and a rattle of grapeshot among the branches high above his head roused him from his dream. The baffled cannoneer had fired him a random farewell. He sprang to his feet, rushed up the sloping bank, and plunged into the forest.

All that day he travelled, laying his course by the rounding sun. The forest seemed interminable; nowhere did he discover a break in it, not even a woodman's road. He had not known that he lived in so wild a region. There was something uncanny in the revelation.

By nightfall he was fatigued, footsore, famished. The thought of his wife and children urged him on. At last he found a road which led him in what he knew to be the right direction. It was as wide and straight as a city street, yet it seemed untravelled. No fields bordered it, no dwelling anywhere. Not so much as the barking of a dog suggested human habitation. The black bodies of the trees formed a straight wall on both sides, terminating on the horizon in a point, like a diagram in a lesson in perspective. Overhead, as he looked up through this rift in the wood, shone great golden stars looking unfamiliar and grouped in strange constellations. He was sure they were arranged in some order which had a secret and malign significance. The wood on either side was full of singular noises, among which – once, twice, and again – he distinctly heard whispers in an unknown tongue.

His neck was in pain and lifting his hand to it found it horribly swollen. He knew that it had a circle of black where the rope had bruised it. His eyes felt congested; he could no longer close them. His tongue was swollen with thirst; he relieved its fever by thrusting it forward from between his teeth into the cold air. How softly the turf had carpeted the untravelled avenue – he could no longer feel the roadway beneath his feet!

Doubtless, despite his suffering, he had fallen asleep while walking, for now he sees another scene – perhaps he has merely recovered from a delirium. He stands at the gate of his own home. All is as he left it, and all bright and beautiful in the morning sunshine. He must have travelled the entire night. As he pushes open the gate and passes up the wide white walk, he sees a flutter of female garments; his wife, looking fresh and cool and sweet, steps down from the veranda to meet him. At the bottom of the steps she stands waiting, with a smile of ineffable joy, an attitude of matchless grace and dignity. Ah, how beautiful she is! He springs forwards with extended arms. As he is about to clasp her he feels a stunning blow upon the back of the neck; a blinding white light blazes all about him with a sound like the shock of a cannon – then all is darkness and silence!

Peyton Farquhar was dead; his body, with a broken neck, swung gently from side to side beneath the timbers of the Owl Creek bridge.

The Moonlit Road

Statement of Joel Hetman, Jr.

I am the most unfortunate of men. Rich, respected, fairly well educated and of sound health – with many other advantages usually valued by those having them and coveted by those who have them not – I sometimes think that I should be less unhappy if they had been denied me, for then the contrast between my outer and my inner life would not be continually demanding a painful attention. In the stress of privation and the need of effort I might sometimes forget the sombre secret ever baffling the conjecture that it compels.

I am the only child of Joel and Julia Hetman. The one was a well-to-do country gentleman, the other a beautiful and accomplished woman to whom he was passionately attached with what I now know to have been a jealous and exacting devotion. The family home was a few miles from Nashville, Tennessee, a large, irregularly built dwelling of no particular order of architecture, a little way off the road, in a park of trees and shrubbery.

At the time of which I write I was nineteen years old, a student at Yale. One day I received a telegram from my father of such urgency that in compliance with its unexplained demand I left at once for home. At the railway station in Nashville a distant relative awaited me to apprise me of the reason for my recall: my mother had been barbarously murdered – why and by whom none could conjecture, but the circumstances were these: My father had gone to Nashville, intending to return the next afternoon. Something prevented his accomplishing the business in hand, so he returned on the same night, arriving just before the dawn. In his testimony before the coroner he explained that having no latchkey and not caring to disturb the sleeping servants, he had, with no clearly defined intention, gone round to the rear of the house. As he turned an angle of the building, he heard a sound as of a door gently closed, and saw in the darkness, indistinctly, the figure of a man, which instantly disappeared among the trees of the lawn. A hasty pursuit and brief search of the grounds in the belief that the trespasser was someone secretly visiting a servant proving fruitless, he entered at the unlocked door and mounted the stairs to my mother's chamber. Its door was open, and stepping into black darkness he fell headlong over some heavy object on the floor. I may spare myself the details; it was my poor mother, dead of strangulation by human hands!

Nothing had been taken from the house, the servants had heard no sound, and excepting those terrible finger-marks upon the dead woman's throat – dear God! that I might forget them! – no trace of the assassin was ever found.

I gave up my studies and remained with my father, who, naturally, was greatly changed. Always of a sedate, taciturn disposition, he now fell into so deep a dejection that nothing could hold his attention, yet anything – a footfall, the sudden closing of a door – aroused in him a fitful interest; one might have called it an apprehension. At any small surprise of the senses he would start visibly and sometimes turn pale, then relapse into a melancholy apathy deeper than before. I suppose he was what is called a 'nervous wreck'. As to me, I was younger then than now – there is much in that. Youth is Gilead, in which is balm for every wound. Ah, that I might again dwell in that enchanted land! Unacquainted with grief, I knew not how to appraise my bereavement; I could not rightly estimate the strength of the stroke.

One night, a few months after the dreadful event, my father and I walked home from the city. The full moon was about three hours above the eastern horizon; the entire countryside had the solemn stillness of a summer night; our footfalls and the ceaseless song of the katydids were the only sound aloof. Black shadows of bordering trees lay athwart the road, which, in the short reaches between, gleamed a ghostly white. As we approached the gate to our dwelling, whose front was in shadow, and in which no light shone, my father suddenly stopped and clutched my arm, saying, hardly above his breath: 'God! God! What is that?'

'I hear nothing,' I replied.

'But see – see!' he said, pointing along the road, directly ahead.

I said: 'Nothing is there. Come, father, let us go in – you are ill.'

He had released my arm and was standing rigid and motionless in the centre of the illuminated roadway, staring like one bereft of sense. His face in the moonlight showed a pallor and fixity inexpressibly distressing. I pulled gently at his sleeve, but he had forgotten my existence. Presently he began to retire backward, step by step, never for an instant removing his eyes from what he saw, or thought he saw. I turned half round to follow, but stood irresolute. I do not recall any feeling of fear, unless a sudden chill was its physical manifestation. It seemed as if an icy wind had touched my face and enfolded my body from head to foot; I could feel the stir of it in my hair.

At that moment my attention was drawn to a light that suddenly streamed from an upper window of the house: one of the servants, awakened by what mysterious premonition of evil who can say, and in obedience to an impulse that she was never able to name, had lit a lamp. When I turned to look for my father he was gone, and in all the years that have passed no whisper of his fate has come across the borderland of conjecture from the realm of the unknown.

2

Statement of Caspar Grattan

Today I am said to live; tomorrow, here in this room, will lie a senseless shape of clay that all too long was I. If anyone lift the cloth from the face of that unpleasant thing it will be in gratification of a mere morbid curiosity. Some, doubtless, will go further and enquire, 'Who was he?' In this writing I supply the only answer that I am able to make – Caspar Grattan. Surely, that should be enough. The name has served my small need for more than twenty years of a life of unknown length. True, I gave it to myself, but lacking another I had the right. In this world one must have a name; it prevents confusion, even when it does not establish identity. Some, though, are known by numbers, which also seem inadequate distinctions.

One day, for illustration, I was passing along a street of a city, far from here, when I met two men in uniform, one of whom, half-pausing and looking curiously into my face, said to his companion, 'That man looks like 767.' Something in the number seemed familiar and horrible. Moved by an uncontrollable impulse, I sprang into a side street and ran until I fell exhausted in a country lane.

I have never forgotten that number, and always it comes to memory attended by gibbering obscenity, peals of joyless laughter, the clang of iron doors. So I say a name, even if self-bestowed, is better than a number. In the register of the potter's field I shall soon have both. What wealth!

Of him who shall find this paper I must beg a little consideration. It is not the history of my life; the knowledge to write that is denied me. This is only a record of broken and apparently unrelated memories, some of them as distinct and sequent as brilliant beads upon a thread, others remote and strange, having the character of crimson dreams with interspaces blank and black – witch-fires glowing still and red in a great desolation.

Standing upon the shore of eternity, I turn for a last look landward over the course by which I came. There are twenty years of foot-prints fairly distinct, the impressions of bleeding feet. They lead through poverty and pain, devious and unsure, as of one staggering beneath a burden –

> Remote, unfriended, melancholy, slow.

Ah, the poet's prophecy of Me – how admirable, how dreadfully admirable!

Backward beyond the beginning of this *via dolorosa* – this epic of suffering with episodes of sin – I see nothing clearly; it comes out of a cloud. I know that it spans only twenty years, yet I am an old man.

One does not remember one's birth – one has to be told. But with me it was different; life came to me full-handed and dowered me with all my faculties and powers. Of a previous existence I know no more than others, for all have stammering intimations that may be memories and may be dreams. I know only that my first conscious-ness was of maturity in body and mind – a consciousness accepted without surprise or conjecture. I merely found myself walking in a forest, half-clad, footsore, unutterably weary and hungry. Seeing a farmhouse, I approached and asked for food, which was given me by one who enquired my name. I did not know, yet knew that all had names. Greatly embarrassed, I retreated, and night coming on, lay down in the forest and slept.

The next day I entered a large town which I shall not name. Nor shall I recount further incidents of the life that is now to end – a life of wandering, always and everywhere haunted by an overmastering sense of crime in punishment of wrong and of terror in punishment of crime. Let me see if I can reduce it to narrative.

I seem once to have lived near a great city, a prosperous planter, married to a woman whom I loved and distrusted. We had, it some-times seems, one child, a youth of brilliant parts and promise. He is at all times a vague figure, never clearly drawn, frequently altogether out of the picture.

One luckless evening it occurred to me to test my wife's fidelity in a vulgar, commonplace way familiar to everyone who has acquaintance with the literature of fact and fiction. I went to the city, telling my wife that I should be absent until the following afternoon. But I returned before daybreak and went to the rear of the house, purposing to enter by a door with which I had secretly so tampered that it would seem to lock, yet not actually fasten. As I approached it, I heard it gently open and close, and saw a man steal away into the darkness. With murder in my heart, I sprang after him, but he had vanished without even the bad luck of identification. Sometimes now I cannot even persuade myself that it was a human being.

Crazed with jealousy and rage, blind and bestial with all the elemental passions of insulted manhood, I entered the house and sprang up the stairs to the door of my wife's chamber. It was closed, but having tampered with its lock also, I easily entered and despite the black darkness soon stood by the side of her bed. My groping hands told me that although disarranged it was unoccupied.

'She is below,' I thought, 'and terrified by my entrance has evaded me in the darkness of the hall.'

With the purpose of seeking her I turned to leave the room, but took a wrong direction – the right one! My foot struck her, cowering in a corner of the room. Instantly my hands were at her throat, stifling a shriek, my knees were upon her struggling body; and there in the darkness, without a word of accusation or reproach, I strangled her till she died!

There ends the dream. I have related it in the past tense, but the present would be the fitter form, for again and again the sombre tragedy re-enacts itself in my consciousness – over and over I lay the plan, I suffer the confirmation, I redress the wrong. Then all is blank; and afterward the rains beat against the grimy window-panes, or the snows fall upon my scant attire, the wheels rattle in the squalid streets where my life lies in poverty and mean employment. If there is ever sunshine I do not recall it; if there are birds they do not sing.

There is another dream, another vision of the night. I stand among the shadows in a moonlit road. I am aware of another presence, but whose I cannot rightly determine. In the shadow of a great dwelling I catch the gleam of white garments; then the figure of a woman confronts me in the road – my murdered wife! There is death in the face; there are marks upon the throat. The eyes are fixed on mine with an infinite gravity which is not reproach, nor hate, nor menace, nor anything less terrible than recognition. Before this awful apparition I retreat in terror – a terror that is upon me as I write. I can no longer rightly shape the words. See! they –

Now I am calm, but truly there is no more to tell: the incident ends where it began – in darkness and in doubt.

Yes, I am again in control of myself: 'the captain of my soul'. But that is not respite; it is another stage and phase of expiation. My penance, constant in degree, is mutable in kind: one of its variants is tranquillity. After all, it is only a life-sentence. 'To Hell for life' – that is a foolish penalty: the culprit chooses the duration of his punishment. Today my term expires.

To each and all, the peace that was not mine.

3
Statement of the late Julia Hetman, through the Medium Bayrolles

I had retired early and fallen almost immediately into a peaceful sleep, from which I awoke with that indefinable sense of peril which is, I think, a common experience in that other, earlier life. Of its unmeaning character, too, I was entirely persuaded, yet that did not banish it. My husband, Joel Hetman, was away from home; the servants slept in another part of the house. But these were familiar conditions; they had never before distressed me. Nevertheless, the strange terror grew so insupportable that conquering my reluctance to move I sat up and lit the lamp at my bedside. Contrary to my expectation this gave me no relief; the light seemed rather an added danger, for I reflected that it would shine out under the door, disclosing my presence to whatever evil thing might lurk outside. You that are still in the flesh, subject to horrors of the imagination, think what a monstrous fear that must be which seeks in darkness security from malevolent existences of the night. That is to spring to close quarters with an unseen enemy – the strategy of despair!

Extinguishing the lamp I pulled the bed-clothing about my head and lay trembling and silent, unable to shriek, forgetful to pray. In this pitiable state I must have lain for what you call hours – with us there are no hours, there is no time.

At last it came – a soft, irregular sound of footfalls on the stairs! They were slow, hesitant, uncertain, as of something that did not see its way; to my disordered reason all the more terrifying for that, as the approach of some blind and mindless malevolence to which is no appeal. I even thought that I must have left the hall lamp burning and the groping of this creature proved it a monster of the night. This was foolish and inconsistent with my previous dread of the light, but what would you have? Fear has no brains; it is an idiot. The dismal witness that it bears and the cowardly counsel that it whispers are unrelated. We know this well, we who have passed into the Realm of Terror, who skulk in eternal dusk among the scenes of our former lives, invisible even to ourselves and one another, yet hiding forlorn in lonely places; yearning for speech with our loved ones, yet dumb, and as fearful of them as they of us. Sometimes the disability is removed, the law suspended: by the deathless power of love or hate we break the spell – we are seen by those whom we would warn, console, or punish. What form we seem to them to bear we know not; we know only that we terrify even those whom we most wish to comfort, and from whom we most crave tenderness and sympathy.

Forgive, I pray you, this inconsequent digression by what was once a woman. You who consult us in this imperfect way – you do not understand. You ask foolish questions about things unknown and things forbidden. Much that we know and could impart in our speech is meaningless in yours. We must communicate with you through a stammering intelligence in that small fraction of our language that you yourselves can speak. You think that we are of another world. No, we have knowledge of no world but yours, though for us it holds no sunlight, no warmth, no music, no laughter, no song of birds, nor any companionship. O God! What a thing it is to be a ghost, cowering and shivering in an altered world, a prey to apprehension and despair!

No, I did not die of fright: the Thing turned and went away. I heard it go down the stairs, hurriedly, I thought, as if itself in sudden fear. Then I rose to call for help. Hardly had my shaking hand found the doorknob when – merciful heaven! – I heard it returning. Its footfalls as it remounted the stairs were rapid, heavy and loud; they shook the house. I fled to an angle of the wall and crouched upon the floor. I tried to pray. I tried to call the name of my dear husband. Then I heard the door thrown open. There was an interval of unconsciousness, and when I revived I felt a strangling clutch upon my throat – felt my arms feebly beating against something that bore me backward – felt my tongue thrusting itself from between my teeth! And then I passed into this life.

No, I have no knowledge of what it was. The sum of what we knew at death is the measure of what we know afterward of all that went before. Of this existence we know many things, but no new light falls upon any page of that; in memory is written all of it that we can read. Here are no heights of truth overlooking the confused landscape of that dubitable domain. We still dwell in the Valley of the Shadow, lurk in its desolate places, peering from brambles and thickets at its mad, malign inhabitants. How should we have new knowledge of that fading past?

What I am about to relate happened on a night. We know when it is night, for then you retire to your houses and we can venture from our places of concealment to move unafraid about our old homes, to look in at the windows, even to enter and gaze upon your faces as you sleep. I had lingered long near the dwelling where I had been so cruelly changed to what I am, as we do while any that we love or hate remain. Vainly I had sought some method of manifestation, some way to make my continued existence and my great love and poignant pity understood by my husband and son. Always if they slept they would wake, or if in my desperation I dared approach them when they were awake, would turn toward me the terrible eyes of the living, frightening me by the glances that I sought from the purpose that I held.

On this night I had searched for them without success, fearing to find them; they were nowhere in the house, nor about the moonlit lawn. For, although the sun is lost to us forever, the moon, full-orbed or slender, remains to us. Sometimes it shines by night, sometimes by day, but always it rises and sets, as in that other life.

I left the lawn and moved in the white light and silence along the road, aimless and sorrowing. Suddenly I heard the voice of my poor husband in exclamations of astonishment, with that of my son in reassurance and dissuasion; and there by the shadow of a group of trees they stood – near, so near! Their faces were toward me, the eyes of the elder man fixed upon mine. He saw me – at last, at last, he saw me! In the consciousness of that, my terror fled as a cruel dream. The death-spell was broken: Love had conquered Law! Mad with exultation I shouted – I *must* have shouted, 'He sees, he sees: he will understand!' Then, controlling myself, I moved forward, smiling and consciously beautiful, to offer myself to his arms, to comfort him with endearments, and, with my son's hand in mine, to speak words that should restore the broken bonds between the living and the dead.

Alas! alas! his face went white with fear, his eyes were as those of a hunted animal. He backed away from me, as I advanced, and at last turned and fled into the wood – whither, it is not given to me to know.

To my poor boy, left doubly desolate, I have never been able to impart a sense of my presence. Soon he, too, must pass to this Life Invisible and be lost to me forever.

Haita the Shepherd

In the heart of Haita the illusions of youth had not been supplanted by those of age and experience. His thoughts were pure and pleasant, for his life was simple and his soul devoid of ambition. He rose with the sun and went forth to pray at the shrine of Hastur, the god of shepherds, who heard and was pleased. After performance of this pious rite Haita unbarred the gate of the fold and with a cheerful mind drove his flock afield, eating his morning meal of curds and oat cake as he went, occasionally pausing to add a few berries, cold with dew, or to drink of the waters that came away from the hills to join the stream in the middle of the valley and be borne along with it, he knew not whither.

During the long summer day, as his sheep cropped the good grass which the gods had made to grow for them, or lay with their forelegs doubled under their breasts and chewed the cud, Haita, reclining in the shadow of a tree, or sitting upon a rock, played so sweet music upon his reed pipe that sometimes from the corner of his eye he got accidental glimpses of the minor sylvan deities, leaning forward out of the copse to hear; but if he looked at them directly they vanished. From this – for he must be thinking if he would not turn into one of his own sheep – he drew the solemn inference that happiness may come if not sought, but if looked for will never be seen; for next to the favour of Hastur, who never disclosed himself, Haita most valued the friendly interest of his neighbours, the shy immortals of the wood and stream. At nightfall he drove his flock back to the fold, saw that the gate was secure and retired to his cave for refreshment and for dreams.

So passed his life, one day like another, save when the storms uttered the wrath of an offended god. Then Haita cowered in his cave, his face hidden in his hands, and prayed that he alone might be punished for his sins and the world saved from destruction. Sometimes when there was a great rain, and the stream came out of its banks, compelling him to urge his terrified flock to the uplands, he interceded for the people in the cities which he had been told lay in the plain beyond the two blue hills forming the gateway of his valley.

'It is kind of thee, O Hastur,' so he prayed, 'to give me mountains so near to my dwelling and my fold that I and my sheep can escape the angry torrents; but the rest of the world thou must thyself deliver in some way that I know not of, or I will no longer worship thee.'

And Hastur, knowing that Haita was a youth who kept his word, spared the cities and turned the waters into the sea.

So he had lived since he could remember. He could not rightly conceive any other mode of existence. The holy hermit who dwelt at the head of the valley, a full hour's journey away, from whom he had heard the tale of the great cities where dwelt people – poor souls! – who had no sheep, gave him no knowledge of that early time, when, so he reasoned, he must have been small and helpless like a lamb.

It was through thinking on these mysteries and marvels, and on that horrible change to silence and decay which he felt sure must some time come to him, as he had seen it come to so many of his flock – as it came to all living things except the birds – that Haita first became conscious how miserable and hopeless was his lot.

'It is necessary,' he said, 'that I know whence and how I came; for how can one perform his duties unless able to judge what they are by the way in which he was entrusted with them? And what contentment can I have when I know not how long it is going to last? Perhaps before another sun I may be changed, and then what will become of the sheep? What, indeed, will have become of me?'

Pondering these things Haita became melancholy and morose. He no longer spoke cheerfully to his flock, nor ran with alacrity to the shrine of Hastur. In every breeze he heard whispers of malign deities whose existence he now first observed. Every cloud was a portent signifying disaster, and the darkness was full of terrors. His reed pipe when applied to his lips gave out no melody, but a dismal wail; the sylvan and riparian intelligences no longer thronged the thicket-side to listen, but fled from the sound, as he knew by the stirred leaves and bent flowers. He relaxed his vigilance and many of his sheep strayed away into the hills and were lost. Those that remained became lean and ill for lack of good pasturage, for he would not seek it for them, but conducted them day after day to the same spot, through mere abstraction, while puzzling about life and death – of immortality he knew not.

One day while indulging in the gloomiest reflections he suddenly sprang from the rock upon which he sat, and with a determined gesture of the right hand exclaimed: 'I will no longer be a suppliant for knowledge which the gods withhold. Let them look to it that they do me no wrong. I will do my duty as best I can and if I err upon their own heads be it!'

Suddenly, as he spoke, a great brightness fell about him, causing him to look upward, thinking the sun had burst through a rift in the clouds; but there were no clouds. No more than an arm's length away stood a beautiful maiden. So beautiful she was that the flowers about her feet folded their petals in despair and bent their heads in token of submission; so sweet her look that the humming birds thronged her eyes, thrusting their thirsty bills almost into them, and the wild bees were about her lips. And such was her brightness that the shadows of all objects lay divergent from her feet, turning as she moved.

Haita was entranced. Rising, he knelt before her in adoration, and she laid her hand upon his head.

'Come,' she said in a voice that had the music of all the bells of his flock – 'come, thou art not to worship me, who am no goddess, but if thou art truthful and dutiful I will abide with thee.'

Haita seized her hand, and stammering his joy and gratitude arose, and hand in hand they stood and smiled into each other's eyes. He gazed on her with reverence and rapture. He said: 'I pray thee, lovely maid, tell me thy name and whence and why thou comest.'

At this she laid a warning finger on her lip and began to withdraw. Her beauty underwent a visible alteration that made him shudder, he knew not why, for still she was beautiful. The landscape was darkened by a giant shadow sweeping across the valley with the speed of a vulture. In the obscurity the maiden's figure grew dim and indistinct and her voice seemed to come from a distance, as she said, in a tone of sorrowful reproach: 'Presumptuous and ungrateful youth! Must I then so soon leave thee? Would nothing do but thou must at once break the eternal compact?'

Inexpressibly grieved, Haita fell upon his knees and implored her to remain – rose and sought her in the deepening darkness – ran in circles, calling to her aloud, but all in vain. She was no longer visible, but out of the gloom he heard her voice saying: 'Nay, thou shalt not have me by seeking. Go to thy duty, faithless shepherd, or we shall never meet again.'

Night had fallen; the wolves were howling in the hills and the terrified sheep crowding about Haita's feet. In the demands of the hour he forgot his disappointment, drove his sheep to the fold and repairing to the place of worship poured out his heart in gratitude to Hastur for permitting him to save his flock, then retired to his cave and slept.

When Haita awoke the sun was high and shone in at the cave, illuminating it with a great glory. And there, beside him, sat the maiden. She smiled upon him with a smile that seemed the visible music of his pipe of reeds. He dared not speak, fearing to offend her as before, for he knew not what he could venture to say.

'Because,' she said, 'thou didst thy duty by the flock, and didst not forget to thank Hastur for staying the wolves of the night, I am come to thee again. Wilt thou have me for a companion?'

'Who would not have thee forever?' replied Haita. 'Oh! never again leave me until – until I – change and become silent and motionless.'

Haita had no word for death.

'I wish, indeed,' he continued, 'that thou wert of my own sex, that we might wrestle and run races and so never tire of being together.'

At these words the maiden arose and passed out of the cave, and Haita, springing from his couch of fragrant boughs to overtake and detain her, observed to his astonishment that the rain was falling and the stream in the middle of the valley had come out of its banks. The sheep were bleating in terror, for the rising waters had invaded their fold. And there was danger for the unknown cities of the distant plain.

It was many days before Haita saw the maiden again. One day he was returning from the head of the valley, where he had gone with ewe's milk and oat cake and berries for the holy hermit, who was too old and feeble to provide himself with food.

'Poor old man!' he said aloud, as he trudged along homeward. 'I will return tomorrow and bear him on my back to my own dwelling, where I can care for him. Doubtless it is for this that Hastur has reared me all these many years, and gives me health and strength.'

As he spoke, the maiden, clad in glittering garments, met him in the path with a smile that took away his breath.

'I am come again,' she said, 'to dwell with thee if thou wilt now have me, for none else will. Thou mayest have learned wisdom, and art willing to take me as I am, nor care to know.'

Haita threw himself at her feet. 'Beautiful being,' he cried, 'if thou wilt but deign to accept all the devotion of my heart and soul – after Hastur be served – it is thine forever. But, alas! thou art capricious and wayward. Before tomorrow's sun I may lose thee again. Promise, I beseech thee, that however in my ignorance I may offend, thou wilt forgive and remain always with me.'

Scarcely had he finished speaking when a troop of bears came out of the hills, racing toward him with crimson mouths and fiery eyes. The maiden again vanished, and he turned and fled for his life. Nor did he stop until he was in the cot of the holy hermit, whence he had set out. Hastily barring the door against the bears he cast himself upon the ground and wept.

'My son,' said the hermit from his couch of straw, freshly gathered that morning by Haita's hands, 'it is not like thee to weep for bears – tell me what sorrow hath befallen thee, that age may minister to the hurts of youth with such balms as it hath of its wisdom.'

Haita told him all: how thrice he had met the radiant maid, and thrice she had left him forlorn. He related minutely all that had passed between them, omitting no word of what had been said.

When he had ended, the holy hermit was a moment silent, then said: 'My son, I have attended to thy story, and I know the maiden. I have myself seen her, as have many. Know, then, that her name, which she would not even permit thee to enquire, is Happiness. Thou saidst the truth to her, that she is capricious, for she imposeth conditions that man cannot fulfil, and delinquency is punished by desertion. She cometh only when unsought, and will not be questioned. One manifestation of curiosity, one sign of doubt, one expression of misgiving, and she is away! How long didst thou have her at any time before she fled?'

'Only a single instant,' answered Haita, blushing with shame at the confession. 'Each time I drove her away in one moment.'

'Unfortunate youth!' said the holy hermit, 'but for thine indiscretion thou mightst have had her for two.'

The Secret of Macarger's Gulch

North-westwardly from Indian Hill, about nine miles as the crow flies, is Macarger's Gulch. It is not much of a gulch – a mere depression between two wooded ridges of inconsiderable height. From its mouth up to its head – for gulches, like rivers, have an anatomy of their own – the distance does not exceed two miles, and the width at bottom is at only one place more than a dozen yards; for most of the distance on either side of the little brook which drains it in winter, and goes dry in the early spring, there is no level ground at all; the steep slopes of the hills, covered with an almost impenetrable growth of manzanita and chemisal, are parted by nothing but the width of the water course. No-one but an occasional enterprising hunter of the vicinity ever goes into Macarger's Gulch, and five miles away it is unknown, even by name. Within that distance in any direction are far more conspicuous topographical features without names, and one might try in vain to ascertain by local enquiry the origin of the name of this one.

About midway between the head and the mouth of Macarger's Gulch, the hill on the right as you ascend is cloven by another gulch, a short dry one, and at the junction of the two is a level space of two or three acres, and there a few years ago stood an old board house containing one small room. How the component parts of the house, few and simple as they were, had been assembled at that almost inaccessible point is a problem in the solution of which there would be greater satisfaction than advantage. Possibly the creek bed is a reformed road. It is certain that the gulch was at one time pretty thoroughly prospected by miners, who must have had some means of getting in with at least pack animals carrying tools and supplies; their profits, apparently, were not such as would have justified any considerable outlay to connect Macarger's Gulch with any centre of civilisation enjoying the distinction of a sawmill. The house, however, was there, most of it. It lacked a door and a window frame, and the chimney of mud and stones had fallen into an unlovely heap, overgrown with rank weeds. Such humble furniture as there may once have been and much of the lower weatherboarding, had served as fuel in the camp fires of hunters; as had also, probably, the curbing of an old well, which at the time I write of existed in the form of a rather wide but not very deep depression nearby.

One afternoon in the summer of 1874, I passed up Macarger's Gulch from the narrow valley into which it opens, by following the dry bed of the brook. I was quail-shooting and had made a bag of about a dozen birds by the time I had reached the house described, of whose existence I was until then unaware. After rather carelessly inspecting the ruin I resumed my sport, and having fairly good success prolonged it until near sunset, when it occurred to me that I was a long way from any human habitation – too far to reach one by nightfall. But in my game bag was food, and the old house would afford shelter, if shelter were needed on a warm and dewless night in the foothills of the Sierra Nevada, where one may sleep in comfort on the pine needles, without covering. I am fond of solitude and love the night, so my resolution to 'camp out' was soon taken, and by the time that it was dark I had made my bed of boughs and grasses in a corner of the room and was roasting a quail at a fire that I had kindled on the hearth. The smoke escaped out of the ruined chimney, the light illuminated the room with a kindly glow, and as I ate my simple meal of plain bird and drank the remains of a bottle of red wine which had served me all the afternoon in place of the water, which the region did not supply, I experienced a sense of comfort which better fare and accommodations do not always give.

Nevertheless, there was something lacking. I had a sense of comfort, but not of security. I detected myself staring more frequently at the open doorway and blank window than I could find warrant for doing. Outside these apertures all was black, and I was unable to repress a certain feeling of apprehension as my fancy pictured the outer world and filled it with unfriendly entities, natural and supernatural – chief among which, in their respective classes, were the grizzly bear, which I knew was occasionally still seen in that region, and the ghost, which I had reason to think was not. Unfortunately, our feelings do not always respect the law of probabilities, and to me that evening, the possible and the impossible were equally disquieting.

Everyone who has had experience in the matter must have observed that one confronts the actual and imaginary perils of the night with far less apprehension in the open air than in a house with an open doorway. I felt this now as I lay on my leafy couch in a corner of the room next to the chimney and permitted my fire to die out. So strong became my sense of the presence of something malign and menacing in the place, that I found myself almost unable to withdraw my eyes from the opening, as in the deepening darkness it became more and more indistinct. And when the last little flame flickered and went out I grasped the shotgun which I had laid at my side and actually turned the muzzle in the direction of the now invisible entrance, my thumb on one of the hammers, ready to cock the piece, my breath suspended, my muscles rigid and tense. But later I laid down the weapon with a sense of shame and mortification. What did I fear, and why? – I, to whom the night had been

> a more familiar face
> Than that of man –

I, in whom that element of hereditary superstition from which none of us is altogether free had given to solitude and darkness and silence only a more alluring interest and charm! I was unable to comprehend my folly, and losing in the conjecture the thing conjectured of, I fell asleep. And then I dreamed.

I was in a great city in a foreign land – a city whose people were of my own race, with minor differences of speech and costume; yet precisely what these were I could not say; my sense of them was indistinct. The city was dominated by a great castle upon an overlooking height whose name I knew, but could not speak. I walked through many streets, some broad and straight with high, modern buildings, some narrow, gloomy, and tortuous, between the gables of quaint old houses whose overhanging storeys, elaborately ornamented with carvings in wood and stone, almost met above my head.

I sought someone whom I had never seen, yet knew that I should recognise when found. My quest was not aimless and fortuitous; it had a definite method. I turned from one street into another without hesitation and threaded a maze of intricate passages, devoid of the fear of losing my way.

Presently I stopped before a low door in a plain stone house which might have been the dwelling of an artisan of the better sort, and without announcing myself, entered. The room, rather sparely furnished, and lighted by a single window with small diamond-shaped panes, had but two occupants; a man and a woman. They took no notice of my intrusion, a circumstance which, in the manner of dreams, appeared entirely natural. They were not conversing; they sat apart, unoccupied and sullen.

The woman was young and rather stout, with fine large eyes and a certain grave beauty; my memory of her expression is exceedingly vivid, but in dreams one does not observe the details of faces. About her shoulders was a plaid shawl. The man was older, dark, with an evil face made more forbidding by a long scar extending from near the left temple diagonally downward into the black mustache; though in my dreams it seemed rather to haunt the face as a thing apart – I can express it no otherwise – than to belong to it. The moment that I found the man and woman I knew them to be husband and wife.

What followed, I remember indistinctly; all was confused and inconsistent – made so, I think, by gleams of consciousness. It was as if two pictures, the scene of my dream, and my actual surroundings, had been blended, one overlying the other, until the former, gradually fading, disappeared, and I was broad awake in the deserted cabin, entirely and tranquilly conscious of my situation.

My foolish fear was gone, and opening my eyes I saw that my fire, not altogether burned out, had revived by the falling of a stick and was again lighting the room. I had probably slept only a few minutes, but my commonplace dream had somehow so strongly impressed me that I was no longer drowsy; and after a little while I rose, pushed the embers of my fire together, and lighting my pipe proceeded in a rather ludicrously methodical way to meditate upon my vision.

It would have puzzled me then to say in what respect it was worth attention. In the first moment of serious thought that I gave to the matter I recognised the city of my dream as Edinburgh, where I had never been; so if the dream was a memory it was a memory of pictures and description. The recognition somehow deeply impressed me; it was as if something in my mind insisted rebelliously against will and reason on the importance of all this. And that faculty, whatever it was, asserted also a control of my speech. 'Surely,' I said aloud, quite involuntarily, 'the MacGregors must have come here from Edinburgh.'

At the moment, neither the substance of this remark nor the fact of my making it, surprised me in the least; it seemed entirely natural that I should know the name of my dreamfolk and something of their history. But the absurdity of it all soon dawned upon me: I laughed aloud, knocked the ashes from my pipe and again stretched myself upon my bed of boughs and grass, where I lay staring absently into my failing fire, with no further thought of either my dream or my surroundings. Suddenly the single remaining flame crouched for a moment, then, springing upward, lifted itself clear of its embers and expired in air. The darkness was absolute.

At that instant – almost, it seemed, before the gleam of the blaze had faded from my eyes – there was a dull, dead sound, as of some heavy body falling upon the floor, which shook beneath me as I lay. I sprang to a sitting posture and groped at my side for my gun; my notion was that some wild beast had leaped in through the open window. While the flimsy structure was still shaking from the impact I heard the sound of blows, the scuffling of feet upon the floor, and then – it seemed to come from almost within reach of my hand, the sharp shrieking of a woman in mortal agony. So horrible a cry I had never heard nor conceived; it utterly unnerved me; I was conscious for a moment of nothing but my own terror! Fortunately my hand now found the weapon of which it was in search, and the familiar touch somewhat restored me. I leaped to my feet, straining my eyes to pierce the darkness. The violent sounds had ceased, but more terrible than these, I heard, at what seemed long intervals, the faint intermittent gasping of some living, dying thing!

As my eyes grew accustomed to the dim light of the coals in the fireplace, I saw first the shapes of the door and window, looking blacker than the black of the walls. Next, the distinction between wall and floor became discernible, and at last I was sensible to the form and full expanse of the floor from end to end and side to side. Nothing was visible and the silence was unbroken.

With a hand that shook a little, the other still grasping my gun, I restored my fire and made a critical examination of the place. There was nowhere any sign that the cabin had been entered. My own tracks were visible in the dust covering the floor, but there were no others. I relit my pipe, provided fresh fuel by ripping a thin board or two from the inside of the house – I did not care to go into the darkness out of doors – and passed the rest of the night smoking and thinking, and feeding my fire; not for added years of life would I have permitted that little flame to expire again.

Some years afterward I met in Sacramento a man named Morgan, to whom I had a note of introduction from a friend in San Francisco. Dining with him one evening at his home I observed various 'trophies' upon the wall, indicating that he was fond of shooting. It turned out that he was, and in relating some of his feats he mentioned having been in the region of my adventure.

'Mr Morgan,' I asked abruptly, 'do you know a place up there called Macarger's Gulch?'

'I have good reason to,' he replied; 'it was I who gave to the newspapers, last year, the accounts of the finding of the skeleton there.'

I had not heard of it; the accounts had been published, it appeared, while I was absent in the East.

'By the way,' said Morgan, 'the name of the gulch is a corruption; it should have been called "MacGregor's". My dear,' he added, speaking to his wife, 'Mr Elderson has upset his wine.'

That was hardly accurate – I had simply dropped it, glass and all.

'There was an old shanty once in the gulch,' Morgan resumed when the ruin wrought by my awkwardness had been repaired, 'but just previously to my visit it had been blown down, or rather blown away, for its debris was scattered all about, the very floor being parted, plank from plank. Between two of the sleepers still in position I and my companion observed the remnant of a plaid shawl, and examining it found that it was wrapped about the shoulders of the body of a woman, of which but little remained besides the bones, partly covered with fragments of clothing, and brown dry skin. But we will spare Mrs Morgan,' he added with a smile. The lady had indeed exhibited signs of disgust rather than sympathy.

'It is necessary to say, however,' he went on, 'that the skull was fractured in several places, as by blows of some blunt instrument; and that instrument itself – a pick-handle, still stained with blood – lay under the boards nearby.'

Mr Morgan turned to his wife. 'Pardon me, my dear,' he said with affected solemnity, 'for mentioning these disagreeable particulars, the natural though regrettable incidents of a conjugal quarrel – resulting, doubtless, from the luckless wife's insubordination.'

'I ought to be able to overlook it,' the lady replied with composure; 'you have so many times asked me to in those very words.'

I thought he seemed rather glad to go on with his story.

'From these and other circumstances,' he said, 'the coroner's jury found that the deceased, Janet MacGregor, came to her death from blows inflicted by some person to the jury unknown; but it was added that the evidence pointed strongly to her husband, Thomas Mac-Gregor, as the guilty person. But Thomas MacGregor has never been found nor heard of. It was learned that the couple came from Edinburgh, but not – my dear, do you not observe that Mr Elderson's boneplate has water in it?'

I had deposited a chicken bone in my finger bowl.

'In a little cupboard I found a photograph of MacGregor, but it did not lead to his capture.'

'Will you let me see it?' I said.

The picture showed a dark man with an evil face made more forbidding by a long scar extending from near the temple diagonally downward into the black mustache.

'By the way, Mr Elderson,' said my affable host, 'may I know why you asked about "Macarger's Gulch"?'

'I lost a mule near there once,' I replied, 'and the mischance has – has quite – upset me.'

'My dear,' said Mr Morgan, with the mechanical intonation of an interpreter translating, 'the loss of Mr Elderson's mule has peppered his coffee.'

The Eyes of the Panther

One does not always marry when insane

A man and a woman – nature had done the grouping – sat on a rustic seat, in the late afternoon. The man was middle-aged, slender, swarthy, with the expression of a poet and the complexion of a pirate – a man at whom one would look again. The woman was young, blonde, graceful, with something in her figure and movements suggesting the word 'lithe.' She was habited in a grey gown with odd brown markings in the texture. She may have been beautiful; one could not readily say, for her eyes denied attention to all else. They were grey-green, long and narrow, with an expression defying analysis. One could only know that they were disquieting. Cleopatra may have had such eyes.

The man and the woman talked. 'Yes,' said the woman, 'I love you, God knows! But marry you, no. I cannot, will not.'

'Irene, you have said that many times, yet always have denied me a reason. I've a right to know, to understand, to feel and prove my fortitude if I have it. Give me a reason.'

'For loving you?'

The woman was smiling through her tears and her pallor. That did not stir any sense of humour in the man.

'No; there is no reason for that. A reason for not marrying me. I've a right to know. I must know. I will know!'

He had risen and was standing before her with clenched hands, on his face a frown – it might have been called a scowl. He looked as if he might attempt to learn by strangling her. She smiled no more – merely sat looking up into his face with a fixed, set regard that was utterly without emotion or sentiment. Yet it had something in it that tamed his resentment and made him shiver.

'You are determined to have my reason?' she asked in a tone that was entirely mechanical – a tone that might have been her look made audible.

'If you please – if I'm not asking too much.'

Apparently this lord of creation was yielding some part of his dominion over his co-creature.

'Very well, you shall know: I am insane.'

The man started, then looked incredulous and was conscious that he ought to be amused. But, again, the sense of humour failed him in his need and despite his disbelief he was profoundly disturbed by that which he did not believe. Between our convictions and our feelings there is no good understanding.

'That is what the physicians would say,' the woman continued – 'if they knew. I might myself prefer to call it a case of "possession". Sit down and hear what I have to say.'

The man silently resumed his seat beside her on the rustic bench by the wayside. Over-against them on the eastern side of the valley the hills were already sunset-flushed and the stillness all about was of that peculiar quality that foretells the twilight. Something of its mysterious and significant solemnity had imparted itself to the man's mood. In the spiritual, as in the material world, are signs and presages of night. Rarely meeting her look, and whenever he did so conscious of the indefinable dread with which, despite their feline beauty, her eyes always affected him, Jenner Brading listened in silence to the story told by Irene Marlowe. In deference to the reader's possible prejudice against the artless method of an unpractised historian the author ventures to substitute his own version for hers.

2

A room may be too narrow for three, though one is outside

In a little log house containing a single room sparely and rudely furnished, crouching on the floor against one of the walls, was a woman, clasping to her breast a child. Outside, a dense unbroken forest extended for many miles in every direction. This was at night and the room was black dark: no human eye could have discerned the woman and the child. Yet they were observed, narrowly, vigilantly, with never even a momentary slackening of attention; and that is the pivotal fact upon which this narrative turns.

Charles Marlowe was of the class, now extinct in this country, of woodmen pioneers – men who found their most acceptable surroundings in sylvan solitudes that stretched along the eastern slope of the Mississippi Valley, from the Great Lakes to the Gulf of Mexico. For

more than a hundred years these men pushed ever westward, generation after generation, with rifle and axe, reclaiming from Nature and
her savage children here and there an isolated acreage for the plough,
no sooner reclaimed than surrendered to their less venturesome but
more thrifty successors. At last they burst through the edge of the
forest into the open country and vanished as if they had fallen over a
cliff. The woodman pioneer is no more; the pioneer of the plains – he
whose easy task it was to subdue for occupancy two-thirds of the
country in a single generation – is another and inferior creation. With
Charles Marlowe in the wilderness, sharing the dangers, hardships
and privations of that strange, unprofitable life, were his wife and
child, to whom, in the manner of his class, in which the domestic
virtues were a religion, he was passionately attached. The woman was
still young enough to be comely, new enough to the awful isolation of
her lot to be cheerful. By withholding the large capacity for happiness
which the simple satisfactions of the forest life could not have filled,
Heaven had dealt honourably with her. In her light household tasks,
her child, her husband and her few foolish books, she found abundant
provision for her needs.

One morning in midsummer Marlowe took down his rifle from the
wooden hooks on the wall and signified his intention of getting game.

'We've meat enough,' said the wife; 'please don't go out today. I
dreamed last night, O, such a dreadful thing! I cannot recollect it,
but I'm almost sure that it will come to pass if you go out.'

It is painful to confess that Marlowe received this solemn statement with less of gravity than was due to the mysterious nature of the
calamity foreshadowed. In truth, he laughed.

'Try to remember,' he said. 'Maybe you dreamed that Baby had
lost the power of speech.'

The conjecture was obviously suggested by the fact that Baby,
clinging to the fringe of his hunting-coat with all her ten pudgy
thumbs, was at that moment uttering her sense of the situation in a
series of exultant goo-goos inspired by sight of her father's raccoon-
skin cap.

The woman yielded: lacking the gift of humour she could not hold
out against his kindly badinage. So, with a kiss for the mother and a
kiss for the child, he left the house and closed the door upon his
happiness forever.

At nightfall he had not returned. The woman prepared supper and
waited. Then she put Baby to bed and sang softly to her until she
slept. By this time the fire on the hearth, at which she had cooked

supper, had burned out and the room was lighted by a single candle. This she afterward placed in the open window as a sign and welcome to the hunter if he should approach from that side. She had thoughtfully closed and barred the door against such wild animals as might prefer it to an open window – of the habits of beasts of prey in entering a house uninvited she was not advised, though with true female prevision she may have considered the possibility of their entrance by way of the chimney. As the night wore on she became not less anxious, but more drowsy, and at last rested her arms upon the bed by the child and her head upon the arms. The candle in the window burned down to the socket, sputtered and flared a moment and went out unobserved; for the woman slept and dreamed.

In her dreams she sat beside the cradle of a second child. The first one was dead. The father was dead. The home in the forest was lost and the dwelling in which she lived was unfamiliar. There were heavy oaken doors, always closed, and outside the windows, fastened into the thick stone walls, were iron bars, obviously (so she thought) a provision against Indians. All this she noted with an infinite self-pity, but without surprise – an emotion unknown in dreams. The child in the cradle was invisible under its coverlet which something impelled her to remove. She did so, disclosing the face of a wild animal! In the shock of this dreadful revelation the dreamer awoke, trembling in the darkness of her cabin in the wood.

As a sense of her actual surroundings came slowly back to her she felt for the child that was not a dream, and assured herself by its breathing that all was well with it; nor could she forbear to pass a hand lightly across its face. Then, moved by some impulse for which she probably could not have accounted, she rose and took the sleeping babe in her arms, holding it close against her breast. The head of the child's cot was against the wall to which the woman now turned her back as she stood. Lifting her eyes she saw two bright objects starring the darkness with a reddish-green glow. She took them to be two coals on the hearth, but with her returning sense of direction came the disquieting consciousness that they were not in that quarter of the room, moreover were too high, being nearly at the level of the eyes – of her own eyes. For these were the eyes of a panther.

The beast was at the open window directly opposite and not five paces away. Nothing but those terrible eyes was visible, but in the dreadful tumult of her feelings as the situation disclosed itself to her understanding she somehow knew that the animal was standing on its hinder feet, supporting itself with its paws on the window-ledge. That signified a malign interest – not the mere gratification of an indolent curiosity. The consciousness of the attitude was an added horror, accentuating the menace of those awful eyes, in whose steadfast fire her strength and courage were alike consumed. Under their silent questioning she shuddered and turned sick. Her knees failed her, and by degrees, instinctively striving to avoid a sudden movement that might bring the beast upon her, she sank to the floor, crouched against the wall and tried to shield the babe with her trembling body without withdrawing her gaze from the luminous orbs that were killing her. No thought of her husband came to her in her agony – no hope nor suggestion of rescue or escape. Her capacity for thought and feeling had narrowed to the dimensions of a single emotion – fear of the animal's spring, of the impact of its body, the buffeting of its great arms, the feel of its teeth in her throat, the mangling of her babe. Motionless now and in absolute silence, she awaited her doom, the moments growing to hours, to years, to ages; and still those devilish eyes maintained their watch.

Returning to his cabin late at night with a deer on his shoulders Charles Marlowe tried the door. It did not yield. He knocked; there was no answer. He laid down his deer and went round to the window. As he turned the angle of the building he fancied he heard a sound as of stealthy footfalls and a rustling in the undergrowth of the forest, but they were too slight for certainty, even to his practised ear. Approaching the window, and to his surprise finding it open, he threw his leg over the sill and entered. All was darkness and silence. He groped his way to the fire-place, struck a match and lit a candle.

Then he looked about. Cowering on the floor against a wall was his wife, clasping his child. As he sprang toward her she rose and broke into laughter, long, loud, and mechanical, devoid of gladness and devoid of sense – the laughter that is not out of keeping with the clanking of a chain. Hardly knowing what he did he extended his arms. She laid the babe in them. It was dead – pressed to death in its mother's embrace.

3

The theory of the defence

That is what occurred during a night in a forest, but not all of it did Irene Marlowe relate to Jenner Brading; not all of it was known to her. When she had concluded the sun was below the horizon and the

long summer twilight had begun to deepen in the hollows of the
land. For some moments Brading was silent, expecting the narrative
to be carried forward to some definite connection with the conversation introducing it; but the narrator was as silent as he, her face
averted, her hands clasping and unclasping themselves as they lay
in her lap, with a singular suggestion of an activity independent
of her will.

'It is a sad, a terrible story,' said Brading at last, 'but I do not
understand. You call Charles Marlowe father; that I know. That he is
old before his time, broken by some great sorrow, I have seen, or
thought I saw. But, pardon me, you said that you – that you – '

'That I am insane,' said the girl, without a movement of head
or body.

'But, Irene, you say – please, dear, do not look away from me – you
say that the child was dead, not demented.'

'Yes, that one – I am the second. I was born three months after that
night, my mother being mercifully permitted to lay down her life in
giving me mine.'

Brading was again silent; he was a trifle dazed and could not at
once think of the right thing to say. Her face was still turned away. In
his embarrassment he reached impulsively toward the hands that lay
closing and unclosing in her lap, but something – he could not have
said what – restrained him. He then remembered, vaguely, that he
had never altogether cared to take her hand.

'Is it likely,' she resumed, 'that a person born under such circumstances is like others – is what you call sane?'

Brading did not reply; he was preoccupied with a new thought that
was taking shape in his mind – what a scientist would have called an
hypothesis; a detective, a theory. It might throw an added light,
albeit a lurid one, upon such doubt of her sanity as her own assertion
had not dispelled.

The country was still new and, outside the villages, sparsely
populated. The professional hunter was still a familiar figure, and
among his trophies were heads and pelts of the larger kinds of
game. Tales variously credible of nocturnal meetings with savage
animals in lonely roads were sometimes current, passed through
the customary stages of growth and decay, and were forgotten. A
recent addition to these popular apocrypha, originating, apparently,
by spontaneous generation in several households, was of a panther
which had frightened some of their members by looking in at
windows by night. The yarn had caused its little ripple of excite-

ment – had even attained to the distinction of a place in the local newspaper; but Brading had given it no attention. Its likeness to the story to which he had just listened now impressed him as perhaps more than accidental. Was it not possible that the one story had suggested the other – that finding congenial conditions in a morbid mind and a fertile fancy, it had grown to the tragic tale that he had heard?

Brading recalled certain circumstances of the girl's history and disposition, of which, with love's incuriosity, he had hitherto been heedless – such as her solitary life with her father, at whose house no-one, apparently, was an acceptable visitor, and her strange fear of the night, by which those who knew her best accounted for her never being seen after dark. Surely in such a mind imagination once kindled might burn with a lawless flame, penetrating and enveloping the entire structure. That she was mad, though the conviction gave him the acutest pain, he could no longer doubt; she had only mistaken an effect of her mental disorder for its cause, bringing into imaginary relation with her own personality the vagaries of the local myth-makers. With some vague intention of testing his new 'theory', and no very definite notion of how to set about it he said, gravely, but with hesitation: 'Irene, dear, tell me – I beg you will not take offence, but tell me – '

'I have told you,' she interrupted, speaking with a passionate earnestness that he had not known her to show – 'I have already told you that we cannot marry; is anything else worth saying?'

Before he could stop her she had sprung from her seat and without another word or look was gliding away among the trees toward her father's house. Brading had risen to detain her; he stood watching her in silence until she had vanished in the gloom. Suddenly he started as if he had been shot; his face took on an expression of amazement and alarm: in one of the black shadows into which she had disappeared he had caught a quick, brief glimpse of shining eyes! For an instant he was dazed and irresolute; then he dashed into the wood after her, shouting: 'Irene, Irene, look out! The panther! The panther!'

In a moment he had passed through the fringe of forest into open ground and saw the girl's grey skirt vanishing into her father's door. No panther was visible.

4

An Appeal to the Conscience of God

Jenner Brading, attorney-at-law, lived in a cottage at the edge of the town. Directly behind the dwelling was the forest. Being a bachelor, and therefore, by the Draconian moral code of the time and place denied the services of the only species of domestic servant known thereabout, the 'hired girl', he boarded at the village hotel, where also was his office. The woodside cottage was merely a lodging maintained – at no great cost, to be sure – as an evidence of prosperity and respectability. It would hardly do for one to whom the local newspaper had pointed with pride as 'the foremost jurist of his time' to be 'homeless', albeit he may sometimes have suspected that the words 'home' and 'house' were not strictly synonymous. Indeed, his consciousness of the disparity and his will to harmonise it were matters of logical inference, for it was generally reported that soon after the cottage was built its owner had made a futile venture in the direction of marriage – had, in truth, gone so far as to be rejected by the beautiful but eccentric daughter of Old Man Marlowe, the recluse. This was publicly believed because he had told it himself and she had not – a reversal of the usual order of things which could hardly fail to carry conviction.

Brading's bedroom was at the rear of the house, with a single window facing the forest.

One night he was awakened by a noise at that window; he could hardly have said what it was like. With a little thrill of the nerves he sat up in bed and laid hold of the revolver which, with a fore-thought most commendable in one addicted to the habit of sleeping on the ground floor with an open window, he had put under his pillow. The room was in absolute darkness, but being unterrified he knew where to direct his eyes, and there he held them, awaiting in silence what further might occur. He could now dimly discern the aperture – a square of lighter black. Presently there appeared at its lower edge two gleaming eyes that burned with a malignant lustre inexpressibly terrible! Brading's heart gave a great jump, then seemed to stand still. A chill passed along his spine and through his hair; he felt the blood forsake his cheeks. He could not have cried out – not to save his life; but being a man of courage he would not, to save his life, have done so if he had been able. Some trepidation his coward body might feel, but his spirit was of sterner stuff. Slowly the shining eyes rose with a steady motion that seemed an approach, and slowly rose Brading's right hand, holding the pistol. He fired!

Blinded by the flash and stunned by the report, Brading nevertheless heard, or fancied that he heard, the wild, high scream of the panther, so human in sound, so devilish in suggestion. Leaping from the bed he hastily clothed himself and, pistol in hand, sprang from the door, meeting two or three men who came running up from the road. A brief explanation was followed by a cautious search of the house. The grass was wet with dew; beneath the window it had been trodden and partly levelled for a wide space, from which a devious trail, visible in the light of a lantern, led away into the bushes. One of the men stumbled and fell upon his hands, which as he rose and rubbed them together were slippery. On examination they were seen to be red with blood.

An encounter, unarmed, with a wounded panther was not agreeable to their taste; all but Brading turned back. He, with lantern and pistol, pushed courageously forward into the wood. Passing through a difficult undergrowth he came into a small opening, and there his courage had its reward, for there he found the body of his victim. But it was no panther. What it was is told, even to this day, upon a weather-worn headstone in the village churchyard, and for many years was attested daily at the graveside by the bent figure and sorrow-seamed face of Old Man Marlowe, to whose soul, and to the soul of his strange, unhappy child, peace. Peace and reparation.

The Stranger

A man stepped out of the darkness into the little illuminated circle about our failing campfire and seated himself upon a rock.

'You are not the first to explore this region,' he said, gravely.

Nobody controverted his statement; he was himself proof of its truth, for he was not of our party and must have been somewhere near when we camped. Moreover, he must have companions not far away; it was not a place where one would be living or travelling alone. For more than a week we had seen, besides ourselves and our animals, only such living things as rattlesnakes and horned toads. In an Arizona desert one does not long coexist with only such creatures as these: one must have pack animals, supplies, arms – 'an outfit.' And all these imply comrades. It was perhaps a doubt as to what manner of men this unceremonious stranger's comrades might be, together with something in his words interpretable as a challenge, that caused every man of our half-dozen 'gentlemen adventurers' to rise to a sitting posture and lay his hand upon a weapon – an act signifying, in that time and place, a policy of expectation. The stranger gave the matter no attention and began again to speak in the same deliberate, uninflected monotone in which he had delivered his first sentence: 'Thirty years ago Ramon Gallegos, William Shaw, George W. Kent and Berry Davis, all of Tucson, crossed the Santa Catalina mountains and travelled due west, as nearly as the configuration of the country permitted. We were prospecting and it was our intention, if we found nothing, to push through to the Gila river at some point near Big Bend, where we understood there was a settlement. We had a good outfit but no guide – just Ramon Gallegos, William Shaw, George W. Kent and Berry Davis.'

The man repeated the names slowly and distinctly, as if to fix them in the memories of his audience, every member of which was now attentively observing him, but with a slackened apprehension regarding his possible companions somewhere in the darkness that seemed to enclose us like a black wall; in the manner of this volunteer historian was no suggestion of an unfriendly purpose. His act was rather that of a harmless lunatic than an enemy. We were not so new to the country as not to know that the solitary life of many a plainsman had a tendency to develop eccentricities of conduct and character not always easily distinguishable from mental aberration. A man is like a tree: in a forest of his fellows he will grow as straight as his generic and individual nature permits; alone in the open, he yields to the deforming stresses and torsions that environ him. Some such thoughts were in my mind as I watched the man from the shadow of my hat, pulled low to shut out the firelight. A witless fellow, no doubt, but what could he be doing there in the heart of a desert?

Having undertaken to tell this story, I wish that I could describe the man's appearance; that would be a natural thing to do. Unfortunately, and somewhat strangely, I find myself unable to do so with any degree of confidence, for afterward no two of us agreed as to what he wore and how he looked; and when I try to set down my own impressions they elude me. Anyone can tell some kind of story; narration is one of the elemental powers of the race. But the talent for description is a gift.

Nobody having broken silence the visitor went on to say: 'This country was not then what it is now. There was not a ranch between the Gila and the Gulf. There was a little game here and there in the mountains, and near the infrequent waterholes grass enough to keep our animals from starvation. If we should be so fortunate as to encounter no Indians we might get through. But within a week the purpose of the expedition had altered from discovery of wealth to preservation of life. We had gone too far to go back, for what was ahead could be no worse than what was behind; so we pushed on, riding by night to avoid Indians and the intolerable heat, and concealing ourselves by day as best we could. Sometimes, having exhausted our supply of wild meat and emptied our casks, we were days without food or drink; then a water-hole or a shallow pool in the bottom of an arroyo so restored our strength and sanity that we were able to shoot some of the wild animals that sought it also. Sometimes it was a bear, sometimes an antelope, a coyote, a cougar – that was as God pleased; all were food.

'One morning as we skirted a mountain range, seeking a practicable pass, we were attacked by a band of Apaches who had followed our trail up a gulch – it is not far from here. Knowing that they outnumbered us ten to one, they took none of their usual cowardly precautions, but dashed upon us at a gallop, firing and yelling. Fighting was out of the question: we urged our feeble animals up the gulch as far as there was footing for a hoof, then threw ourselves out of our saddles and took to the chaparral on one of the slopes, abandoning our entire outfit to the enemy. But we retained our rifles, every man – Ramon Gallegos, William Shaw, George W. Kent and Berry Davis.'

'Same old crowd,' said the humorist of our party. He was an Eastern man, unfamiliar with the decent observances of social inter-course. A gesture of disapproval from our leader silenced him and the stranger proceeded with his tale.

'The savages dismounted also, and some of them ran up the gulch beyond the point at which we had left it, cutting off further retreat in that direction and forcing us on up the side. Unfortunately the chaparral extended only a short distance up the slope, and as we came into the open ground above we took the fire of a dozen rifles; but Apaches shoot badly when in a hurry, and God so willed it that none of us fell. Twenty yards up the slope, beyond the edge of the brush, were vertical cliffs, in which, directly in front of us, was a narrow opening. Into that we ran, finding ourselves in a cavern about as large as an ordinary room in a house. Here for a time we were safe: a single man with a repeating rifle could defend the entrance against all the Apaches in the land. But against hunger and thirst we had no defence. Courage we still had, but hope was a memory.

'Not one of those Indians did we afterward see, but by the smoke and glare of their fires in the gulch we knew that by day and by night they watched with ready rifles in the edge of the bush – knew that if we made a sortie not a man of us would live to take three steps into the open. For three days, watching in turn, we held out before our suffering became insupportable. Then – it was the morning of the fourth day – Ramon Gallegos said: ' "Señores, I know not well of the good God and what please him. I have live without religion, and I am not acquaint with that of you. Pardon, señores, if I shock you, but for me the time is come to beat the game of the Apache."

'He knelt upon the rock floor of the cave and pressed his pistol against his temple. "Madre de Dios," he said, "comes now the soul of Ramon Gallegos."

'And so he left us – William Shaw, George W. Kent and Berry Davis.

'I was the leader: it was for me to speak.

' "He was a brave man," I said – "he knew when to die, and how. It is foolish to go mad from thirst and fall by Apache bullets, or be skinned alive – it is in bad taste. Let us join Ramon Gallegos."

' "That is right," said William Shaw.

' "That is right," said George W. Kent.

'I straightened the limbs of Ramon Gallegos and put a handkerchief over his face. Then William Shaw said: "I should like to look like that – a little while."

'And George W. Kent said that he felt that way, too.

' "It shall be so," I said: "the red devils will wait a week. William Shaw and George W. Kent, draw and kneel."

'They did so and I stood before them.

' "Almighty God, our Father," said I.

' "Almighty God, our Father," said William Shaw.

' "Almighty God, our Father," said George W. Kent.

' "Forgive us our sins," said I.

' "Forgive us our sins," said they.

' "And receive our souls."

' "And receive our souls."

' "Amen!"

' "Amen!"

'I laid them beside Ramon Gallegos and covered their faces.'

There was a quick commotion on the opposite side of the campfire: one of our party had sprung to his feet, pistol in hand.

'And you!' he shouted – '*You* dared to escape? – You dare to be alive? You cowardly hound, I'll send you to join them if I hang for it!'

But with the leap of a panther the captain was upon him, grasping his wrist. 'Hold it in, Sam Yountsey, hold it in!'

We were now all upon our feet – except the stranger, who sat motionless and apparently inattentive. Someone seized Yountsey's other arm.

'Captain,' I said, 'there is something wrong here. This fellow is either a lunatic or merely a liar – just a plain, everyday liar whom Yountsey has no call to kill. If this man was of that party it had five members, one of whom – probably himself – he has not named.'

'Yes,' said the captain, releasing the insurgent, who sat down, 'there is something – unusual. Years ago four dead bodies of white men, scalped and shamefully mutilated, were found about the mouth of that cave. They are buried there; I have seen the graves – we shall all see them tomorrow.'

The stranger rose, standing tall in the light of the expiring fire, which in our breathless attention to his story we had neglected to keep going.

'There were four,' he said – 'Ramon Gallegos, William Shaw, George W. Kent and Berry Davis.'

With this reiterated roll-call of the dead he walked into the darkness and we saw him no more.

At that moment one of our party, who had been on guard, strode in among us, rifle in hand and somewhat excited.

'Captain,' he said, 'for the last half-hour three men have been standing out there on the *mesa*.' He pointed in the direction taken by the stranger. 'I could see them distinctly, for the moon is up, but as they had no guns and I had them covered with mine I thought it was their move. They have made none, but, damn it! they have got on to my nerves.'

'Go back to your post, and stay till you see them again,' said the captain. 'The rest of you lie down again, or I'll kick you all into the fire.'

The sentinel obediently withdrew, swearing, and did not return. As we were arranging our blankets the fiery Yountsey said: 'I beg your pardon, Captain, but who the devil do you take them to be?'

'Ramon Gallegos, William Shaw and George W. Kent.'

'But how about Berry Davis? I ought to have shot him.'

'Quite needless; you couldn't have made him any deader. Go to sleep.'

An Inhabitant of Carcosa

For there be divers sorts of death – some wherein the body remaineth; and in some it vanisheth quite away with the spirit. This commonly occurreth only in solitude (such is God's will) and, none seeing the end, we say the man is lost, or gone on a long journey – which indeed he hath; but sometimes it hath happened in sight of many, as abundant testimony showeth. In one kind of death the spirit also dieth, and this it hath been known to do while yet the body was in vigour for many years. Sometimes, as is veritably attested, it dieth with the body, but after a season is raised up again in that place where the body did decay.

Pondering these words of Hali (whom God rest) and questioning their full meaning, as one who, having an intimation, yet doubts if there be not something behind, other than that which he has discerned, I noted not whither I had strayed until a sudden chill wind striking my face revived in me a sense of my surroundings. I observed with astonishment that everything seemed unfamiliar. On every side of me stretched a bleak and desolate expanse of plain, covered with a tall overgrowth of sere grass, which rustled and whistled in the autumn wind with heaven knows what mysterious and disquieting suggestion. Protruded at long intervals above it, stood strangely-shaped and sombre-coloured rocks, which seemed to have an understanding with one another and to exchange looks of uncomfortable significance, as if they had reared their heads to watch the issue of some foreseen event. A few blasted trees here and there appeared as leaders in this malevolent conspiracy of silent expectation.

The day, I thought, must be far advanced, though the sun was invisible; and although sensible that the air was raw and chill my consciousness of that fact was rather mental than physical – I had no feeling of discomfort. Over all the dismal landscape a canopy of low, lead-coloured clouds hung like a visible curse. In all this there were a menace and a portent – a hint of evil, an intimation of doom.

Bird, beast, or insect there was none. The wind sighed in the bare branches of the dead trees and the grey grass bent to whisper its dread secret to the earth; but no other sound nor motion broke the awful repose of that dismal place.

I observed in the herbage a number of weather-worn stones, evidently shaped with tools. They were broken, covered with moss and half-sunken in the earth. Some lay prostrate, some leaned at various angles, none was vertical. They were obviously headstones of graves, though the graves themselves no longer existed as either mounds or depressions; the years had levelled all. Scattered here and there, more massive blocks showed where some pompous tomb or ambitious monument had once flung its feeble defiance at oblivion. So old seemed these relics, these vestiges of vanity and memorials of affection and piety, so battered and worn and stained – so neglected, deserted, forgotten the place, that I could not help thinking myself the discoverer of the burial-ground of a prehistoric race of men whose very name was long extinct.

Filled with these reflections, I was for some time heedless of the sequence of my own experiences, but soon I thought, 'How came I hither?' A moment's reflection seemed to make this all clear and explain at the same time, though in a disquieting way, the singular character with which my fancy had invested all that I saw or heard. I was ill. I remembered now that I had been prostrated by a sudden fever, and that my family had told me that in my periods of delirium I had constantly cried out for liberty and air, and had been held in bed to prevent my escape out of doors. Now I had eluded the vigilance of my attendants and had wandered hither to – to where? I could not conjecture. Clearly I was at a considerable distance from the city where I dwelt – the ancient and famous city of Carcosa.

No signs of human life were anywhere visible nor audible; no rising smoke, no watchdog's bark, no lowing of cattle, no shouts of children at play – nothing but that dismal burial-place, with its air of mystery and dread, due to my own disordered brain. Was I not becoming again delirious, there beyond human aid? Was it not indeed *all* an illusion of my madness? I called aloud the names of my wives and sons, reached out my hands in search of theirs, even as I walked among the crumbling stones and in the withered grass.

A noise behind me caused me to turn about. A wild animal – a lynx – was approaching. The thought came to me: if I break down here in the desert – if the fever return and I fail, this beast will be at my throat. I sprang toward it, shouting. It trotted tranquilly by within a hand's breadth of me and disappeared behind a rock.

A moment later a man's head appeared to rise out of the ground a short distance away. He was ascending the farther slope of a low hill whose crest was hardly to be distinguished from the general level. His whole figure soon came into view against the background of grey cloud. He was half-naked, half-clad in skins. His hair was unkempt, his beard long and ragged. In one hand he carried a bow and arrow; the other held a blazing torch with a long trail of black smoke. He walked slowly and with caution, as if he feared falling into some open grave concealed by the tall grass. This strange apparition surprised but did not alarm, and taking such a course as to intercept him I met him almost face to face, accosting him with the familiar salutation, 'God keep you.'

He gave no heed, nor did he arrest his pace.

'Good stranger,' I continued, 'I am ill and lost. Direct me, I beseech you, to Carcosa.'

The man broke into a barbarous chant in an unknown tongue, passing on and away.

An owl on the branch of a decayed tree hooted dismally and was answered by another in the distance. Looking upward, I saw through a sudden rift in the clouds Aldebaran and the Hyades! In all this there was a hint of night – the lynx, the man with the torch, the owl. Yet I saw – I saw even the stars in absence of the darkness. I saw, but was apparently not seen nor heard. Under what awful spell did I exist?

I seated myself at the root of a great tree, seriously to consider what it were best to do. That I was mad I could no longer doubt, yet recognised a ground of doubt in the conviction. Of fever I had no trace. I had, withal, a sense of exhilaration and vigour altogether unknown to me – a feeling of mental and physical exaltation. My senses seemed all alert; I could feel the air as a ponderous substance; I could hear the silence.

A great root of the giant tree against whose trunk I leaned as I sat held enclosed in its grasp a slab of stone, a part of which protruded into a recess formed by another root. The stone was thus partly protected from the weather, though greatly decomposed. Its edges were worn round, its corners eaten away, its surface deeply furrowed and scaled. Glittering particles of mica were visible in the earth about it – vestiges of its decomposition. This stone had apparently marked the grave out of which the tree had sprung ages ago. The tree's exacting roots had robbed the grave and made the stone a prisoner.

A sudden wind pushed some dry leaves and twigs from the upper-most face of the stone; I saw the low-relief letters of an inscription and bent to read it. God in Heaven! *My* name in full! – The date of *my* birth! – The date of *my* death!

A level shaft of light illuminated the whole side of the tree as I sprang to my feet in terror. The sun was rising in the rosy east. I stood between the tree and his broad red disk – no shadow darkened the trunk!

A chorus of howling wolves saluted the dawn. I saw them sitting on their haunches, singly and in groups, on the summits of irregular mounds and tumuli filling a half of my desert prospect and extending to the horizon. And then I knew that these were ruins of the ancient and famous city of Carcosa.

Such are the facts imparted to the medium Bayrolles by the spirit Hoseib Alar Robardin.

The Applicant

Pushing his adventurous shins through the deep snow that had fallen overnight, and encouraged by the glee of his little sister, following in the open way that he made, a sturdy small boy, the son of Grayville's most distinguished citizen, struck his foot against something of which there was no visible sign on the surface of the snow. It is the purpose of this narrative to explain how it came to be there.

No-one who has had the advantage of passing through Grayville by day can have failed to observe the large stone building crowning the low hill to the north of the railway station – that is to say, to the right in going toward Great Mowbray. It is a somewhat dull-looking edifice, of the Early Comatose order, and appears to have been designed by an architect who shrank from publicity, and although unable to conceal his work – even compelled, in this instance, to set it on an eminence in the sight of men – did what he honestly could to insure it against a second look. So far as concerns its outer and visible aspect, the Abersush Home for Old Men is unquestionably inhospitable to human attention. But it is a building of great magnitude, and cost its benevolent founder the profit of many a cargo of the teas and silks and spices that his ships brought up from the under-world when he was in trade in Boston; though the main expense was its endowment. Altogether, this reckless person had robbed his heirs-at-law of no less a sum than half a million dollars and flung it away in riotous giving. Possibly it was with a view to get out of sight of the silent big witness to his extravagance that he shortly afterward disposed of all his Grayville property that remained to him, turned his back upon the scene of his prodigality and went off across the sea in one of his own ships. But the gossips who got their inspiration most directly from Heaven declared that he went in search of a wife – a theory not easily reconciled with that of the village humorist, who solemnly averred that the bachelor philanthropist had departed this life (left Grayville, to wit) because the marriageable maidens had made it too hot to hold him. However this may have been, he had not returned, and although at long intervals there had come to Gray-ville, in a desultory way, vague rumours of his wanderings in strange lands, no-one seemed certainly to know about him, and to the new generation he was no more than a name. But from above the portal of the Home for Old Men the name shouted in stone.

Despite its unpromising exterior, the Home is a fairly commodious place of retreat from the ills that its inmates have incurred by being poor and old and men. At the time embraced in this brief chronicle they were in number about a score, but in acerbity, querulousness, and general ingratitude they could hardly be reckoned at fewer than a hundred; at least that was the estimate of the superintendent, Mr Silas Tilbody. It was Mr Tilbody's steadfast conviction that always, in admitting new old men to replace those who had gone to another and a better Home, the trustees had distinctly in will the infraction of his peace, and the trial of his patience. In truth, the longer the institution was connected with him, the stronger was his feeling that the founder's scheme of benevolence was sadly impaired by providing any inmates at all. He had not much imagination, but with what he had he was addicted to the reconstruction of the Home for Old Men into a kind of 'castle in Spain', with himself as castellan, hospitably entertaining about a score of sleek and prosperous middle-aged gentlemen, consummately good-humoured and civilly willing to pay for their board and lodging. In this revised project of philanthropy the trustees, to whom he was indebted for his office and responsible for his conduct, had not the happiness to appear. As to them, it was held by the village humorist aforementioned that in their management of the great charity Providence had thoughtfully supplied an incentive to thrift. With the inference which he expected to be drawn from that view we have nothing to do; it had neither support nor denial from the inmates, who certainly were most concerned. They lived out their little remnant of life, crept into graves neatly numbered, and were succeeded by other old men as like them as could be desired by the Adversary of Peace. If the Home was a place of punishment for the sin of unthrift the veteran offenders sought justice with a persistence that attested the sincerity of their penitence. It is to one of these that the reader's attention is now invited.

In the matter of attire this person was not altogether engaging. But for this season, which was midwinter, a careless observer might have looked upon him as a clever device of the husbandman indisposed to share the fruits of his toil with the crows that toil not, neither spin – an error that might not have been dispelled without longer and closer observation than he seemed to court; for his progress up Abersush Street, toward the Home in the gloom of the winter evening, was not visibly faster than what might have been expected of a scarecrow blessed with youth, health, and discontent. The man was indisputably ill-clad, yet not without a certain fitness and good taste, withal; for he was obviously an applicant for admittance to the Home, where poverty was a qualification. In the army of indigence the uniform is rags; they serve to distinguish the rank and file from the recruiting officers.

As the old man, entering the gate of the grounds, shuffled up the broad walk, already white with the fast-falling snow, which from time to time he feebly shook from its various coigns of vantage on his person, he came under inspection of the large globe lamp that burned always by night over the great door of the building. As if unwilling to incur its revealing beams, he turned to the left and, passing a considerable distance along the face of the building, rang at a smaller door emitting a dimmer ray that came from within, through the fanlight, and expended itself incuriously overhead. The door was opened by no less a personage than the great Mr Tilbody himself. Observing his visitor, who at once uncovered, and somewhat shortened the radius of the permanent curvature of his back, the great man gave visible token of neither surprise nor displeasure. Mr Tilbody was, indeed, in an uncommonly good humour, a phenomenon ascribable doubtless to the cheerful influence of the season; for this was Christmas Eve, and the morrow would be that blessed 365th part of the year that all Christian souls set apart for mighty feats of goodness and joy. Mr Tilbody was so full of the spirit of the season that his fat face and pale blue eyes, whose ineffectual fire served to distinguish it from an untimely summer squash, effused so genial a glow that it seemed a pity that he could not have lain down in it, basking in the consciousness of his own identity. He was hatted, booted, overcoated, and umbrellaed, as became a person who was about to expose himself to the night and the storm on an errand of charity; for Mr Tilbody had just parted from his wife and children to go 'down town' and purchase the wherewithal to confirm the annual falsehood about the hunch-bellied saint who frequents the chimneys to reward little boys and girls who are good, and especially truthful. So he did not invite the old man in, but saluted him cheerily: 'Hello! Just in time; a moment later and you would have missed me. Come, I have no time to waste; we'll walk a little way together.'

'Thank you,' said the old man, upon whose thin and white but not ignoble face the light from the open door showed an expression that was perhaps disappointment; 'but if the trustees – if my application –'

'The trustees,' Mr Tilbody said, closing more doors than one, and cutting off two kinds of light, 'have agreed that your application disagrees with them.'

Certain sentiments are inappropriate to Christmastide, but Humour, like Death, has all seasons for his own.

'Oh, my God!' cried the old man, in so thin and husky a tone that the invocation was anything but impressive, and to at least one of his two auditors sounded, indeed, somewhat ludicrous. To the Other – but that is a matter which laymen are devoid of the light to expound.

'Yes,' continued Mr Tilbody, accommodating his gait to that of his companion, who was mechanically, and not very successfully, retracing the track that he had made through the snow; 'they have decided that, under the circumstances – under the very peculiar circumstances, you understand – it would be inexpedient to admit you. As superintendent and *ex officio* secretary of the honourable board' – as Mr Tilbody 'read his title clear' the magnitude of the big building, seen through its veil of falling snow, appeared to suffer somewhat in comparison – 'it is my duty to inform you that, in the words of Deacon Byram, the chairman, your presence in the Home would – under the circumstances – be peculiarly embarrassing. I felt it my duty to submit to the honourable board the statement that you made to me yesterday of your needs, your physical condition, and the trials which it has pleased Providence to send upon you in your very proper effort to present your claims in person; but, after careful, and I may say prayerful, consideration of your case – with something too, I trust, of the large charitableness appropriate to the season – it was decided that we would not be justified in doing anything likely to impair the usefulness of the institution entrusted (under Providence) to our care.'

They had now passed out of the grounds; the street lamp opposite the gate was dimly visible through the snow. Already the old man's former track was obliterated, and he seemed uncertain as to which way he should go. Mr Tilbody had drawn a little away from him, but paused and turned half toward him, apparently reluctant to forego the continuing opportunity.

'Under the circumstances,' he resumed, 'the decision –'

But the old man was inaccessible to the suasion of his verbosity; he had crossed the street into a vacant lot and was going forward, rather deviously toward nowhere in particular – which, he having nowhere in particular to go to, was not so reasonless a proceeding as it looked.

And that is how it happened that the next morning, when the church bells of all Grayville were ringing with an added unction appropriate to the day, the sturdy little son of Deacon Byram, breaking a way through the snow to the place of worship, struck his foot against the body of Amasa Abersush, philanthropist.

The Death of Halpin Frayser

For by death is wrought greater change than hath been shown. Whereas in general the spirit that removed cometh back upon occasion, and is sometimes seen of those in flesh (appearing in the form of the body it bore) yet it hath happened that the veritable body without the spirit hath walked. And it is attested of those encountering who have lived to speak thereon that a lich so raised up hath no natural affection, nor remembrance thereof, but only hate. Also, it is known that some spirits which in life were benign become by death evil altogether. – *Hali*.

One dark night in midsummer a man waking from a dreamless sleep in a forest lifted his head from the earth, and staring a few moments into the blackness, said: 'Catherine Larue'. He said nothing more; no reason was known to him why he should have said so much.

The man was Halpin Frayser. He lived in St Helena, but where he lives now is uncertain, for he is dead. One who practises sleeping in the woods with nothing under him but the dry leaves and the damp earth, and nothing over him but the branches from which the leaves have fallen and the sky from which the earth has fallen, cannot hope for great longevity, and Frayser had already attained the age of thirty-two. There are persons in this world, millions of persons, and far and away the best persons, who regard that as a very advanced age. They are the children. To those who view the voyage of life from the port of departure the bark that has accomplished any considerable distance appears already in close approach to the farther shore. However, it is not certain that Halpin Frayser came to his death by exposure.

He had been all day in the hills west of the Napa Valley, looking for doves and such small game as was in season. Late in the afternoon it had come on to be cloudy, and he had lost his bearings; and although he had only to go always downhill – everywhere the way to safety when one is lost – the absence of trails had so impeded him that he was overtaken by night while still in the forest. Unable in the darkness to penetrate the thickets of manzanita and other undergrowth, utterly bewildered and overcome with fatigue, he had lain down near the root of a large madrono and fallen into a dreamless sleep. It was hours later, in the very middle of the night, that one of God's mysterious messengers, gliding ahead of the incalculable host of his companions sweeping westward with the dawn line, pronounced the awakening word in the ear of the sleeper, who sat upright and spoke, he knew not why, a name, he knew not whose.

Halpin Frayser was not much of a philosopher, nor a scientist. The circumstance that, waking from a deep sleep at night in the midst of a forest, he had spoken aloud a name that he had not in memory and hardly had in mind did not arouse an enlightened curiosity to investigate the phenomenon. He thought it odd, and with a little perfunctory shiver, as if in deference to a seasonal presumption that the night was chill, he lay down again and went to sleep. But his sleep was no longer dreamless.

He thought he was walking along a dusty road that showed white in the gathering darkness of a summer night. Whence and whither it led, and why he travelled it, he did not know, though all seemed simple and natural, as is the way in dreams; for in the Land Beyond the Bed surprises cease from troubling and the judgement is at rest. Soon he came to a parting of the ways; leading from the highway was a road less travelled, having the appearance, indeed, of having been long abandoned, because, he thought, it led to something evil; yet he turned into it without hesitation, impelled by some imperious necessity.

As he pressed forward he became conscious that his way was haunted by invisible existences whom he could not definitely figure to his mind. From among the trees on either side he caught broken and incoherent whispers in a strange tongue which yet he partly understood. They seemed to him fragmentary utterances of a monstrous conspiracy against his body and soul.

It was now long after nightfall, yet the interminable forest through which he journeyed was lit with a wan glimmer having no point of diffusion, for in its mysterious lumination nothing cast a shadow. A shallow pool in the guttered depression of an old wheel rut, as from a recent rain, met his eye with a crimson gleam. He stooped and plunged his hand into it. It stained his fingers; it was blood! Blood, he then observed, was about him everywhere. The weeds growing rankly by the roadside showed it in blots and splashes on their big, broad leaves. Patches of dry dust between the wheelways were pitted and spattered as with a red rain. Defiling the trunks of the trees were broad maculations of crimson, and blood dripped like dew from their foliage.

All this he observed with a terror which seemed not incompatible with the fulfilment of a natural expectation. It seemed to him that it was all in expiation of some crime which, though conscious of his guilt, he could not rightly remember. To the menaces and mysteries of his surroundings the consciousness was an added horror. Vainly he sought by tracing life backward in memory, to reproduce the moment of his sin; scenes and incidents came crowding tumultuously into his mind, one picture effacing another, or commingling with it in confusion and obscurity, but nowhere could he catch a glimpse of what he sought. The failure augmented his terror; he felt as one who has murdered in the dark, not knowing whom nor why. So frightful was the situation – the mysterious light burned with so silent and awful a menace; the noxious plants, the trees that by common consent are invested with a melancholy or baleful character, so openly in his sight conspired against his peace; from overhead and all about came so audible and startling whispers and the sighs of creatures so obviously not of earth – that he could endure it no longer, and with a great effort to break some malign spell that bound his faculties to silence and inaction, he shouted with the full strength of his lungs! His voice broken, it seemed, into an infinite multitude of unfamiliar sounds, went babbling and stammering away into the distant reaches of the forest, died into silence, and all was as before. But he had made a beginning at resistance and was encouraged. He said: 'I will not submit unheard. There may be powers that are not malignant travelling this accursed road. I shall leave them a record and an appeal. I shall relate my wrongs, the persecutions that I endure – I, a helpless mortal, a penitent, an unoffending poet!' Halpin Frayser was a poet only as he was a penitent: in his dream.

Taking from his clothing a small red-leather pocketbook, one half of which was leaved for memoranda, he discovered that he was without a pencil. He broke a twig from a bush, dipped it into a pool of blood and wrote rapidly. He had hardly touched the paper with the point of his twig when a low, wild peal of laughter broke out at a measureless distance away, and growing ever louder, seemed approaching ever nearer; a soulless, heartless, and unjoyous laugh, like that of the loon, solitary by the lakeside at midnight; a laugh which culminated in an unearthly shout close at hand, then died away by slow gradations, as if the accursed being that uttered it had withdrawn over the verge of the world whence it had come. But the man felt that this was not so – that it was nearby and had not moved.

A strange sensation began slowly to take possession of his body and his mind. He could not have said which, if any, of his senses was affected; he felt it rather as a consciousness – a mysterious mental assurance of some overpowering presence – some super-natural malevolence different in kind from the invisible existences that swarmed about him, and superior to them in power. He knew that it had uttered that hideous laugh. And now it seemed to be approaching him; from what direction he did not know – dared not conjecture. All his former fears were forgotten or merged in the gigantic terror that now held him in thrall. Apart from that, he had but one thought: to complete his written appeal to the benign powers who, traversing the haunted wood, might some time rescue him if he should be denied the blessing of annihilation. He wrote with terrible rapidity, the twig in his fingers rilling blood without renewal; but in the middle of a sentence his hands denied their service to his will, his arms fell to his sides, the book to the earth; and powerless to move or cry out, he found himself staring into the sharply drawn face and blank, dead eyes of his own mother, standing white and silent in the garments of the grave!

2

In his youth Halpin Frayser had lived with his parents in Nashville, Tennessee. The Fraysers were well-to-do, having a good position in such society as had survived the wreck wrought by civil war. Their children had the social and educational opportunities of their time and place, and had responded to good associations and in-struction with agreeable manners and cultivated minds. Halpin being the youngest and not over-robust was perhaps a trifle 'spoiled'. He had the double disadvantage of a mother's assiduity and a father's neglect. Frayser père was what no Southern man of means is not – a politician. His country, or rather his section and State, made demands upon his time and attention so exacting that to those of his family he was compelled to turn an ear partly deafened by the thunder of the political captains and the shouting, his own included.

Young Halpin was of a dreamy, indolent and rather romantic turn, somewhat more addicted to literature than law, the profession to which he was bred. Among those of his relations who professed the modern faith of heredity it was well understood that in him the character of the late Myron Bayne, a maternal great-grandfather, had revisited the glimpses of the moon – by which orb Bayne had in his lifetime been sufficiently affected to be a poet of no small Colonial distinction. If not specially observed, it was observable that while a Frayser who was not the proud possessor of a sumptuous copy of the ancestral 'poetical works' (printed at the family expense, and long ago withdrawn from an inhospitable market) was a rare Frayser indeed, there was an illogical indisposition to honour the great deceased in the person of his spiritual successor. Halpin was pretty generally deprecated as an intellectual black sheep who was likely at any moment to disgrace the flock by bleating in metre. The Tennessee Fraysers were a practical folk – not practical in the popular sense of devotion to sordid pursuits, but having a robust contempt for any qualities unfitting a man for the wholesome vocation of politics.

In justice to young Halpin it should be said that while in him were pretty faithfully reproduced most of the mental and moral characteristics ascribed by history and family tradition to the famous Colonial bard, his succession to the gift and faculty divine was purely inferential. Not only had he never been known to court the muse, but in truth he could not have written correctly a line of verse to save himself from the Killer of the Wise. Still, there was no knowing when the dormant faculty might wake and smite the lyre.

In the meantime the young man was rather a loose fish, anyhow. Between him and his mother was the most perfect sympathy, for secretly the lady was herself a devout disciple of the late and great Myron Bayne, though with the tact so generally and justly admired in her sex (despite the hardy calumniators who insist that it is essentially the same thing as cunning) she had always taken care to conceal her weakness from all eyes but those of him who shared it. Their common guilt in respect of that was an added tie between them. If in Halpin's youth his mother had 'spoiled' him, he had assuredly done his part toward being spoiled. As he grew to such manhood as is attainable by a Southerner who does not care which way elections go the attachment between him and his beautiful mother – whom from early childhood he had called Katy – became yearly stronger and more tender. In these two romantic natures was manifest in a signal way that neglected phenomenon, the dominance of the sexual element in all the relations of life, strengthening, softening, and beautifying even those of consanguinity. The two were nearly inseparable, and by strangers observing their manner were not infrequently mistaken for lovers.

Entering his mother's boudoir one day Halpin Frayser kissed her upon the forehead, toyed for a moment with a lock of her dark hair which had escaped from its confining pins, and said, with an obvious effort at calmness: 'Would you greatly mind, Katy, if I were called away to California for a few weeks?'

It was hardly needful for Katy to answer with her lips a question to which her telltale cheeks had made instant reply. Evidently she would greatly mind; and the tears, too, sprang into her large brown eyes as corroborative testimony.

'Ah, my son,' she said, looking up into his face with infinite tenderness, 'I should have known that this was coming. Did I not lie awake a half of the night weeping because, during the other half, Grandfather Bayne had come to me in a dream, and standing by his portrait – young, too, and handsome as that – pointed to yours on the same wall? And when I looked it seemed that I could not see the features; you had been painted with a face cloth, such as we put upon the dead. Your father has laughed at me, but you and I, dear, know that such things are not for nothing. And I saw below the edge of the cloth the marks of hands on your throat – forgive me, but we have not been used to keep such things from each other. Perhaps you have another interpretation. Perhaps it does not mean that you will go to California. Or maybe you will take me with you?'

It must be confessed that this ingenious interpretation of the dream in the light of newly discovered evidence did not wholly commend itself to the son's more logical mind; he had, for the moment at least, a conviction that it foreshadowed a more simple and immediate, if less tragic, disaster than a visit to the Pacific Coast. It was Halpin Frayser's impression that he was to be garrotted on his native heath.

'Are there not medicinal springs in California?' Mrs Frayser resumed before he had time to give her the true reading of the dream – 'places where one recovers from rheumatism and neuralgia? Look – my fingers feel so stiff; and I am almost sure they have been giving me great pain while I slept.'

She held out her hands for his inspection. What diagnosis of her case the young man may have thought it best to conceal with a smile the historian is unable to state, but for himself he feels bound to say that fingers looking less stiff, and showing fewer evidences of even insensible pain, have seldom been submitted for medical inspection by even the fairest patient desiring a prescription of unfamiliar scenes.

The outcome of it was that of these two odd persons having equally odd notions of duty, the one went to California, as the interest of his client required, and the other remained at home in compliance with a wish that her husband was scarcely conscious of entertaining.

While in San Francisco Halpin Frayser was walking one dark night along the waterfront of the city, when, with a suddenness that surprised and disconcerted him, he became a sailor. He was in fact 'shanghaied' aboard a gallant, gallant ship, and sailed for a far countree. Nor did his misfortunes end with the voyage; for the ship was cast ashore on an island of the South Pacific, and it was six years afterward when the survivors were taken off by a venturesome trading schooner and brought back to San Francisco.

Though poor in purse, Frayser was no less proud in spirit than he had been in the years that seemed ages and ages ago. He would accept no assistance from strangers, and it was while living with a fellow survivor near the town of St Helena, awaiting news and remittances from home, that he had gone gunning and dreaming.

3

The apparition confronting the dreamer in the haunted wood – the thing so like, yet so unlike his mother – was horrible! It stirred no love nor longing in his heart; it came unattended with pleasant memories of a golden past – inspired no sentiment of any kind; all the finer emotions were swallowed up in fear. He tried to turn and run from before it, but his legs were as lead; he was unable to lift his feet from the ground. His arms hung helpless at his sides; of his eyes only he retained control, and these he dared not remove from the lustreless orbs of the apparition, which he knew was not a soul without a body, but that most dreadful of all existences infesting that haunted wood – a body without a soul! In its blank stare was neither love, nor pity, nor intelligence – nothing to which to address an appeal for mercy. 'An appeal will not lie,' he thought, with an absurd reversion to professional slang, making the situation more horrible, as the fire of a cigar might light up a tomb.

For a time, which seemed so long that the world grew grey with age and sin, and the haunted forest, having fulfilled its purpose in this monstrous culmination of its terrors, vanished out of his consciousness with all its sights and sounds, the apparition stood within a pace, regarding him with the mindless malevolence of a wild brute; then thrust its hands forward and sprang upon him with appalling ferocity! The act released his physical energies without unfettering his will; his mind was still spellbound, but his powerful body and agile limbs, endowed with a blind, insensate life of their own, resisted stoutly and well. For an instant he seemed to see this unnatural contest between a dead intelligence and a breathing mechanism only as a spectator – such fancies are in dreams; then he regained his identity almost as if by a leap forward into his body, and the straining automaton had a directing will as alert and fierce as that of its hideous antagonist.

But what mortal can cope with a creature of his dream? The imagination creating the enemy is already vanquished; the combat's result is the combat's cause. Despite his struggles – despite his strength and activity, which seemed wasted in a void, he felt the cold fingers close upon his throat. Borne backward to the earth, he saw above him the dead and drawn face within a hand's breadth of his own, and then all was black. A sound as of the beating of distant drums – a murmur of swarming voices, a sharp, far cry signing all to silence, and Halpin Frayser dreamed that he was dead.

4

A warm, clear night had been followed by a morning of drenching fog. At about the middle of the afternoon of the preceding day a little whiff of light vapour – a mere thickening of the atmosphere, the ghost of a cloud – had been observed clinging to the western side of Mount St Helena, away up along the barren altitudes near the summit. It was so thin, so diaphanous, so like a fancy made visible, that one would have said: 'Look quickly! In a moment it will be gone.'

In a moment it was visibly larger and denser. While with one edge it clung to the mountain, with the other it reached farther and farther out into the air above the lower slopes. At the same time it extended itself to north and south, joining small patches of mist that appeared to come out of the mountainside on exactly the same level, with an intelligent design to be absorbed. And so it grew and grew until the summit was shut out of view from the valley, and over the valley itself was an ever-extending canopy, opaque and grey. At Calistoga, which lies near the head of the valley and the foot of the mountain, there were a starless night and a sunless morning. The fog, sinking into the valley, had reached southward, swallowing up ranch after ranch, until it had blotted out the town of St Helena, nine miles away. The dust in the road was laid; trees were adrip with moisture; birds sat silent in their coverts; the morning light was wan and ghastly, with neither colour nor fire.

Two men left the town of St Helena at the first glimmer of dawn, and walked along the road northward up the valley toward Calistoga. They carried guns on their shoulders, yet no-one having knowledge of such matters could have mistaken them for hunters of bird or beast. They were a deputy sheriff from Napa and a detective from San Francisco – Holker and Jaralson, respectively. Their business was man-hunting.

'How far is it?' enquired Holker, as they strode along, their feet stirring white the dust beneath the damp surface of the road.

'The White Church? Only a half-mile farther,' the other answered. 'By the way,' he added, 'it is neither white nor a church; it is an abandoned schoolhouse, grey with age and neglect. Religious services were once held in it – when it was white, and there is a graveyard that would delight a poet. Can you guess why I sent for you, and told you to come heeled?'

'Oh, I never have bothered you about things of that kind. I've always found you communicative when the time came. But if I may hazard a guess, you want me to help you arrest one of the corpses in the graveyard.'

'You remember Branscom?' said Jaralson, treating his companion's wit with the inattention that it deserved.

'The chap who cut his wife's throat? I ought; I wasted a week's work on him and had my expenses for my trouble. There is a reward of five hundred dollars, but none of us ever got a sight of him. You don't mean to say – '

'Yes, I do. He has been under the noses of you fellows all the time. He comes by night to the old graveyard at the White Church.'

'The devil! That's where they buried his wife.'

'Well, you fellows might have had sense enough to suspect that he would return to her grave some time.'

'The very last place that anyone would have expected him to return to.'

'But you had exhausted all the other places. Learning your failure at them, I "laid for him" there.'

'And you found him?'

'Damn it! He found *me*. The rascal got the drop on me – regularly held me up and made me travel. It's God's mercy that he didn't go through me. Oh, he's a good one, and I fancy the half of that reward is enough for me if you're needy.'

Holker laughed good-humouredly, and explained that his creditors were never more importunate.

'I wanted merely to show you the ground, and arrange a plan with you,' the detective explained. 'I thought it as well for us to be heeled, even in daylight.'

'The man must be insane,' said the deputy sheriff. 'The reward is for his capture and conviction. If he's mad he won't be convicted.'

Mr Holker was so profoundly affected by that possible failure of justice that he involuntarily stopped in the middle of the road, then resumed his walk with abated zeal.

'Well, he looks it,' assented Jaralson. 'I'm bound to admit that a more unshaven, unshorn, unkempt, and uneverything wretch I never saw outside the ancient and honourable order of tramps. But I've gone in for him, and can't make up my mind to let go. There's glory in it for us, anyhow. Not another soul knows that he is this side of the Mountains of the Moon.'

'All right,' Holker said; 'we will go and view the ground,' and he added, in the words of a once favourite inscription for tombstones: ' "where you must shortly lie" – I mean, if old Branscom ever gets tired of you and your impertinent intrusion. By the way, I heard the other day that "Branscom" was not his real name.'

'What is?'

'I can't recall it. I had lost all interest in the wretch, and it did not fix itself in my memory – something like Pardee. The woman whose throat he had the bad taste to cut was a widow when he met her. She had come to California to look up some relatives – there are persons who will do that sometimes. But you know all that.'

'Naturally.'

'But not knowing the right name, by what happy inspiration did you find the right grave? The man who told me what the name was said it had been cut on the headboard.'

'I don't know the right grave.' Jaralson was apparently a trifle reluctant to admit his ignorance of so important a point of his plan. 'I have been watching about the place generally. A part of our work this morning will be to identify that grave. Here is the White Church.'

For a long distance the road had been bordered by fields on both sides, but now on the left there was a forest of oaks, madroños, and gigantic spruces whose lower parts only could be seen, dim and ghostly in the fog. The undergrowth was, in places, thick, but nowhere impenetrable. For some moments Holker saw nothing of the building, but as they turned into the woods it revealed itself in faint grey outline through the fog, looking huge and far away. A few steps more, and it was within an arm's length, distinct, dark with moisture, and insignificant in size. It had the usual country-school-house form – belonged to the packing-box order of architecture; had an underpinning of stones, a moss-grown roof, and blank window spaces, whence both glass and sash had long departed. It was ruined, but not a ruin – a typical Californian substitute for what are known to guide-bookers abroad as 'monuments of the past'. With scarcely a glance at this uninteresting structure Jaralson moved on into the dripping undergrowth beyond.

'I will show you where he held me up,' he said. 'This is the graveyard.'

Here and there among the bushes were small enclosures containing graves, sometimes no more than one. They were recognised as graves by the discoloured stones or rotting boards at head and foot, leaning at all angles, some prostrate; by the ruined picket fences surrounding them; or, infrequently, by the mound itself showing its gravel through the fallen leaves. In many instances nothing marked the spot where lay the vestiges of some poor mortal – who, leaving 'a large circle of sorrowing friends', had been left by them in turn – except a depression in the earth, more lasting than that in the spirits of the mourners. The paths, if any paths had been, were long obliterated; trees of a considerable size had been permitted to grow up from the graves and thrust aside with root or branch the inclosing fences. Over all was that air of abandonment and decay which seems nowhere so fit and significant as in a village of the forgotten dead.

As the two men, Jaralson leading, pushed their way through the growth of young trees, that enterprising man suddenly stopped and brought up his shotgun to the height of his breast, uttered a low note of warning, and stood motionless, his eyes fixed upon something ahead. As well as he could, obstructed by brush, his companion, though seeing nothing, imitated the posture and so stood, prepared for what might ensue. A moment later Jaralson moved cautiously forward, the other following.

Under the branches of an enormous spruce lay the dead body of a man. Standing silent above it they noted such particulars as first strike the attention – the face, the attitude, the clothing; whatever most promptly and plainly answers the unspoken question of a sympathetic curiosity.

The body lay upon its back, the legs wide apart. One arm was thrust upward, the other outward; but the latter was bent acutely, and the hand was near the throat. Both hands were tightly clenched. The whole attitude was that of desperate but ineffectual resistance to – what?

Nearby lay a shotgun and a game bag through the meshes of which was seen the plumage of shot birds. All about were evidences of a furious struggle; small sprouts of poison-oak were bent and denuded of leaf and bark; dead and rotting leaves had been pushed into heaps and ridges on both sides of the legs by the action of other feet than theirs; alongside the hips were unmistakable impressions of human knees.

The nature of the struggle was made clear by a glance at the dead man's throat and face. While breast and hands were white, those were purple – almost black. The shoulders lay upon a low mound, and the head was turned back at an angle otherwise impossible, the expanded eyes staring blankly backward in a direction opposite to that of the feet. From the froth filling the open mouth the tongue protruded, black and swollen. The throat showed horrible contusions; not mere fingermarks, but bruises and lacerations wrought by two strong hands that must have buried themselves in the yielding flesh, maintaining their terrible grasp until long after death. Breast, throat, face, were wet; the clothing was saturated; drops of water, condensed from the fog, studded the hair and mustache.

All this the two men observed without speaking – almost at a glance. Then Holker said: 'Poor devil! he had a rough deal.'

Jaralson was making a vigilant circumspection of the forest, his shotgun held in both hands and at full cock, his finger upon the trigger.

'The work of a maniac,' he said, without withdrawing his eyes from the enclosing wood. 'It was done by Branscom – Pardee.'

Something half-hidden by the disturbed leaves on the earth caught Holker's attention. It was a red-leather pocketbook. He picked it up and opened it. It contained leaves of white paper for memoranda, and upon the first leaf was the name 'Halpin Frayser'. Written in red on several succeeding leaves – scrawled as if in haste and barely legible – were the following lines, which Holker read aloud, while his companion continued scanning the dim grey confines of their

narrow world and hearing matter of apprehension in the drip of
water from every burdened branch:

> 'Enthralled by some mysterious spell, I stood
> In the lit gloom of an enchanted wood.
>   The cypress there and myrtle twined their boughs,
> Significant, in baleful brotherhood.
>
> 'The brooding willow whispered to the yew;
> Beneath, the deadly nightshade and the rue,
>   With immortelles self-woven into strange
> Funereal shapes, and horrid nettles grew.
>
> 'No song of bird nor any drone of bees,
> Nor light leaf lifted by the wholesome breeze:
>   The air was stagnant all, and Silence was
> A living thing that breathed among the trees.
>
> 'Conspiring spirits whispered in the gloom,
> Half-heard, the stilly secrets of the tomb.
>   With blood the trees were all adrip; the leaves
> Shone in the witch-light with a ruddy bloom.
>
> 'I cried aloud! – the spell, unbroken still,
> Rested upon my spirit and my will.
>   Unsouled, unhearted, hopeless and forlorn,
> I strove with monstrous presages of ill!
>
> 'At last the viewless – '

Holker ceased reading; there was no more to read. The manuscript
broke off in the middle of a line.

'That sounds like Bayne,' said Jaralson, who was something of a
scholar in his way. He had abated his vigilance and stood looking
down at the body.

'Who's Bayne?' Holker asked rather incuriously.

'Myron Bayne, a chap who flourished in the early years of the
nation – more than a century ago. Wrote mighty dismal stuff; I have
his collected works. That poem is not among them, but it must have
been omitted by mistake.'

'It is cold,' said Holker; 'let us leave here; we must have up the
coroner from Napa.'

Jaralson said nothing, but made a movement in compliance. Passing
the end of the slight elevation of earth upon which the dead man's

head and shoulders lay, his foot struck some hard substance under the rotting forest leaves, and he took the trouble to kick it into view. It was a fallen headboard, and painted on it were the hardly decipherable words, 'Catharine Larue'.

'Larue, Larue!' exclaimed Holker, with sudden animation. 'Why, that is the real name of Branscom – not Pardee. And – bless my soul! how it all comes to me – the murdered woman's name had been Frayser!'

'There is some rascally mystery here,' said Detective Jaralson. 'I hate anything of that kind.'

There came to them out of the fog – seemingly from a great distance – the sound of a laugh, a low, deliberate, soulless laugh, which had no more of joy than that of a hyena night-prowling in the desert; a laugh that rose by slow gradation, louder and louder, clearer, more distinct and terrible, until it seemed barely outside the narrow circle of their vision; a laugh so unnatural, so unhuman, so devilish, that it filled those hardy man-hunters with a sense of dread unspeakable! They did not move their weapons nor think of them; the menace of that horrible sound was not of the kind to be met with arms. As it had grown out of silence, so now it died away; from a culminating shout which had seemed almost in their ears, it drew itself away into the distance, until its failing notes, joyless and mechanical to the last, sank to silence at a measureless remove.

A Watcher by the Dead

In an upper room of an unoccupied dwelling in the part of San Francisco known as North Beach lay the body of a man, under a sheet. The hour was near nine in the evening; the room was dimly lighted by a single candle. Although the weather was warm, the two windows, contrary to the custom which gives the dead plenty of air, were closed and the blinds drawn down. The furniture of the room consisted of but three pieces – an armchair, a small reading-stand supporting the candle, and a long kitchen table, supporting the body of the man. All these, as also the corpse, seemed to have been recently brought in, for an observer, had there been one, would have seen that all were free from dust, whereas everything else in the room was pretty thickly coated with it, and there were cobwebs in the angles of the walls.

Under the sheet the outlines of the body could be traced, even the features, these having that unnaturally sharp definition which seems to belong to faces of the dead, but is really characteristic of those only that have been wasted by disease. From the silence of the room one would rightly have inferred that it was not in the front of the house, facing a street. It really faced nothing but a high breast of rock, the rear of the building being set into a hill.

As a neighbouring church clock was striking nine with an indolence which seemed to imply such an indifference to the flight of time that one could hardly help wondering why it took the trouble to strike at all, the single door of the room was opened and a man entered, advancing toward the body. As he did so the door closed, apparently of its own volition; there was a grating, as of a key turned with difficulty, and the snap of the lock bolt as it shot into its socket. A sound of retiring footsteps in the passage outside ensued, and the man was to all appearance a prisoner. Advancing to the table, he stood a moment looking down at the body; then with a slight shrug of the shoulders walked over to one of the windows and hoisted the blind. The darkness outside was absolute, the panes were covered with dust, but by wiping this away he could see that the window was fortified with strong iron bars crossing it within a few inches of the glass and embedded in the masonry on each side. He examined the other window. It was the same. He manifested no great curiosity in the matter, did not even so much as raise the sash. If he was a prisoner he was apparently a tractable one. Having completed his examination of the room, he seated himself in the armchair, took a book from his pocket, drew the stand with its candle alongside and began to read.

The man was young – not more than thirty – dark in complexion, smooth-shaven, with brown hair. His face was thin and high-nosed, with a broad forehead and a 'firmness' of the chin and jaw which is said by those having it to denote resolution. The eyes were grey and steadfast, not moving except with definitive purpose. They were now for the greater part of the time fixed upon his book, but he occasionally withdrew them and turned them to the body on the table, not, apparently, from any dismal fascination which under such circumstances it might be supposed to exercise upon even a courageous person, nor with a conscious rebellion against the contrary influence which might dominate a timid one. He looked at it as if in his reading he had come upon something recalling him to a sense of his surroundings. Clearly this watcher by the dead was discharging his trust with intelligence and composure, as became him.

After reading for perhaps a half-hour he seemed to come to the end of a chapter and quietly laid away the book. He then rose and taking the reading-stand from the floor carried it into a corner of the room near one of the windows, lifted the candle from it and returned to the empty fireplace before which he had been sitting.

A moment later he walked over to the body on the table, lifted the sheet and turned it back from the head, exposing a mass of dark hair and a thin face-cloth, beneath which the features showed with even sharper definition than before. Shading his eyes by interposing his free hand between them and the candle, he stood looking at his motionless companion with a serious and tranquil regard. Satisfied with his inspection, he pulled the sheet over the face again and returning to the chair, took some matches off the candlestick, put them in the side pocket of his sack-coat and sat down. He then lifted the candle from its socket and looked at it critically, as if calculating how long it would last. It was barely two inches long; in another hour he would be in darkness. He replaced it in the candlestick and blew it out.

2

In a physician's office in Kearny Street three men sat about a table, drinking punch and smoking. It was late in the evening, almost midnight, indeed, and there had been no lack of punch. The gravest of the three, Dr Helberson, was the host – it was in his rooms they sat. He was about thirty years of age; the others were even younger; all were physicians.

'The superstitious awe with which the living regard the dead,' said Dr Helberson, 'is hereditary and incurable. One needs no more be ashamed of it than of the fact that he inherits, for example, an incapacity for mathematics, or a tendency to lie.'

The others laughed. 'Oughtn't a man to be ashamed to lie?' asked the youngest of the three, who was in fact a medical student not yet graduated.

'My dear Harper, I said nothing about that. The tendency to lie is one thing; lying is another.'

'But do you think,' said the third man, 'that this superstitious feeling, this fear of the dead, reasonless as we know it to be, is universal? I am myself not conscious of it.'

'Oh, but it is "in your system" for all that,' replied Helberson; 'it needs only the right conditions – what Shakespeare calls the "confederate season" – to manifest itself in some very disagreeable way that will open your eyes. Physicians and soldiers are of course more nearly free from it than others.'

'Physicians and soldiers! – why don't you add hangmen and headsmen? Let us have in all the assassin classes.'

'No, my dear Mancher; the juries will not let the public executioners acquire sufficient familiarity with death to be altogether unmoved by it.'

Young Harper, who had been helping himself to a fresh cigar at the sideboard, resumed his seat. 'What would you consider conditions under which any man of woman born would become insupportably conscious of his share of our common weakness in this regard?' he asked, rather verbosely.

'Well, I should say that if a man were locked up all night with a corpse – alone – in a dark room – of a vacant house – with no bedcovers to pull over his head – and lived through it without going altogether mad, he might justly boast himself not of woman born, nor yet, like Macduff, a product of Caesarean section.'

'I thought you never would finish piling up conditions,' said Harper, 'but I know a man who is neither a physician nor a soldier who will accept them all, for any stake you like to name.'

'Who is he?'

'His name is Jarette – a stranger here; comes from my town in New York. I have no money to back him, but he will back himself with loads of it.'

'How do you know that?'

'He would rather bet than eat. As for fear – I dare say he thinks it some cutaneous disorder, or possibly a particular kind of religious heresy.'

'What does he look like?' Helberson was evidently becoming interested.

'Like Mancher, here – might be his twin brother.'

'I accept the challenge,' said Helberson, promptly.

'Awfully obliged to you for the compliment, I'm sure,' drawled Mancher, who was growing sleepy. 'Can't I get into this?'

'Not against me,' Helberson said. 'I don't want *your* money.'

'All right,' said Mancher; 'I'll be the corpse.'

The others laughed.

The outcome of this crazy conversation we have seen.

3

In extinguishing his meagre allowance of candle Mr Jarette's object was to preserve it against some unforeseen need. He may have thought, too, or half thought, that the darkness would be no worse at one time than another, and if the situation became insupportable it would be better to have a means of relief, or even release. At any rate it was wise to have a little reserve of light, even if only to enable him to look at his watch.

No sooner had he blown out the candle and set it on the floor at his side than he settled himself comfortably in the armchair, leaned back and closed his eyes, hoping and expecting to sleep. In this he was disappointed; he had never in his life felt less sleepy, and in a few minutes he gave up the attempt. But what could he do? He could not go groping about in absolute darkness at the risk of bruising himself – at the risk, too, of blundering against the table and rudely disturbing the dead. We all recognise their right to lie at rest, with immunity from all that is harsh and violent. Jarette almost succeeded in making himself believe that considerations of this kind restrained him from risking the collision and fixed him to the chair.

While thinking of this matter he fancied that he heard a faint sound in the direction of the table – what kind of sound he could hardly have explained. He did not turn his head. Why should he – in the darkness? But he listened – why should he not? And listening he grew giddy and grasped the arms of the chair for support. There was a strange ringing in his ears; his head seemed bursting; his chest was oppressed by the constriction of his clothing. He wondered why it was so, and whether these were symptoms of fear. Then, with a long and strong expiration, his chest appeared to collapse, and with the great gasp with which he refilled his exhausted lungs the vertigo left him and he knew that so intently had he listened that he had held his breath almost to suffocation. The revelation was vexatious; he arose, pushed away the chair with his foot and strode to the centre of the room. But one does not stride far in darkness; he began to grope, and finding the wall followed it to an angle, turned, followed it past the two windows and there in another corner came into violent contact with the reading-stand, overturning it. It made a clatter that startled him. He was annoyed. 'How the devil could I have forgotten where it was?' he muttered, and groped his way along the third wall to the fireplace. 'I must put things to rights,' said he, feeling the floor for the candle.

Having recovered that, he lighted it and instantly turned his eyes to the table, where, naturally, nothing had undergone any change. The reading-stand lay unobserved upon the floor: he had forgotten to 'put it to rights'. He looked all about the room, dispersing the deeper shadows by movements of the candle in his hand, and crossing over to the door tested it by turning and pulling the knob with all his strength. It did not yield and this seemed to afford him a certain satisfaction; indeed, he secured it more firmly by a bolt which he had not before observed. Returning to his chair, he looked at his watch; it was half-past nine. With a start of surprise he held the watch at his ear. It had not stopped. The candle was now visibly shorter. He again extinguished it, placing it on the floor at his side as before.

Mr Jarette was not at his ease; he was distinctly dissatisfied with his surroundings, and with himself for being so. 'What have I to fear?' he thought. 'This is ridiculous and disgraceful; I will not be so great a fool.' But courage does not come of saying, 'I will be courageous,' nor of recognising its appropriateness to the occasion. The more Jarette condemned himself, the more reason he gave himself for condemnation; the greater the number of variations which he played upon the simple theme of the harmlessness of the dead, the more insupportable grew the discord of his emotions. 'What!' he cried aloud in the anguish of his spirit, 'What! Shall I, who have not a shade of superstition in my nature – I, who have no belief in immortality – I, who know (and never more clearly than now) that the afterlife is the dream of a desire – shall I lose at once my bet, my honour and my self-respect, perhaps my reason, because certain savage ancestors dwelling in caves and burrows conceived the monstrous notion that the dead walk by night? – that – ' Distinctly, unmistakably, Mr Jarette heard behind him a light, soft sound of footfalls, deliberate, regular, successively nearer!

4

Just before daybreak the next morning Dr Helberson and his young friend Harper were driving slowly through the streets of North Beach in the doctor's coupé.

'Have you still the confidence of youth in the courage or stolidity of your friend?' said the elder man. 'Do you believe that I have lost this wager?'

'I *know* you have,' replied the other, with enfeebling emphasis.

'Well, upon my soul, I hope so.'

It was spoken earnestly, almost solemnly. There was a silence for a few moments.

'Harper,' the doctor resumed, looking very serious in the shifting half-lights that entered the carriage as they passed the street lamps, 'I don't feel altogether comfortable about this business. If your friend had not irritated me by the contemptuous manner in which he treated my doubt of his endurance – a purely physical quality – and by the cool incivility of his suggestion that the corpse be that of a physician, I should not have gone on with it. If anything should happen we are ruined, as I fear we deserve to be.'

'What can happen? Even if the matter should be taking a serious turn, of which I am not at all afraid, Mancher has only to "resurrect" himself and explain matters. With a genuine "subject" from the dissecting-room, or one of your late patients, it might be different.'

Dr Mancher, then, had been as good as his promise; he was the 'corpse'.

Dr Helberson was silent for a long time, as the carriage, at a snail's pace, crept along the same street it had travelled two or three times already. Presently he spoke: 'Well, let us hope that Mancher, if he has had to rise from the dead, has been discreet about it. A mistake in that might make matters worse instead of better.'

'Yes,' said Harper, 'Jarette would kill him. But, Doctor' – looking at his watch as the carriage passed a gas lamp – 'it is nearly four o'clock at last.'

A moment later the two had quitted the vehicle and were walking briskly toward the long-unoccupied house belonging to the doctor in which they had immured Mr Jarette in accordance with the terms of the mad wager. As they neared it they met a man running. 'Can you tell me,' he cried, suddenly checking his speed, 'where I can find a doctor?'

'What's the matter?' Helberson asked, noncommittal.

'Go and see for yourself,' said the man, resuming his running.

They hastened on. Arrived at the house, they saw several persons entering in haste and excitement. In some of the dwellings nearby and across the way the chamber windows were thrown up, showing a protrusion of heads. All heads were asking questions, none heeding the questions of the others. A few of the windows with closed blinds were illuminated; the inmates of those rooms were dressing to come down. Exactly opposite the door of the house that they sought a street lamp threw a yellow, insufficient light upon the scene, seeming to say that it could disclose a good deal more if it wished. Harper paused at the door and laid a hand upon his companion's arm. 'It is all up with us, Doctor,' he said in extreme agitation, which contrasted strangely with his free-and-easy words; 'the game has gone against us all. Let's not go in there; I'm for lying low.'

'I'm a physician,' said Dr Helberson, calmly; 'there may be need of one.'

They mounted the doorsteps and were about to enter. The door was open; the street lamp opposite lighted the passage into which it opened. It was full of men. Some had ascended the stairs at the farther end, and, denied admittance above, waited for better fortune. All were talking, none listening. Suddenly, on the upper landing there was a great commotion; a man had sprung out of a door and was breaking away from those endeavouring to detain him. Down through the mass of affrighted idlers he came, pushing them aside, flattening them against the wall on one side, or compelling them to cling to the rail on the other, clutching them by the throat, striking them savagely, thrusting them back down the stairs and walking over the fallen. His clothing was in disorder, he was without a hat. His eyes, wild and restless, had in them something more terrifying than his apparently superhuman strength. His face, smooth-shaven, was bloodless, his hair frost-white.

As the crowd at the foot of the stairs, having more freedom, fell away to let him pass Harper sprang forward. 'Jarette! Jarette!' he cried.

Dr Helberson seized Harper by the collar and dragged him back. The man looked into their faces without seeming to see them and sprang through the door, down the steps, into the street, and away. A stout policeman, who had had inferior success in conquering his way down the stairway, followed a moment later and started in pursuit, all the heads in the windows – those of women and children now – screaming in guidance.

The stairway being now partly cleared, most of the crowd having rushed down to the street to observe the flight and pursuit, Dr Helberson mounted to the landing, followed by Harper. At a door in the upper passage an officer denied them admittance. 'We are physicians,' said the doctor, and they passed in. The room was full of men, dimly seen, crowded about a table. The newcomers edged their way forward and looked over the shoulders of those in the front rank. Upon the table, the lower limbs covered with a sheet, lay the body of a man, brilliantly illuminated by the beam of a bull's-eye lantern held by a policeman standing at the feet. The others, excepting those near the head – the officer himself – all were in darkness. The face of the body showed yellow, repulsive, horrible! The eyes were partly open and upturned and the jaw fallen; traces of froth defiled the lips, the chin, the cheeks. A tall man, evidently a doctor, bent over the body with his hand thrust under the shirt front. He withdrew it and placed two fingers in the open mouth. 'This man has been about six hours dead,' said he. 'It is a case for the coroner.'

He drew a card from his pocket, handed it to the officer and made his way toward the door.

'Clear the room – out, all!' said the officer, sharply, and the body disappeared as if it had been snatched away, as shifting the lantern he flashed its beam of light here and there against the faces of the crowd. The effect was amazing! The men, blinded, confused, almost terrified, made a tumultuous rush for the door, pushing, crowding, and tumbling over one another as they fled, like the hosts of Night before the shafts of Apollo. Upon the struggling, trampling mass the officer poured his light without pity and without cessation. Caught in the current, Helberson and Harper were swept out of the room and cascaded down the stairs into the street.

'Good God, Doctor! did I not tell you that Jarette would kill him?' said Harper, as soon as they were clear of the crowd.

'I believe you did,' replied the other, without apparent emotion.

They walked on in silence, block after block. Against the greying east the dwellings of the hill tribes showed in silhouette. The familiar milk wagon was already astir in the streets; the baker's man would soon come upon the scene; the newspaper carrier was abroad in the land.

'It strikes me, youngster,' said Helberson, 'that you and I have been having too much of the morning air lately. It is unwholesome; we need a change. What do you say to a tour in Europe?'

'When?'

'I'm not particular. I should suppose that four o'clock this afternoon would be early enough.'

'I'll meet you at the boat,' said Harper.

Seven years afterward these two men sat upon a bench in Madison Square, New York, in familiar conversation. Another man, who had been observing them for some time, himself unobserved, approached and, courteously lifting his hat from locks as white as frost, said: 'I beg your pardon, gentlemen, but when you have killed a man by coming to life, it is best to change clothes with him, and at the first opportunity make a break for liberty.'

Helberson and Harper exchanged significant glances. They were obviously amused. The former then looked the stranger kindly in the eye and replied: 'That has always been my plan. I entirely agree with you as to its advant – '

He stopped suddenly, rose and went white. He stared at the man, open-mouthed; he trembled visibly.

'Ah!' said the stranger, 'I see that you are indisposed, Doctor. If you cannot treat yourself Dr Harper can do something for you, I am sure.'

'Who the devil are you?' said Harper, bluntly.

The stranger came nearer and, bending toward them, said in a whisper: 'I call myself Jarette sometimes, but I don't mind telling you, for old friendship, that I am Dr William Mancher.'

The revelation brought Harper to his feet. 'Mancher!' he cried; and Helberson added: 'It is true, by God!'

'Yes,' said the stranger, smiling vaguely, 'it is true enough, no doubt.'

He hesitated and seemed to be trying to recall something, then began humming a popular air. He had apparently forgotten their presence.

'Look here, Mancher,' said the elder of the two, 'tell us just what occurred that night – to Jarette, you know.'

'Oh, yes, about Jarette,' said the other. 'It's odd I should have neglected to tell you – I tell it so often. You see I knew, by over-hearing him talking to himself, that he was pretty badly frightened. So I couldn't resist the temptation to come to life and have a bit of fun out of him – I couldn't really. That was all right, though certainly I did not think he would take it so seriously; I did not, truly. And afterward – well, it was a tough job changing places with him, and then – damn you! you didn't let me out!'

Nothing could exceed the ferocity with which these last words were delivered. Both men stepped back in alarm.

'We? Why – why,' Helberson stammered, losing his self-possession utterly, 'we had nothing to do with it.'

'Didn't I say you were Drs. Hell-born and Sharper?' enquired the man, laughing.

'My name is Helberson, yes; and this gentleman is Mr Harper,' replied the former, reassured by the laugh. 'But we are not physicians now; we are – well, hang it, old man, we are gamblers.'

And that was the truth.

'A very good profession – very good, indeed; and, by the way, I hope Sharper here paid over Jarette's money like an honest stakeholder. A very good and honourable profession,' he repeated, thoughtfully, moving carelessly away; 'but I stick to the old one. I am High Supreme Medical Officer of the Bloomingdale Asylum; it is my duty to cure the superintendent.'

An Imperfect Conflagration

Early one June morning in 1872 I murdered my father – an act which made a deep impression on me at the time. This was before my marriage, while I was living with my parents in Wisconsin. My father and I were in the library of our home, dividing the proceeds of a burglary which we had committed that night. These consisted of household goods mostly, and the task of equitable division was difficult. We got on very well with the napkins, towels and such things, and the silverware was parted pretty nearly equally, but you can see for yourself that when you try to divide a single music-box by two without a remainder you will have trouble. It was that music-box which brought disaster and disgrace upon our family. If we had left it my poor father might now be alive.

It was a most exquisite and beautiful piece of workmanship – inlaid with costly woods and carven very curiously. It would not only play a great variety of tunes, but would whistle like a quail, bark like a dog, crow every morning at daylight whether it was wound up or not, and break the Ten Commandments. It was this last mentioned accomplishment that won my father's heart and caused him to commit the only dishonourable act of his life, though possibly he would have committed more if he had been spared: he tried to conceal that music-box from me, and declared upon his honour that he had not taken it, though I know very well that, so far as he was concerned, the burglary had been undertaken chiefly for the purpose of obtaining it.

My father had the music-box hidden under his cloak; we had worn cloaks by way of disguise. He had solemnly assured me that he did not take it. I knew that he did, and knew something of which he was evidently ignorant; namely, that the box would crow at daylight and betray him if I could prolong the division of profits till that time. All occurred as I wished: as the gaslight began to pale in the library and the shape of the windows was seen dimly behind the curtains, a long cock-a-doodle-doo came from beneath the old gentleman's cloak, followed by a few bars of an aria from *Tannhäuser*, ending with a loud click. A small hand-axe, which we had used to break into the unlucky house, lay between us on the table; I picked it up. The old man seeing that further concealment was useless took the box from under his cloak and set it on the table. 'Cut it in two if you prefer that plan,' said he; 'I tried to save it from destruction.'

He was a passionate lover of music and could himself play the concertina with expression and feeling.

I said: 'I do not question the purity of your motive: it would be presumptuous of me to sit in judgement on my father. But business is business, and with this axe I am going to effect a dissolution of our partnership unless you will consent in all future burglaries to wear a bell-punch.'

'No,' he said, after some reflection, 'no, I could not do that; it would look like a confession of dishonesty. People would say that you distrusted me.'

I could not help admiring his spirit and sensitiveness; for a moment I was proud of him and disposed to overlook his fault, but a glance at the richly jewelled music-box decided me, and, as I said, I removed the old man from this vale of tears. Having done so, I was a trifle uneasy. Not only was he my father – the author of my being – but the body would be certainly discovered. It was now broad daylight and my mother was likely to enter the library at any moment. Under the circumstances, I thought it expedient to remove her also, which I did. Then I paid off all the servants and discharged them.

That afternoon I went to the chief of police, told him what I had done and asked his advice. It would be very painful to me if the facts became publicly known. My conduct would be generally condemned; the newspapers would bring it up against me if ever I should run for office. The chief saw the force of these considerations; he was himself an assassin of wide experience. After consulting with the presiding judge of the Court of Variable Jurisdiction he advised me to conceal the bodies in one of the bookcases, get a heavy insurance on the house and burn it down. This I proceeded to do.

In the library was a book-case which my father had recently purchased of some cranky inventor and had not filled. It was in shape and size something like the old-fashioned 'ward-robes' which one sees in bedrooms without closets, but opened all the way down, like a woman's night-dress. It had glass doors. I had recently laid out my parents and they were now rigid enough to stand erect; so I stood them in this book-case, from which I had removed the shelves. I locked them in and tacked some curtains over the glass doors. The inspector from the insurance office passed a half-dozen times before the case without suspicion.

That night, after getting my policy, I set fire to the house and started through the woods to town, two miles away, where I managed to be found about the time the excitement was at its height. With cries of apprehension for the fate of my parents, I joined the rush and arrived at the fire some two hours after I had kindled it. The whole town was there as I dashed up. The house was entirely consumed, but in one end of the level bed of glowing embers, bolt upright and uninjured, was that book-case! The curtains had burned away, exposing the glass-doors, through which the fierce, red light illuminated the interior. There stood my dear father 'in his habit as he lived', and at his side the partner of his joys and sorrows. Not a hair of them was singed, their clothing was intact. On their heads and throats the injuries which in the accomplishment of my designs I had been compelled to inflict were conspicuous. As in the presence of a miracle, the people were silent; awe and terror had stilled every tongue. I was myself greatly affected.

Some three years later, when the events herein related had nearly faded from my memory, I went to New York to assist in passing some counterfeit United States bonds. Carelessly looking into a furniture store one day, I saw the exact counterpart of that book-case. 'I bought it for a trifle from a reformed inventor,' the dealer explained. 'He said it was fireproof, the pores of the wood being filled with alum under hydraulic pressure and the glass made of asbestos. I don't suppose it is really fireproof – you can have it at the price of an ordinary book-case.'

'No,' I said, 'if you cannot warrant it fireproof I won't take it' – and I bade him good-morning.

I would not have had it at any price: it revived memories that were exceedingly disagreeable.

The Man and the Snake

I

It is of veritabyll report, and attested of so many that there be nowe of wyse and learned none to gaynsaye it, that ye serpente hys eye hath a magnetick propertie that whosoe falleth into its svasion is drawn forwards in despyte of his wille, and perisheth miserabyll by ye creature hys byte.

Stretched at ease upon a sofa, in gown and slippers, Harker Brayton smiled as he read the foregoing sentence in old Morryster's *Marvells of Science*. 'The only marvel in the matter,' he said to himself, 'is that the wise and learned in Morryster's day should have believed such nonsense as is rejected by most of even the ignorant in ours.'

A train of reflections followed – for Brayton was a man of thought – and he unconsciously lowered his book without altering the direction of his eyes. As soon as the volume had gone below the line of sight, something in an obscure corner of the room recalled his attention to his surroundings. What he saw, in the shadow under his bed, were two small points of light, apparently about an inch apart. They might have been reflections of the gas jet above him, in metal nail heads; he gave them but little thought and resumed his reading. A moment later something – some impulse which it did not occur to him to analyse – impelled him to lower the book again and seek for what he saw before. The points of light were still there. They seemed to have become brighter than before, shining with a greenish lustre which he had not at first observed. He thought, too, that they might have moved a trifle – were somewhat nearer. They were still too much in the shadow, however, to reveal their nature and origin to an indolent attention, and he resumed his reading. Suddenly something in the text suggested a thought which made him start and drop the book for the third time to the side of the sofa, whence, escaping from his hand, it fell sprawling to the floor, back upward. Brayton, half-risen, was staring intently into the obscurity beneath the bed, where the

points of light shone with, it seemed to him, an added fire. His
attention was now fully aroused, his gaze eager and imperative. It
disclosed, almost directly beneath the foot rail of the bed, the coils of
a large serpent – the points of light were its eyes! Its horrible head,
thrust flatly forth from the innermost coil and resting upon the
outermost, was directed straight toward him, the definition of the
wide, brutal jaw and the idiotlike forehead serving to show the
direction of its malevolent gaze. The eyes were no longer merely
luminous points; they looked into his own with a meaning, a malign
significance.

2

A snake in a bedroom of a modern city dwelling of the better sort is,
happily, not so common a phenomenon as to make explanation
altogether needless. Harker Brayton, a bachelor of thirty-five, a
scholar, idler, and something of an athlete, rich, popular, and of
sound health, had returned to San Francisco from all manner of
remote and unfamiliar countries. His tastes, always a trifle luxurious,
had taken on an added exuberance from long privation; and the
resources of even the Castle Hotel being inadequate for their perfect
gratification, he had gladly accepted the hospitality of his friend,
Dr Druring, the distinguished scientist. Dr Druring's house, a large,
old-fashioned one in what was now an obscure quarter of the city,
had an outer and visible aspect of reserve. It plainly would not
associate with the contiguous elements of its altered environment, and appeared to have developed some of the eccentricities
which come of isolation. One of these was a 'wing', conspicuously
irrelevant in point of architecture, and no less rebellious in the
matter of purpose; for it was a combination of laboratory, menagerie,
and museum. It was here that the doctor indulged the scientific side
of his nature in the study of such forms of animal life as engaged his
interest and comforted his taste – which, it must be confessed, ran
rather to the lower forms. For one of the higher types nimbly and
sweetly to recommend itself unto his gentle senses, it had at least to
retain certain rudimentary characteristics allying it to such 'dragons
of the prime' as toads and snakes. His scientific sympathies were
distinctly reptilian; he loved nature's vulgarians and described himself as the Zola of zoology. His wife and daughters, not having the
advantage to share his enlightened curiosity regarding the works
and ways of our ill-starred fellow-creatures, were, with needless

austerity, excluded from what he called the Snakery, and doomed to companionship with their own kind; though, to soften the rigors of their lot, he had permitted them, out of his great wealth, to outdo the reptiles in the gorgeousness of their surroundings and to shine with a superior splendour.

Architecturally, and in point of 'furnishing', the Snakery had a severe simplicity befitting the humble circumstances of its occupants, many of whom, indeed, could not safely have been entrusted with the liberty which is necessary to the full enjoyment of luxury, for they had the troublesome peculiarity of being alive. In their own apartments, however, they were under as little personal restraint as was compatible with their protection from the baneful habit of swallowing one another; and, as Brayton had thoughtfully been apprised, it was more than a tradition that some of them had at divers times been found in parts of the premises where it would have embarrassed them to explain their presence. Despite the Snakery and its uncanny associations – to which, indeed, he gave little attention – Brayton found life at the Druring mansion very much to his mind.

3

Beyond a smart shock of surprise and a shudder of mere loathing, Mr Brayton was not greatly affected. His first thought was to ring the call bell and bring a servant; but, although the bell cord dangled within easy reach, he made no movement toward it; it had occurred to his mind that the act might subject him to the suspicion of fear, which he certainly did not feel. He was more keenly conscious of the incongruous nature of the situation than affected by its perils; it was revolting, but absurd.

The reptile was of a species with which Brayton was unfamiliar. Its length he could only conjecture; the body at the largest visible part seemed about as thick as his forearm. In what way was it dangerous, if in any way? Was it venomous? Was it a constrictor? His knowledge of nature's danger signals did not enable him to say; he had never deciphered the code.

If not dangerous, the creature was at least offensive. It was *de trop* – 'matter out of place' – an impertinence. The gem was unworthy of the setting. Even the barbarous taste of our time and country, which had loaded the walls of the room with pictures, the floor with furniture, and the furniture with bric-a-brac, had not quite fitted the

place for this bit of the savage life of the jungle. Besides – insupportable thought! – the exhalations of its breath mingled with
the atmosphere which he himself was breathing!

These thoughts shaped themselves with greater or less definition
in Brayton's mind, and begot action. The process is what we call
consideration and decision. It is thus that we are wise and unwise. It
is thus that the withered leaf in an autumn breeze shows greater
or less intelligence than its fellows, falling upon the land or upon
the lake. The secret of human action is an open one – something
contracts our muscles. Does it matter if we give to the preparatory
molecular changes the name of will?

Brayton rose to his feet and prepared to back softly away from the
snake, without disturbing it, if possible, and through the door. People
retire so from the presence of the great, for greatness is power, and
power is a menace. He knew that he could walk backward without
obstruction, and find the door without error. Should the monster
follow, the taste which had plastered the walls with paintings had
consistently supplied a rack of murderous Oriental weapons from
which he could snatch one to suit the occasion. In the meantime the
snake's eyes burned with a more pitiless malevolence than ever.

Brayton lifted his right foot free of the floor to step backward.
That moment he felt a strong aversion to doing so.

'I am accounted brave,' he murmured; 'is bravery, then, no more
than pride? Because there are none to witness the shame shall I
retreat?'

He was steadying himself with his right hand upon the back of a
chair, his foot suspended.

'Nonsense!' he said aloud; 'I am not so great a coward as to fear to
seem to myself afraid.'

He lifted the foot a little higher by slightly bending the knee,
and thrust it sharply to the floor – an inch in front of the other!
He could not think how that occurred. A trial with the left foot
had the same result; it was again in advance of the right. The hand
upon the chair back was grasping it; the arm was straight, reaching
somewhat backward. One might have seen that he was reluctant
to lose his hold. The snake's malignant head was still thrust forth
from the inner coil as before, the neck level. It had not moved, but
its eyes were now electric sparks, radiating an infinity of luminous
needles.

The man had an ashy pallor. Again he took a step forward, and
another, partly dragging the chair, which, when finally released, fell

upon the floor with a crash. The man groaned; the snake made neither sound nor motion, but its eyes were two dazzling suns. The reptile itself was wholly concealed by them. They gave off enlarging rings of rich and vivid colours, which at their greatest expansion successively vanished like soap bubbles; they seemed to approach his very face, and anon were an immeasurable distance away. He heard, somewhere, the continual throbbing of a great drum, with desultory bursts of far music, inconceivably sweet, like the tones of an Aeolian harp. He knew it for the sunrise melody of Memnon's statue, and thought he stood in the Nileside reeds, hearing, with exalted sense, that immortal anthem through the silence of the centuries.

The music ceased; rather, it became by insensible degrees the distant roll of a retreating thunderstorm. A landscape, glittering with sun and rain, stretched before him, arched with a vivid rainbow, framing in its giant curve a hundred visible cities. In the middle distance a vast serpent, wearing a crown, reared its head out of its voluminous convolutions and looked at him with his dead mother's eyes. Suddenly this enchanting landscape seemed to rise swiftly upward, like the drop scene at a theatre, and vanished in a blank. Something struck him a hard blow upon the face and breast. He had fallen to the floor; the blood ran from his broken nose and his bruised lips. For a moment he was dazed and stunned, and lay with closed eyes, his face against the door. In a few moments he had recovered, and then realised that his fall, by withdrawing his eyes, had broken the spell which held him. He felt that now, by keeping his gaze averted, he would be able to retreat. But the thought of the serpent within a few feet of his head, yet unseen – perhaps in the very act of springing upon him and throwing its coils about his throat – was too horrible. He lifted his head, stared again into those baleful eyes, and was again in bondage.

The snake had not moved, and appeared somewhat to have lost its power upon the imagination; the gorgeous illusions of a few moments before were not repeated. Beneath that flat and brainless brow its black, beady eyes simply glittered, as at first, with an expression unspeakably malignant. It was as if the creature, knowing its triumph assured, had determined to practise no more alluring wiles.

Now ensued a fearful scene. The man, prone upon the floor, within a yard of his enemy, raised the upper part of his body upon his elbows, his head thrown back, his legs extended to their full length. His face was white between its gouts of blood; his eyes were strained open to their uttermost expansion. There was froth upon his lips; it dropped off in flakes. Strong convulsions ran through his body, making almost serpentine undulations. He bent himself at the waist, shifting his legs from side to side. And every movement left him a little nearer to the snake. He thrust his hands forward to brace himself back, yet constantly advanced upon his elbows.

4

Dr Druring and his wife sat in the library. The scientist was in rare good humour.

'I have just obtained, by exchange with another collector,' he said, 'a splendid specimen of the Ophiophagus.'

'And what may that be?' the lady enquired with a somewhat languid interest.

'Why, bless my soul, what profound ignorance! My dear, a man who ascertains after marriage that his wife does not know Greek, is entitled to a divorce. The Ophiophagus is a snake which eats other snakes.'

'I hope it will eat all yours,' she said, absently shifting the lamp. 'But how does it get the other snakes? By charming them, I suppose.'

'That is just like you, dear,' said the doctor, with an affectation of petulance. 'You know how irritating to me is any allusion to that vulgar superstition about the snake's power of fascination.'

The conversation was interrupted by a mighty cry which rang through the silent house like the voice of a demon shouting in a tomb. Again and yet again it sounded, with terrible distinctness. They sprang to their feet, the man confused, the lady pale and speechless with fright. Almost before the echoes of the last cry had died away the doctor was out of the room, springing up the staircase two steps at a time. In the corridor, in front of Brayton's chamber, he met some servants who had come from the upper floor. Together they rushed at the door without knocking. It was unfastened, and gave way. Brayton lay upon his stomach on the floor, dead. His head and arms were partly concealed under the foot rail of the bed. They pulled the body away, turning it upon the back. The face was daubed with blood and froth, the eyes were wide open, staring – a dreadful sight!

'Died in a fit,' said the scientist, bending his knee and placing his hand upon the heart. While in that position he happened to glance under the bed. 'Good God!' he added; 'how did this thing get in here?'

He reached under the bed, pulled out the snake, and flung it, still coiled, to the centre of the room, whence, with a harsh, shuffling sound, it slid across the polished floor till stopped by the wall, where it lay without motion. It was a stuffed snake; its eyes were two shoe buttons.

John Mortonson's Funeral

John Mortonson was dead: his lines in 'the tragedy *Man*' had all been spoken and he had left the stage.

The body rested in a fine mahogany coffin fitted with a plate of glass. All arrangements for the funeral had been so well attended to that had the deceased known he would doubtless have approved. The face, as it showed under the glass, was not disagreeable to look upon: it bore a faint smile, and as the death had been painless, had not been distorted beyond the repairing power of the undertaker. At two o'clock of the afternoon the friends were to assemble to pay their last tribute of respect to one who had no further need of friends and respect. The surviving members of the family came severally every few minutes to the casket and wept above the placid features beneath the glass. This did them no good; it did no good to John Mortonson; but in the presence of death reason and philosophy are silent.

As the hour of two approached the friends began to arrive and after offering such consolation to the stricken relatives as the proprieties of the occasion required, solemnly seated themselves about the room with an augmented consciousness of their importance in the scheme funereal. Then the minister came, and in that overshadowing presence the lesser lights went into eclipse. His entrance was followed by that of the widow, whose lamentations filled the room. She approached the casket and after leaning her face against the cold glass for a moment was gently led to a seat near her daughter. Mournfully and low the man of God began his eulogy of the dead, and his doleful voice, mingled with the sobbing which it was its purpose to stimulate and sustain, rose and fell, seemed to come and go, like the sound of a sullen sea. The gloomy day grew darker as he spoke; a curtain of cloud underspread the sky and a few drops of rain fell audibly. It seemed as if all nature were weeping for John Mortonson.

When the minister had finished his eulogy with prayer a hymn was sung and the pall-bearers took their places beside the bier. As the last notes of the hymn died away the widow ran to the coffin, cast herself upon it and sobbed hysterically. Gradually, however, she yielded to dissuasion, becoming more composed; and as the minister was in the act of leading her away her eyes sought the face of the dead beneath the glass. She threw up her arms and with a shriek fell backward insensible.

The mourners sprang forward to the coffin, the friends followed, and as the clock on the mantel solemnly struck three all were staring down upon the face of John Mortonson, deceased.

They turned away, sick and faint. One man, trying in his terror to escape the awful sight, stumbled against the coffin so heavily as to knock away one of its frail supports. The coffin fell to the floor, the glass was shattered to bits by the concussion.

From the opening crawled John Mortonson's cat, which lazily leapt to the floor, sat up, tranquilly wiped its crimson muzzle with a forepaw, then walked with dignity from the room.

Moxon's Master

'Are you serious? Do you really believe that a machine thinks?'

I got no immediate reply; Moxon was apparently intent upon the coals in the grate, touching them deftly here and there with the fire-poker till they signified a sense of his attention by a brighter glow. For several weeks I had been observing in him a growing habit of delay in answering even the most trivial of commonplace questions. His air, however, was that of preoccupation rather than deliberation: one might have said that he had 'something on his mind'.

Presently he said: 'What is a "machine"? The word has been variously defined. Here is one definition from a popular dictionary: "Any instrument or organisation by which power is applied and made effective, or a desired effect produced". Well, then, is not a man a machine? And you will admit that he thinks – or thinks he thinks.'

'If you do not wish to answer my question,' I said, rather testily, 'why not say so? – all that you say is mere evasion. You know well enough that when I say "machine" I do not mean a man, but something that man has made and controls.'

'When it does not control him,' he said, rising abruptly and looking out of a window, whence nothing was visible in the blackness of a stormy night. A moment later he turned about and with a smile said: 'I beg your pardon; I had no thought of evasion. I considered the dictionary man's unconscious testimony suggestive and worth something in the discussion. I can give your question a direct answer easily enough: I do believe that a machine thinks about the work that it is doing.'

That was direct enough, certainly. It was not altogether pleasing, for it tended to confirm a sad suspicion that Moxon's devotion to study and work in his machine-shop had not been good for him. I knew, for one thing, that he suffered from insomnia, and that is no light affliction. Had it affected his mind? His reply to my question seemed to me then evidence that it had; perhaps I should think differently about it now. I was younger then, and among the blessings that are not denied to youth is ignorance. Incited by that great stimulant to controversy, I said: 'And what, pray, does it think within the absence of a brain?'

The reply, coming with less than his customary delay, took his favourite form of counter-interrogation: 'With what does a plant think – in the absence of a brain?'

'Ah, plants also belong to the philosopher class! I should be pleased to know some of their conclusions; you may omit the premises.'

'Perhaps,' he replied, apparently unaffected by my foolish irony, 'you may be able to infer their convictions from their acts. I will spare you the familiar examples of the sensitive mimosa, the several insectivorous flowers and those whose stamens bend down and shake their pollen upon the entering bee in order that he may fertilise their distant mates. But observe this. In an open spot in my garden I planted a climbing vine. When it was barely above the surface I set a stake into the soil a yard away. The vine at once made for it, but as it was about to reach it after several days I removed it a few feet. The vine at once altered its course, making an acute angle, and again made for the stake. This manoeuvre was repeated several times, but finally, as if discouraged, the vine abandoned the pursuit and ignoring further attempts to divert it travelled to a small tree, further away, which it climbed.

'Roots of the eucalyptus will prolong themselves incredibly in search of moisture. A well-known horticulturist relates that one entered an old drain pipe and followed it until it came to a break, where a section of the pipe had been removed to make way for a stone wall that had been built across its course. The root left the drain and followed the wall until it found an opening where a stone had fallen out. It crept through and following the other side of the wall back to the drain, entered the unexplored part and resumed its journey.'

'And all this?'

'Can you miss the significance of it? It shows the consciousness of plants. It proves that they think.'

'Even if it did – what then? We were speaking, not of plants, but of machines. They may be composed partly of wood – wood that has no longer vitality – or wholly of metal. Is thought an attribute also of the mineral kingdom?'

'How else do you explain the phenomena, for example, of crystallisation?'

'I do not explain them.'

'Because you cannot without affirming what you wish to deny, namely, intelligent cooperation among the constituent elements of the crystals. When soldiers form lines, or hollow squares, you call it reason. When wild geese in flight take the form of a letter V you say instinct. When the homogeneous atoms of a mineral, moving freely in solution, arrange themselves into shapes mathematically perfect, or particles of frozen moisture into the symmetrical and beautiful forms of snowflakes, you have nothing to say. You have not even invented a name to conceal your heroic unreason.'

Moxon was speaking with unusual animation and earnestness. As he paused I heard in an adjoining room known to me as his 'machine-shop,' which no-one but himself was permitted to enter, a singular thumping sound, as of someone pounding upon a table with an open hand. Moxon heard it at the same moment and, visibly agitated, rose and hurriedly passed into the room whence it came. I thought it odd that anyone else should be in there, and my interest in my friend – with doubtless a touch of unwarrantable curiosity – led me to listen intently, though, I am happy to say, not at the keyhole. There were confused sounds, as of a struggle or scuffle; the floor shook. I distinctly heard hard breathing and a hoarse whisper which said 'Damn you!' Then all was silent, and presently Moxon reappeared and said, with a rather sorry smile: 'Pardon me for leaving you so abruptly. I have a machine in there that lost its temper and cut up rough.'

Fixing my eyes steadily upon his left cheek, which was traversed by four parallel excoriations showing blood, I said: 'How would it do to trim its nails?'

I could have spared myself the jest; he gave it no attention, but seated himself in the chair that he had left and resumed the interrupted monologue as if nothing had occurred: 'Doubtless you do not hold with those (I need not name them to a man of your reading) who have taught that all matter is sentient, that every atom is a living, feeling, conscious being. *I* do. There is no such thing as dead, inert matter: it is all alive; all instinct with force, actual and potential; all sensitive to the same forces in its environment and susceptible to the contagion of higher and subtler ones residing in such superior organisms as it may be brought into relation with, as those of man when he is fashioning it into an instrument of his will. It absorbs something of his intelligence and purpose – more of them in proportion to the complexity of the resulting machine and that of its work.

'Do you happen to recall Herbert Spencer's definition of "Life"? I read it thirty years ago. He may have altered it afterward, for anything I know, but in all that time I have been unable to think of a single word that could profitably be changed or added or removed. It seems to me not only the best definition, but the only possible one.

' "Life," he says, "is a definite combination of heterogeneous changes, both simultaneous and successive, in correspondence with external coexistences and sequences." '

'That defines the phenomenon,' I said, 'but gives no hint of its cause.'

'That,' he replied, 'is all that any definition can do. As Mill points out, we know nothing of cause except as an antecedent – nothing of effect except as a consequent. Of certain phenomena, one never occurs without another, which is dissimilar: the first in point of time we call cause, the second, effect. One who had many times seen a rabbit pursued by a dog, and had never seen rabbits and dogs otherwise, would think the rabbit the cause of the dog.

'But I fear,' he added, laughing naturally enough, 'that my rabbit is leading me a long way from the track of my legitimate quarry: I'm indulging in the pleasure of the chase for its own sake. What I want you to observe is that in Herbert Spencer's definition of "life" the activity of a machine is included – there is nothing in the definition that is not applicable to it. According to this sharpest of observers and deepest of thinkers, if a man during his period of activity is alive, so is a machine when in operation. As an inventor and constructor of machines I know that to be true.'

Moxon was silent for a long time, gazing absently into the fire. It was growing late and I thought it time to be going, but somehow I did not like the notion of leaving him in that isolated house, all alone except for the presence of some person of whose nature my conjectures could go no further than that it was unfriendly, perhaps malign. Leaning toward him and looking earnestly into his eyes while making a motion with my hand through the door of his workshop, I said: 'Moxon, whom have you in there?'

Somewhat to my surprise he laughed lightly and answered without hesitation: 'Nobody; the incident that you have in mind was caused by my folly in leaving a machine in action with nothing to act upon, while I undertook the interminable task of enlightening your understanding. Do you happen to know that Consciousness is the creature of Rhythm?'

'Oh, bother them both!' I replied, rising and laying hold of my overcoat. 'I'm going to wish you good-night; and I'll add the hope that the machine which you inadvertently left in action will have her gloves on the next time you think it needful to stop her.'

Without waiting to observe the effect of my shot I left the house.

Rain was falling, and the darkness was intense. In the sky beyond the crest of a hill toward which I groped my way along precarious plank sidewalks and across miry, unpaved streets I could see the faint glow of the city's lights, but behind me nothing was visible but a single window of Moxon's house. It glowed with what seemed to me a mysterious and fateful meaning. I knew it was an uncurtained aperture in my friend's 'machine-shop', and I had little doubt that he had resumed the studies interrupted by his duties as my instructor in mechanical consciousness and the fatherhood of Rhythm. Odd, and in some degree humorous, as his convictions seemed to me at that time, I could not wholly divest myself of the feeling that they had some tragic relation to his life and character – perhaps to his destiny – although I no longer entertained the notion that they were the vagaries of a disordered mind. Whatever might be thought of his views, his exposition of them was too logical for that. Over and over, his last words came back to me: 'Consciousness is the creature of Rhythm.' Bald and terse as the statement was, I now found it infinitely alluring. At each recurrence it broadened in meaning and deepened in suggestion. Why, here, (I thought) is something upon which to found a philosophy. If consciousness is the product of rhythm all things *are* conscious, for all have motion, and all motion is rhythmic. I wondered if Moxon knew the significance and breadth of his thought – the scope of this momentous generalisation; or had he arrived at his philosophic faith by the tortuous and uncertain road of observation?

That faith was then new to me, and all Moxon's expounding had failed to make me a convert; but now it seemed as if a great light shone about me, like that which fell upon Saul of Tarsus; and out there in the storm and darkness and solitude I experienced what Lewes calls 'the endless variety and excitement of philosophic thought.' I exulted in a new sense of knowledge, a new pride of reason. My feet seemed hardly to touch the earth; it was as if I were uplifted and borne through the air by invisible wings.

Yielding to an impulse to seek further light from him whom I now recognised as my master and guide, I had unconsciously turned about, and almost before I was aware of having done so found myself again at Moxon's door. I was drenched with rain, but felt no discomfort. Unable in my excitement to find the doorbell I instinctively tried the knob. It turned and, entering, I mounted the stairs to the room that I had so recently left. All was dark and silent; Moxon, as I had supposed, was in the adjoining room – the 'machine-shop'. Groping along the wall until I found the communicating door I knocked loudly several times, but got no response, which I attributed to the uproar outside, for the wind was blowing a gale and dashing the rain against the thin walls in sheets. The drumming upon the shingle roof spanning the unceiled room was loud and incessant.

I had never been invited into the machine-shop – had, indeed, been denied admittance, as had all others, with one exception, a skilled metal worker, of whom no-one knew anything except that his name was Haley and his habit silence. But in my spiritual exaltation, discretion and civility were alike forgotten and I opened the door. What I saw took all philosophical speculation out of me in short order.

Moxon sat facing me at the farther side of a small table upon which a single candle made all the light that was in the room. Opposite him, his back toward me, sat another person. On the table between the two was a chessboard; the men were playing. I knew little of chess, but as only a few pieces were on the board it was obvious that the game was near its close. Moxon was intensely interested – not so much, it seemed to me, in the game as in his antagonist, upon whom he had fixed so intent a look that, standing though I did directly in the line of his vision, I was altogether unobserved. His face was ghastly white, and his eyes glittered like diamonds. Of his antagonist I had only a back view, but that was sufficient; I should not have cared to see his face.

He was apparently not more than five feet in height, with proportions suggesting those of a gorilla – a tremendous breadth of shoulders, thick, short neck and broad, squat head, which had a tangled growth of black hair and was topped with a crimson fez. A tunic of the same colour, belted tightly to the waist, reached the seat – apparently a box – upon which he sat; his legs and feet were not seen. His left forearm appeared to rest in his lap; he moved his pieces with his right hand, which seemed disproportionately long.

I had shrunk back and now stood a little to one side of the doorway and in shadow. If Moxon had looked farther than the face of his opponent he could have observed nothing now, except that the door was open. Something forbade me either to enter or to retire, a feeling – I know not how it came – that I was in the presence of an imminent tragedy and might serve my friend by remaining. With a scarcely conscious rebellion against the indelicacy of the act I remained.

The play was rapid. Moxon hardly glanced at the board before making his moves, and to my unskilled eye seemed to move the piece most convenient to his hand, his motions in doing so being quick, nervous and lacking in precision. The response of his antagonist, while equally prompt in the inception, was made with a slow, uniform, mechanical and, I thought, somewhat theatrical movement of the arm, that was a sore trial to my patience. There was something un-earthly about it all, and I caught myself shuddering. But I was wet and cold.

Two or three times after moving a piece the stranger slightly inclined his head, and each time I observed that Moxon shifted his king. All at once the thought came to me that the man was dumb. And then that he was a machine – an automaton chess-player! Then I remembered that Moxon had once spoken to me of having invented such a piece of mechanism, though I did not understand that it had actually been constructed. Was all his talk about the consciousness and intelligence of machines merely a prelude to eventual exhibition of this device – only a trick to intensify the effect of its mechanical action upon me in my ignorance of its secret?

A fine end, this, of all my intellectual transports – my 'endless variety and excitement of philosophic thought!' I was about to retire in disgust when something occurred to hold my curiosity. I observed a shrug of the thing's great shoulders, as if it were irritated: and so natural was this – so entirely human – that in my new view of the matter it startled me. Nor was that all, for a moment later it struck the table sharply with its clenched hand. At that gesture Moxon seemed even more startled than I: he pushed his chair a little back-ward, as in alarm.

Presently Moxon, whose play it was, raised his hand high above the board, pounced upon one of his pieces like a sparrow-hawk and with the exclamation 'checkmate!' rose quickly to his feet and stepped behind his chair. The automaton sat motionless.

The wind had now gone down, but I heard, at lessening intervals and progressively louder, the rumble and roll of thunder. In the pauses between I now became conscious of a low humming or buzz-ing which, like the thunder, grew momentarily louder and more distinct. It seemed to come from the body of the automaton, and was unmistakably a whirring of wheels. It gave me the impression of a disordered mechanism which had escaped the repressive and regulating action of some controlling part – an effect such as might be expected if a pawl should be jostled from the teeth of a ratchet-wheel. But before I had time for much conjecture as to its nature my attention was taken by the strange motions of the automaton itself. A slight but continuous convulsion appeared to have possession of it. In body and head it shook like a man with palsy or an ague chill, and the motion augmented every moment until the entire figure was in violent agitation. Suddenly it sprang to its feet and with a movement almost too quick for the eye to follow shot forward across table and chair, with both arms thrust forth to their full length – the posture and lunge of a diver. Moxon tried to throw himself backward out of reach, but he was too late: I saw the horrible thing's hands close upon his throat, his own clutch its wrists. Then the table was overturned, the candle thrown to the floor and extinguished, and all was black dark. But the noise of the struggle was dreadfully distinct, and most terrible of all were the raucous, squawking sounds made by the strangled man's efforts to breathe. Guided by the infernal hubbub, I sprang to the rescue of my friend, but had hardly taken a stride in the darkness when the whole room blazed with a blinding white light that burned into my brain and heart and memory a vivid picture of the combatants on the floor, Moxon underneath, his throat still in the clutch of those iron hands, his head forced backward, his eyes protruding, his mouth wide open and his tongue thrust out; and – horrible contrast! – upon the painted face of his assassin an expression of tranquil and profound thought, as in the solution of a problem in chess! This I observed, then all was blackness and silence.

Three days later I recovered consciousness in a hospital. As the memory of that tragic night slowly evolved in my ailing brain, I recognised in my attendant Moxon's confidential workman, Haley. Responding to a look he approached, smiling.

'Tell me about it,' I managed to say, faintly – 'all about it.'

'Certainly,' he said; 'you were carried unconscious from a burning house – Moxon's. Nobody knows how you came to be there. You may have to do a little explaining. The origin of the fire is a bit mysterious, too. My own notion is that the house was struck by lightning.'

'And Moxon?'

'Buried yesterday – what was left of him.'

Apparently this reticent person could unfold himself on occasion. When imparting shocking intelligence to the sick he was affable enough. After some moments of the keenest mental suffering I ventured to ask another question: 'Who rescued me?'

'Well, if that interests you – I did.'

'Thank you, Mr Haley, and may God bless you for it. Did you rescue, also, that charming product of your skill, the automaton chess-player that murdered its inventor?'

The man was silent a long time, looking away from me. Presently he turned and gravely said: 'Do you know that?'

'I do,' I replied; 'I saw it done.'

That was many years ago. If asked today I should answer less confidently.

The Damned Thing

One does not always eat what is on the table

By the light of a tallow candle which had been placed on one end of a rough table a man was reading something written in a book. It was an old account book, greatly worn; and the writing was not, apparently, very legible, for the man sometimes held the page close to the flame of the candle to get a stronger light on it. The shadow of the book would then throw into obscurity a half of the room, darkening a number of faces and figures; for besides the reader, eight other men were present. Seven of them sat against the rough log walls, silent, motionless, and the room being small, not very far from the table. By extending an arm any one of them could have touched the eighth man, who lay on the table, face upward, partly covered by a sheet, his arms at his sides. He was dead.

The man with the book was not reading aloud, and no-one spoke; all seemed to be waiting for something to occur; the dead man only was without expectation. From the blank darkness outside came in, through the aperture that served for a window, all the ever-unfamiliar noises of night in the wilderness – the long nameless note of a distant coyote; the stilly pulsing thrill of tireless insects in trees; strange cries of night birds, so different from those of the birds of day; the drone of great blundering beetles, and all that mysterious chorus of small sounds that seem always to have been but half heard when they have suddenly ceased, as if conscious of an indiscretion. But nothing of all this was noted in that company; its members were not over-much addicted to idle interest in matters of no practical importance; that was obvious in every line of their rugged faces – obvious even in the dim light of the single candle. They were evidently men of the vicinity – farmers and woodsmen.

The person reading was a trifle different; one would have said of him that he was of the world, worldly, albeit there was that in his attire which attested a certain fellowship with the organisms of his environment. His coat would hardly have passed muster in San Francisco; his foot-gear was not of urban origin, and the hat that lay by him on the floor (he was the only one uncovered) was such that if one had considered it as an article of mere personal adornment he would have missed its meaning. In countenance the man was rather prepossessing, with just a hint of sternness; though that he may have assumed or cultivated, as appropriate to one in authority. For he was a coroner. It was by virtue of his office that he had possession of the book in which he was reading; it had been found among the dead man's effects – in his cabin, where the inquest was now taking place.

When the coroner had finished reading he put the book into his breast pocket. At that moment the door was pushed open and a young man entered. He, clearly, was not of mountain birth and breeding: he was clad as those who dwell in cities. His clothing was dusty, however, as from travel. He had, in fact, been riding hard to attend the inquest.

The coroner nodded; no-one else greeted him.

'We have waited for you,' said the coroner. 'It is necessary to have done with this business tonight.'

The young man smiled. 'I am sorry to have kept you,' he said. 'I went away, not to evade your summons, but to post to my newspaper an account of what I suppose I am called back to relate.'

The coroner smiled.

'The account that you posted to your newspaper,' he said, 'differs, probably, from that which you will give here under oath.'

'That,' replied the other, rather hotly and with a visible flush, 'is as you please. I used manifold paper and have a copy of what I sent. It was not written as news, for it is incredible, but as fiction. It may go as a part of my testimony under oath.'

'But you say it is incredible.'

'That is nothing to you, sir, if I also swear that it is true.'

The coroner was silent for a time, his eyes upon the floor. The men about the sides of the cabin talked in whispers, but seldom withdrew their gaze from the face of the corpse. Presently the coroner lifted his eyes and said: 'We will resume the inquest.'

The men removed their hats. The witness was sworn.

'What is your name?' the coroner asked.

'William Harker.'

'Age?'

'Twenty-seven.'

'You knew the deceased, Hugh Morgan?'

'Yes.'

'You were with him when he died?'

'Near him.'

'How did that happen – your presence, I mean?'

'I was visiting him at this place to shoot and fish. A part of my purpose, however, was to study him and his odd, solitary way of life. He seemed a good model for a character in fiction. I sometimes write stories.'

'I sometimes read them.'

'Thank you.'

'Stories in general – not yours.'

Some of the jurors laughed. Against a sombre background humour shows highlights. Soldiers in the intervals of battle laugh easily, and a jest in the death chamber conquers by surprise.

'Relate the circumstances of this man's death,' said the coroner. 'You may use any notes or memoranda that you please.'

The witness understood. Pulling a manuscript from his breast pocket he held it near the candle and turning the leaves until he found the passage that he wanted began to read.

2
What may happen in a field of wild oats

' . . . The sun had hardly risen when we left the house. We were looking for quail, each with a shotgun, but we had only one dog. Morgan said that our best ground was beyond a certain ridge that he pointed out, and we crossed it by a trail through the chaparral. On the other side was comparatively level ground, thickly covered with wild oats. As we emerged from the chaparral Morgan was but a few yards in advance. Suddenly we heard, at a little distance to our right and partly in front, a noise as of some animal thrashing about in the bushes, which we could see were violently agitated.

' "We've started a deer," ' I said. "I wish we had brought a rifle."

'Morgan, who had stopped and was intently watching the agitated chaparral, said nothing, but had cocked both barrels of his gun and was holding it in readiness to aim. I thought him a trifle excited, which surprised me, for he had a reputation for exceptional coolness, even in moments of sudden and imminent peril.

' "O, come," I said. "You are not going to fill up a deer with quail-shot, are you?"

'Still he did not reply; but catching a sight of his face as he turned it slightly toward me I was struck by the intensity of his look. Then I understood that we had serious business in hand and my first conjecture was that we had "jumped" a grizzly. I advanced to Morgan's side, cocking my piece as I moved.

'The bushes were now quiet and the sounds had ceased, but Morgan was as attentive to the place as before.

' "What is it? What the devil is it?" I asked.

' "That Damned Thing!" he replied, without turning his head. His voice was husky and unnatural. He trembled visibly.

'I was about to speak further, when I observed the wild oats near the place of the disturbance moving in the most inexplicable way. I can hardly describe it. It seemed as if stirred by a streak of wind, which not only bent it, but pressed it down – crushed it so that it did not rise; and this movement was slowly prolonging itself directly toward us.

'Nothing that I had ever seen had affected me so strangely as this unfamiliar and unaccountable phenomenon, yet I am unable to recall any sense of fear. I remember – and tell it here because, singularly enough, I recollected it then – that once in looking carelessly out of an open window I momentarily mistook a small tree close at hand for one of a group of larger trees at a little distance away. It looked the same size as the others, but being more distinctly and sharply defined in mass and detail seemed out of harmony with them. It was a mere falsification of the law of aerial perspective, but it startled, almost terrified me. We so rely upon the orderly operation of familiar natural laws that any seeming suspension of them is noted as a menace to our safety, a warning of unthinkable calamity. So now the apparently causeless movement of the herbage and the slow, undeviating approach of the line of disturbance were distinctly disquieting. My companion appeared actually frightened, and I could hardly credit my senses when I saw him suddenly throw his gun to his shoulder and fire both barrels at the agitated grain! Before the smoke of the discharge had cleared away I heard a loud savage cry – a scream like that of a wild animal – and flinging his gun upon the ground Morgan sprang away and ran swiftly from the spot. At the same instant I was thrown violently to the ground by the impact of something unseen in the smoke – some soft, heavy substance that seemed thrown against me with great force.

'Before I could get upon my feet and recover my gun, which seemed to have been struck from my hands, I heard Morgan crying out as if in mortal agony, and mingling with his cries were such hoarse, savage sounds as one hears from fighting dogs. Inexpressibly terrified, I struggled to my feet and looked in the direction of Morgan's retreat; and may Heaven in mercy spare me from another sight like that! At a distance of less than thirty yards was my friend, down upon one knee, his head thrown back at a frightful angle, hatless, his long hair in disorder and his whole body in violent movement from side to side, backward and forward. His right arm was lifted and seemed to lack the hand – at least, I could see none. The other arm was invisible. At times, as my memory now reports this extraordinary scene, I could discern but a part of his body; it was as if he had been partly blotted out – I cannot otherwise express it – then a shifting of his position would bring it all into view again.

'All this must have occurred within a few seconds, yet in that time Morgan assumed all the postures of a determined wrestler vanquished by superior weight and strength. I saw nothing but him, and him not always distinctly. During the entire incident his shouts and curses were heard, as if through an enveloping uproar of such sounds of rage and fury as I had never heard from the throat of man or brute!

'For a moment only I stood irresolute, then throwing down my gun I ran forward to my friend's assistance. I had a vague belief that he was suffering from a fit, or some form of convulsion. Before I could reach his side he was down and quiet. All sounds had ceased, but with a feeling of such terror as even these awful events had not inspired I now saw again the mysterious movement of the wild oats, prolonging itself from the trampled area about the prostrate man toward the edge of a wood. It was only when it had reached the wood that I was able to withdraw my eyes and look at my companion. He was dead.'

3

A man though naked may be in rags

The coroner rose from his seat and stood beside the dead man. Lifting an edge of the sheet he pulled it away, exposing the entire body, altogether naked and showing in the candle-light a claylike yellow. It had, however, broad maculations of bluish black, obviously caused by extravasated blood from contusions. The chest and sides looked as if they had been beaten with a bludgeon. There were dreadful lacerations; the skin was torn in strips and shreds.

The coroner moved round to the end of the table and undid a silk handkerchief which had been passed under the chin and knotted on the top of the head. When the handkerchief was drawn away it exposed what had been the throat. Some of the jurors who had risen to get a better view repented their curiosity and turned away their faces. Witness Harker went to the open window and leaned out across the sill, faint and sick. Dropping the handkerchief upon the dead man's neck the coroner stepped to an angle of the room and from a pile of clothing produced one garment after another, each of which he held up a moment for inspection. All were torn, and stiff with blood. The jurors did not make a closer inspection. They seemed rather uninterested. They had, in truth, seen all this before; the only thing that was new to them being Harker's testimony.

'Gentlemen,' the coroner said, 'we have no more evidence, I think. Your duty has been already explained to you; if there is nothing you wish to ask you may go outside and consider your verdict.'

The foreman rose – a tall, bearded man of sixty, coarsely clad.

'I should like to ask one question, Mr Coroner,' he said. 'What asylum did this yer last witness escape from?'

'Mr Harker,' said the coroner, gravely and tranquilly, 'from what asylum did you last escape?'

Harker flushed crimson again, but said nothing, and the seven jurors rose and solemnly filed out of the cabin.

'If you have done insulting me, sir,' said Harker, as soon as he and the officer were left alone with the dead man, 'I suppose I am at liberty to go?'

'Yes.'

Harker started to leave, but paused, with his hand on the door latch. The habit of his profession was strong in him – stronger than his sense of personal dignity. He turned about and said: 'The book that you have there – I recognise it as Morgan's diary. You seemed greatly interested in it; you read in it while I was testifying. May I see it? The public would like – '

'The book will cut no figure in this matter,' replied the official, slipping it into his coat pocket; 'all the entries in it were made before the writer's death.'

As Harker passed out of the house the jury re-entered and stood about the table, on which the now covered corpse showed under the sheet with sharp definition. The foreman seated himself near the candle, produced from his breast pocket a pencil and scrap of paper and wrote rather laboriously the following verdict, which with various degrees of effort all signed:

'We, the jury, do find that the remains come to their death at the hands of a mountain lion, but some of us thinks, all the same, they had fits.'

4

An explanation from the tomb

In the diary of the late Hugh Morgan are certain interesting entries having, possibly, a scientific value as suggestions. At the inquest upon his body the book was not put in evidence; possibly the coroner thought it not worth while to confuse the jury. The date of the first of the entries mentioned cannot be ascertained; the upper part of the leaf is torn away; the part of the entry remaining follows:

' . . . would run in a half-circle, keeping his head turned always toward the centre, and again he would stand still, barking furiously. At last he ran away into the brush as fast as he could go. I thought at first that he had gone mad, but on returning to the house found no other alteration in his manner than what was obviously due to fear of punishment.

'Can a dog see with his nose? Do odours impress some cerebral centre with images of the thing that emitted them? . . .

'Sept. 2 – Looking at the stars last night as they rose above the crest of the ridge east of the house, I observed them successively disappear – from left to right. Each was eclipsed but an instant, and only a few at the same time, but along the entire length of the ridge all that were within a degree or two of the crest were blotted out. It was as if something had passed along between me and them; but I could not see it, and the stars were not thick enough to define its outline. Ugh! I don't like this . . . '

Several weeks' entries are missing, three leaves being torn from the book.

'Sept. 27 – It has been about here again – I find evidences of its presence every day. I watched again all last night in the same cover, gun in hand, double-charged with buckshot. In the morning the fresh footprints were there, as before. Yet I would have sworn that I did not sleep – indeed, I hardly sleep at all. It is terrible,

insupportable! If these amazing experiences are real I shall go mad;
if they are fanciful I am mad already.

'Oct. 3 – I shall not go – it shall not drive me away. No, this is
my house, *my* land. God hates a coward . . .

'Oct. 5 – I can stand it no longer; I have invited Harker to pass
a few weeks with me – he has a level head. I can judge from his
manner if he thinks me mad.

'Oct. 7 – I have the solution of the mystery; it came to me
last night – suddenly, as by revelation. How simple – how
terribly simple!

'There are sounds that we cannot hear. At either end of the scale
are notes that stir no chord of that imperfect instrument, the
human ear. They are too high or too grave. I have observed a flock
of blackbirds occupying an entire tree-top – the tops of several
trees – and all in full song. Suddenly – in a moment – at absolutely
the same instant – all spring into the air and fly away. How? They
could not all see one another – whole tree-tops intervened. At no
point could a leader have been visible to all. There must have been
a signal of warning or command, high and shrill above the din, but
by me unheard. I have observed, too, the same simultaneous flight
when all were silent, among not only blackbirds, but other birds –
quail, for example, widely separated by bushes – even on opposite
sides of a hill.

'It is known to seamen that a school of whales basking or sport-
ing on the surface of the ocean, miles apart, with the convexity
of the earth between, will sometimes dive at the same instant – all
gone out of sight in a moment. The signal has been sounded – too
grave for the ear of the sailor at the masthead and his comrades on
the deck – who nevertheless feel its vibrations in the ship as the
stones of a cathedral are stirred by the bass of the organ.

'As with sounds, so with colours. At each end of the solar
spectrum the chemist can detect the presence of what are known
as "actinic" rays. They represent colours – integral colours in the
composition of light – which we are unable to discern. The
human eye is an imperfect instrument; its range is but a few
octaves of the real "chromatic scale". I am not mad; there are
colours that we cannot see.

'And, God help me! the Damned Thing is of such a colour!'

The Realm of the Unreal

I

For a part of the distance between Auburn and Newcastle the road –
first on one side of a creek and then on the other – occupies
the whole bottom of the ravine, being partly cut out of the steep
hillside, and partly built up with boulders removed from the creek-
bed by the miners. The hills are wooded, the course of the ravine is
sinuous. In a dark night careful driving is required in order not to
go off into the water. The night that I have in memory was dark, the
creek a torrent, swollen by a recent storm. I had driven up from
Newcastle and was within about a mile of Auburn in the darkest
and narrowest part of the ravine, looking intently ahead of my
horse for the roadway. Suddenly I saw a man almost under the
animal's nose, and reined in with a jerk that came near setting the
creature upon its haunches.

'I beg your pardon,' I said; 'I did not see you, sir.'

'You could hardly be expected to see me,' the man replied, civilly,
approaching the side of the vehicle; 'and the noise of the creek
prevented my hearing you.'

I at once recognised the voice, although five years had passed since
I had heard it. I was not particularly well pleased to hear it now.

'You are Dr Dorrimore, I think,' said I.

'Yes; and you are my good friend Mr Manrich. I am more than
glad to see you – the excess,' he added, with a light laugh, 'being
due to the fact that I am going your way, and naturally expect an
invitation to ride with you.'

'Which I extend with all my heart.'

That was not altogether true.

Dr Dorrimore thanked me as he seated himself beside me, and I
drove cautiously forward, as before. Doubtless it is fancy, but it
seems to me now that the remaining distance was made in a chill fog;
that I was uncomfortably cold; that the way was longer than ever
before, and the town, when we reached it, cheerless, forbidding, and

desolate. It must have been early in the evening, yet I do not recollect a light in any of the houses nor a living thing in the streets. Dorrimore explained at some length how he happened to be there, and where he had been during the years that had elapsed since I had seen him. I recall the fact of the narrative, but none of the facts narrated. He had been in foreign countries and had returned – this is all that my memory retains, and this I already knew. As to myself I cannot remember that I spoke a word, though doubtless I did. Of one thing I am distinctly conscious: the man's presence at my side was strangely distasteful and disquieting – so much so that when I at last pulled up under the lights of the Putnam House I experienced a sense of having escaped some spiritual peril of a nature peculiarly forbidding. This sense of relief was somewhat modified by the discovery that Dr Dorrimore was living at the same hotel.

2

In partial explanation of my feelings regarding Dr Dorrimore I will relate briefly the circumstances under which I had met him some years before. One evening a half-dozen men of whom I was one were sitting in the library of the Bohemian Club in San Francisco. The conversation had turned to the subject of sleight-of-hand and the feats of the *prestidigitateurs*, one of whom was then exhibiting at a local theatre.

'These fellows are pretenders in a double sense,' said one of the party; 'they can do nothing which it is worth one's while to be made a dupe by. The humblest wayside juggler in India could mystify them to the verge of lunacy.'

'For example, how?' asked another, lighting a cigar.

'For example, by all their common and familiar performances – throwing large objects into the air which never come down; causing plants to sprout, grow visibly and blossom, in bare ground chosen by spectators; putting a man into a wicker basket, piercing him through and through with a sword while he shrieks and bleeds, and then – the basket being opened nothing is there; tossing the free end of a silken ladder into the air, mounting it and disappearing.'

'Nonsense!' I said, rather uncivilly, I fear. 'You surely do not believe such things?'

'Certainly not: I have seen them too often.'

'But I do,' said a journalist of considerable local fame as a picturesque reporter. 'I have so frequently related them that nothing but observation could shake my conviction. Why, gentlemen, I have my own word for it.'

Nobody laughed – all were looking at something behind me. Turning in my seat I saw a man in evening dress who had just entered the room. He was exceedingly dark, almost swarthy, with a thin face, black-bearded to the lips, an abundance of coarse black hair in some disorder, a high nose and eyes that glittered with as soulless an expression as those of a cobra. One of the group rose and introduced him as Dr Dorrimore, of Calcutta. As each of us was presented in turn he acknowledged the fact with a profound bow in the Oriental manner, but with nothing of Oriental gravity. His smile impressed me as cynical and a trifle contemptuous. His whole demeanour I can describe only as disagreeably engaging.

His presence led the conversation into other channels. He said little – I do not recall anything of what he did say. I thought his voice singularly rich and melodious, but it affected me in the same way as his eyes and smile. In a few minutes I rose to go. He also rose and put on his overcoat.

'Mr Manrich,' he said, 'I am going your way.'

'The devil you are!' I thought. 'How do you know which way I am going?' Then I said, 'I shall be pleased to have your company.'

We left the building together. No cabs were in sight, the street-cars had gone to bed, there was a full moon and the cool night air was delightful; we walked up the California street hill. I took that direction thinking he would naturally wish to take another, toward one of the hotels.

'You do not believe what is told of the Hindu jugglers,' he said abruptly.

'How do you know that?' I asked.

Without replying he laid his hand lightly upon my arm and with the other pointed to the stone sidewalk directly in front. There, almost at our feet, lay the dead body of a man, the face upturned and white in the moonlight! A sword whose hilt sparkled with gems stood fixed and upright in the breast; a pool of blood had collected on the stones of the sidewalk.

I was startled and terrified – not only by what I saw, but by the circumstances under which I saw it. Repeatedly during our ascent of the hill my eyes, I thought, had traversed the whole reach of that sidewalk, from street to street. How could they have been insensible to this dreadful object now so conspicuous in the white moonlight?

As my dazed faculties cleared I observed that the body was in evening dress; the overcoat thrown wide open revealed the dress-coat, the white tie, the broad expanse of shirt front pierced by the sword. And – horrible revelation! – the face, except for its pallor, was that of my companion! It was to the minutest detail of dress and feature Dr Dorrimore himself. Bewildered and horrified, I turned to look for the living man. He was nowhere visible, and with an added terror I retired from the place, down the hill in the direction whence I had come. I had taken but a few strides when a strong grasp upon my shoulder arrested me. I came near crying out with terror: the dead man, the sword still fixed in his breast, stood beside me! Pulling out the sword with his disengaged hand, he flung it from him, the moonlight glinting upon the jewels of its hilt and the unsullied steel of its blade. It fell with a clang upon the sidewalk ahead and – vanished! The man, swarthy as before, relaxed his grasp upon my shoulder and looked at me with the same cynical regard that I had observed on first meeting him. The dead have not that look – it partly restored me, and turning my head backward, I saw the smooth white expanse of sidewalk, unbroken from street to street.

'What is all this nonsense, you devil?' I demanded, fiercely enough, though weak and trembling in every limb.

'It is what some are pleased to call jugglery,' he answered, with a light, hard laugh.

He turned down Dupont street and I saw him no more until we met in the Auburn ravine.

3

On the day after my second meeting with Dr Dorrimore I did not see him: the clerk in the Putnam House explained that a slight illness confined him to his rooms. That afternoon at the railway station I was surprised and made happy by the unexpected arrival of Miss Margaret Corray and her mother, from Oakland.

This is not a love story. I am no storyteller, and love as it is cannot be portrayed in a literature dominated and enthralled by the debasing tyranny which 'sentences letters' in the name of the Young Girl. Under the Young Girl's blighting reign – or rather under the rule of those false Ministers of the Censure who have appointed themselves to the custody of her welfare –

love veils her sacred fires,
And, unaware, Morality expires,

famished upon the sifted meal and distilled water of a prudish purveyance.

Let it suffice that Miss Corray and I were engaged in marriage. She and her mother went to the hotel at which I lived, and for two weeks I saw her daily. That I was happy needs hardly be said; the only bar to my perfect enjoyment of those golden days was the presence of Dr Dorrimore, whom I had felt compelled to introduce to the ladies.

By them he was evidently held in favour. What could I say? I knew absolutely nothing to his discredit. His manners were those of a cultivated and considerate gentleman; and to women a man's manner is the man. On one or two occasions when I saw Miss Corray walking with him I was furious, and once had the indiscretion to protest. Asked for reasons, I had none to give and fancied I saw in her expression a shade of contempt for the vagaries of a jealous mind. In time I grew morose and consciously disagreeable, and resolved in my madness to return to San Francisco the next day. Of this, however, I said nothing.

4

There was at Auburn an old, abandoned cemetery. It was nearly in the heart of the town, yet by night it was as gruesome a place as the most dismal of human moods could crave. The railings about the plots were prostrate, decayed, or altogether gone. Many of the graves were sunken, from others grew sturdy pines, whose roots had committed unspeakable sin. The headstones were fallen and broken across; brambles overran the ground; the fence was mostly gone, and cows and pigs wandered there at will; the place was a dishonour to the living, a calumny on the dead, a blasphemy against God.

The evening of the day on which I had taken my madman's resolution to depart in anger from all that was dear to me found me in that congenial spot. The light of the half moon fell ghostly through the foliage of trees in spots and patches, revealing much that was unsightly, and the black shadows seemed conspiracies withholding to the proper time revelations of darker import. Passing along what had been a gravel path, I saw emerging from shadow the figure of Dr Dorrimore. I was myself in shadow, and stood still with clenched hands and set teeth, trying to control the impulse to leap upon and strangle him. A moment later a second figure joined him and clung to his arm. It was Margaret Corray!

I cannot rightly relate what occurred. I know that I sprang forward, bent upon murder; I know that I was found in the grey of the morning, bruised and bloody, with finger marks upon my throat. I was taken to the Putnam House, where for days I lay in a delirium. All this I know, for I have been told. And of my own knowledge I know that when consciousness returned with convalescence I sent for the clerk of the hotel.

'Are Mrs Corray and her daughter still here?' I asked.

'What name did you say?'

'Corray.'

'Nobody of that name has been here.'

'I beg you will not trifle with me,' I said petulantly. 'You see that I am all right now; tell me the truth.'

'I give you my word,' he replied with evident sincerity, 'we have had no guests of that name.'

His words stupefied me. I lay for a few moments in silence; then I asked: 'Where is Dr Dorrimore?'

'He left on the morning of your fight and has not been heard of since. It was a rough deal he gave you.'

5

Such are the facts of this case. Margaret Corray is now my wife. She has never seen Auburn, and during the weeks whose history as it shaped itself in my brain I have endeavoured to relate, was living at her home in Oakland, wondering where her lover was and why he did not write. The other day I saw in the *Baltimore Sun* the following paragraph:

Professor Valentine Dorrimore, the hypnotist, had a large audience last night. The lecturer, who has lived most of his life in India, gave some marvellous exhibitions of his power, hypnotising anyone who chose to submit himself to the experiment, by merely looking at him. In fact, he twice hypnotised the entire audience (reporters alone exempted), making all entertain the most extraordinary illusions. The most valuable feature of the lecture was the disclosure of the methods of the Hindu jugglers in their famous performances, familiar in the mouths of travellers. The professor declares that these thaumaturgists have acquired such skill in the art which he learned at their feet that they perform their miracles by simply throwing the "spectators" into a state of hypnosis and telling them what to see and hear. His assertion that a peculiarly susceptible subject may be kept in the realm of the unreal for weeks, months, and even years, dominated by whatever delusions and hallucinations the operator may from time to time suggest, is a trifle disquieting.

Chickamauga

One sunny autumn afternoon a child strayed away from its rude home in a small field and entered a forest unobserved. It was happy in a new sense of freedom from control, happy in the opportunity of exploration and adventure; for this child's spirit, in bodies of its ancestors, had for thousands of years been trained to memorable feats of discovery and conquest – victories in battles whose critical moments were centuries, whose victors' camps were cities of hewn stone. From the cradle of its race it had conquered its way through two continents and passing a great sea had penetrated a third, there to be born to war and dominion as a heritage.

The child was a boy aged about six years, the son of a poor planter. In his younger manhood the father had been a soldier, had fought against naked savages and followed the flag of his country into the capital of a civilised race to the far South. In the peaceful life of a planter the warrior-fire survived; once kindled, it is never extinguished. The man loved military books and pictures and the boy had understood enough to make himself a wooden sword, though even the eye of his father would hardly have known it for what it was. This weapon he now bore bravely, as became the son of an heroic race, and pausing now and again in the sunny space of the forest assumed, with some exaggeration, the postures of aggression and defence that he had been taught by the engraver's art. Made reckless by the ease with which he overcame invisible foes attempting to stay his advance, he committed the common enough military error of pushing the pursuit to a dangerous extreme, until he found himself upon the margin of a wide but shallow brook, whose rapid waters barred his direct advance against the flying foe that had crossed with illogical ease. But the intrepid victor was not to be baffled; the spirit of the race which had passed the great sea burned unconquerable in that small breast and would not be denied. Finding a place where some boulders in the bed of the stream lay but a step or a leap apart, he made his way across and fell again upon the rearguard of his imaginary foe, putting all to the sword.

Now that the battle had been won, prudence required that he withdraw to his base of operations. Alas; like many a mightier conqueror, and like one, the mightiest, he could not curb the lust for war, Nor learn that tempted Fate will leave the loftiest star.

Advancing from the bank of the creek he suddenly found himself confronted with a new and more formidable enemy: in the path that he was following, sat, bolt upright, with ears erect and paws suspended before it, a rabbit! With a startled cry the child turned and fled, he knew not in what direction, calling with inarticulate cries for his mother, weeping, stumbling, his tender skin cruelly torn by brambles, his little heart beating hard with terror – breathless, blind with tears – lost in the forest! Then, for more than an hour, he wandered with erring feet through the tangled undergrowth, till at last, overcome by fatigue, he lay down in a narrow space between two rocks, within a few yards of the stream and still grasping his toy sword, no longer a weapon but a companion, sobbed himself to sleep. The wood birds sang merrily above his head; the squirrels, whisking their bravery of tail, ran barking from tree to tree, unconscious of the pity of it, and somewhere far away was a strange, muffled thunder, as if the partridges were drumming in celebration of nature's victory over the son of her immemorial enslavers. And back at the little plantation, where white men and black were hastily searching the fields and hedges in alarm, a mother's heart was breaking for her missing child.

Hours passed, and then the little sleeper rose to his feet. The chill of the evening was in his limbs, the fear of the gloom in his heart. But he had rested, and he no longer wept. With some blind instinct which impelled to action he struggled through the undergrowth about him and came to a more open ground – on his right the brook, to the left a gentle acclivity studded with infrequent trees; over all, the gathering gloom of twilight. A thin, ghostly mist rose along the water. It frightened and repelled him; instead of recrossing, in the direction whence he had come, he turned his back upon it, and went forward toward the dark enclosing wood. Suddenly he saw before him a strange moving object which he took to be some large animal – a dog, a pig – he could not name it; perhaps it was a bear. He had seen pictures of bears, but knew of nothing to their discredit and had vaguely wished to meet one. But something in form or movement of this object – something in the awkwardness of its approach – told him that it was not a bear, and curiosity was stayed by fear. He stood still and as it came slowly on gained courage every moment, for he saw that at least it had not the long, menacing ears of the rabbit. Possibly his impressionable mind was half-conscious of something familiar in its shambling, awkward gait. Before it had approached near enough to resolve his doubts he saw that it was followed by another and another. To right and to left were many more; the whole open space about him was alive with them – all moving toward the brook.

They were men. They crept upon their hands and knees. They used their hands only, dragging their legs. They used their knees only, their arms hanging idle at their sides. They strove to rise to their feet, but fell prone in the attempt. They did nothing naturally, and nothing alike, save only to advance foot by foot in the same direction. Singly, in pairs and in little groups, they came on through the gloom, some halting now and again while others crept slowly past them, then resuming their movement. They came by dozens and by hundreds; as far on either hand as one could see in the deepening gloom they extended and the black wood behind them appeared to be inexhaustible. The very ground seemed in motion toward the creek. Occasionally one who had paused did not again go on, but lay motionless. He was dead. Some, pausing, made strange gestures with their hands, erected their arms and lowered them again, clasped their heads; spread their palms upward, as men are sometimes seen to do in public prayer.

Not all of this did the child note; it is what would have been noted by an elder observer; he saw little but that these were men, yet crept like babes. Being men, they were not terrible, though unfamiliarly clad. He moved among them freely, going from one to another and peering into their faces with childish curiosity. All their faces were singularly white and many were streaked and gouted with red. Something in this – something too, perhaps, in their grotesque attitudes and movements – reminded him of the painted clown whom he had seen last summer in the circus, and he laughed as he watched them. But on and ever on they crept, these maimed and bleeding men, as heedless as he of the dramatic contrast between his laughter and their own ghastly gravity. To him it was a merry spectacle. He had seen his father's negroes creep upon their hands and knees for his amuse-ment – had ridden them so, 'making believe' they were his horses. He now approached one of these crawling figures from behind and with an agile movement mounted it astride. The man sank upon his breast, recovered, flung the small boy fiercely to the ground as an unbroken colt might have done, then turned upon him a face that lacked a lower jaw – from the upper teeth to the throat was a great red gap fringed with hanging shreds of flesh and splinters of bone. The unnatural prominence of nose, the absence of chin, the fierce eyes, gave this man the appearance of a great bird of prey crimsoned in throat and breast by the blood of its quarry. The man rose to his knees, the child to his feet. The man shook his fist at the child; the child, terrified at last, ran to a tree nearby, got upon the farther side of it and took a more serious view of the situation. And so the clumsy multitude dragged itself slowly and painfully along in hideous panto-mime – moved forward down the slope like a swarm of great black beetles, with never a sound of going – in silence profound, absolute.

Instead of darkening, the haunted landscape began to brighten. Through the belt of trees beyond the brook shone a strange red light, the trunks and branches of the trees making a black lacework against it. It struck the creeping figures and gave them monstrous shadows, which caricatured their movements on the lit grass. It fell upon their faces, touching their whiteness with a ruddy tinge, accentuating the stains with which so many of them were freaked and maculated. It sparkled on buttons and bits of metal in their clothing. Instinctively the child turned toward the growing splendour and moved down the slope with his horrible companions; in a few moments had passed the foremost of the throng – not much of a feat, considering his advantages. He placed himself in the lead, his wooden sword still in hand, and solemnly directed the march, conforming his pace to theirs and occasionally turning as if to see that his forces did not straggle. Surely such a leader never before had such a following.

Scattered about upon the ground now slowly narrowing by the encroachment of this awful march to water, were certain articles to which, in the leader's mind, were coupled no significant assoc-iations: an occasional blanket, tightly rolled lengthwise, doubled and the ends bound together with a string; a heavy knapsack here, and there a broken rifle – such things, in short, as are found in the rear of retreating troops, the 'spoor' of men flying from their hunters. Everywhere near the creek, which here had a margin of lowland, the earth was trodden into mud by the feet of men and horses. An observer of better experience in the use of his eyes would have noticed that these footprints pointed in both directions; the ground had been twice passed over – in advance and in retreat. A few hours before, these desperate, stricken men, with their more fortunate and now distant comrades, had penetrated the forest in thousands. Their successive battalions, breaking into swarms and re-forming in lines, had passed the child on every side – had almost trodden on him as he slept. The rustle and murmur of their march had not awakened him. Almost within a stone's throw of where he lay they had fought a battle; but all unheard by him were the roar of the musketry, the shock of the cannon, 'the thunder of the captains and the shouting'. He had slept through it all, grasping his little wooden sword with perhaps a tighter clutch in unconscious sympathy with his martial environment, but as heedless of the grandeur of the struggle as the dead who had died to make the glory.

The fire beyond the belt of woods on the farther side of the creek, reflected to earth from the canopy of its own smoke, was now suffusing the whole landscape. It transformed the sinuous line of mist to the vapour of gold. The water gleamed with dashes of red, and red, too, were many of the stones protruding above the surface. But that was blood; the less desperately wounded had stained them in crossing. On them, too, the child now crossed with eager steps; he was going to the fire. As he stood upon the farther bank he turned about to look at the companions of his march. The advance was arriving at the creek. The stronger had already drawn themselves to the brink and plunged their faces into the flood. Three or four who lay without motion appeared to have no heads. At this the child's eyes expanded with wonder; even his hospitable understanding could not accept a phenomenon implying such vitality as that. After slaking their thirst these men had not had the strength to back away from the water, nor to keep their heads above it. They were drowned. In rear of these, the open spaces of the forest showed the leader as many formless figures of his grim command as at first; but not nearly so many were in motion. He waved his cap for their encouragement and smilingly pointed with his weapon in the direction of the guiding light – a pillar of fire to this strange exodus.

Confident of the fidelity of his forces, he now entered the belt of woods, passed through it easily in the red illumination, climbed a fence, ran across a field, turning now and again to coquet with his responsive shadow, and so approached the blazing ruin of a dwelling. Desolation everywhere! In all the wide glare not a living thing was visible. He cared nothing for that; the spectacle pleased, and he danced with glee in imitation of the wavering flames. He ran about, collecting fuel, but every object that he found was too heavy for him to cast in from the distance to which the heat limited his approach. In despair he flung in his sword – a surrender to the superior forces of nature. His military career was at an end.

Shifting his position, his eyes fell upon some outbuildings which had an oddly familiar appearance, as if he had dreamed of them. He stood considering them with wonder, when suddenly the entire plantation, with its enclosing forest, seemed to turn as if upon a pivot. His little world swung half around; the points of the compass were reversed. He recognised the blazing building as his own home!

For a moment he stood stupefied by the power of the revelation, then ran with stumbling feet, making a half-circuit of the ruin. There, conspicuous in the light of the conflagration, lay the dead body of a woman – the white face turned upward, the hands thrown out and clutched full of grass, the clothing deranged, the long dark hair in tangles and full of clotted blood. The greater part of the forehead was torn away, and from the jagged hole the brain protruded, overflowing the temple, a frothy mass of grey, crowned with clusters of crimson bubbles – the work of a shell.

The child moved his little hands, making wild, uncertain gestures. He uttered a series of inarticulate and indescribable cries – something between the chattering of an ape and the gobbling of a turkey – a startling, soulless, unholy sound, the language of a devil. The child was a deaf mute.

Then he stood motionless, with quivering lips, looking down upon the wreck.

A Fruitless Assignment

Henry Saylor, who was killed in Covington, in a quarrel with Antonio Finch, was a reporter on the Cincinnati Commercial. In the year 1859 a vacant dwelling in Vine street, in Cincinnati, became the centre of a local excitement because of the strange sights and sounds said to be observed in it nightly. According to the testimony of many reputable residents of the vicinity these were inconsistent with any other hypothesis than that the house was haunted. Figures with something singularly unfamiliar about them were seen by crowds on the sidewalk to pass in and out. No-one could say just where they appeared upon the open lawn on their way to the front door by which they entered, nor at exactly what point they vanished as they came out; or rather, while each spectator was positive enough about these matters, no two agreed. They were all similarly at variance in their descriptions of the figures themselves. Some of the bolder of the curious throng ventured on several evenings to stand upon the doorsteps to intercept them, or failing in this, get a nearer look at them. These courageous men, it was said, were unable to force the door by their united strength, and always were hurled from the steps by some invisible agency and severely injured; the door immediately afterward opening, apparently of its own volition, to admit or free some ghostly guest. The dwelling was known as the Roscoe house, a family of that name having lived there for some years, and then, one by one, disappeared, the last to leave being an old woman. Stories of foul play and successive murders had always been rife, but never were authenticated.

One day during the prevalence of the excitement Saylor presented himself at the office of the Commercial for orders. He received a note from the city editor which read as follows: 'Go and pass the night alone in the haunted house in Vine street and if anything occurs worth while make two columns.' Saylor obeyed his superior; he could not afford to lose his position on the paper.

Apprising the police of his intention, he effected an entrance through a rear window before dark, walked through the deserted rooms, bare of furniture, dusty and desolate, and seating himself at last in the parlour on an old sofa which he had dragged in from another room watched the deepening of the gloom as night came on. Before it was altogether dark the curious crowd had collected in the street, silent, as a rule, and expectant, with here and there a scoffer uttering his incredulity and courage with scornful remarks or ribald cries. None knew of the anxious watcher inside. He feared to make a light; the uncurtained windows would have betrayed his presence, subjecting him to insult, possibly to injury. Moreover, he was too conscientious to do anything to enfeeble his impressions and unwilling to alter any of the customary conditions under which the manifestations were said to occur.

It was now dark outside, but light from the street faintly illuminated the part of the room that he was in. He had set open every door in the whole interior, above and below, but all the outer ones were locked and bolted. Sudden exclamations from the crowd caused him to spring to the window and look out. He saw the figure of a man moving rapidly across the lawn toward the building – saw it ascend the steps; then a projection of the wall concealed it. There was a noise as of the opening and closing of the hall door; he heard quick, heavy footsteps along the passage – heard them ascend the stairs – heard them on the uncarpeted floor of the chamber immediately overhead.

Saylor promptly drew his pistol, and groping his way up the stairs entered the chamber, dimly lighted from the street. No-one was there. He heard footsteps in an adjoining room and entered that. It was dark and silent. He struck his foot against some object on the floor, knelt by it, passed his hand over it. It was a human head – that of a woman. Lifting it by the hair this iron-nerved man returned to the half-lighted room below, carried it near the window and attentively examined it. While so engaged he was half-conscious of the rapid opening and closing of the outer door, of footfalls sounding all about him. He raised his eyes from the ghastly object of his attention and saw himself the centre of a crowd of men and women dimly seen; the room was thronged with them. He thought the people had broken in.

'Ladies and gentlemen,' he said, coolly, 'you see me under suspicious circumstances, but – ' his voice was drowned in peals of laughter – such laughter as is heard in asylums for the insane. The persons about him pointed at the object in his hand and their merriment increased as he dropped it and it went rolling among their feet. They danced about it with gestures grotesque and attitudes obscene and indescribable. They struck it with their feet, urging it about the room from wall to wall; pushed and overthrew one another in their struggles to kick it; cursed and screamed and sang snatches of ribald songs as the battered head bounded about the room as if in terror and trying to escape. At last it shot out of the door into the hall, followed by all, with tumultuous haste. That moment the door closed with a sharp concussion. Saylor was alone, in dead silence.

Carefully putting away his pistol, which all the time he had held in his hand, he went to a window and looked out. The street was deserted and silent; the lamps were extinguished; the roofs and chimneys of the houses were sharply outlined against the dawn-light in the east. He left the house, the door yielding easily to his hand, and walked to the Commercial office. The city editor was still in his office – asleep. Saylor waked him and said: 'I have been at the haunted house.'

The editor stared blankly as if not wholly awake. 'Good God!' he cried, 'are you Saylor?'

'Yes – why not?'

The editor made no answer, but continued staring.

'I passed the night there – it seems,' said Saylor.

'They say that things were uncommonly quiet out there,' the editor said, trifling with a paperweight upon which he had dropped his eyes, 'did anything occur?'

'Nothing whatever.'

A Vine on a House

About three miles from the little town of Norton, in Missouri, on the road leading to Maysville, stands an old house that was last occupied by a family named Harding. Since 1886 no-one has lived in it, nor is anyone likely to live in it again. Time and the disfavour of persons dwelling thereabout are converting it into a rather picturesque ruin. An observer unacquainted with its history would hardly put it into the category of 'haunted houses', yet in all the region round such is its evil reputation. Its windows are without glass, its doorways without doors; there are wide breaches in the shingle roof, and for lack of paint the weatherboarding is a dun grey. But these unfailing signs of the supernatural are partly concealed and greatly softened by the abundant foliage of a large vine overrunning the entire structure. This vine – of a species which no botanist has ever been able to name – has an important part in the story of the house.

The Harding family consisted of Robert Harding, his wife Matilda, Miss Julia Went, who was her sister, and two young children. Robert Harding was a silent, cold-mannered man who made no friends in the neighbourhood and apparently cared to make none. He was about forty years old, frugal and industrious, and made a living from the little farm which is now overgrown with brush and brambles. He and his sister-in-law were rather tabooed by their neighbours, who seemed to think that they were seen too frequently together – not entirely their fault, for at these times they evidently did not challenge observation. The moral code of rural Missouri is stern and exacting.

Mrs Harding was a gentle, sad-eyed woman, lacking a left foot.

At some time in 1884 it became known that she had gone to visit her mother in Iowa. That was what her husband said in reply to enquiries, and his manner of saying it did not encourage further questioning. She never came back, and two years later, without selling his farm or anything that was his, or appointing an agent to look after his interests, or removing his household goods, Harding, with the rest of the family, left the country. Nobody knew whither he went; nobody at that time cared. Naturally, whatever was movable about the place soon disappeared and the deserted house became 'haunted' in the manner of its kind.

One summer evening, four or five years later, the Rev. J. Gruber, of Norton, and a Maysville attorney named Hyatt met on horseback in front of the Harding place. Having business matters to discuss, they hitched their animals and going to the house sat on the porch to talk. Some humorous reference to the sombre reputation of the place was made and forgotten as soon as uttered, and they talked of their business affairs until it grew almost dark. The evening was oppressively warm, the air stagnant.

Presently both men started from their seats in surprise: a long vine that covered half the front of the house and dangled its branches from the edge of the porch above them was visibly and audibly agitated, shaking violently in every stem and leaf.

'We shall have a storm,' Hyatt exclaimed.

Gruber said nothing, but silently directed the other's attention to the foliage of adjacent trees, which showed no movement; even the delicate tips of the boughs silhouetted against the clear sky were motionless. They hastily passed down the steps to what had been a lawn and looked upward at the vine, whose entire length was now visible. It continued in violent agitation, yet they could discern no disturbing cause.

'Let us leave,' said the minister.

And leave they did. Forgetting that they had been travelling in opposite directions, they rode away together. They went to Norton, where they related their strange experience to several discreet friends. The next evening, at about the same hour, accompanied by two others whose names are not recalled, they were again on the porch of the Harding house, and again the mysterious phenomenon occurred: the vine was violently agitated while under the closest scrutiny from root to tip, nor did their combined strength applied to the trunk serve to still it. After an hour's observation they retreated, no less wise, it is thought, than when they had come.

No great time was required for these singular facts to rouse the curiosity of the entire neighbourhood. By day and by night crowds of persons assembled at the Harding house 'seeking a sign'. It does not appear that any found it, yet so credible were the witnesses mentioned that none doubted the reality of the 'manifestations' to which they testified.

By either a happy inspiration or some destructive design, it was one day proposed – nobody appeared to know from whom the suggestion came – to dig up the vine, and after a good deal of debate this was done. Nothing was found but the root, yet nothing could have been more strange!

For five or six feet from the trunk, which had at the surface of the ground a diameter of several inches, it ran downward, single and straight, into a loose, friable earth; then it divided and subdivided into rootlets, fibres and filaments, most curiously interwoven. When carefully freed from soil they showed a singular formation. In their ramifications and doublings back upon themselves they made a compact network, having in size and shape an amazing resemblance to the human figure. Head, trunk and limbs were there; even the fingers and toes were distinctly defined; and many professed to see in the distribution and arrangement of the fibres in the globular mass representing the head a grotesque suggestion of a face. The figure was horizontal; the smaller roots had begun to unite at the breast.

In point of resemblance to the human form this image was imperfect. At about ten inches from one of the knees, the cilia forming that leg had abruptly doubled backward and inward upon their course of growth. The figure lacked the left foot.

There was but one inference – the obvious one; but in the ensuing excitement as many courses of action were proposed as there were incapable counsellors. The matter was settled by the sheriff of the county, who as the lawful custodian of the abandoned estate ordered the root replaced and the excavation filled with the earth that had been removed.

Later enquiry brought out only one fact of relevancy and significance: Mrs Harding had never visited her relatives in Iowa, nor did they know that she was supposed to have done so.

Of Robert Harding and the rest of his family nothing is known. The house retains its evil reputation, but the replanted vine is as orderly and well-behaved a vegetable as a nervous person could wish to sit under of a pleasant night, when the katydids grate out their immemorial revelation and the distant whippoorwill signifies his notion of what ought to be done about it.

One of Twins

[a letter found among the papers of the late Mortimer Barr]

You ask me if in my experience as one of a pair of twins I ever observed anything unaccountable by the natural laws with which we have acquaintance. As to that you shall judge; perhaps we have not all acquaintance with the same natural laws. You may know some that I do not, and what is to me unaccountable may be very clear to you.

You knew my brother John – that is, you knew him when you knew that I was not present; but neither you nor, I believe, any human being could distinguish between him and me if we chose to seem alike. Our parents could not; ours is the only instance of which I have any knowledge of so close resemblance as that. I speak of my brother John, but I am not at all sure that his name was not Henry and mine John. We were regularly christened, but afterward, in the very act of tattooing us with small distinguishing marks, the operator lost his reckoning; and although I bear upon my forearm a small 'H' and he bore a 'J,' it is by no means certain that the letters ought not to have been transposed. During our boyhood our parents tried to distinguish us more obviously by our clothing and other simple devices, but we would so frequently exchange suits and otherwise circumvent the enemy that they abandoned all such ineffectual attempts, and during all the years that we lived together at home everybody recognised the difficulty of the situation and made the best of it by calling us both 'Jehnry'. I have often wondered at my father's forbearance in not branding us conspicuously upon our unworthy brows, but as we were tolerably good boys and used our power of embarrassment and annoyance with commendable moderation, we escaped the iron. My father was, in fact, a singularly good-natured man, and I think quietly enjoyed nature's practical joke.

Soon after we had come to California, and settled at San Jose (where the only good fortune that awaited us was our meeting with so kind a friend as you) the family, as you know, was broken up by the death of both my parents in the same week. My father died insolvent and the homestead was sacrificed to pay his debts. My sisters returned to relatives in the East, but owing to your kindness John and I, then twenty-two years of age, obtained employment in San Francisco, in different quarters of the town. Circumstances did not permit us to live together, and we saw each other infrequently, sometimes not oftener than once a week. As we had few acquaintances in common, the fact of our extraordinary likeness was little known. I come now to the matter of your enquiry.

One day soon after we had come to this city I was walking down Market street late in the afternoon, when I was accosted by a well-dressed man of middle age, who after greeting me cordially said: 'Stevens, I know, of course, that you do not go out much, but I have told my wife about you, and she would be glad to see you at the house. I have a notion, too, that my girls are worth knowing. Suppose you come out tomorrow at six and dine with us, *en famille*; and then if the ladies can't amuse you afterward I'll stand in with a few games of billiards.'

This was said with so bright a smile and so engaging a manner that I had not the heart to refuse, and although I had never seen the man in my life I promptly replied: 'You are very good, sir, and it will give me great pleasure to accept the invitation. Please present my compliments to Mrs Margovan and ask her to expect me.'

With a shake of the hand and a pleasant parting word the man passed on. That he had mistaken me for my brother was plain enough. That was an error to which I was accustomed and which it was not my habit to rectify unless the matter seemed important. But how had I known that this man's name was Margovan? It certainly is not a name that one would apply to a man at random, with a probability that it would be right. In point of fact, the name was as strange to me as the man.

The next morning I hastened to where my brother was employed and met him coming out of the office with a number of bills that he was to collect. I told him how I had 'committed' him and added that if he didn't care to keep the engagement I should be delighted to continue the impersonation.

'That's queer,' he said thoughtfully. 'Margovan is the only man in the office here whom I know well and like. When he came in this morning and we had passed the usual greetings some singular impulse prompted me to say: "Oh, I beg your pardon, Mr Margovan, but I neglected to ask your address." I got the address, but what under the sun I was to do with it, I did not know until now. It's good of you to offer to take the consequence of your impudence, but I'll eat that dinner myself, if you please.'

He ate a number of dinners at the same place – more than were good for him, I may add without disparaging their quality; for he fell in love with Miss Margovan, proposed marriage to her and was heartlessly accepted.

Several weeks after I had been informed of the engagement, but before it had been convenient for me to make the acquaintance of the young woman and her family, I met one day on Kearney street a handsome but somewhat dissipated-looking man whom something prompted me to follow and watch, which I did without any scruple whatever. He turned up Geary street and followed it until he came to Union square. There he looked at his watch, then entered the square. He loitered about the paths for some time, evidently waiting for someone. Presently he was joined by a fashionably dressed and beautiful young woman and the two walked away up Stockton street, I following. I now felt the necessity of extreme caution, for although the girl was a stranger it seemed to me that she would recognise me at a glance. They made several turns from one street to another and finally, after both had taken a hasty look all about – which I narrowly evaded by stepping into a doorway – they entered a house of which I do not care to state the location. Its location was better than its character.

I protest that my action in playing the spy upon these two strangers was without assignable motive. It was one of which I might or might not be ashamed, according to my estimate of the character of the person finding it out. As an essential part of a narrative educed by your question it is related here without hesitancy or shame.

A week later John took me to the house of his prospective father-in-law, and in Miss Margovan, as you have already surmised, but to my profound astonishment, I recognised the heroine of that discreditable adventure. A gloriously beautiful heroine of a discreditable adventure I must in justice admit that she was; but that fact has only this importance: her beauty was such a surprise to me that it cast a doubt upon her identity with the young woman I had seen before; how could the marvellous fascination of her face have failed to strike me at that time? But no – there was no possibility of error; the difference was due to costume, light and general surroundings.

John and I passed the evening at the house, enduring, with the fortitude of long experience, such delicate enough banter as our likeness naturally suggested. When the young lady and I were left alone for a few minutes I looked her squarely in the face and said with sudden gravity: 'You, too, Miss Margovan, have a double: I saw her last Tuesday afternoon in Union Square.'

She trained her great grey eyes upon me for a moment, but her glance was a trifle less steady than my own and she withdrew it, fixing it on the tip of her shoe.

'Was she very like me?' she asked, with an indifference which I thought a little overdone.

'So like,' said I, 'that I greatly admired her, and being unwilling to lose sight of her I confess that I followed her until – Miss Margovan, are you sure that you understand?'

She was now pale, but entirely calm. She again raised her eyes to mine, with a look that did not falter.

'What do you wish me to do?' she asked. 'You need not fear to name your terms. I accept them.'

It was plain, even in the brief time given me for reflection, that in dealing with this girl ordinary methods would not do, and ordinary exactions were needless.

'Miss Margovan,' I said, doubtless with something of the compassion in my voice that I had in my heart, 'it is impossible not to think you the victim of some horrible compulsion. Rather than impose new embarrassments upon you I would prefer to aid you to regain your freedom.'

She shook her head, sadly and hopelessly, and I continued, with agitation: 'Your beauty unnerves me. I am disarmed by your frankness and your distress. If you are free to act upon conscience you will, I believe, do what you conceive to be best; if you are not – well, Heaven help us all! You have nothing to fear from me but such opposition to this marriage as I can try to justify on – on other grounds.'

These were not my exact words, but that was the sense of them, as nearly as my sudden and conflicting emotions permitted me to express it. I rose and left her without another look at her, met the others as they re-entered the room and said, as calmly as I could: 'I have been bidding Miss Margovan good-evening; it is later than I thought.'

John decided to go with me. In the street he asked if I had observed anything singular in Julia's manner.

'I thought her ill,' I replied; 'that is why I left.' Nothing more was said.

The next evening I came late to my lodgings. The events of the previous evening had made me nervous and ill; I had tried to cure myself and attain to clear thinking by walking in the open air, but I was oppressed with a horrible presentiment of evil – a presentiment which I could not formulate. It was a chill, foggy night; my clothing and hair were damp and I shook with cold. In my dressing-gown and slippers before a blazing grate of coals I was even more uncomfortable. I no longer shivered but shuddered – there is a difference. The dread of some impending calamity was so strong and dispiriting that I tried to drive it away by inviting a real sorrow – tried to dispel the conception of a terrible future by substituting the memory of a painful past. I recalled the death of my parents and endeavoured to fix my mind upon the last sad scenes at their bedsides and their graves. It all seemed vague and unreal, as having occurred ages ago and to another person. Suddenly, striking through my thought and parting it as a tense cord is parted by the stroke of steel – I can think of no other comparison – I heard a sharp cry as of one in mortal agony! The voice was that of my brother and seemed to come from the street outside my window. I sprang to the window and threw it open. A street lamp directly opposite threw a wan and ghastly light upon the wet pavement and the fronts of the houses. A single policeman, with upturned collar, was leaning against a gatepost, quietly smoking a cigar. No-one else was in sight. I closed the window and pulled down the shade, seated myself before the fire and tried to fix my mind upon my surroundings. By way of assisting, by performance of some familiar act, I looked at my watch; it marked half-past eleven. Again I heard that awful cry! It seemed in the room – at my side. I was frightened and for some moments had not the power to move. A few minutes later – I have no recollection of the intermediate time – I found myself hurrying along an unfamiliar street as fast as I could walk. I did not know where I was, nor whither I was going, but presently sprang up the steps of a house before which were two or three carriages and in which were moving lights and a subdued confusion of voices. It was the house of Mr Margovan.

You know, good friend, what had occurred there. In one chamber lay Julia Margovan, hours dead by poison; in another John Stevens, bleeding from a pistol wound in the chest, inflicted by his own hand. As I burst into the room, pushed aside the physicians and laid my hand upon his forehead he unclosed his eyes, stared blankly, closed them slowly and died without a sign.

I knew no more until six weeks afterward, when I had been nursed back to life by your own saintly wife in your own beautiful home. All of that you know, but what you do not know is this – which, however, has no bearing upon the subject of your psychological researches – at least not upon that branch of them in which, with a delicacy and consideration all your own, you have asked for less assistance than I think I have given you.

One moonlight night several years afterward I was passing through Union Square. The hour was late and the square deserted. Certain memories of the past naturally came into my mind as I came to the spot where I had once witnessed that fateful assignation, and with that unaccountable perversity which prompts us to dwell upon thoughts of the most painful character I seated myself upon one of the benches to indulge them. A man entered the square and came along the walk toward me. His hands were clasped behind him, his head was bowed; he seemed to observe nothing. As he approached the shadow in which I sat I recognised him as the man whom I had seen meet Julia Margovan years before at that spot. But he was terribly altered – grey, worn and haggard. Dissipation and vice were in evidence in every look; illness was no less apparent. His clothing was in disorder, his hair fell across his forehead in a derangement which was at once uncanny and picturesque. He looked fitter for restraint than liberty – the restraint of a hospital.

With no defined purpose I rose and confronted him. He raised his head and looked me full in the face. I have no words to describe the ghastly change that came over his own; it was a look of unspeakable terror – he thought himself eye to eye with a ghost. But he was a courageous man. 'Damn you, John Stevens!' he cried, and lifting his trembling arm he dashed his fist feebly at my face and fell headlong upon the gravel as I walked away.

Somebody found him there, stone-dead. Nothing more is known of him, not even his name. To know of a man that he is dead should be enough.

Present at a Hanging

An old man named Daniel Baker, living near Lebanon, Iowa, was
suspected by his neighbours of having murdered a pedlar who had
obtained permission to pass the night at his house. This was in 1853,
when peddling was more common in the Western country than it is
now, and was attended with considerable danger. The pedlar with his
pack traversed the country by all manner of lonely roads, and
was compelled to rely upon the country people for hospitality. This
brought him into relation with queer characters, some of whom were
not altogether scrupulous in their methods of making a living, murder
being an acceptable means to that end. It occasionally occurred that a
pedlar with diminished pack and swollen purse would be traced to the
lonely dwelling of some rough character and never could be traced
beyond. This was so in the case of 'old man Baker', as he was always
called. (Such names are given in the western 'settlements' only to
elderly persons who are not esteemed; to the general disrepute of
social unworth is affixed the special reproach of age.) A pedlar came to
his house and none went away – that is all that anybody knew.

Seven years later the Rev. Mr Cummings, a Baptist minister well
known in that part of the country, was driving by Baker's farm one
night. It was not very dark: there was a bit of moon somewhere above
the light veil of mist that lay along the earth. Mr Cummings, who was
at all times a cheerful person, was whistling a tune, which he would
occasionally interrupt to speak a word of friendly encouragement to
his horse. As he came to a little bridge across a dry ravine he saw the
figure of a man standing upon it, clearly outlined against the grey
background of a misty forest. The man had something strapped on
his back and carried a heavy stick – obviously an itinerant pedlar.
His attitude had in it a suggestion of abstraction, like that of a sleep-
walker. Mr Cummings reined in his horse when he arrived in front of
him, gave him a pleasant salutation and invited him to a seat in the
vehicle – 'if you are going my way,' he added. The man raised his
head, looked him full in the face, but neither answered nor made

any further movement. The minister, with good-natured persistence, repeated his invitation. At this the man threw his right hand forward from his side and pointed downward as he stood on the extreme edge of the bridge. Mr Cummings looked past him, over into the ravine, saw nothing unusual and withdrew his eyes to address the man again. He had disappeared. The horse, which all this time had been uncommonly restless, gave at the same moment a snort of terror and started to run away. Before he had regained control of the animal the minister was at the crest of the hill a hundred yards along. He looked back and saw the figure again, at the same place and in the same attitude as when he had first observed it. Then for the first time he was conscious of a sense of the supernatural and drove home as rapidly as his willing horse would go.

On arriving at home he related his adventure to his family, and early the next morning, accompanied by two neighbours, John White Corwell and Abner Raiser, returned to the spot. They found the body of old man Baker hanging by the neck from one of the beams of the bridge, immediately beneath the spot where the apparition had stood. A thick coating of dust, slightly dampened by the mist, covered the floor of the bridge, but the only footprints were those of Mr Cummings' horse.

In taking down the body the men disturbed the loose, friable earth of the slope below it, disclosing human bones already nearly uncovered by the action of water and frost. They were identified as those of the lost pedlar. At the double inquest the coroner's jury found that Daniel Baker died by his own hand while suffering from temporary insanity, and that Samuel Morritz was murdered by some person or persons to the jury unknown.

A Wireless Message

In the summer of 1896 Mr William Holt, a wealthy manufacturer of Chicago, was living temporarily in a little town of central New York, the name of which the writer's memory has not retained. Mr Holt had had 'trouble with his wife', from whom he had parted a year before. Whether the trouble was anything more serious than 'incompatibility of temper', he is probably the only living person that knows: he is not addicted to the vice of confidences. Yet he has related the incident herein set down to at least one person without exacting a pledge of secrecy. He is now living in Europe.

One evening he had left the house of a brother whom he was visiting, for a stroll in the country. It may be assumed – whatever the value of the assumption in connection with what is said to have occurred – that his mind was occupied with reflections on his domestic infelicities and the distressing changes that they had wrought in his life.

Whatever may have been his thoughts, they so possessed him that he observed neither the lapse of time nor whither his feet were carrying him; he knew only that he had passed far beyond the town limits and was traversing a lonely region by a road that bore no resemblance to the one by which he had left the village. In brief, he was 'lost'.

Realising his mischance, he smiled; central New York is not a region of perils, nor does one long remain lost in it. He turned about and went back the way that he had come. Before he had gone far he observed that the landscape was growing more distinct – was brightening. Everything was suffused with a soft, red glow in which he saw his shadow projected in the road before him. 'The moon is rising,' he said to himself. Then he remembered that it was about the time of the new moon, and if that tricksy orb was in one of its stages of visibility it had set long before. He stopped and faced about, seeking the source of the rapidly broadening light. As he did so, his shadow turned and lay along the road in front of him as before. The light still came from behind him. That was surprising; he could not understand. Again he turned, and again, facing successively to every point of the horizon. Always the shadow was before – always the light behind, 'a still and awful red'.

Holt was astonished – 'dumbfounded' is the word that he used in telling it – yet seems to have retained a certain intelligent curiosity. To test the intensity of the light whose nature and cause he could not determine, he took out his watch to see if he could make out the figures on the dial. They were plainly visible, and the hands indicated the hour of eleven o'clock and twenty-five minutes. At that moment the mysterious illumination suddenly flared to an intense, an almost blinding splendour, flushing the entire sky, extinguishing the stars and throwing the monstrous shadow of himself athwart the landscape. In that unearthly illumination he saw near him, but apparently in the air at a considerable elevation, the figure of his wife, clad in her night-clothing and holding to her breast the figure of his child. Her eyes were fixed upon his with an expression which he afterward professed himself unable to name or describe, further than that it was 'not of this life'.

The flare was momentary, followed by black darkness, in which, however, the apparition still showed white and motionless; then by insensible degrees it faded and vanished, like a bright image on the retina after the closing of the eyes. A peculiarity of the apparition, hardly noted at the time, but afterward recalled, was that it showed only the upper half of the woman's figure: nothing was seen below the waist.

The sudden darkness was comparative, not absolute, for gradually all objects of his environment became again visible.

In the dawn of the morning Holt found himself entering the village at a point opposite to that at which he had left it. He soon arrived at the house of his brother, who hardly knew him. He was wild-eyed, haggard, and grey as a rat. Almost incoherently, he related his night's experience.

'Go to bed, my poor fellow,' said his brother, 'and – wait. We shall hear more of this.'

An hour later came the predestined telegram. Holt's dwelling in one of the suburbs of Chicago had been destroyed by fire. Her escape cut off by the flames, his wife had appeared at an upper window, her child in her arms. There she had stood, motionless, apparently dazed. Just as the firemen had arrived with a ladder, the floor had given way, and she was seen no more.

The moment of this culminating horror was eleven o'clock and twenty-five minutes, standard time.

One of the Missing

Jerome Searing, a private soldier of General Sherman's army, then confronting the enemy at and about Kennesaw Mountain, Georgia, turned his back upon a small group of officers with whom he had been talking in low tones, stepped across a light line of earthworks, and disappeared in a forest. None of the men in line behind the works had said a word to him, nor had he so much as nodded to them in passing, but all who saw understood that this brave man had been entrusted with some perilous duty. Jerome Searing, though a private, did not serve in the ranks; he was detailed for service at division headquarters, being borne upon the rolls as an orderly. 'Orderly' is a word covering a multitude of duties. An orderly may be a messenger, a clerk, an officer's servant – anything. He may perform services for which no provision is made in orders and army regulations. Their nature may depend upon his aptitude, upon favour, upon accident. Private Searing, an incomparable marksman, young, hardy, intelligent and insensible to fear, was a scout. The general commanding his division was not content to obey orders blindly without knowing what was in his front, even when his command was not on detached service, but formed a fraction of the line of the army; nor was he satisfied to receive his knowledge of his *vis-a-vis* through the customary channels; he wanted to know more than he was apprised of by the corps commander and the collisions of pickets and skirmishers. Hence Jerome Searing, with his extraordinary daring, his woodcraft, his sharp eyes, and truthful tongue. On this occasion his instructions were simple: to get as near the enemy's lines as possible and learn all that he could.

In a few moments he had arrived at the picket-line, the men on duty there lying in groups of two and four behind little banks of earth scooped out of the slight depression in which they lay, their rifles protruding from the green boughs with which they had masked their small defences. The forest extended without a break toward the front, so solemn and silent that only by an effort of the imagination could it be conceived as populous with armed men, alert and vigilant – a forest formidable with possibilities of battle. Pausing a moment in one of these rifle-pits to apprise the men of his intention Searing crept stealthily forward on his hands and knees and was soon lost to view in a dense thicket of underbrush.

'That is the last of him,' said one of the men; 'I wish I had his rifle; those fellows will hurt some of us with it.'

Searing crept on, taking advantage of every accident of ground and growth to give himself better cover. His eyes penetrated everywhere, his ears took note of every sound. He stilled his breathing, and at the cracking of a twig beneath his knee stopped his progress and hugged the earth. It was slow work, but not tedious; the danger made it exciting, but by no physical signs was the excitement manifest. His pulse was as regular, his nerves were as steady as if he were trying to trap a sparrow.

'It seems a long time,' he thought, 'but I cannot have come very far; I am still alive.'

He smiled at his own method of estimating distance, and crept forward. A moment later he suddenly flattened himself upon the earth and lay motionless, minute after minute. Through a narrow opening in the bushes he had caught sight of a small mound of yellow clay – one of the enemy's rifle-pits. After some little time he cautiously raised his head, inch by inch, then his body upon his hands, spread out on each side of him, all the while intently regarding the hillock of clay. In another moment he was upon his feet, rifle in hand, striding rapidly forward with little attempt at conceal- ment. He had rightly interpreted the signs, whatever they were; the enemy was gone.

To assure himself beyond a doubt before going back to report upon so important a matter, Searing pushed forward across the line of abandoned pits, running from cover to cover in the more open forest, his eyes vigilant to discover possible stragglers. He came to the edge of a plantation – one of those forlorn, deserted homesteads of the last years of the war, upgrown with brambles, ugly with broken fences and desolate with vacant buildings having blank apertures in place of doors and windows. After a keen reconnaissance from the safe seclusion of a clump of young pines Searing ran lightly across a field and through an orchard to a small structure which stood apart from the other farm buildings, on a slight elevation. This he thought would enable him to overlook a large scope of country in the direc- tion that he supposed the enemy to have taken in withdrawing. This building, which had originally consisted of a single room elevated upon four posts about ten feet high, was now little more than a roof; the floor had fallen away, the joists and planks loosely piled on the ground below or resting on end at various angles, not wholly torn from their fastenings above. The supporting posts were themselves no longer vertical. It looked as if the whole edifice would go down at the touch of a finger.

Concealing himself in the debris of joists and flooring Searing looked across the open ground between his point of view and a spur of Kennesaw Mountain, a half-mile away. A road leading up and across this spur was crowded with troops – the rearguard of the retiring enemy, their gun-barrels gleaming in the morning sunlight.

Searing had now learned all that he could hope to know. It was his duty to return to his own command with all possible speed and report his discovery. But the grey column of Confederates toiling up the mountain road was singularly tempting. His rifle – an ordinary 'Springfield', but fitted with a globe sight and hair-trigger – would easily send its ounce and a quarter of lead hissing into their midst. That would probably not affect the duration and result of the war, but it is the business of a soldier to kill. It is also his habit if he is a good soldier. Searing cocked his rifle and 'set' the trigger.

But it was decreed from the beginning of time that Private Searing was not to murder anybody that bright summer morning, nor was the Confederate retreat to be announced by him. For countless ages events had been so matching themselves together in that wondrous mosaic to some parts of which, dimly discernible, we give the name of history, that the acts which he had in will would have marred the harmony of the pattern. Some twenty-five years previously the Power charged with the execution of the work according to the design had provided against that mischance by causing the birth of a certain male child in a little village at the foot of the Carpathian Mountains, had carefully reared it, supervised its education, directed its desires into a military channel, and in due time made it an officer of artillery. By the concurrence of an infinite number of favouring influences and their preponderance over an infinite number of opposing ones, this officer of artillery had been made to commit a breach of discipline and flee from his native country to avoid punishment. He had been directed to New Orleans (instead of New York), where a recruiting officer awaited him on the wharf. He was enlisted and promoted, and things were so ordered that he now commanded a Confederate battery some two miles along the line from where Jerome Searing, the Federal scout, stood cocking his rifle. Nothing had been neglected – at every step in the progress of both these men's lives, and in the lives of their contemporaries and ancestors, and in the lives of the contemporaries of their ancestors, the right thing had been done to bring about the desired result. Had anything in all this vast concatenation been overlooked Private Searing might have fired on the retreating Confederates that morning, and would perhaps have missed. As it fell out, a Confederate captain of artillery, having nothing better to do while awaiting his turn to pull out and be off, amused himself by sighting a field-piece obliquely to his right at what he mistook for some Federal officers on the crest of a hill, and discharged it. The shot flew high of its mark.

As Jerome Searing drew back the hammer of his rifle and with his eyes upon the distant Confederates considered where he could plant his shot with the best hope of making a widow or an orphan or a childless mother – perhaps all three, for Private Searing, although he had repeatedly refused promotion, was not without a certain kind of ambition – he heard a rushing sound in the air, like that made by the wings of a great bird swooping down upon its prey. More quickly than he could apprehend the gradation, it increased to a hoarse and horrible roar, as the missile that made it sprang at him out of the sky, striking with a deafening impact one of the posts supporting the confusion of timbers above him, smashing it into matchwood, and bringing down the crazy edifice with a loud clatter, in clouds of blinding dust!

When Jerome Searing recovered consciousness he did not at once understand what had occurred. It was, indeed, some time before he opened his eyes. For a while he believed that he had died and been buried, and he tried to recall some portions of the burial service. He thought that his wife was kneeling upon his grave, adding her weight to that of the earth upon his breast. The two of them, widow and earth, had crushed his coffin. Unless the children should persuade her to go home he would not much longer be able to breathe. He felt a sense of wrong. 'I cannot speak to her,' he thought; 'the dead have no voice; and if I open my eyes I shall get them full of earth.'

He opened his eyes. A great expanse of blue sky, rising from a fringe of the tops of trees. In the foreground, shutting out some of the trees, a high, dun mound, angular in outline and crossed by an intricate, patternless system of straight lines; the whole an immeasurable distance away – a distance so inconceivably great that it fatigued him, and he closed his eyes. The moment that he did so he was conscious of an insufferable light. A sound was in his ears like the low, rhythmic thunder of a distant sea breaking in successive waves upon the beach, and out of this noise, seeming a part of it, or possibly coming from beyond it, and intermingled with its ceaseless undertone, came the articulate words: 'Jerome Searing, you are caught like a rat in a trap – in a trap, trap, trap.'

Suddenly there fell a great silence, a black darkness, an infinite tranquillity, and Jerome Searing, perfectly conscious of his rathood, and well assured of the trap that he was in, remembering all and nowise alarmed, again opened his eyes to reconnoitre, to note the strength of his enemy, to plan his defence.

He was caught in a reclining posture, his back firmly supported by a solid beam. Another lay across his breast, but he had been able to shrink a little away from it so that it no longer oppressed him, though it was immovable. A brace joining it at an angle had wedged him against a pile of boards on his left, fastening the arm on that side. His legs, slightly parted and straight along the ground, were covered upward to the knees with a mass of debris which towered above his narrow horizon. His head was as rigidly fixed as in a vice; he could move his eyes, his chin – no more. Only his right arm was partly free. 'You must help us out of this,' he said to it. But he could not get it from under the heavy timber athwart his chest, nor move it outward more than six inches at the elbow.

Searing was not seriously injured, nor did he suffer pain. A smart rap on the head from a flying fragment of the splintered post, incurred simultaneously with the frightfully sudden shock to the nervous system, had momentarily dazed him. His term of unconsciousness, including the period of recovery, during which he had had the strange fancies, had probably not exceeded a few seconds, for the dust of the wreck had not wholly cleared away as he began an intelligent survey of the situation.

With his partly free right hand he now tried to get hold of the beam that lay across, but not quite against, his breast. In no way could he do so. He was unable to depress the shoulder so as to push the elbow beyond that edge of the timber which was nearest his knees; failing in that, he could not raise the forearm and hand to grasp the beam. The brace that made an angle with it downward and backward prevented him from doing anything in that direction, and between it and his body the space was not half so wide as the length of his forearm. Obviously he could not get his hand under the beam nor over it; the hand could not, in fact, touch it at all. Having demonstrated his inability, he desisted, and began to think whether he could reach any of the debris piled upon his legs.

In surveying the mass with a view to determining that point, his attention was arrested by what seemed to be a ring of shining metal immediately in front of his eyes. It appeared to him at first to surround some perfectly black substance, and it was somewhat more than a half-inch in diameter. It suddenly occurred to his mind that the blackness was simply shadow and that the ring was in fact the muzzle of his rifle protruding from the pile of debris. He was not long in satisfying himself that this was so – if it was a satisfaction. By closing either eye he could look a little way along the barrel – to the point where it was hidden by the rubbish that held it. He could see the one side, with the corresponding eye, at apparently the same angle as the other side with the other eye. Looking with the right eye, the weapon seemed to be directed at a point to the left of his head, and *vice-versa*. He was unable to see the upper surface of the barrel, but could see the under surface of the stock at a slight angle. The piece was, in fact, aimed at the exact centre of his forehead.

In the perception of this circumstance, in the recollection that just previously to the mischance of which this uncomfortable situation was the result he had cocked the rifle and set the trigger so that a touch would discharge it, Private Searing was affected with a feeling of uneasiness. But that was as far as possible from fear; he was a brave man, somewhat familiar with the aspect of rifles from that point of view, and of cannon too. And now he recalled, with something like amusement, an incident of his experience at the storming of Missionary Ridge, where, walking up to one of the enemy's embrasures from which he had seen a heavy gun throw charge after charge of grape among the assailants he had thought for a moment that the piece had been withdrawn; he could see nothing in the opening but a brazen circle. What that was he had understood just in time to step aside as it pitched another peck of iron down that swarming slope. To face firearms is one of the commonest incidents in a soldier's life – firearms, too, with male-volent eyes blazing behind them. That is what a soldier is for. Still, Private Searing did not altogether relish the situation, and turned away his eyes.

After groping, aimless, with his right hand for a time he made an ineffectual attempt to release his left. Then he tried to disengage his head, the fixity of which was the more annoying from his ignorance of what held it. Next he tried to free his feet, but while exerting the powerful muscles of his legs for that purpose it occurred to him that a disturbance of the rubbish which held them might discharge the rifle; how it could have endured what had already befallen it he could not understand, although memory assisted him with several instances in point. One in particular he recalled, in which in a moment of mental abstraction he had clubbed his rifle and beaten out another gentleman's brains, observing afterward that the weapon which he had been diligently swinging by the muzzle was loaded, capped, and at full cock – knowledge of which circumstance would doubtless have cheered his antagonist to longer endurance. He had always smiled in recalling that blunder of his 'green and salad days' as a soldier, but now he did not smile. He turned his eyes again to the muzzle of the rifle and for a moment fancied that it had moved; it seemed somewhat nearer.

Again he looked away. The tops of the distant trees beyond the bounds of the plantation interested him: he had not before observed how light and feathery they were, nor how darkly blue the sky was, even among their branches, where they somewhat paled it with their green; above him it appeared almost black. 'It will be uncomfortably hot here,' he thought, 'as the day advances. I wonder which way I am looking.'

Judging by such shadows as he could see, he decided that his face was due north; he would at least not have the sun in his eyes, and north – well, that was toward his wife and children.

'Bah!' he exclaimed aloud, 'what have they to do with it?'

He closed his eyes. 'As I can't get out I may as well go to sleep. The rebels are gone and some of our fellows are sure to stray out here foraging. They'll find me.'

But he did not sleep. Gradually he became sensible of a pain in his forehead – a dull ache, hardly perceptible at first, but growing more and more uncomfortable. He opened his eyes and it was gone – closed them and it returned. 'The devil!' he said, irrelevantly, and stared again at the sky. He heard the singing of birds, the strange metallic note of the meadow lark, suggesting the clash of vibrant blades. He fell into pleasant memories of his childhood, played again with his brother and sister, raced across the fields, shouting to alarm the sedentary larks, entered the sombre forest beyond and with timid steps followed the faint path to Ghost Rock, standing at last with audible heart-throbs before the Dead Man's Cave and seeking to penetrate its awful mystery. For the first time he observed that the opening of the haunted cavern was encircled by a ring of metal. Then all else vanished and left him gazing into the barrel of his rifle as before. But whereas before it had seemed nearer, it now seemed an inconceivable distance away, and all the more sinister for that. He cried out and, startled by something in his own voice – the note of fear – lied to himself in denial: 'If I don't sing out I may stay here till I die.'

He now made no further attempt to evade the menacing stare of the gun barrel. If he turned away his eyes an instant it was to look for assistance (although he could not see the ground on either side the ruin), and he permitted them to return, obedient to the imperative fascination. If he closed them it was from weariness, and instantly the poignant pain in his forehead – the prophecy and menace of the bullet – forced him to reopen them.

The tension of nerve and brain was too severe; nature came to his relief with intervals of unconsciousness. Reviving from one of these he became sensible of a sharp, smarting pain in his right hand, and when he worked his fingers together, or rubbed his palm with them, he could feel that they were wet and slippery. He could not see the hand, but he knew the sensation; it was running blood. In his delirium he had beaten it against the jagged fragments of the wreck, had clutched it full of splinters. He resolved that he would meet his fate more manly. He was a plain, common soldier, had no religion and not much philosophy; he could not die like a hero, with great and wise last words, even if there had been someone to hear them, but he could die 'game', and he would. But if he could only know when to expect the shot!

Some rats which had probably inhabited the shed came sneaking and scampering about. One of them mounted the pile of debris that held the rifle; another followed and another. Searing regarded them at first with indifference, then with friendly interest; then, as the thought flashed into his bewildered mind that they might touch the trigger of his rifle, he cursed them and ordered them to go away. 'It is no business of yours,' he cried.

The creatures went away; they would return later, attack his face, gnaw away his nose, cut his throat – he knew that, but he hoped by that time to be dead.

Nothing could now unfix his gaze from the little ring of metal with its black interior. The pain in his forehead was fierce and incessant. He felt it gradually penetrating the brain more and more deeply, until at last its progress was arrested by the wood at the back of his head. It grew momentarily more insufferable: he began wantonly beating his lacerated hand against the splinters again to counteract that horrible ache. It seemed to throb with a slow, regular recurrence, each pulsation sharper than the preceding, and sometimes he cried out, thinking he felt the fatal bullet. No thoughts of home, of wife and children, of country, of glory. The whole record of memory was effaced. The world had passed away – not a vestige remained. Here in this confusion of timbers and boards is the sole universe. Here is immortality in time – each pain an everlasting life. The throbs tick off eternities.

Jerome Searing, the man of courage, the formidable enemy, the strong, resolute warrior, was as pale as a ghost. His jaw was fallen; his eyes protruded; he trembled in every fibre; a cold sweat bathed his entire body; he screamed with fear. He was not insane – he was terrified.

In groping about with his torn and bleeding hand he seized at last a strip of board, and, pulling, felt it give way. It lay parallel with his body, and by bending his elbow as much as the contracted space would permit, he could draw it a few inches at a time. Finally it was altogether loosened from the wreckage covering his legs; he could lift it clear of the ground its whole length. A great hope came into his mind: perhaps he could work it upward, that is to say backward, far enough to lift the end and push aside the rifle; or, if that were too tightly wedged, so place the strip of board as to deflect the bullet. With this object he passed it backward inch by inch, hardly daring to breathe lest that act somehow defeat his intent, and more than ever unable to remove his eyes from the rifle, which might perhaps now hasten to improve its waning opportunity. Something at least had been gained: in the occupation of his mind in this attempt at self-defence he was less sensible of the pain in his head and had ceased to wince. But he was still dreadfully frightened and his teeth rattled like castanets.

The strip of board ceased to move to the suasion of his hand. He tugged at it with all his strength, changed the direction of its length all he could, but it had met some extended obstruction behind him and the end in front was still too far away to clear the pile of debris and reach the muzzle of the gun. It extended, indeed, nearly as far as the trigger guard, which, uncovered by the rubbish, he could imperfectly see with his right eye. He tried to break the strip with his hand, but had no leverage. In his defeat, all his terror returned, augmented tenfold. The black aperture of the rifle appeared to threaten a sharper and more imminent death in punishment of his rebellion. The track of the bullet through his head ached with an intenser anguish. He began to tremble again.

Suddenly he became composed. His tremor subsided. He clenched his teeth and drew down his eyebrows. He had not exhausted his means of defence; a new design had shaped itself in his mind – another plan of battle. Raising the front end of the strip of board, he carefully pushed it forward through the wreckage at the side of the rifle until it pressed against the trigger guard. Then he moved the end slowly outward until he could feel that it had cleared it, then, closing his eyes, thrust it against the trigger with all his strength! There was no explosion; the rifle had been discharged as it dropped from his hand when the building fell. But it did its work.

*   *   *

Lieutenant Adrian Searing, in command of the picket-guard on that part of the line through which his brother Jerome had passed on his mission, sat with attentive ears in his breastwork behind the line. Not the faintest sound escaped him; the cry of a bird, the barking of a squirrel, the noise of the wind among the pines – all were anxiously noted by his overstrained sense. Suddenly, directly in front of his line, he heard a faint, confused rumble, like the clatter of a falling building translated by distance. The lieutenant mechanically looked at his watch. Six o'clock and eighteen minutes. At the same moment an officer approached him on foot from the rear and saluted.

'Lieutenant,' said the officer, 'the colonel directs you to move forward your line and feel the enemy if you find him. If not, continue the advance until directed to halt. There is reason to think that the enemy has retreated.'

The lieutenant nodded and said nothing; the other officer retired. In a moment the men, apprised of their duty by the non-commissioned officers in low tones, had deployed from their rifle-pits and were moving forward in skirmishing order, with set teeth and beating hearts.

This line of skirmishers sweeps across the plantation toward the mountain. They pass on both sides of the wrecked building, observing nothing. At a short distance in their rear their commander comes. He casts his eyes curiously upon the ruin and sees a dead body half-buried in boards and timbers. It is so covered with dust that its clothing is Confederate grey. Its face is yellowish white; the cheeks are fallen in, the temples sunken, too, with sharp ridges about them, making the forehead forbiddingly narrow; the upper lip, slightly lifted, shows the white teeth, rigidly clenched. The hair is heavy with moisture, the face as wet as the dewy grass all about. From his point of view the officer does not observe the rifle; the man was apparently killed by the fall of the building.

'Dead a week,' said the officer curtly, moving on and absently pulling out his watch as if to verify his estimate of time. Six o'clock and forty minutes.

An Arrest

Having murdered his brother-in-law, Orrin Brower of Kentucky was a fugitive from justice. From the county jail where he had been confined to await his trial he had escaped by knocking down his jailer with an iron bar, robbing him of his keys and, opening the outer door, walking out into the night. The jailer being unarmed, Brower got no weapon with which to defend his recovered liberty. As soon as he was out of the town he had the folly to enter a forest; this was many years ago, when that region was wilder than it is now.

The night was pretty dark, with neither moon nor stars visible, and as Brower had never dwelt thereabout, and knew nothing of the lay of the land, he was, naturally, not long in losing himself. He could not have said if he were getting farther away from the town or going back to it – a most important matter to Orrin Brower. He knew that in either case a posse of citizens with a pack of bloodhounds would soon be on his track and his chance of escape was very slender; but he did not wish to assist in his own pursuit. Even an added hour of freedom was worth having.

Suddenly he emerged from the forest into an old road, and there before him saw, indistinctly, the figure of a man, motionless in the gloom. It was too late to retreat: the fugitive felt that at the first movement back toward the wood he would be, as he afterward explained, 'filled with buckshot'. So the two stood there like trees, Brower nearly suffocated by the activity of his own heart; the other – the emotions of the other are not recorded.

A moment later – it may have been an hour – the moon sailed into a patch of unclouded sky and the hunted man saw that visible embodiment of Law lift an arm and point significantly toward and beyond him. He understood. Turning his back to his captor, he walked submissively away in the direction indicated, looking to neither the right nor the left; hardly daring to breathe, his head and back actually aching with a prophecy of buckshot.

Brower was as courageous a criminal as ever lived to be hanged; that was shown by the conditions of awful personal peril in which he had coolly killed his brother-in-law. It is needless to relate them here; they came out at his trial, and the revelation of his calmness in confronting them came near to saving his neck. But what would you have? – When a brave man is beaten, he submits.

So they pursued their journey jailward along the old road through the woods. Only once did Brower venture a turn of the head: just once, when he was in deep shadow and he knew that the other was in moonlight, he looked backward. His captor was Burton Duff, the jailer, as white as death and bearing upon his brow the livid mark of the iron bar. Orrin Brower had no further curiosity.

Eventually they entered the town, which was all alight, but deserted; only the women and children remained, and they were off the streets. Straight toward the jail the criminal held his way. Straight up to the main entrance he walked, laid his hand upon the knob of the heavy iron door, pushed it open without command, entered and found himself in the presence of a half-dozen armed men. Then he turned. Nobody else entered.

On a table in the corridor lay the dead body of Burton Duff.

A Jug of Sirup

This narrative begins with the death of its hero. Silas Deemer died on the 16th day of July, 1863, and two days later his remains were buried. As he had been personally known to every man, woman and well-grown child in the village, the funeral, as the local newspaper phrased it, 'was largely attended'. In accordance with a custom of the time and place, the coffin was opened at the graveside and the entire assembly of friends and neighbours filed past, taking a last look at the face of the dead. And then, before the eyes of all, Silas Deemer was put into the ground. Some of the eyes were a trifle dim, but in a general way it may be said that at that interment there was lack of neither observance nor observation; Silas was indubitably dead, and none could have pointed out any ritual delinquency that would have justified him in coming back from the grave. Yet if human testimony is good for anything (and certainly it once put an end to witchcraft in and about Salem) he came back.

I forgot to state that the death and burial of Silas Deemer occurred in the little village of Hillbrook, where he had lived for thirty-one years. He had been what is known in some parts of the Union (which is admittedly a free country) as a 'merchant'; that is to say, he kept a retail shop for the sale of such things as are commonly sold in shops of that character. His honesty had never been questioned, so far as is known, and he was held in high esteem by all. The only thing that could be urged against him by the most censorious was a too close attention to business. It was not urged against him, though many another, who manifested it in no greater degree, was less leniently judged. The business to which Silas was devoted was mostly his own – that, possibly, may have made a difference.

At the time of Deemer's death nobody could recollect a single day, Sundays excepted, that he had not passed in his 'store', since he had opened it more than a quarter-century before. His health having been perfect during all that time, he had been unable to discern any validity in whatever may or might have been urged to lure him astray from his counter and it is related that once when he was summoned to the county seat as a witness in an important law case and did not attend, the lawyer who had the hardihood to move that he be 'admonished' was solemnly informed that the Court regarded the proposal with 'surprise'. Judicial surprise being an emotion that attorneys are not commonly ambitious to arouse, the motion was hastily withdrawn and an agreement with the other side effected as to what Mr Deemer would have said if he had been there – the other side pushing its advantage to the extreme and making the supposititious testimony distinctly damaging to the interests of its proponents. In brief, it was the general feeling in all that region that Silas Deemer was the one immobile verity of Hillbrook, and that his translation in space would precipitate some dismal public ill or strenuous calamity.

Mrs Deemer and two grown daughters occupied the upper rooms of the building, but Silas had never been known to sleep elsewhere than on a cot behind the counter of the store. And there, quite by accident, he was found one night, dying, and passed away just before the time for taking down the shutters. Though speechless, he appeared conscious, and it was thought by those who knew him best that if the end had unfortunately been delayed beyond the usual hour for opening the store the effect upon him would have been deplorable.

Such had been Silas Deemer – such the fixity and invariety of his life and habit, that the village humorist (who had once attended college) was moved to bestow upon him the sobriquet of 'Old Ibidem', and, in the first issue of the local newspaper after the death, to explain without offence that Silas had taken 'a day off'. It was more than a day, but from the record it appears that well within a month Mr Deemer made it plain that he had not the leisure to be dead.

One of Hillbrook's most respected citizens was Alvan Creede, a banker. He lived in the finest house in town, kept a carriage and was a most estimable man variously. He knew something of the advantages of travel, too, having been frequently in Boston, and once, it was thought, in New York, though he modestly disclaimed that glittering distinction. The matter is mentioned here merely as a contribution to an understanding of Mr Creede's worth, for either way it is creditable to him – to his intelligence if he had put himself, even temporarily, into contact with metropolitan culture; to his candour if he had not.

One pleasant summer evening at about the hour of ten Mr Creede, entering at his garden gate, passed up the gravel walk, which looked

very white in the moonlight, mounted the stone steps of his fine
house and pausing a moment inserted his latchkey in the door. As he
pushed this open he met his wife, who was crossing the passage from
the parlour to the library. She greeted him pleasantly and pulling
the door further back held it for him to enter. Instead he turned
and, looking about his feet in front of the threshold, uttered an
exclamation of surprise.

'Why! – What the devil,' he said, 'has become of that jug?'

'What jug, Alvan?' his wife enquired, not very sympathetically.

'A jug of maple sirup – I brought it along from the store and set it
down here to open the door. What the – '

'There, there, Alvan, please don't swear again,' said the lady, interrupting. Hillbrook, by the way, is not the only place in Christendom
where a vestigial polytheism forbids the taking in vain of the Evil
One's name.

The jug of maple sirup which the easy ways of village life had
permitted Hillbrook's foremost citizen to carry home from the store
was not there.

'Are you quite sure, Alvan?'

'My dear, do you suppose a man does not know when he is carrying
a jug? I bought that sirup at Deemer's as I was passing. Deemer
himself drew it and lent me the jug, and I – '

The sentence remains to this day unfinished. Mr Creede staggered
into the house, entered the parlour and dropped into an armchair,
trembling in every limb. He had suddenly remembered that Silas
Deemer was three weeks dead.

Mrs Creede stood by her husband, regarding him with surprise
and anxiety.

'For Heaven's sake,' she said, 'what ails you?'

Mr Creede's ailment having no obvious relation to the interests of
the better land he did not apparently deem it necessary to expound it
on that demand; he said nothing – merely stared. There were long
moments of silence broken by nothing but the measured ticking of the
clock, which seemed somewhat slower than usual, as if it were civilly
granting them an extension of time in which to recover their wits.

'Jane, I have gone mad – that is it.' He spoke thickly and hurriedly.
'You should have told me; you must have observed my symptoms
before they became so pronounced that I have observed them myself. I thought I was passing Deemer's store; it was open and lit up –
that is what I thought; of course it is never open now. Silas Deemer
stood at his desk behind the counter. My God, Jane, I saw him as

distinctly as I see you. Remembering that you had said you wanted some maple sirup, I went in and bought some – that is all – I bought two quarts of maple sirup from Silas Deemer, who is dead and underground, but nevertheless drew that sirup from a cask and handed it to me in a jug. He talked with me, too, rather gravely, I remember, even more so than was his way, but not a word of what he said can I now recall. But I saw him – good Lord, I saw and talked with him – and he is dead! So I thought, but I'm mad, Jane, I'm as crazy as a beetle; and you have kept it from me.'

This monologue gave the woman time to collect what faculties she had.

'Alvan,' she said, 'you have given no evidence of insanity, believe me. This was undoubtedly an illusion – how should it be anything else? That would be too terrible! But there is no insanity; you are working too hard at the bank. You should not have attended the meeting of directors this evening; anyone could see that you were ill; I knew something would occur.'

It may have seemed to him that the prophecy had lagged a bit, awaiting the event, but he said nothing of that, being concerned with his own condition. He was calm now, and could think coherently.

'Doubtless the phenomenon was subjective,' he said, with a some-what ludicrous transition to the slang of science. 'Granting the possibility of spiritual apparition and even materialisation, yet the apparition and materialisation of a half-gallon brown clay jug – a piece of coarse, heavy pottery evolved from nothing – that is hardly thinkable.'

As he finished speaking, a child ran into the room – his little daughter. She was clad in a bedgown. Hastening to her father she threw her arms about his neck, saying: 'You naughty papa, you forgot to come in and kiss me. We heard you open the gate and got up and looked out. And, papa dear, Eddy says mayn't he have the little jug when it is empty?'

As the full import of that revelation imparted itself to Alvan Creede's understanding he visibly shuddered. For the child could not have heard a word of the conversation.

The estate of Silas Deemer being in the hands of an administrator who had thought it best to dispose of the 'business', the store had been closed ever since the owner's death, the goods having been removed by another 'merchant' who had purchased them en bloc. The rooms above were vacant as well, for the widow and daughters had gone to another town.

On the evening immediately after Alvan Creede's adventure (which had somehow 'got out') a crowd of men, women and children thronged the sidewalk opposite the store. That the place was haunted by the spirit of the late Silas Deemer was now well known to every resident of Hillbrook, though many affected disbelief. Of these the hardiest, and in a general way the youngest, threw stones against the front of the building, the only part accessible, but carefully missed the unshuttered windows. Incredulity had not grown to malice. A few venturesome souls crossed the street and rattled the door in its frame; struck matches and held them near the window; attempted to view the black interior. Some of the spectators invited attention to their wit by shouting and groaning and challenging the ghost to a footrace.

After a considerable time had elapsed without any manifestation, and many of the crowd had gone away, all those remaining began to observe that the interior of the store was suffused with a dim, yellow light. At this all demonstrations ceased; the intrepid souls about the door and windows fell back to the opposite side of the street and were merged in the crowd; the small boys ceased throwing stones. Nobody spoke above his breath; all whispered excitedly and pointed to the now steadily growing light. How long a time had passed since the first faint glow had been observed none could have guessed, but eventually the illumination was bright enough to reveal the whole interior of the store; and there, standing at his desk behind the counter, Silas Deemer was distinctly visible!

The effect upon the crowd was marvellous. It began rapidly to melt away at both flanks, as the timid left the place. Many ran as fast as their legs would let them; others moved off with greater dignity, turning occasionally to look backward over the shoulder. At last a score or more, mostly men, remained where they were, speechless, staring, excited. The apparition inside gave them no attention; it was apparently occupied with a book of accounts.

Presently three men left the crowd on the sidewalk as if by a common impulse and crossed the street. One of them, a heavy man, was about to set his shoulder against the door when it opened, apparently without human agency, and the courageous investigators passed in. No sooner had they crossed the threshold than they were seen by the awed observers outside to be acting in the most unaccountable way. They thrust out their hands before them, pursued devious courses, came into violent collision with the counter, with boxes and barrels on the floor, and with one another. They turned awkwardly hither and thither and seemed trying to escape, but unable to retrace their steps. Their voices were heard in exclamations and curses. But in no way did the apparition of Silas Deemer manifest an interest in what was going on.

By what impulse the crowd was moved none ever recollected, but the entire mass – men, women, children, dogs – made a simultaneous and tumultuous rush for the entrance. They congested the doorway, pushing for precedence – resolving themselves at length into a line and moving up step by step. By some subtle spiritual or physical alchemy observation had been transmuted into action – the sight-seers had become participants in the spectacle – the audience had usurped the stage.

To the only spectator remaining on the other side of the street – Alvan Creede, the banker – the interior of the store with its inpouring crowd continued in full illumination; all the strange things going on there were clearly visible. To those inside all was black darkness. It was as if each person as he was thrust in at the door had been stricken blind, and was maddened by the mischance. They groped with aimless imprecision, tried to force their way out against the current, pushed and elbowed, struck at random, fell and were trampled, rose and trampled in their turn. They seized one another by the garments, the hair, the beard – fought like animals, cursed, shouted, called one another opprobrious and obscene names. When, finally, Alvan Creede had seen the last person of the line pass into that awful tumult the light that had illuminated it was suddenly quenched and all was as black to him as to those within. He turned away and left the place.

In the early morning a curious crowd had gathered about 'Deemer's'. It was composed partly of those who had run away the night before, but now had the courage of sunshine, partly of honest folk going to their daily toil. The door of the store stood open; the place was vacant, but on the walls, the floor, the furniture, were shreds of clothing and tangles of hair. Hillbrook militant had managed somehow to pull itself out and had gone home to medicine its hurts and swear that it had been all night in bed. On the dusty desk, behind the counter, was the sales-book. The entries in it, in Deemer's handwriting, had ceased on the 16th day of July, the last of his life. There was no record of a later sale to Alvan Creede.

That is the entire story – except that men's passions having subsided and reason having resumed its immemorial sway, it was confessed in Hillbrook that, considering the harmless and honourable character of his first commercial transaction under the new conditions, Silas

Deemer, deceased, might properly have been suffered to resume business at the old stand without mobbing. In that judgement the local historian from whose unpublished work these facts are compiled had the thoughtfulness to signify his concurrence.

The Isle of Pines

For many years there lived near the town of Gallipolis, Ohio, an old man named Herman Deluse. Very little was known of his history, for he would neither speak of it himself nor suffer others. It was a common belief among his neighbours that he had been a pirate – if upon any better evidence than his collection of boarding pikes, cutlasses, and ancient flintlock pistols, no-one knew. He lived entirely alone in a small house of four rooms, falling rapidly into decay and never repaired further than was required by the weather. It stood on a slight elevation in the midst of a large, stony field overgrown with brambles, and cultivated in patches and only in the most primitive way. It was his only visible property, but could hardly have yielded him a living, simple and few as were his wants. He seemed always to have ready money, and paid cash for all his purchases at the village stores roundabout, seldom buying more than two or three times at the same place until after the lapse of a considerable time. He got no commendation, however, for this equitable distribution of his patronage; people were disposed to regard it as an ineffectual attempt to conceal his possession of so much money. That he had great hoards of ill-gotten gold buried somewhere about his tumbledown dwelling was not reasonably to be doubted by any honest soul conversant with the facts of local tradition and gifted with a sense of the fitness of things.

On the 9th of November, 1867, the old man died; at least his dead body was discovered on the 10th, and physicians testified that death had occurred about twenty-four hours previously – precisely how, they were unable to say; for the post-mortem examination showed every organ to be absolutely healthy, with no indication of disorder or violence. According to them, death must have taken place about noonday, yet the body was found in bed. The verdict of the coroner's jury was that he 'came to his death by a visitation of God'. The body was buried and the public administrator took charge of the estate.

A rigorous search disclosed nothing more than was already known about the dead man, and much patient excavation here and there about the premises by thoughtful and thrifty neighbours went unrewarded. The administrator locked up the house against the time when the property, real and personal, should be sold by law with a view to defraying, partly, the expenses of the sale.

The night of November 20 was boisterous. A furious gale stormed across the country, scourging it with desolating drifts of sleet. Great trees were torn from the earth and hurled across the roads. So wild a night had never been known in all that region, but toward morning the storm had blown itself out of breath and day dawned bright and clear. At about eight o'clock that morning the Rev. Henry Galbraith, a well-known and highly esteemed Lutheran minister, arrived on foot at his house, a mile and a half from the Deluse place. Mr Galbraith had been for a month in Cincinnati. He had come up the river in a steamboat, and landing at Gallipolis the previous evening had immediately obtained a horse and buggy and set out for home. The violence of the storm had delayed him overnight, and in the morning the fallen trees had compelled him to abandon his conveyance and continue his journey afoot.

'But where did you pass the night?' enquired his wife, after he had briefly related his adventure.

'With old Deluse at the "Isle of Pines" ' was the laughing reply; 'and a glum enough time I had of it. He made no objection to my remaining, but not a word could I get out of him.'

Fortunately for the interests of truth there was present at this conversation Mr Robert Mosely Maren, a lawyer and litterateur of Columbus, the same who wrote the delightful *Mellowcraft Papers*. Noting, but apparently not sharing, the astonishment caused by Mr Galbraith's answer this ready-witted person checked by a gesture the exclamations that would naturally have followed, and tranquilly enquired: 'How came you to go in there?'

This is Mr Maren's version of Mr Galbraith's reply.

'I saw a light moving about the house, and being nearly blinded by the sleet, and half-frozen besides, drove in at the gate and put up my horse in the old rail stable, where it is now. I then rapped at the door, and getting no invitation went in without one. The room was dark, but having matches I found a candle and lit it. I tried to enter the adjoining room, but the door was fast, and although I heard the old man's heavy footsteps in there he made no response to my calls. There was no fire on the hearth, so I made one and laying [sic] down before it with my overcoat under my head, prepared myself for sleep. Pretty soon the door that I had tried silently opened and the old man came in, carrying a candle. I spoke to him pleasantly, apologising for my intrusion, but he took no notice of me. He seemed to be searching for something, though his eyes were unmoved in their sockets. I wonder if he ever walks in his sleep. He took a circuit a part of the way round the room, and went out the same way he had come in. Twice more before I slept he came back into the room, acting precisely the same way, and departing as at first. In the intervals I heard him tramping all over the house, his footsteps distinctly audible in the pauses of the storm. When I woke in the morning he had already gone out.'

Mr Maren attempted some further questioning, but was unable longer to restrain the family's tongues; the story of Deluse's death and burial came out, greatly to the good minister's astonishment.

'The explanation of your adventure is very simple,' said Mr Maren. 'I don't believe old Deluse walks in his sleep – not in his present one; but you evidently dream in yours.'

And to this view of the matter Mr Galbraith was compelled reluctantly to assent.

Nevertheless, a late hour of the next night found these two gentlemen, accompanied by a son of the minister, in the road in front of the old Deluse house. There was a light inside; it appeared now at one window and now at another. The three men advanced to the door. Just as they reached it there came from the interior a confusion of the most appalling sounds – the clash of weapons, steel against steel, sharp explosions as of firearms, shrieks of women, groans and the curses of men in combat! The investigators stood a moment, irresolute, frightened. Then Mr Galbraith tried the door. It was fast. But the minister was a man of courage, a man, moreover, of Herculean strength. He retired a pace or two and rushed against the door, striking it with his right shoulder and bursting it from the frame with a loud crash. In a moment the three were inside. Darkness and silence! The only sound was the beating of their hearts.

Mr Maren had provided himself with matches and a candle. With some difficulty, begotten of his excitement, he made a light, and they proceeded to explore the place, passing from room to room. Everything was in orderly arrangement, as it had been left by the sheriff; nothing had been disturbed. A light coating of dust was everywhere. A back door was partly open, as if by neglect, and their first thought was that the authors of the awful revelry might have escaped. The door was opened, and the light of the candle shone through upon the ground. The expiring effort of the previous night's storm had been a light fall of snow; there were no footprints; the white surface was unbroken. They closed the door and entered the last room of the four that the house contained – that farthest from the road, in an angle of the building. Here the candle in Mr Maren's hand was suddenly extinguished as by a draught of air. Almost immediately followed the sound of a heavy fall. When the candle had been hastily relighted young Mr Galbraith was seen prostrate on the floor at a little distance from the others. He was dead. In one hand the body grasped a heavy sack of coins, which later examination showed to be all of old Spanish mintage. Directly over the body as it lay, a board had been torn from its fastenings in the wall, and from the cavity so disclosed it was evident that the bag had been taken.

Another inquest was held: another post-mortem examination failed to reveal a probable cause of death. Another verdict of 'the visitation of God' left all at liberty to form their own conclusions. Mr Maren contended that the young man died of excitement.

At Old Man Eckert's

Philip Eckert lived for many years in an old, weather-stained wooden house about three miles from the little town of Marion, in Vermont. There must be quite a number of persons living who remember him, not unkindly, I trust, and know something of the story that I am about to tell.

'Old Man Eckert', as he was always called, was not of a sociable disposition and lived alone. As he was never known to speak of his own affairs nobody thereabout knew anything of his past, nor of his relatives if he had any. Without being particularly ungracious or repellent in manner or speech, he managed somehow to be immune to impertinent curiosity, yet exempt from the evil repute with which it commonly revenges itself when baffled; so far as I know, Mr Eckert's renown as a reformed assassin or a retired pirate of the Spanish Main had not reached any ear in Marion. He got his living cultivating a small and not very fertile farm.

One day he disappeared and a prolonged search by his neighbours failed to turn him up or throw any light upon his whereabouts or whyabouts. Nothing indicated preparation to leave: all was as he might have left it to go to the spring for a bucket of water. For a few weeks little else was talked of in that region; then 'old man Eckert' became a village tale for the ear of the stranger. I do not know what was done regarding his property – the correct legal thing, doubtless. The house was standing, still vacant and conspicuously unfit, when I last heard of it, some twenty years afterward.

Of course it came to be considered 'haunted', and the customary tales were told of moving lights, dolorous sounds and startling apparitions. At one time, about five years after the disappearance, these stories of the supernatural became so rife, or through some attesting circumstances seemed so important, that some of Marion's most serious citizens deemed it well to investigate, and to that end arranged for a night session on the premises. The parties to this undertaking were John Holcomb, an apothecary; Wilson Merle, a lawyer, and Andrus C. Palmer, the teacher of the public school, all men of consequence and repute. They were to meet at Holcomb's house at eight o'clock in the evening of the appointed day and go together to the scene of their vigil, where certain arrangements for their comfort, a provision of fuel and the like, for the season was winter, had been already made.

Palmer did not keep the engagement, and after waiting a half-hour for him the others went to the Eckert house without him. They established themselves in the principal room, before a glowing fire, and without other light than it gave, awaited events. It had been agreed to speak as little as possible: they did not even renew the exchange of views regarding the defection of Palmer, which had occupied their minds on the way.

Probably an hour had passed without incident when they heard (not without emotion, doubtless) the sound of an opening door in the rear of the house, followed by footfalls in the room adjoining that in which they sat. The watchers rose to their feet, but stood firm, prepared for whatever might ensue. A long silence followed – how long neither would afterward undertake to say. Then the door between the two rooms opened and a man entered.

It was Palmer. He was pale, as if from excitement – as pale as the others felt themselves to be. His manner, too, was singularly distrait: he neither responded to their salutations nor so much as looked at them, but walked slowly across the room in the light of the failing fire and opening the front door passed out into the darkness.

It seems to have been the first thought of both men that Palmer was suffering from fright – that something seen, heard or imagined in the back room had deprived him of his senses. Acting on the same friendly impulse both ran after him through the open door. But neither they nor anyone ever again saw or heard of Andrus Palmer!

This much was ascertained the next morning. During the session of Messrs. Holcomb and Merle at the 'haunted house' a new snow had fallen to a depth of several inches upon the old. In this snow Palmer's trail from his lodging in the village to the back door of the Eckert house was conspicuous. But there it ended: from the front door nothing led away but the tracks of the two men who swore that he preceded them. Palmer's disappearance was as complete as that of 'old man Eckert' himself – whom, indeed, the editor of the local paper somewhat graphically accused of having 'reached out and pulled him in.'

Three and One are One

In the year 1861 Barr Lassiter, a young man of twenty-two, lived with his parents and an elder sister near Carthage, Tennessee. The family were in somewhat humble circumstances, subsisting by cultivation of a small and not very fertile plantation. Owning no slaves, they were not rated among 'the best people' of their neighbourhood; but they were honest persons of good education, fairly well-mannered and as respectable as any family could be if uncredentialled by personal dominion over the sons and daughters of Ham. The elder Lassiter had that severity of manner that so frequently affirms an uncompromising devotion to duty, and conceals a warm and affectionate disposition. He was of the iron of which martyrs are made, but in the heart of the matrix had lurked a nobler metal, fusible at a milder heat, yet never colouring nor softening the hard exterior. By both heredity and environment something of the man's inflexible character had touched the other members of the family; the Lassiter home, though not devoid of domestic affection, was a veritable citadel of duty, and duty – ah, duty is as cruel as death!

When the war came on it found in the family, as in so many others in that State, a divided sentiment; the young man was loyal to the Union, the others savagely hostile. This unhappy division begot an insupportable domestic bitterness, and when the offending son and brother left home with the avowed purpose of joining the Federal army not a hand was laid in his, not a word of farewell was spoken, not a good wish followed him out into the world whither he went to meet with such spirit as he might whatever fate awaited him.

Making his way to Nashville, already occupied by the Army of General Buell, he enlisted in the first organisation that he found, a Kentucky regiment of cavalry, and in due time passed through all the stages of military evolution from raw recruit to experienced trooper. A right good trooper he was, too, although in his oral narrative from which this tale is made there was no mention of that;

the fact was learned from his surviving comrades. For Barr Lassiter
has answered 'Here' to the sergeant whose name is Death.

Two years after he had joined it his regiment passed through the
region whence he had come. The country thereabout had suffered
severely from the ravages of war, having been occupied alternately
(and simultaneously) by the belligerent forces, and a sanguinary
struggle had occurred in the immediate vicinity of the Lassiter
homestead. But of this the young trooper was not aware.

Finding himself in camp near his home, he felt a natural longing
to see his parents and sister, hoping that in them, as in him, the
unnatural animosities of the period had been softened by time and
separation. Obtaining a leave of absence, he set foot in the late
summer afternoon, and soon after the rising of the full moon was
walking up the gravel path leading to the dwelling in which he
had been born.

Soldiers in war age rapidly, and in youth two years are a long time.
Barr Lassiter felt himself an old man, and had almost expected to find
the place a ruin and a desolation. Nothing, apparently, was changed.
At the sight of each dear and familiar object he was profoundly affected. His heart beat audibly, his emotion nearly suffocated him; an
ache was in his throat. Unconsciously he quickened his pace until
he almost ran, his long shadow making grotesque efforts to keep its
place beside him.

The house was unlighted, the door open. As he approached and
paused to recover control of himself his father came out and stood
bareheaded in the moonlight.

'Father!' cried the young man, springing forward with outstretched
hand – 'Father!'

The elder man looked him sternly in the face, stood a moment
motionless and without a word withdrew into the house. Bitterly
disappointed, humiliated, inexpressibly hurt and altogether unnerved,
the soldier dropped upon a rustic seat in deep dejection, supporting
his head upon his trembling hand. But he would not have it so: he was
too good a soldier to accept repulse as defeat. He rose and entered the
house, passing directly to the 'sitting-room'.

It was dimly lighted by an uncurtained east window. On a low stool
by the hearthside, the only article of furniture in the place, sat his
mother, staring into a fireplace strewn with blackened embers and
cold ashes. He spoke to her – tenderly, interrogatively, and with
hesitation, but she neither answered, nor moved, nor seemed in any
way surprised. True, there had been time for her husband to apprise

her of their guilty son's return. He moved nearer and was about to lay his hand upon her arm, when his sister entered from an adjoining room, looked him full in the face, passed him without a sign of recognition and left the room by a door that was partly behind him. He had turned his head to watch her, but when she was gone his eyes again sought his mother. She too had left the place.

Barr Lassiter strode to the door by which he had entered. The moonlight on the lawn was tremulous, as if the sward were a rippling sea. The trees and their black shadows shook as in a breeze. Blended with its borders, the gravel walk seemed unsteady and insecure to step on. This young soldier knew the optical illusions produced by tears. He felt them on his cheek, and saw them sparkle on the breast of his trooper's jacket. He left the house and made his way back to camp.

The next day, with no very definite intention, with no dominant feeling that he could rightly have named, he again sought the spot. Within a half-mile of it he met Bushrod Albro, a former playfellow and schoolmate, who greeted him warmly.

'I am going to visit my home,' said the soldier.

The other looked at him rather sharply, but said nothing.

'I know,' continued Lassiter, 'that my folks have not changed, but – '

'There have been changes,' Albro interrupted. 'Everything changes. I'll go with you if you don't mind. We can talk as we go.'

But Albro did not talk.

Instead of a house they found only fire-blackened foundations of stone, enclosing an area of compact ashes pitted by rains.

Lassiter's astonishment was extreme.

'I could not find the right way to tell you,' said Albro. 'In the fight a year ago your house was burned by a Federal shell.'

'And my family – where are they?'

'In Heaven, I hope. All were killed by the shell.'

The Spook House

On the road leading north from Manchester, in eastern Kentucky, to Booneville, twenty miles away, stood, in 1862, a wooden plantation house of a somewhat better quality than most of the dwellings in that region. The house was destroyed by fire in the year following – probably by some stragglers from the retreating column of General George W. Morgan, when he was driven from Cumberland Gap to the Ohio river by General Kirby Smith. At the time of its destruction, it had for four or five years been vacant. The fields about it were overgrown with brambles, the fences gone, even the few negro quarters, and outhouses generally, fallen partly into ruin by neglect and pillage; for the negroes and poor whites of the vicinity found in the building and fences an abundant supply of fuel, of which they availed themselves without hesitation, openly and by daylight. By daylight alone; after nightfall no human being except passing strangers ever went near the place.

It was known as the 'Spook House'. That it was tenanted by evil spirits, visible, audible and active, no-one in all that region doubted any more than he doubted what he was told of Sundays by the travelling preacher. Its owner's opinion of the matter was unknown; he and his family had disappeared one night and no trace of them had ever been found. They left everything – household goods, clothing, provisions, the horses in the stable, the cows in the field, the negroes in the quarters – all as it stood; nothing was missing – except a man, a woman, three girls, a boy and a babe! It was not altogether surprising that a plantation where seven human beings could be simultaneously effaced and nobody the wiser should be under some suspicion.

One night in June, 1859, two citizens of Frankfort, Col. J. C. McArdle, a lawyer, and Judge Myron Veigh, of the State Militia, were driving from Booneville to Manchester. Their business was so important that they decided to push on, despite the darkness and the mutterings of an approaching storm, which eventually broke upon them just as they arrived opposite the 'Spook House'. The lightning was so incessant that they easily found their way through the gateway and into a shed, where they hitched and unharnessed their team. They then went to the house, through the rain, and knocked at all the doors without getting any response. Attributing this to the continuous uproar of the thunder they pushed at one of the doors, which yielded. They entered without further ceremony and closed the door. That instant they were in darkness and silence. Not a gleam of the lightning's unceasing blaze penetrated the windows or crevices; not a whisper of the awful tumult without reached them there. It was as if they had suddenly been stricken blind and deaf, and McArdle afterward said that for a moment he believed himself to have been killed by a stroke of lightning as he crossed the threshold. The rest of this adventure can as well be related in his own words, from the *Frankfort Advocate* of August 6, 1876.

When I had somewhat recovered from the dazing effect of the transition from uproar to silence, my first impulse was to reopen the door which I had closed, and from the knob of which I was not conscious of having removed my hand; I felt it distinctly, still in the clasp of my fingers. My notion was to ascertain by stepping again into the storm whether I had been deprived of sight and hearing. I turned the doorknob and pulled open the door. It led into another room!

This apartment was suffused with a faint greenish light, the source of which I could not determine, making everything distinctly visible, though nothing was sharply defined. Everything, I say, but in truth the only objects within the blank stone walls of that room were human corpses. In number they were perhaps eight or ten – it may well be understood that I did not truly count them. They were of different ages, or rather sizes, from infancy up, and of both sexes. All were prostrate on the floor, excepting one, apparently a young woman, who sat up, her back supported by an angle of the wall. A babe was clasped in the arms of another and older woman. A half-grown lad lay face downward across the legs of a full-bearded man. One or two were nearly naked, and the hand of a young girl held the fragment of a gown which she had torn open at the breast. The bodies were in various stages of decay, all greatly shrunken in face and figure. Some were but little more than skeletons.

While I stood stupefied with horror by this ghastly spectacle and still holding open the door, by some unaccountable perversity my attention was diverted from the shocking scene and concerned itself with trifles and details. Perhaps my mind, with an instinct of self-preservation, sought relief in matters which would relax its dangerous tension. Among other things, I observed that the door that I was holding open was of heavy iron plates, riveted. Equidistant from one another and from the top and bottom, three strong bolts protruded from the bevelled edge. I turned the knob and they were retracted flush with the edge; released it, and they shot out. It was a spring lock. On the inside there was no knob, nor any kind of projection – a smooth surface of iron.

While noting these things with an interest and attention which it now astonishes me to recall I felt myself thrust aside, and Judge Veigh, whom in the intensity and vicissitudes of my feelings I had altogether forgotten, pushed by me into the room. "For God's sake," I cried, "do not go in there! Let us get out of this dreadful place!"

He gave no heed to my entreaties, but (as fearless a gentleman as lived in all the South) walked quickly to the centre of the room, knelt beside one of the bodies for a closer examination and tenderly raised its blackened and shrivelled head in his hands. A strong disagreeable odour came through the doorway, completely overpowering me. My senses reeled; I felt myself falling, and in clutching at the edge of the door for support pushed it shut with a sharp click!

I remember no more: six weeks later I recovered my reason in a hotel at Manchester, whither I had been taken by strangers the next day. For all these weeks I had suffered from a nervous fever, attended with constant delirium. I had been found lying in the road several miles away from the house; but how I had escaped from it to get there I never knew. On recovery, or as soon as my physicians permitted me to talk, I enquired the fate of Judge Veigh, whom (to quiet me, as I now know) they represented as well and at home.

No-one believed a word of my story, and who can wonder? And who can imagine my grief when, arriving at my home in Frankfort two months later, I learned that Judge Veigh had never been heard of since that night? I then regretted bitterly the pride which since the first few days after the recovery of my reason had forbidden me to repeat my discredited story and insist upon its truth.

With all that afterward occurred – the examination of the house; the failure to find any room corresponding to that which

I have described; the attempt to have me adjudged insane, and my triumph over my accusers – the readers of the *Advocate* are familiar. After all these years I am still confident that excavations which I have neither the legal right to undertake nor the wealth to make would disclose the secret of the disappearance of my unhappy friend, and possibly of the former occupants and owners of the deserted and now destroyed house. I do not despair of yet bringing about such a search, and it is a source of deep grief to me that it has been delayed by the undeserved hostility and unwise incredulity of the family and friends of the late Judge Veigh.

Colonel McArdle died in Frankfort on the thirteenth day of December, in the year 1879.

The Middle Toe of the Right Foot

It is well known that the old Manton house is haunted. In all the rural district near about, and even in the town of Marshall, a mile away, not one person of unbiased mind entertains a doubt of it; incredulity is confined to those opinionated persons who will be called 'cranks' as soon as the useful word shall have penetrated the intellectual demesne of the Marshall *Advance*. The evidence that the house is haunted is of two kinds: the testimony of disinterested witnesses who have had ocular proof, and that of the house itself. The former may be disregarded and ruled out on any of the various grounds of objection which may be urged against it by the ingenious; but facts within the observation of all are material and controlling.

In the first place, the Manton house has been unoccupied by mortals for more than ten years, and with its outbuildings is slowly falling into decay – a circumstance which in itself the judicious will hardly venture to ignore. It stands a little way off the loneliest reach of the Marshall and Harriston road, in an opening which was once a farm and is still disfigured with strips of rotting fence and half-covered with brambles overrunning a stony and sterile soil long unacquainted with the plough. The house itself is in tolerably good condition, though badly weather-stained and in dire need of attention from the glazier, the smaller male population of the region having attested in the manner of its kind its disapproval of dwelling without dwellers. It is two stories in height, nearly square, its front pierced by a single doorway flanked on each side by a window boarded up to the very top. Corresponding windows above, not protected, serve to admit light and rain to the rooms of the upper floor. Grass and weeds grow pretty rankly all about, and a few shade trees, somewhat the worse for wind, and leaning all in one direction, seem to be making a concerted effort to run away. In short, as the Marshall town humorist explained in the columns of the *Advance*, 'the proposition that the Manton house is badly haunted is the only logical conclusion from the premises.' The fact that in this dwelling Mr Manton thought it expedient one night some ten years ago to rise and cut the throats of his wife and two small children, removing at once to another part of the country, has no doubt done its share in directing public attention to the fitness of the place for supernatural phenomena.

To this house, one summer evening, came four men in a wagon. Three of them promptly alighted, and the one who had been driving hitched the team to the only remaining post of what had been a fence. The fourth remained seated in the wagon. 'Come,' said one of his companions, approaching him, while the others moved away in the direction of the dwelling – 'this is the place.'

The man addressed did not move. 'By God!' he said harshly, 'this is a trick, and it looks to me as if you were in it.'

'Perhaps I am,' the other said, looking him straight in the face and speaking in a tone which had something of contempt in it. 'You will remember, however, that the choice of place was with your own assent left to the other side. Of course if you are afraid of spooks – '

'I am afraid of nothing,' the man interrupted with another oath, and sprang to the ground. The two then joined the others at the door, which one of them had already opened with some difficulty, caused by rust of lock and hinge. All entered. Inside it was dark, but the man who had unlocked the door produced a candle and matches and made a light. He then unlocked a door on their right as they stood in the passage. This gave them entrance to a large, square room that the candle but dimly lighted. The floor had a thick carpeting of dust, which partly muffled their footfalls. Cobwebs were in the angles of the walls and depended from the ceiling like strips of rotting lace, making undulatory movements in the disturbed air. The room had two windows in adjoining sides, but from neither could anything be seen except the rough inner surfaces of boards a few inches from the glass. There was no fireplace, no furniture; there was nothing: besides the cobwebs and the dust, the four men were the only objects there which were not a part of the structure.

Strange enough they looked in the yellow light of the candle. The one who had so reluctantly alighted was especially spectacular – he might have been called sensational. He was of middle age, heavily built, deep-chested and broad-shouldered. Looking at his figure, one would have said that he had a giant's strength; at his features, that he would use it like a giant. He was clean-shaven, his hair rather closely cropped and grey. His low forehead was seamed with wrinkles above the eyes, and over the nose these became vertical. The heavy black brows followed the same law, saved from meeting only by an upward turn at what would otherwise have been the point of contact. Deeply sunken beneath these, glowed in the obscure light a pair of eyes of uncertain colour, but obviously enough too small. There was something forbidding in their expression, which was not bettered by the cruel mouth and wide jaw. The nose was well enough, as noses go; one does not expect much of noses. All that was sinister in the man's face seemed accentuated by an unnatural pallor – he appeared altogether bloodless.

The appearance of the other men was sufficiently commonplace: they were such persons as one meets and forgets that he met. All were younger than the man described, between whom and the eldest of the others, who stood apart, there was apparently no kindly feeling. They avoided looking at each other.

'Gentlemen,' said the man holding the candle and keys, 'I believe everything is right. Are you ready, Mr Rosser?'

The man standing apart from the group bowed and smiled.

'And you, Mr Grossmith?'

The heavy man bowed and scowled.

'You will be pleased to remove your outer clothing.'

Their hats, coats, waistcoats and neckwear were soon removed and thrown outside the door, in the passage. The man with the candle now nodded, and the fourth man – he who had urged Grossmith to leave the wagon – produced from the pocket of his overcoat two long, murderous-looking bowie-knives, which he drew now from their leather scabbards.

'They are exactly alike,' he said, presenting one to each of the two principals – for by this time the dullest observer would have understood the nature of this meeting. It was to be a duel to the death.

Each combatant took a knife, examined it critically near the candle and tested the strength of blade and handle across his lifted knee. Their persons were then searched in turn, each by the second of the other.

'If it is agreeable to you, Mr Grossmith,' said the man holding the light, 'you will place yourself in that corner.'

He indicated the angle of the room farthest from the door, whither Grossmith retired, his second parting from him with a grasp of the hand which had nothing of cordiality in it. In the angle nearest the door Mr Rosser stationed himself, and after a whispered consultation his second left him, joining the other near the door. At that moment the candle was suddenly extinguished, leaving all in profound darkness. This may have been done by a draught from the opened door; whatever the cause, the effect was startling.

'Gentlemen,' said a voice which sounded strangely unfamiliar in the altered condition affecting the relations of the senses – 'gentlemen, you will not move until you hear the closing of the outer door.'

A sound of trampling ensued, then the closing of the inner door; and finally the outer one closed with a concussion which shook the entire building.

A few minutes afterward a belated farmer's boy met a light wagon which was being driven furiously toward the town of Marshall. He declared that behind the two figures on the front seat stood a third, with its hands upon the bowed shoulders of the others, who appeared to struggle vainly to free themselves from its grasp. This figure, unlike the others, was clad in white, and had undoubtedly boarded the wagon as it passed the haunted house. As the lad could boast a considerable former experience with the supernatural thereabouts his word had the weight justly due to the testimony of an expert. The story (in connection with the next day's events) eventually appeared in the *Advance*, with some slight literary embellishments and a concluding intimation that the gentlemen referred to would be allowed the use of the paper's columns for their version of the night's adventure. But the privilege remained without a claimant.

2

The events that led up to this 'duel in the dark' were simple enough. One evening three young men of the town of Marshall were sitting in a quiet corner of the porch of the village hotel, smoking and discussing such matters as three educated young men of a Southern village would naturally find interesting. Their names were King, Sancher and Rosser. At a little distance, within easy hearing, but taking no part in the conversation, sat a fourth. He was a stranger to the others. They merely knew that on his arrival by the stage-coach that afternoon he had written in the hotel register the name Robert Grossmith. He had not been observed to speak to anyone except the hotel clerk. He seemed, indeed, singularly fond of his own company – or, as the *personnel* of the Advance expressed it, 'grossly addicted to evil associations.' But then it should be said in justice to the stranger that the *personnel* was himself of a too convivial disposition fairly to judge one differently gifted, and had, moreover, experienced a slight rebuff in an effort at an 'interview'.

'I hate any kind of deformity in a woman,' said King, 'whether natural or – acquired. I have a theory that any physical defect has its correlative mental and moral defect.'

'I infer, then,' said Rosser, gravely, 'that a lady lacking the moral advantage of a nose would find the struggle to become Mrs King an arduous enterprise.'

'Of course you may put it that way,' was the reply; 'but, seriously, I once threw over a most charming girl on learning quite accidentally that she had suffered amputation of a toe. My conduct was brutal if you like, but if I had married that girl I should have been miserable for life and should have made her so.'

'Whereas,' said Sancher, with a light laugh, 'by marrying a gentleman of more liberal views she escaped with a parted throat.'

'Ah, you know to whom I refer. Yes, she married Manton, but I don't know about his liberality; I'm not sure but he cut her throat because he discovered that she lacked that excellent thing in woman, the middle toe of the right foot.'

'Look at that chap!' said Rosser in a low voice, his eyes fixed upon the stranger.

That chap was obviously listening intently to the conversation.

'Damn his impudence!' muttered King – 'what ought we to do?'

'That's an easy one,' Rosser replied, rising. 'Sir,' he continued, addressing the stranger, 'I think it would be better if you would remove your chair to the other end of the veranda. The presence of gentlemen is evidently an unfamiliar situation to you.'

The man sprang to his feet and strode forward with clenched hands, his face white with rage. All were now standing. Sancher stepped between the belligerents.

'You are hasty and unjust,' he said to Rosser; 'this gentleman has done nothing to deserve such language.'

But Rosser would not withdraw a word. By the custom of the country and the time there could be but one outcome to the quarrel.

'I demand the satisfaction due to a gentleman,' said the stranger, who had become more calm. 'I have not an acquaintance in this region. Perhaps you, sir,' bowing to Sancher, 'will be kind enough to represent me in this matter.'

Sancher accepted the trust – somewhat reluctantly it must be confessed, for the man's appearance and manner were not at all to his liking. King, who during the colloquy had hardly removed his eyes from the stranger's face and had not spoken a word, consented with a nod to act for Rosser, and the upshot of it was that, the principals having retired, a meeting was arranged for the next evening. The nature of the arrangements has been already disclosed. The duel with knives in a dark room was once a commoner feature of South-western life than it is likely to be again. How thin a veneering of 'chivalry' covered the essential brutality of the code under which such encounters were possible we shall see.

3

In the blaze of a midsummer noonday the old Manton house was hardly true to its traditions. It was of the earth, earthy. The sunshine caressed it warmly and affectionately, with evident disregard of its bad reputation. The grass greening all the expanse in its front seemed to grow, not rankly, but with a natural and joyous exuberance, and the weeds blossomed quite like plants. Full of charming lights and shadows and populous with pleasant-voiced birds, the neglected shade trees no longer struggled to run away, but bent reverently beneath their burdens of sun and song. Even in the glassless upper windows was an expression of peace and contentment, due to the light within. Over the stony fields the visible heat danced with a lively tremor incompatible with the gravity which is an attribute of the supernatural.

Such was the aspect under which the place presented itself to Sheriff Adams and two other men who had come out from Marshall to look at it. One of these men was Mr King, the sheriff's deputy; the other, whose name was Brewer, was a brother of the late Mrs Manton. Under a beneficent law of the State relating to property which has been for a certain period abandoned by an owner whose residence cannot be ascertained, the sheriff was legal custodian of the Manton farm and appurtenances thereunto belonging. His present visit was in mere perfunctory compliance with some order of a court in which Mr Brewer had an action to get possession of the property as heir to his deceased sister. By a mere coincidence, the visit was made on the day after the night that Deputy King had unlocked the house for another and very different purpose. His presence now was not of his own choosing: he had been ordered to accompany his superior and at the moment could think of nothing more prudent than simulated alacrity in obedience to the command.

Carelessly opening the front door, which to his surprise was not locked, the sheriff was amazed to see, lying on the floor of the passage into which it opened, a confused heap of men's apparel.

Examination showed it to consist of two hats, and the same number of coats, waistcoats and scarves, all in a remarkably good state of preservation, albeit somewhat defiled by the dust in which they lay. Mr Brewer was equally astonished, but Mr King's emotion is not of record. With a new and lively interest in his own actions the sheriff now unlatched and pushed open a door on the right, and the three entered. The room was apparently vacant – no; as their eyes became accustomed to the dimmer light something was visible in the farthest angle of the wall. It was a human figure – that of a man crouching close in the corner. Something in the attitude made the intruders halt when they had barely passed the threshold. The figure more and more clearly defined itself. The man was upon one knee, his back in the angle of the wall, his shoulders elevated to the level of his ears, his hands before his face, palms outward, the fingers spread and crooked like claws; the white face turned upward on the retracted neck had an expression of unutterable fright, the mouth half-open, the eyes incredibly expanded. He was stone dead. Yet, with the exception of a bowie-knife, which had evidently fallen from his own hand, not another object was in the room.

In thick dust that covered the floor were some confused footprints near the door and along the wall through which it opened. Along one of the adjoining walls, too, past the boarded-up windows, was the trail made by the man himself in reaching his corner. Instinctively in approaching the body the three men followed that trail. The sheriff grasped one of the outthrown arms; it was as rigid as iron, and the application of a gentle force rocked the entire body without altering the relation of its parts. Brewer, pale with excitement, gazed intently into the distorted face. 'God of mercy!' he suddenly cried, 'it is Manton!'

'You are right,' said King, with an evident attempt at calmness: 'I knew Manton. He then wore a full beard and his hair long, but this is he.'

He might have added: 'I recognised him when he challenged Rosser. I told Rosser and Sancher who he was before we played him this horrible trick. When Rosser left this dark room at our heels, forgetting his outer clothing in the excitement, and driving away with us in his shirt sleeves – all through the discreditable proceedings we knew whom we were dealing with, murderer and coward that he was!'

But nothing of this did Mr King say. With his better light he was trying to penetrate the mystery of the man's death. That he had not once moved from the corner where he had been stationed; that his posture was that of neither attack nor defence; that he had dropped his weapon; that he had obviously perished of sheer horror of something that he saw – these were circumstances which Mr King's disturbed intelligence could not rightly comprehend.

Groping in intellectual darkness for a clue to his maze of doubt, his gaze, directed mechanically downward in the way of one who ponders momentous matters, fell upon something which, there, in the light of day and in the presence of living companions, affected him with terror. In the dust of years that lay thick upon the floor – leading from the door by which they had entered, straight across the room to within a yard of Manton's crouching corpse – were three parallel lines of footprints – light but definite impressions of bare feet, the outer ones those of small children, the inner a woman's. From the point at which they ended they did not return; they pointed all one way. Brewer, who had observed them at the same moment, was leaning forward in an attitude of rapt attention, horribly pale.

'Look at that!' he cried, pointing with both hands at the nearest print of the woman's right foot, where she had apparently stopped and stood. 'The middle toe is missing – it was Gertrude!'

Gertrude was the late Mrs Manton, sister to Mr Brewer.

The Thing at Nolan

To the south of where the road between Leesville and Hardy, in the State of Missouri, crosses the east fork of May Creek stands an abandoned house. Nobody has lived in it since the summer of 1879, and it is fast going to pieces. For some three years before the date mentioned above, it was occupied by the family of Charles May, from one of whose ancestors the creek near which it stands took its name.

Mr May's family consisted of a wife, an adult son and two young girls. The son's name was John – the names of the daughters are unknown to the writer of this sketch.

John May was of a morose and surly disposition, not easily moved to anger, but having an uncommon gift of sullen, implacable hate. His father was quite otherwise; of a sunny, jovial disposition, but with a quick temper like a sudden flame kindled in a wisp of straw, which consumes it in a flash and is no more. He cherished no resentments, and his anger gone, was quick to make overtures for reconciliation. He had a brother living nearby who was unlike him in respect of all this, and it was a current witticism in the neighbourhood that John had inherited his disposition from his uncle.

One day a misunderstanding arose between father and son, harsh words ensued, and the father struck the son full in the face with his fist. John quietly wiped away the blood that followed the blow, fixed his eyes upon the already penitent offender and said with cold composure, 'You will die for that.'

The words were overheard by two brothers named Jackson, who were approaching the men at the moment; but seeing them engaged in a quarrel they retired, apparently unobserved. Charles May afterward related the unfortunate occurrence to his wife and explained that he had apologised to the son for the hasty blow, but without avail; the young man not only rejected his overtures, but refused to withdraw his terrible threat. Nevertheless, there was no open rupture of relations: John continued living with the family, and things went on very much as before.

One Sunday morning in June, 1879, about two weeks after what has been related, May senior left the house immediately after breakfast, taking a spade. He said he was going to make an excavation at a certain spring in a wood about a mile away, so that the cattle could obtain water. John remained in the house for some hours, variously occupied in shaving himself, writing letters and reading a newspaper. His manner was very nearly what it usually was; perhaps he was a trifle more sullen and surly.

At two o'clock he left the house. At five, he returned. For some reason not connected with any interest in his movements, and which is not now recalled, the time of his departure and that of his return were noted by his mother and sisters, as was attested at his trial for murder. It was observed that his clothing was wet in spots, as if (so the prosecution afterward pointed out) he had been removing bloodstains from it. His manner was strange, his look wild. He complained of illness, and going to his room took to his bed.

May senior did not return. Later that evening the nearest neighbours were aroused, and during that night and the following day a search was prosecuted through the wood where the spring was. It resulted in little but the discovery of both men's footprints in the clay about the spring. John May in the meantime had grown rapidly worse with what the local physician called brain fever, and in his delirium raved of murder, but did not say whom he conceived to have been murdered, nor whom he imagined to have done the deed. But his threat was recalled by the brothers Jackson and he was arrested on suspicion and a deputy sheriff put in charge of him at his home. Public opinion ran strongly against him and but for his illness he would probably have been hanged by a mob. As it was, a meeting of the neighbours was held on Tuesday and a committee appointed to watch the case and take such action at any time as circumstances might seem to warrant.

On Wednesday all was changed. From the town of Nolan, eight miles away, came a story which put a quite different light on the matter. Nolan consisted of a school house, a blacksmith's shop, a 'store' and a half-dozen dwellings. The store was kept by one Henry Odell, a cousin of the elder May. On the afternoon of the Sunday of May's disappearance Mr Odell and four of his neighbours, men of credibility, were sitting in the store smoking and talking. It was a warm day; and both the front and the back door were open. At about three o'clock Charles May, who was well known to three of them, entered at the front door and passed out at the rear. He was without hat or coat. He did not look at them, nor return their greeting, a circumstance which did not surprise, for he was evidently seriously hurt. Above the left eyebrow was a wound – a deep gash from which the blood flowed, covering the whole left side of the face and neck and saturating his light-grey shirt. Oddly enough, the thought uppermost in the minds of all was that he had been fighting and was going to the brook directly at the back of the store, to wash himself.

Perhaps there was a feeling of delicacy – a backwoods etiquette which restrained them from following him to offer assistance; the court records, from which, mainly, this narrative is drawn, are silent as to anything but the fact. They waited for him to return, but he did not return.

Bordering the brook behind the store is a forest extending for six miles back to the Medicine Lodge Hills. As soon as it became known in the neighbourhood of the missing man's dwelling that he had been seen in Nolan there was a marked alteration in public sentiment and feeling. The vigilance committee went out of existence without the formality of a resolution. Search along the wooded bottom lands of May Creek was stopped and nearly the entire male population of the region took to beating the bush about Nolan and in the Medicine Lodge Hills. But of the missing man no trace was found.

One of the strangest circumstances of this strange case is the formal indictment and trial of a man for murder of one whose body no human being professed to have seen – one not known to be dead. We are all more or less familiar with the vagaries and eccentricities of frontier law, but this instance, it is thought, is unique. However that may be, it is of record that on recovering from his illness John May was indicted for the murder of his missing father. Counsel for the defence appears not to have demurred and the case was tried on its merits. The prosecution was spiritless and perfunctory; the defence easily established – with regard to the deceased – an alibi. If during the time in which John May must have killed Charles May, if he killed him at all, Charles May was miles away from where John May must have been, it is plain that the deceased must have come to his death at the hands of someone else.

John May was acquitted, immediately left the country, and has never been heard of from that day. Shortly afterward his mother and sisters removed to St Louis. The farm having passed into the possession of a man who owns the land adjoining, and has a dwelling of his own, the May house has ever since been vacant, and has the sombre reputation of being haunted.

One day after the May family had left the country, some boys, playing in the woods along May Creek, found concealed under a mass of dead leaves, but partly exposed by the rooting of hogs, a spade, nearly new and bright, except for a spot on one edge, which was rusted and stained with blood. The implement had the initials C. M. cut into the handle.

This discovery renewed, in some degree, the public excitement of a few months before. The earth near the spot where the spade was found was carefully examined, and the result was the finding of the dead body of a man. It had been buried under two or three feet of soil and the spot covered with a layer of dead leaves and twigs. There was but little decomposition, a fact attributed to some preservative property in the mineral-bearing soil.

Above the left eyebrow was a wound – a deep gash from which blood had flowed, covering the whole left side of the face and neck and saturating the light-grey shirt. The skull had been cut through by the blow. The body was that of Charles May.

But what was it that passed through Mr Odell's store at Nolan?

The Difficulty of Crossing a Field

One morning in July, 1854, a planter named Williamson, living six miles from Selma, Alabama, was sitting with his wife and a child on the veranda of his dwelling. Immediately in front of the house was a lawn, perhaps fifty yards in extent between the house and public road, or, as it was called, the 'pike'. Beyond this road lay a close-cropped pasture of some ten acres, level and without a tree, rock, or any natural or artificial object on its surface. At the time there was not even a domestic animal in the field. In another field, beyond the pasture, a dozen slaves were at work under an overseer.

Throwing away the stump of a cigar, the planter rose, saying: 'I forgot to tell Andrew about those horses.' Andrew was the overseer.

Williamson strolled leisurely down the gravel walk, plucking a flower as he went, passed across the road and into the pasture, pausing a moment as he closed the gate leading into it, to greet a passing neighbour, Armour Wren, who lived on an adjoining plantation. Mr Wren was in an open carriage with his son James, a lad of thirteen. When he had driven some two hundred yards from the point of meeting, Mr Wren said to his son: 'I forgot to tell Mr Williamson about those horses.'

Mr Wren had sold to Mr Williamson some horses, which were to have been sent for that day, but for some reason not now remembered it would be inconvenient to deliver them until the morrow. The coachman was directed to drive back, and as the vehicle turned Williamson was seen by all three, walking leisurely across the pasture. At that moment one of the coach horses stumbled and came near falling. It had no more than fairly recovered itself when James Wren cried: 'Why, father, what has become of Mr Williamson?'

It is not the purpose of this narrative to answer that question.

Mr Wren's strange account of the matter, given under oath in the course of legal proceedings relating to the Williamson estate, here follows:

My son's exclamation caused me to look toward the spot where I had seen the deceased [sic] an instant before, but he was not there, nor was he anywhere visible. I cannot say that at the moment I was greatly startled, or realised the gravity of the occurrence, though I thought it singular. My son, however, was greatly astonished and kept repeating his question in different forms until we arrived at the gate. My black boy Sam was similarly affected, even in a greater degree, but I reckon more by my son's manner than by anything he had himself observed. [This sentence in the testimony was stricken out.] As we got out of the carriage at the gate of the field, and while Sam was hanging [sic] the team to the fence, Mrs Williamson, with her child in her arms and followed by several servants, came running down the walk in great excitement, crying: "He is gone, he is gone! O God! what an awful thing!" and many other such exclamations, which I do not distinctly recollect. I got from them the impression that they related to something more – than the mere disappearance of her husband, even if that had occurred before her eyes. Her manner was wild, but not more so, I think, than was natural under the circumstances. I have no reason to think she had at that time lost her mind. I have never since seen nor heard of Mr Williamson.

This testimony, as might have been expected, was corroborated in almost every particular by the only other eyewitness (if that is a proper term) – the lad James. Mrs Williamson had lost her reason and the servants were, of course, not competent to testify. The boy James Wren had declared at first that he *saw* the disappearance, but there is nothing of this in his testimony given in court. None of the field hands working in the field to which Williamson was going had seen him at all, and the most rigorous search of the entire plantation and adjoining country failed to supply a clue. The most monstrous and grotesque fictions, originating with the blacks, were current in that part of the State for many years, and probably are to this day; but what has been here related is all that is certainly known of the matter. The courts decided that Williamson was dead, and his estate was distributed according to law.

The Affair at Coulter's Notch

'Do you think, Colonel, that your brave Coulter would like to put one of his guns in here?' the general asked.

He was apparently not altogether serious; it certainly did not seem a place where any artillerist, however brave, would like to put a gun. The colonel thought that possibly his division commander meant good-humouredly to intimate that in a recent conversation between them Captain Coulter's courage had been too highly extolled.

'General,' he replied warmly, 'Coulter would like to put a gun anywhere within reach of those people', with a motion of his hand in the direction of the enemy.

'It is the only place,' said the general. He was serious, then.

The place was a depression, a 'notch', in the sharp crest of a hill. It was a pass, and through it ran a turnpike, which reaching this highest point in its course by a sinuous ascent through a thin forest made a similar, though less steep, descent toward the enemy. For a mile to the left and a mile to the right, the ridge, though occupied by Federal infantry lying close behind the sharp crest and appearing as if held in place by atmospheric pressure, was inaccessible to artillery. There was no place but the bottom of the notch, and that was barely wide enough for the roadbed. From the Confederate side this point was commanded by two batteries posted on a slightly lower elevation beyond a creek, and a half-mile away. All the guns but one were masked by the trees of an orchard; that one – it seemed a bit of impudence – was on an open lawn directly in front of a rather grandiose building, the planter's dwelling. The gun was safe enough in its exposure – but only because the Federal infantry had been forbidden to fire. Coulter's Notch – it came to be called so – was not, that pleasant summer afternoon, a place where one would 'like to put a gun'.

Three or four dead horses lay there sprawling in the road, three or four dead men in a trim row at one side of it, and a little back, down the hill. All but one were cavalrymen belonging to the Federal advance. One was a quartermaster. The general commanding the division and the colonel commanding the brigade, with their staffs and escorts, had ridden into the notch to have a look at the enemy's guns – which had straightway obscured themselves in towering clouds of smoke. It was hardly profitable to be curious about guns which had the trick of the cuttlefish, and the season of observation had been brief. At its conclusion – a short remove backward from where it began – occurred the conversation already partly reported. 'It is the only place,' the general repeated thoughtfully, 'to get at them.'

The colonel looked at him gravely. 'There is room for only one gun, General – one against twelve.'

'That is true – for only one at a time,' said the commander with something like, yet not altogether like, a smile. 'But then, your brave Coulter – a whole battery in himself.'

The tone of irony was now unmistakable. It angered the colonel, but he did not know what to say. The spirit of military subordination is not favourable to retort, nor even to deprecation.

At this moment a young officer of artillery came riding slowly up the road attended by his bugler. It was Captain Coulter. He could not have been more than twenty-three years of age. He was of medium height, but very slender and lithe, and sat his horse with something of the air of a civilian. In face he was of a type singularly unlike the men about him; thin, high-nosed, grey-eyed, with a slight blond mustache, and long, rather straggling hair of the same colour. There was an apparent negligence in his attire. His cap was worn with the visor a trifle askew; his coat was buttoned only at the sword-belt, showing a considerable expanse of white shirt, tolerably clean for that stage of the campaign. But the negligence was all in his dress and bearing; in his face was a look of intense interest in his surroundings. His grey eyes, which seemed occasionally to strike right and left across the landscape, like searchlights, were for the most part fixed upon the sky beyond the Notch; until he should arrive at the summit of the road there was nothing else in that direction to see. As he came opposite his division and brigade commanders at the roadside he saluted mechanically and was about to pass on. The colonel signed to him to halt.

'Captain Coulter,' he said, 'the enemy has twelve pieces over there on the next ridge. If I rightly understand the general, he directs that you bring up a gun and engage them.'

There was a blank silence; the general looked stolidly at a distant regiment swarming slowly up the hill through rough undergrowth,

like a torn and draggled cloud of blue smoke; the captain appeared
not to have observed him. Presently the captain spoke, slowly and
with apparent effort: 'On the next ridge, did you say, sir? Are the
guns near the house?'

'Ah, you have been over this road before. Directly at the house.'

'And it is – necessary – to engage them? The order is imperative?'

His voice was husky and broken. He was visibly paler. The colonel
was astonished and mortified. He stole a glance at the commander. In
that set, immobile face was no sign; it was as hard as bronze. A
moment later the general rode away, followed by his staff and escort.
The colonel, humiliated and indignant, was about to order Captain
Coulter in arrest, when the latter spoke a few words in a low tone to
his bugler, saluted, and rode straight forward into the Notch, where,
presently, at the summit of the road, his field-glass at his eyes,
he showed against the sky, he and his horse, sharply defined and
statuesque. The bugler had dashed down at speed and disappeared
behind a wood. Presently his bugle was heard singing in the cedars,
and in an incredibly short time a single gun with its caisson, each
drawn by six horses and manned by its full complement of gunners,
came bounding and banging up the grade in a storm of dust, un-
limbered under cover, and was run forward by hand to the fatal crest
among the dead horses. A gesture of the captain's arm, some strangely
agile movements of the men in loading, and almost before the troops
along the way had ceased to hear the rattle of the wheels, a great white
cloud sprang forward down the slope, and with a deafening report the
affair at Coulter's Notch had begun.

It is not intended to relate in detail the progress and incidents of
that ghastly contest – a contest without vicissitudes, its alternations
only different degrees of despair. Almost at the instant when Captain
Coulter's gun blew its challenging cloud twelve answering clouds
rolled upward from among the trees about the plantation house, a
deep multiple report roared back like a broken echo, and thenceforth
to the end the Federal cannoneers fought their hopeless battle in an
atmosphere of living iron whose thoughts were lightnings and whose
deeds were death.

Unwilling to see the efforts which he could not aid and the
slaughter which he could not stay, the colonel ascended the ridge at
a point a quarter of a mile to the left, whence the Notch, itself
invisible, but pushing up successive masses of smoke, seemed the
crater of a volcano in thundering eruption. With his glass he watched
the enemy's guns, noting as he could the effects of Coulter's fire –

if Coulter still lived to direct it. He saw that the Federal gunners, ignoring those of the enemy's pieces whose positions could be determined by their smoke only, gave their whole attention to the one that maintained its place in the open – the lawn in front of the house. Over and about that hardy piece the shells exploded at intervals of a few seconds. Some exploded in the house, as could be seen by thin ascensions of smoke from the breached roof. Figures of prostrate men and horses were plainly visible.

'If our fellows are doing so good work with a single gun,' said the colonel to an aide who happened to be nearest, 'they must be suffering like the devil from twelve. Go down and present the commander of that piece with my congratulations on the accuracy of his fire.'

Turning to his adjutant-general he said, 'Did you observe Coulter's damned reluctance to obey orders?'

'Yes, sir, I did.'

'Well, say nothing about it, please. I don't think the general will care to make any accusations. He will probably have enough to do in explaining his own connection with this uncommon way of amusing the rear-guard of a retreating enemy.'

A young officer approached from below, climbing breathless up the acclivity. Almost before he had saluted, he gasped out: 'Colonel, I am directed by Colonel Harmon to say that the enemy's guns are within easy reach of our rifles, and most of them visible from several points along the ridge.'

The brigade commander looked at him without a trace of interest in his expression. 'I know it,' he said quietly.

The young adjutant was visibly embarrassed. 'Colonel Harmon would like to have permission to silence those guns,' he stammered.

'So should I,' the colonel said in the same tone. 'Present my compliments to Colonel Harmon and say to him that the general's orders for the infantry not to fire are still in force.'

The adjutant saluted and retired. The colonel ground his heel into the earth and turned to look again at the enemy's guns.

'Colonel,' said the adjutant-general, 'I don't know that I ought to say anything, but there is something wrong in all this. Do you happen to know that Captain Coulter is from the South?'

'No; *was* he, indeed?'

'I heard that last summer the division which the general then commanded was in the vicinity of Coulter's home – camped there for weeks, and – '

'Listen!' said the colonel, interrupting with an upward gesture. 'Do you hear *that*?'

'That' was the silence of the Federal gun. The staff, the order-lies, the lines of infantry behind the crest – all had 'heard', and were looking curiously in the direction of the crater, whence no smoke now ascended except desultory cloudlets from the enemy's shells. Then came the blare of a bugle, a faint rattle of wheels; a minute later the sharp reports recommenced with double activity. The demolished gun had been replaced with a sound one.

'Yes,' said the adjutant-general, resuming his narrative, 'the general made the acquaintance of Coulter's family. There was trouble – I don't know the exact nature of it – something about Coulter's wife. She is a red-hot Secessionist, as they all are, except Coulter himself, but she is a good wife and high-bred lady. There was a complaint to army headquarters. The general was transferred to this division. It is odd that Coulter's battery should afterward have been assigned to it.'

The colonel had risen from the rock upon which they had been sitting. His eyes were blazing with a generous indignation.

'See here, Morrison,' said he, looking his gossiping staff officer straight in the face, 'did you get that story from a gentleman or a liar?'

'I don't want to say how I got it, Colonel, unless it is necessary' – he was blushing a trifle – 'but I'll stake my life upon its truth in the main.'

The colonel turned toward a small knot of officers some distance away. 'Lieutenant Williams!' he shouted.

One of the officers detached himself from the group and coming forward saluted, saying: 'Pardon me, Colonel, I thought you had been informed. Williams is dead down there by the gun. What can I do, sir?'

Lieutenant Williams was the aide who had had the pleasure of conveying to the officer in charge of the gun his brigade comman-der's congratulations.

'Go,' said the colonel, 'and direct the withdrawal of that gun instantly. No – I'll go myself.'

He strode down the declivity toward the rear of the Notch at a breakneck pace, over rocks and through brambles, followed by his little retinue in tumultuous disorder. At the foot of the declivity they mounted their waiting animals and took to the road at a lively trot, round a bend and into the Notch. The spectacle which they encoun-tered there was appalling!

Within that defile, barely broad enough for a single gun, were piled the wrecks of no fewer than four. They had noted the silencing of only the last one disabled – there had been a lack of men to replace it quickly with another. The debris lay on both sides of the road; the men had managed to keep an open way between, through which the fifth piece was now firing. The men? – They looked like demons of the pit! All were hatless, all stripped to the waist, their reeking skins black with blotches of powder and spattered with gouts of blood. They worked like madmen, with rammer and cartridge, lever and lanyard. They set their swollen shoulders and bleeding hands against the wheels at each recoil and heaved the heavy gun back to its place. There were no commands; in that awful environment of whooping shot, exploding shells, shrieking fragments of iron, and flying splinters of wood, none could have been heard. Officers, if officers there were, were indistinguishable; all worked together – each while he lasted – governed by the eye. When the gun was sponged, it was loaded; when loaded, aimed and fired. The colonel observed something new to his military experience – something horrible and unnatural: the gun was bleeding at the mouth! In temporary default of water, the man sponging had dipped his sponge into a pool of comrade's blood. In all this work there was no clashing; the duty of the instant was obvious. When one fell, another, looking a trifle cleaner, seemed to rise from the earth in the dead man's tracks, to fall in his turn.

With the ruined guns lay the ruined men – alongside the wreckage, under it and atop of it; and back down the road – a ghastly procession! – crept on hands and knees such of the wounded as were able to move. The colonel – he had compassionately sent his cavalcade to the right about – had to ride over those who were entirely dead in order not to crush those who were partly alive. Into that hell he tranquilly held his way, rode up alongside the gun, and, in the obscurity of the last discharge, tapped upon the cheek the man holding the rammer – who straightway fell, thinking himself killed. A fiend seven times damned sprang out of the smoke to take his place, but paused and gazed up at the mounted officer with an unearthly regard, his teeth flashing between his black lips, his eyes, fierce and expanded, burning like coals beneath his bloody brow. The colonel made an authoritative gesture and pointed to the rear. The fiend bowed in token of obedience. It was Captain Coulter.

Simultaneously with the colonel's arresting sign, silence fell upon the whole field of action. The procession of missiles no longer streamed into that defile of death, for the enemy also had ceased firing. His army had been gone for hours, and the commander of his rearguard, who had held his position perilously long in hope to silence the Federal fire, at that strange moment had silenced his own. 'I was not aware of the breadth of my authority,' said the colonel to anybody, riding forward to the crest to see what had really happened. An hour later his brigade was in bivouac on the enemy's ground, and its idlers were examining, with something of awe, as the faithful inspect a saint's relics, a score of straddling dead horses and three disabled guns, all spiked. The fallen men had been carried away; their torn and broken bodies would have given too great satisfaction.

Naturally, the colonel established himself and his military family in the plantation house. It was somewhat shattered, but it was better than the open air. The furniture was greatly deranged and broken. Walls and ceilings were knocked away here and there, and a lingering odour of powder smoke was everywhere. The beds, the closets of women's clothing, the cupboards were not greatly damaged. The new tenants for a night made themselves comfortable, and the virtual effacement of Coulter's battery supplied them with an interesting topic.

During supper an orderly of the escort showed himself into the dining-room and asked permission to speak to the colonel.

'What is it, Barbour?' said that officer pleasantly, having overheard the request.

'Colonel, there is something wrong in the cellar; I don't know what – somebody there. I was down there rummaging about.'

'I will go down and see,' said a staff officer, rising.

'So will I,' the colonel said; 'let the others remain. Lead on, orderly.'

They took a candle from the table and descended the cellar stairs, the orderly in visible trepidation. The candle made but a feeble light, but presently, as they advanced, its narrow circle of illumination revealed a human figure seated on the ground against the black stone wall which they were skirting, its knees elevated, its head bowed sharply forward. The face, which should have been seen in profile, was invisible, for the man was bent so far forward that his long hair concealed it; and, strange to relate, the beard, of a much darker hue, fell in a great tangled mass and lay along the ground at his side. They involuntarily paused; then the colonel, taking the candle from the orderly's shaking hand, approached the man and attentively considered him. The long dark beard was the hair of a woman – dead.

The dead woman clasped in her arms a dead babe. Both were clasped in the arms of the man, pressed against his breast, against his lips. There was blood in the hair of the woman; there was blood in the hair of the man. A yard away, near an irregular depression in the beaten earth which formed the cellar's floor – fresh excavation with a convex bit of iron, having jagged edges, visible in one of the sides – lay an infant's foot. The colonel held the light as high as he could. The floor of the room above was broken through, the splinters pointing at all angles downward. 'This casemate is not bomb-proof,' said the colonel gravely. It did not occur to him that his summing up of the matter had any levity in it.

They stood about the group awhile in silence; the staff officer was thinking of his unfinished supper, the orderly of what might possibly be in one of the casks on the other side of the cellar. Suddenly the man whom they had thought dead raised his head and gazed tranquilly into their faces. His complexion was coal black; the cheeks were apparently tattooed in irregular sinuous lines from the eyes downward. The lips, too, were white, like those of a stage negro. There was blood upon his forehead.

The staff officer drew back a pace, the orderly two paces.

'What are you doing here, my man?' said the colonel, unmoved.

'This house belongs to me, sir,' was the reply, civilly delivered.

'To you? Ah, I see! And these?'

'My wife and child. I am Captain Coulter.'

An Unfinished Race

James Burne Worson was a shoemaker who lived in Leamington, Warwickshire, England. He had a little shop in one of the byways leading off the road to Warwick. In his humble sphere he was esteemed an honest man, although like many of his class in English towns he was somewhat addicted to drink. When in liquor he would make foolish wagers. On one of these too frequent occasions he was boasting of his prowess as a pedestrian and athlete, and the outcome was a match against nature. For a stake of one sovereign he undertook to run all the way to Coventry and back, a distance of something more than forty miles. This was on the 3rd day of September in 1873. He set out at once, the man with whom he had made the bet – whose name is not remembered – accompanied by Barham Wise, a linen draper, and Hamerson Burns, a photographer, I think, following in a light cart or wagon.

For several miles Worson went on very well, at an easy gait, without apparent fatigue, for he had really great powers of endurance and was not sufficiently intoxicated to enfeeble them. The three men in the wagon kept a short distance in the rear, giving him occasional friendly 'chaff' or encouragement, as the spirit moved them. Suddenly – in the very middle of the roadway, not a dozen yards from them, and with their eyes full upon him – the man seemed to stumble, pitched headlong forward, uttered a terrible cry and vanished! He did not fall to the earth – he vanished before touching it. No trace of him was ever discovered.

After remaining at and about the spot for some time, with aimless irresolution, the three men returned to Leamington, told their astonishing story and were afterward taken into custody. But they were of good standing, had always been considered truthful, were sober at the time of the occurrence, and nothing ever transpired to discredit their sworn account of their extraordinary adventure, concerning the truth of which, nevertheless, public opinion was divided, throughout the United Kingdom. If they had something to conceal, their choice of means is certainly one of the most amazing ever made by sane human beings.

Charles Ashmore's Trail

The family of Christian Ashmore consisted of his wife, his mother, two grown daughters, and a son of sixteen years. They lived in Troy, New York, were well-to-do, respectable persons, and had many friends, some of whom, reading these lines, will doubtless learn for the first time the extraordinary fate of the young man. From Troy the Ashmores moved in 1871 or 1872 to Richmond, Indiana, and a year or two later to the vicinity of Quincy, Illinois, where Mr Ashmore bought a farm and lived on it. At some little distance from the farmhouse was a spring with a constant flow of clear, cold water, whence the family derived its supply for domestic use at all seasons.

On the evening of the 9th of November in 1878, at about nine o'clock, young Charles Ashmore left the family circle about the hearth, took a tin bucket and started toward the spring. As he did not return, the family became uneasy, and going to the door by which he had left the house, his father called without receiving an answer. He then lighted a lantern and with the eldest daughter, Martha, who insisted on accompanying him, went in search. A light snow had fallen, obliterating the path, but making the young man's trail conspicuous; each footprint was plainly defined. After going a little more than halfway – perhaps seventy-five yards – the father, who was in advance, halted, and elevating his lantern stood peering intently into the darkness ahead.

'What is the matter, father?' the girl asked.

This was the matter: the trail of the young man had abruptly ended, and all beyond was smooth, unbroken snow. The last footprints were as conspicuous as any in the line; the very nail-marks were distinctly visible. Mr Ashmore looked upward, shading his eyes with his hat held between them and the lantern. The stars were shining; there was not a cloud in the sky; he was denied the explanation which had suggested itself, doubtful as it would have been – a new snowfall with a limit so plainly defined. Taking a wide circuit round the ultimate tracks, so as to leave them undisturbed for further examination, the man proceeded to the spring, the girl following, weak and terrified. Neither had spoken a word of what both had observed. The spring was covered with ice, hours old.

Returning to the house they noted the appearance of the snow on both sides of the trail its entire length. No tracks led away from it.

The morning light showed nothing more. Smooth, spotless, unbroken, the shallow snow lay everywhere.

Four days later the grief-stricken mother herself went to the spring for water. She came back and related that in passing the spot where the footprints had ended she had heard the voice of her son and had been eagerly calling to him, wandering about the place, as she had fancied the voice to be now in one direction, now in another, until she was exhausted with fatigue and emotion.

Questioned as to what the voice had said, she was unable to tell, yet averred that the words were perfectly distinct. In a moment the entire family was at the place, but nothing was heard, and the voice was believed to be an hallucination caused by the mother's great anxiety and her disordered nerves. But for months afterward, at irregular intervals of a few days, the voice was heard by the several members of the family, and by others. All declared it unmistakably the voice of Charles Ashmore; all agreed that it seemed to come from a great distance, faintly, yet with entire distinctness of articulation; yet none could determine its direction, nor repeat its words. The intervals of silence grew longer and longer, the voice fainter and farther, and by midsummer it was heard no more.

If anybody knows the fate of Charles Ashmore it is probably his mother. She is dead.

Staley Fleming's Hallucination

Of two men who were talking one was a physician.

'I sent for you, Doctor,' said the other, 'but I don't think you can do me any good. Maybe you can recommend a specialist in psychopathy. I fancy I'm a bit loony.'

'You look all right,' the physician said.

'You shall judge – I have hallucinations. I wake every night and see in my room, intently watching me, a big black Newfoundland dog with a white forefoot.'

'You say you wake; are you sure about that? "Hallucinations" are sometimes only dreams.'

'Oh, I wake, all right. Sometimes I lie still a long time, looking at the dog as earnestly as the dog looks at me – I always leave the light going. When I can't endure it any longer I sit up in bed – and nothing is there!'

' 'M, 'm – what is the beast's expression?'

'It seems to me sinister. Of course I know that, except in art, an animal's face in repose has always the same expression. But this is not a real animal. Newfoundland dogs are pretty mild-looking, you know; what's the matter with this one?'

'Really, my diagnosis would have no value: I am not going to treat the dog.'

The physician laughed at his own pleasantry, but narrowly watched his patient from the corner of his eye. Presently he said: 'Fleming, your description of the beast fits the dog of the late Atwell Barton.'

Fleming half-rose from his chair, sat again and made a visible attempt at indifference. 'I remember Barton,' he said; 'I believe he was – it was reported that – wasn't there something suspicious in his death?'

Looking squarely now into the eyes of his patient, the physician said: 'Three years ago the body of your old enemy, Atwell Barton, was found in the woods near his house and yours. He had been stabbed to death. There have been no arrests; there was no clue. Some of us had "theories". I had one. Have you?'

'I? Why, bless your soul, what could I know about it? You remember that I left for Europe almost immediately afterward – a considerable time afterward. In the few weeks since my return you could not expect me to construct a "theory". In fact, I have not given the matter a thought. What about his dog?'

'It was first to find the body. It died of starvation on his grave.'

We do not know the inexorable law underlying coincidences. Staley Fleming did not, or he would perhaps not have sprung to his feet as the night wind brought in through the open window the long wailing howl of a distant dog. He strode several times across the room in the steadfast gaze of the physician; then, abruptly confronting him, almost shouted: 'What has all this to do with my trouble, Dr Halderman? You forget why you were sent for.'

Rising, the physician laid his hand upon his patient's arm and said, gently: 'Pardon me. I cannot diagnose your disorder offhand – tomorrow, perhaps. Please go to bed, leaving your door unlocked; I will pass the night here with your books. Can you call me without rising?'

'Yes, there is an electric bell.'

'Good. If anything disturbs you push the button without sitting up. Good-night.'

Comfortably installed in an armchair the man of medicine stared into the glowing coals and thought deeply and long, but apparently to little purpose, for he frequently rose and opening a door leading to the staircase, listened intently; then resumed his seat. Presently, however, he fell asleep, and when he woke it was past midnight. He stirred the failing fire, lifted a book from the table at his side and looked at the title. It was Denneker's *Meditations*. He opened it at random and began to read:

Forasmuch as it is ordained of God that all flesh hath spirit and thereby taketh on spiritual powers, so, also, the spirit hath powers of the flesh, even when it is gone out of the flesh and liveth as a thing apart, as many a violence performed by wraith and lemure sheweth. And there be who say that man is not single in this, but the beasts have the like evil inducement, and –

The reading was interrupted by a shaking of the house, as by the fall of a heavy object. The reader flung down the book, rushed from the room and mounted the stairs to Fleming's bedchamber. He tried the door, but contrary to his instructions it was locked. He set his shoulder against it with such force that it gave way. On the floor near the disordered bed, in his nightclothes, lay Fleming gasping away his life.

The physician raised the dying man's head from the floor and observed a wound in the throat. 'I should have thought of this,' he said, believing it suicide.

When the man was dead an examination disclosed the unmistakeable marks of an animal's fangs deeply sunken into the jugular vein.

But there was no animal.

The Night-Doings at 'Deadman's'

A story that is untrue

It was a singularly sharp night, and clear as the heart of a diamond. Clear nights have a trick of being keen. In darkness you may be cold and not know it; when you see, you suffer. This night was bright enough to bite like a serpent. The moon was moving mysteriously along behind the giant pines crowning the South Mountain, striking a cold sparkle from the crusted snow, and bringing out against the black west the ghostly outlines of the Coast Range, beyond which lay the invisible Pacific. The snow had piled itself, in the open spaces along the bottom of the gulch, into long ridges that seemed to heave, and into hills that appeared to toss and scatter spray. The spray was sunlight, twice reflected: dashed once from the moon, once from the snow.

In this snow many of the shanties of the abandoned mining camp were obliterated (a sailor might have said they had gone down), and at irregular intervals it had overtopped the tall trestles which had once supported a river called a flume; for, of course, 'flume' is *flumen*. Among the advantages of which the mountains cannot deprive the gold-hunter is the privilege of speaking Latin. He says of his dead neighbour, 'He has gone up the flume.' This is not a bad way to say, 'His life has returned to the Fountain of Life.'

While putting on its armour against the assaults of the wind, this snow had neglected no coign of vantage. Snow pursued by the wind is not wholly unlike a retreating army. In the open field it ranges itself in ranks and battalions; where it can get a foothold it makes a stand; where it can take cover it does so. You may see whole platoons of snow cowering behind a bit of broken wall. The devious old road, hewn out of the mountain side, was full of it. Squadron upon squadron had struggled to escape by this line, when suddenly pursuit had ceased. A more desolate and dreary spot than Deadman's Gulch in a winter midnight it is impossible to imagine. Yet Mr Hiram Beeson elected to live there, the sole inhabitant.

Away up the side of the North Mountain his little pine-log shanty projected from its single pane of glass a long, thin beam of light, and looked not altogether unlike a black beetle fastened to the hillside with a bright new pin. Within it sat Mr Beeson himself, before a roaring fire, staring into its hot heart as if he had never before seen such a thing in all his life. He was not a comely man. He was grey; he was ragged and slovenly in his attire; his face was wan and haggard; his eyes were too bright. As to his age, if one had attempted to guess it, one might have said forty-seven, then corrected himself and said seventy-four. He was really twenty-eight. Emaciated he was; as much, perhaps, as he dared be, with a needy undertaker at Bentley's Flat and a new and enterprising coroner at Sonora. Poverty and zeal are an upper and a nether millstone. It is dangerous to make a third in that kind of sandwich.

As Mr Beeson sat there, with his ragged elbows on his ragged knees, his lean jaws buried in his lean hands, and with no apparent intention of going to bed, he looked as if the slightest movement would tumble him to pieces. Yet during the last hour he had winked no fewer than three times.

There was a sharp rapping at the door. A rap at that time of night and in that weather might have surprised an ordinary mortal who had dwelt two years in the gulch without seeing a human face, and could not fail to know that the country was impassable; but Mr Beeson did not so much as pull his eyes out of the coals. And even when the door was pushed open he only shrugged a little more closely into himself, as one does who is expecting something that he would rather not see. You may observe this movement in women when, in a mortuary chapel, the coffin is borne up the aisle behind them.

But when a long old man in a blanket overcoat, his head tied up in a handkerchief and nearly his entire face in a muffler, wearing green goggles and with a complexion of glittering whiteness where it could be seen, strode silently into the room, laying a hard, gloved hand on Mr Beeson's shoulder, the latter so far forgot himself as to look up with an appearance of no small astonishment; whomever he may have been expecting, he had evidently not counted on meeting anyone like this. Nevertheless, the sight of this unexpected guest produced in Mr Beeson the following sequence: a feeling of astonishment; a sense of gratification; a sentiment of profound good will. Rising from his seat, he took the knotty hand from his shoulder, and shook it up and down with a fervour quite unaccountable; for in the old man's aspect was nothing to attract, much to repel. However, attraction is too general a property for repulsion to be without it. The most attractive object in the world is the face we instinctively cover with a cloth. When it becomes still more attractive – fascinating – we put seven feet of earth above it.

'Sir,' said Mr Beeson, releasing the old man's hand, which fell passively against his thigh with a quiet clack, 'it is an extremely disagreeable night. Pray be seated; I am very glad to see you.'

Mr Beeson spoke with an easy good breeding that one would hardly have expected, considering all things. Indeed, the contrast between his appearance and his manner was sufficiently surprising to be one of the commonest of social phenomena in the mines. The old man advanced a step toward the fire, glowing cavernously in the green goggles. Mr Beeson resumed: 'You bet your life I am!'

Mr Beeson's elegance was not too refined; it had made reasonable concessions to local taste. He paused a moment, letting his eyes drop from the muffled head of his guest, down along the row of mouldy buttons confining the blanket overcoat, to the greenish cowhide boots powdered with snow, which had begun to melt and run along the floor in little rills. He took an inventory of his guest, and appeared satisfied. Who would not have been? Then he continued: 'The cheer I can offer you is, unfortunately, in keeping with my surroundings; but I shall esteem myself highly favoured if it is your pleasure to partake of it, rather than seek better at Bentley's Flat.'

With a singular refinement of hospitable humility Mr Beeson spoke as if a sojourn in his warm cabin on such a night, as compared with walking fourteen miles up to the throat in snow with a cutting crust, would be an intolerable hardship. By way of reply, his guest unbuttoned the blanket overcoat. The host laid fresh fuel on the fire, swept the hearth with the tail of a wolf, and added: 'But *I* think you'd better skedaddle.'

The old man took a seat by the fire, spreading his broad soles to the heat without removing his hat. In the mines the hat is seldom removed except when the boots are. Without further remark Mr Beeson also seated himself in a chair which had been a barrel, and which, retaining much of its original character, seemed to have been designed with a view to preserving his dust if it should please him to crumble. For a moment there was silence; then, from some-where among the pines, came the snarling yelp of a coyote; and simultaneously the door rattled in its frame. There was no other connection between the two incidents than that the coyote has an aversion to storms, and the wind was rising; yet there seemed somehow a kind of supernatural conspiracy between the two, and Mr Beeson shuddered with a vague sense of terror. He recovered himself in a moment and again addressed his guest.

'There are strange doings here. I will tell you everything, and then if you decide to go I shall hope to accompany you over the worst of the way; as far as where Baldy Peterson shot Ben Hike – I dare say you know the place.'

The old man nodded emphatically, as intimating not merely that he did, but that he did indeed.

'Two years ago,' began Mr Beeson, 'I, with two companions, occupied this house; but when the rush to the Flat occurred we left, along with the rest. In ten hours the Gulch was deserted. That evening, however, I discovered I had left behind me a valuable pistol (that is it) and returned for it, passing the night here alone, as I have passed every night since. I must explain that a few days before we left, our Chinese domestic had the misfortune to die while the ground was frozen so hard that it was impossible to dig a grave in the usual way. So, on the day of our hasty departure, we cut through the floor there, and gave him such burial as we could. But before putting him down I had the extremely bad taste to cut off his pigtail and spike it to that beam above his grave, where you may see it at this moment, or, preferably, when warmth has given you leisure for observation.

'I stated, did I not, that the Chinaman came to his death from natural causes? I had, of course, nothing to do with that, and returned through no irresistible attraction, or morbid fascination, but only because I had forgotten a pistol. This is clear to you, is it not, sir?'

The visitor nodded gravely. He appeared to be a man of few words, if any. Mr Beeson continued: 'According to the Chinese faith, a man is like a kite: he cannot go to heaven without a tail. Well, to shorten this tedious story – which, however, I thought it my duty to relate – on that night, while I was here alone and thinking of anything but him, that Chinaman came back for his pigtail.

'He did not get it.'

At this point Mr Beeson relapsed into blank silence. Perhaps he was fatigued by the unwonted exercise of speaking; perhaps he had conjured up a memory that demanded his undivided attention. The wind was now fairly abroad, and the pines along the mountainside sang with singular distinctness. The narrator continued: 'You say you do not see much in that, and I must confess I do not myself.

'But he keeps coming!'

There was another long silence, during which both stared into the fire without the movement of a limb. Then Mr Beeson broke out, almost fiercely, fixing his eyes on what he could see of the impassive face of his auditor: 'Give it him? Sir, in this matter I have no intention of troubling anyone for advice. You will pardon me, I am sure' – here he became singularly persuasive – 'but I have ventured to nail that pigtail fast, and have assumed the somewhat onerous obligation of guarding it. So it is quite impossible to act on your considerate suggestion.

'Do you play me for a Modoc?'

Nothing could exceed the sudden ferocity with which he thrust this indignant remonstrance into the ear of his guest. It was as if he had struck him on the side of the head with a steel gauntlet. It was a protest, but it was a challenge. To be mistaken for a coward – to be played for a Modoc: these two expressions are one. Sometimes it is a Chinaman. 'Do you play me for a Chinaman?' is a question frequently addressed to the ear of the suddenly dead.

Mr Beeson's buffet produced no effect, and after a moment's pause, during which the wind thundered in the chimney like the sound of clods upon a coffin, he resumed: 'But, as you say, it is wearing me out. I feel that the life of the last two years has been a mistake – a mistake that corrects itself; you see how. The grave! No; there is no-one to dig it. The ground is frozen, too. But you are very welcome. You may say at Bentley's – but that is not important. It was very tough to cut: they braid silk into their pigtails. Kwaagh.'

Mr Beeson was speaking with his eyes shut, and he wandered. His last word was a snore. A moment later he drew a long breath, opened his eyes with an effort, made a single remark, and fell into a deep sleep. What he said was this: 'They are swiping my dust!'

Then the aged stranger, who had not uttered one word since his arrival, arose from his seat and deliberately laid off his outer clothing, looking as angular in his flannels as the late Signorina Festorazzi, an Irish woman, six feet in height, and weighing fifty-six pounds, who used to exhibit herself in her chemise to the people of San Francisco. He then crept into one of the 'bunks', having first placed a revolver in easy reach, according to the custom of the country. This revolver he took from a shelf, and it was the one which Mr Beeson had mentioned as that for which he had returned to the Gulch two years before.

In a few moments Mr Beeson awoke, and seeing that his guest had retired he did likewise. But before doing so he approached the long, plaited wisp of pagan hair and gave it a powerful tug, to assure himself that it was fast and firm. The two beds – mere shelves covered with blankets not overclean – faced each other from opposite sides of the room, the little square trapdoor that had given access to the China-man's grave being midway between. This, by the way, was crossed by a double row of spike-heads. In his resistance to the supernatural, Mr Beeson had not disdained the use of material precautions.

The fire was now low, the flames burning bluely and petulantly, with occasional flashes, projecting spectral shadows on the walls – shadows that moved mysteriously about, now dividing, now uniting. The shadow of the pendent queue, however, kept moodily apart, near the roof at the further end of the room, looking like a note of admiration. The song of the pines outside had now risen to the dignity of a triumphal hymn. In the pauses the silence was dreadful.

It was during one of these intervals that the trap in the floor began to lift. Slowly and steadily it rose, and slowly and steadily rose the swaddled head of the old man in the bunk to observe it. Then, with a clap that shook the house to its foundation, it was thrown clean back, where it lay with its unsightly spikes pointing threateningly upward. Mr Beeson awoke, and without rising, pressed his fingers into his eyes. He shuddered; his teeth chattered. His guest was now reclining on one elbow, watching the proceedings with the goggles that glowed like lamps.

Suddenly a howling gust of wind swooped down the chimney, scattering ashes and smoke in all directions, for a moment obscuring everything. When the firelight again illuminated the room there was seen, sitting gingerly on the edge of a stool by the hearthside, a swarthy little man of prepossessing appearance and dressed with faultless taste, nodding to the old man with a friendly and engaging smile. 'From San Francisco, evidently,' thought Mr Beeson, who having somewhat recovered from his fright was groping his way to a solution of the evening's events.

But now another actor appeared upon the scene. Out of the square black hole in the middle of the floor protruded the head of the departed Chinaman, his glassy eyes turned upward in their angular slits and fastened on the dangling queue above with a look of yearning unspeakable. Mr Beeson groaned, and again spread his hands upon his face. A mild odour of opium pervaded the place. The phantom, clad only in a short blue tunic quilted and silken but covered with grave-mould, rose slowly, as if pushed by a weak spiral spring. Its knees were at the level of the floor, when with a quick upward impulse like the silent leaping of a flame it grasped the queue with both hands, drew up its body and took the tip in its horrible yellow teeth. To this it clung in a seeming frenzy, grimacing ghastly, surging and plunging from side to side in its efforts to disengage its property from the beam, but uttering no sound. It was like a corpse artificially convulsed by means of a galvanic battery. The contrast between its superhuman activity and its silence was no less than hideous!

Mr Beeson cowered in his bed. The swarthy little gentleman uncrossed his legs, beat an impatient tattoo with the toe of his boot and consulted a heavy gold watch. The old man sat erect and quietly laid hold of the revolver.

Bang!

Like a body cut from the gallows the Chinaman plumped into the black hole below, carrying his tail in his teeth. The trapdoor turned over, shutting down with a snap. The swarthy little gentleman from San Francisco sprang nimbly from his perch, caught something in the air with his hat, as a boy catches a butterfly, and vanished into the chimney as if drawn up by suction.

From away somewhere in the outer darkness floated in through the open door a faint, far cry – a long, sobbing wail, as of a child death-strangled in the desert, or a lost soul borne away by the Adversary. It may have been the coyote.

In the early days of the following spring a party of miners on their way to new diggings passed along the Gulch, and straying through the deserted shanties found in one of them the body of Hiram Beeson, stretched upon a bunk, with a bullet hole through the heart. The ball had evidently been fired from the opposite side of the room, for in one of the oaken beams overhead was a shallow blue dint, where it had struck a knot and been deflected downward to the breast of its victim. Strongly attached to the same beam was what appeared to be an end of a rope of braided horsehair, which had been cut by the bullet in its passage to the knot. Nothing else of interest was noted, excepting a suit of mouldy and incongruous clothing, several articles of which were afterward identified by respectable witnesses as those in which certain deceased citizens of Deadman's had been buried years before. But it is not easy to understand how that could be, unless, indeed, the garments had been worn as a disguise by Death himself – which is hardly credible.

A Baby Tramp

If you had seen little Jo standing at the street corner in the rain, you would hardly have admired him. It was apparently an ordinary autumn rainstorm, but the water which fell upon Jo (who was hardly old enough to be either just or unjust, and so perhaps did not come under the law of impartial distribution) appeared to have some property peculiar to itself: one would have said it was dark and adhesive – sticky. But that could hardly be so, even in Blackburg, where things certainly did occur that were a good deal out of the common.

For example, ten or twelve years before, a shower of small frogs had fallen, as is credibly attested by a contemporaneous chronicle, the record concluding with a somewhat obscure statement to the effect that the chronicler considered it good growing-weather for Frenchmen.

Some years later Blackburg had a fall of crimson snow; it is cold in Blackburg when winter is on, and the snows are frequent and deep. There can be no doubt of it – the snow in this instance was of the colour of blood and melted into water of the same hue, if water it was, not blood. The phenomenon had attracted wide attention, and science had as many explanations as there were scientists who knew nothing about it. But the men of Blackburg – men who for many years had lived right there where the red snow fell, and might be supposed to know a good deal about the matter – shook their heads and said something would come of it.

And something did, for the next summer was made memorable by the prevalence of a mysterious disease – epidemic, endemic, or the Lord knows what, though the physicians didn't – which carried away a full half of the population. Most of the other half carried themselves away and were slow to return, but finally came back, and were now increasing and multiplying as before, but Blackburg had not since been altogether the same.

Of quite another kind, though equally 'out of the common', was the incident of Hetty Parlow's ghost. Hetty Parlow's maiden name had been Brownon, and in Blackburg that meant more than one would think.

The Brownons had from time immemorial – from the very earliest of the old colonial days – been the leading family of the town. It was the richest and it was the best, and Blackburg would have shed the last drop of its plebeian blood in defence of the Brownon fair fame. As few of the family's members had ever been known to live permanently away from Blackburg, although most of them were educated elsewhere and nearly all had travelled, there was quite a number of them. The men held most of the public offices, and the women were foremost in all good works. Of these latter, Hetty was most beloved by reason of the sweetness of her disposition, the purity of her character and her singular personal beauty. She married in Boston a young scapegrace named Parlow, and like a good Brownon brought him to Blackburg forthwith and made a man and a town councilman of him. They had a child which they named Joseph and dearly loved, as was then the fashion among parents in all that region. Then they died of the mysterious disorder already mentioned, and at the age of one whole year Joseph set up as an orphan.

Unfortunately for Joseph the disease which had cut off his parents did not stop at that; it went on and extirpated nearly the whole Brownon contingent and its allies by marriage; and those who fled did not return. The tradition was broken, the Brownon estates passed into alien hands and the only Brownons remaining in that place were underground in Oak Hill Cemetery, where, indeed, was a colony of them powerful enough to resist the encroachment of surrounding tribes and hold the best part of the grounds. But about the ghost:

One night, about three years after the death of Hetty Parlow, a number of the young people of Blackburg were passing Oak Hill Cemetery in a wagon – if you have been there you will remember that the road to Greenton runs alongside it on the south. They had been attending a May Day festival at Greenton; and that serves to fix the date. Altogether there may have been a dozen, and a jolly party they were, considering the legacy of gloom left by the town's recent sombre experiences. As they passed the cemetery the man driving suddenly reined in his team with an exclamation of surprise. It was sufficiently surprising, no doubt, for just ahead, and almost at the roadside, though inside the cemetery, stood the ghost of Hetty Parlow. There could be no doubt of it, for she had been personally known to every youth and maiden in the party. That established the

thing's identity; its character as ghost was signified by all the customary signs – the shroud, the long, undone hair, the 'faraway look' –
everything. This disquieting apparition was stretching out its arms
toward the west, as if in supplication for the evening star, which,
certainly, was an alluring object, though obviously out of reach. As
they all sat silent (so the story goes) every member of that party of
merrymakers – they had merry-made on coffee and lemonade only –
distinctly heard that ghost call the name 'Joey, Joey!' A moment later
nothing was there. Of course one does not have to believe all that.

Now, at that moment, as was afterward ascertained, Joey was wandering about in the sage-brush on the opposite side of the continent,
near Winnemucca, in the State of Nevada. He had been taken to that
town by some good persons distantly related to his dead father, and by
them adopted and tenderly cared for. But on that evening the poor
child had strayed from home and was lost in the desert.

His after-history is involved in obscurity and has gaps which
conjecture alone can fill. It is known that he was found by a family
of Piute Indians, who kept the little wretch with them for a time
and then sold him – actually sold him for money to a woman on one
of the eastbound trains, at a station a long way from Winnemucca.
The woman professed to have made all manner of enquiries, but all
in vain: so, being childless and a widow, she adopted him herself.
At this point of his career Jo seemed to be getting a long way from
the condition of orphanage; the interposition of a multitude of
parents between himself and that woeful state promised him a long
immunity from its disadvantages.

Mrs Darnell, his newest mother, lived in Cleveland, Ohio. But
her adopted son did not long remain with her. He was seen one
afternoon by a policeman, new to that beat, deliberately toddling
away from her house, and being questioned answered that he was 'a
doin' home'. He must have travelled by rail, somehow, for three
days later he was in the town of Whiteville, which, as you know, is a
long way from Blackburg. His clothing was in pretty fair condition,
but he was sinfully dirty. Unable to give any account of himself he
was arrested as a vagrant and sentenced to imprisonment in the
Infants' Sheltering Home – where he was washed.

Jo ran away from the Infants' Sheltering Home at Whiteville – just
took to the woods one day, and the Home knew him no more forever.

We find him next, or rather get back to him, standing forlorn in
the cold autumn rain at a suburban street corner in Blackburg; and
it seems right to explain now that the raindrops falling upon him

there were really not dark and gummy; they only failed to make
his face and hands less so. Jo was indeed fearfully and wonderfully
besmirched, as by the hand of an artist. And the forlorn little tramp
had no shoes; his feet were bare, red, and swollen, and when he walked
he limped with both legs. As to clothing – ah, you would hardly have
had the skill to name any single garment that he wore, or say by what
magic he kept it upon him. That he was cold all over and all through
did not admit of a doubt; he knew it himself. Anyone would have been
cold there that evening; but, for that reason, no-one else was there.
How Jo came to be there himself, he could not for the flickering little
life of him have told, even if gifted with a vocabulary exceeding a
hundred words. From the way he stared about him one could have
seen that he had not the faintest notion of where (nor why) he was.

Yet he was not altogether a fool in his day and generation; being
cold and hungry, and still able to walk a little by bending his knees
very much indeed and putting his feet down toes first, he decided to
enter one of the houses which flanked the street at long intervals and
looked so bright and warm. But when he attempted to act upon that
very sensible decision a burly dog came bowsing out and disputed his
right. Inexpressibly frightened and believing, no doubt (with some
reason, too) that brutes without meant brutality within, he hobbled
away from all the houses, and with grey, wet fields to right of him
and grey, wet fields to left of him – with the rain half-blinding him
and the night coming in mist and darkness, held his way along the
road that leads to Greenton. That is to say, the road leads those to
Greenton who succeed in passing the Oak Hill Cemetery. A considerable number every year do not.

Jo did not.

They found him there the next morning, very wet, very cold, but
no longer hungry. He had apparently entered the cemetery gate –
hoping, perhaps, that it led to a house where there was no dog – and
gone blundering about in the darkness, falling over many a grave, no
doubt, until he had tired of it all and given up. The little body lay
upon one side, with one soiled cheek upon one soiled hand, the other
hand tucked away among the rags to make it warm, the other cheek
washed clean and white at last, as for a kiss from one of God's great
angels. It was observed – though nothing was thought of it at the
time, the body being as yet unidentified – that the little fellow was
lying upon the grave of Hetty Parlow. The grave, however, had not
opened to receive him. That is a circumstance which, without actual
irreverence, one may wish had been ordered otherwise.

A Psychological Shipwreck

In the summer of 1874 I was in Liverpool, whither I had gone on business for the mercantile house of Bronson & Jarrett, New York. I am William Jarrett; my partner was Zenas Bronson. The firm failed last year, and unable to endure the fall from affluence to poverty he died.

Having finished my business, and feeling the lassitude and exhaustion incident to its dispatch, I felt that a protracted sea voyage would be both agreeable and beneficial, so instead of embarking for my return on one of the many fine passenger steamers I booked for New York on the sailing vessel *Morrow*, upon which I had shipped a large and valuable invoice of the goods I had bought. The *Morrow* was an English ship with, of course, but little accommodation for passengers, of whom there were only myself, a young woman and her servant, who was a middle-aged negress. I thought it singular that a travelling English girl should be so attended, but she afterward explained to me that the woman had been left with her family by a man and his wife from South Carolina, both of whom had died on the same day at the house of the young lady's father in Devonshire – a circumstance in itself sufficiently uncommon to remain rather distinctly in my memory, even had it not afterward transpired in conversation with the young lady that the name of the man was William Jarrett, the same as my own. I knew that a branch of my family had settled in South Carolina, but of them and their history I was ignorant.

The *Morrow* sailed from the mouth of the Mersey on the 15th of June and for several weeks we had fair breezes and unclouded skies. The skipper, an admirable seaman but nothing more, favoured us with very little of his society, except at his table; and the young woman, Miss Janette Harford, and I became very well acquainted. We were, in truth, nearly always together, and being of an introspective turn of mind I often endeavoured to analyze and define the novel feeling with which she inspired me – a secret, subtle, but powerful attraction which constantly impelled me to seek her; but the attempt was hopeless. I could only be sure that at least it was not love. Having assured myself of this and being certain that she was quite as wholehearted, I ventured one evening (I remember it was on the 3rd of July) as we sat on deck to ask her, laughingly, if she could assist me to resolve my psychological doubt.

For a moment she was silent, with averted face, and I began to fear I had been extremely rude and indelicate; then she fixed her eyes gravely on my own. In an instant my mind was dominated by as strange a fancy as ever entered human consciousness. It seemed as if she were looking at me, not *with*, but *through*, those eyes – from an immeasurable distance behind them – and that a number of other persons, men, women and children, upon whose faces I caught strangely familiar evanescent expressions, clustered about her, struggling with gentle eagerness to look at me through the same orbs. Ship, ocean, sky – all had vanished. I was conscious of nothing but the figures in this extraordinary and fantastic scene. Then all at once darkness fell upon me, and anon from out of it, as to one who grows accustomed by degrees to a dimmer light, my former surroundings of deck and mast and cordage slowly resolved themselves. Miss Harford had closed her eyes and was leaning back in her chair, apparently asleep, the book she had been reading open in her lap. Impelled by surely I cannot say what motive, I glanced at the top of the page; it was a copy of that rare and curious work, Denneker's *Meditations*, and the lady's index finger rested on this passage:

To sundry it is given to be drawn away, and to be apart from the body for a season; for, as concerning rills which would flow across each other the weaker is borne along by the stronger, so there be certain of kin whose paths intersecting, their souls do bear company, the while their bodies go fore-appointed ways, unknowing.

Miss Harford arose, shuddering; the sun had sunk below the horizon, but it was not cold. There was not a breath of wind; there were no clouds in the sky, yet not a star was visible. A hurried tramping sounded on the deck; the captain, summoned from below, joined the first officer, who stood looking at the barometer. 'Good God!' I heard him exclaim.

An hour later the form of Janette Harford, invisible in the darkness and spray, was torn from my grasp by the cruel vortex of the sinking ship, and I fainted in the cordage of the floating mast to which I had lashed myself.

It was by lamplight that I awoke. I lay in a berth amid the familiar surroundings of the stateroom of a steamer. On a couch opposite sat a man, half-undressed for bed, reading a book. I recognised the face of my friend Gordon Doyle, whom I had met in Liverpool on the day of my embarkation, when he was himself about to sail on the steamer *City of Prague*, on which he had urged me to accompany him.

After some moments I now spoke his name. He simply said, 'Well?' and turned a leaf in his book without removing his eyes from the page.

'Doyle,' I repeated, 'did they save *her*?'

He now deigned to look at me and smiled as if amused. He evidently thought me but half-awake.

'Her? Whom do you mean?'

'Janette Harford.'

His amusement turned to amazement; he stared at me fixedly, saying nothing.

'You will tell me after a while,' I continued; 'I suppose you will tell me after a while.'

A moment later I asked: 'What ship is this?'

Doyle stared again. 'The steamer *City of Prague*, bound from Liverpool to New York, three weeks out with a broken shaft. Principal passenger, Mr Gordon Doyle; ditto lunatic, Mr William Jarrett. These two distinguished travellers embarked together, but they are about to part, it being the resolute intention of the former to pitch the latter overboard.'

I sat bolt upright. 'Do you mean to say that I have been for three weeks a passenger on this steamer?'

'Yes, pretty nearly; this is the 3rd of July.'

'Have I been ill?'

'Right as a trivet all the time, and punctual at your meals.'

'My God! Doyle, there is some mystery here; do have the goodness to be serious. Was I not rescued from the wreck of the ship *Morrow*?'

Doyle changed colour, and approaching me, laid his fingers on my wrist. A moment later, 'What do you know of Janette Harford?' he asked very calmly.

'First tell me what *you* know of her?'

Mr Doyle gazed at me for some moments as if thinking what to do, then seating himself again on the couch, said: 'Why should I not? I am engaged to marry Janette Harford, whom I met a year ago in London. Her family, one of the wealthiest in Devonshire, cut up rough about it, and we eloped – are eloping rather, for on the day that you and I walked to the landing stage to go aboard this steamer she and her faithful servant, a negress, passed us, driving to the ship *Morrow*. She would not consent to go in the same vessel with me, and it had been deemed best that she take a sailing vessel in order to avoid observation and lessen the risk of detection. I am now alarmed lest this cursed breaking of our machinery may detain us so long that the *Morrow* will get to New York before us, and the poor girl will not know where to go.'

I lay still in my berth – so still I hardly breathed. But the subject was evidently not displeasing to Doyle, and after a short pause he resumed: 'By the way, she is only an adopted daughter of the Harfords. Her mother was killed at their place by being thrown from a horse while hunting, and her father, mad with grief, made away with himself the same day. No-one ever claimed the child, and after a reasonable time they adopted her. She has grown up in the belief that she is their daughter.'

'Doyle, what book are you reading?'

'Oh, it's called Denneker's *Meditations*. It's a rum lot, Janette gave it to me; she happened to have two copies. Want to see it?'

He tossed me the volume, which opened as it fell. On one of the exposed pages was a marked passage:

> To sundry it is given to be drawn away, and to be apart from the body for a season; for, as concerning rills which would flow across each other the weaker is borne along by the stronger, so there be certain of kin whose paths intersecting, their souls do bear company, the while their bodies go fore-appointed ways, unknowing.

'She had – she has – a singular taste in reading,' I managed to say, mastering my agitation.

'Yes. And now perhaps you will have the kindness to explain how you knew her name and that of the ship she sailed in.'

'You talked of her in your sleep,' I said.

A week later we were towed into the port of New York. But the *Morrow* was never heard from.

A Cold Greeting

This is a story told by the late Benson Foley of San Francisco.

'In the summer of 1881 I met a man named James H. Conway, a resident of Franklin, Tennessee. He was visiting San Francisco for his health, deluded man, and brought me a note of introduction from Mr Lawrence Barting. I had known Barting as a captain in the Federal army during the civil war. At its close he had settled in Franklin, and in time became, I had reason to think, somewhat prominent as a lawyer. Barting had always seemed to me an honourable and truthful man, and the warm friendship which he expressed in his note for Mr Conway was to me sufficient evidence that the latter was in every way worthy of my confidence and esteem. At dinner one day Conway told me that it had been solemnly agreed between him and Barting that the one who died first should, if possible, communicate with the other from beyond the grave, in some unmistakable way – just how, they had left (wisely, it seemed to me) to be decided by the deceased, according to the opportunities that his altered circumstances might present.

'A few weeks after the conversation in which Mr Conway spoke of this agreement, I met him one day, walking slowly down Montgomery street, apparently, from his abstracted air, in deep thought. He greeted me coldly with merely a movement of the head and passed on, leaving me standing on the walk, with half-proffered hand, surprised and naturally somewhat piqued. The next day I met him again in the office of the Palace Hotel, and seeing him about to repeat the disagreeable performance of the day before, intercepted him in a doorway, with a friendly salutation, and bluntly requested an explanation of his altered manner. He hesitated a moment; then, looking me frankly in the eyes, said: "I do not think, Mr Foley, that I have any longer a claim to your friendship, since Mr Barting appears to have withdrawn his own from me – for what reason, I protest I do not know. If he has not already informed you he probably will do so."

' "But," I replied, "I have not heard from Mr Barting."

' "Heard from him!" he repeated, with apparent surprise. "Why, he is here. I met him yesterday ten minutes before meeting you. I gave you exactly the same greeting that he gave me. I met him again not a quarter of an hour ago, and his manner was precisely the same: he merely bowed and passed on. I shall not soon forget your civility to me. Good-morning, or – as it may please you – farewell."

'All this seemed to me singularly considerate and delicate behaviour on the part of Mr Conway.

'As dramatic situations and literary effects are foreign to my purpose I will explain at once that Mr Barting was dead. He had died in Nashville four days before this conversation. Calling on Mr Conway, I apprised him of our friend's death, showing him the letters announcing it. He was visibly affected in a way that forbade me to entertain a doubt of his sincerity.

' "It seems incredible," he said, after a period of reflection. "I suppose I must have mistaken another man for Barting, and that man's cold greeting was merely a stranger's civil acknowledgment of my own. I remember, indeed, that he lacked Barting's mustache."

' "Doubtless it was another man," I assented; and the subject was never afterward mentioned between us. But I had in my pocket a photograph of Barting, which had been enclosed in the letter from his widow. It had been taken a week before his death, and was without a mustache.'

Beyond the Wall

Many years ago, on my way from Hongkong to New York, I passed a week in San Francisco. A long time had gone by since I had been in that city, during which my ventures in the Orient had prospered beyond my hope; I was rich and could afford to revisit my own country to renew my friendship with such of the companions of my youth as still lived and remembered me with the old affection. Chief of these, I hoped, was Mohun Dampier, an old schoolmate with whom I had held a desultory correspondence which had long ceased, as is the way of correspondence between men. You may have observed that the indisposition to write a merely social letter is in the ratio of the square of the distance between you and your correspondent. It is a law.

I remembered Dampier as a handsome, strong young fellow of scholarly tastes, with an aversion to work and a marked indifference to many of the things that the world cares for, including wealth, of which, however, he had inherited enough to put him beyond the reach of want. In his family, one of the oldest and most aristocratic in the country, it was, I think, a matter of pride that no member of it had ever been in trade nor politics, nor suffered any kind of distinction. Mohun was a trifle sentimental, and had in him a singular element of superstition, which led him to the study of all manner of occult subjects, although his sane mental health safe-guarded him against fantastic and perilous faiths. He made daring incursions into the realm of the unreal without renouncing his residence in the partly surveyed and charted region of what we are pleased to call certitude.

The night of my visit to him was stormy. The Californian winter was on, and the incessant rain plashed in the deserted streets, or, lifted by irregular gusts of wind, was hurled against the houses with incredible fury. With no small difficulty my cabman found the right place, away out toward the ocean beach, in a sparsely populated suburb. The dwelling, a rather ugly one, apparently, stood in the centre of its grounds, which as nearly as I could make out in the gloom were destitute of either flowers or grass. Three or four trees, writhing and moaning in the torment of the tempest, appeared to be trying to escape from their dismal environment and take the chance of finding a better one out at sea. The house was a two-storey brick structure with a tower, a storey higher, at one corner. In a window of that was the only visible light. Something in the appearance of the place made me shudder, a performance that may have been assisted by a rill of rain-water down my back as I scuttled to cover in the doorway.

In answer to my note apprising him of my wish to call, Dampier had written, 'Don't ring – open the door and come up.' I did so. The staircase was dimly lighted by a single gas-jet at the top of the second flight. I managed to reach the landing without disaster and entered by an open door into the lighted square room of the tower. Dampier came forward in gown and slippers to receive me, giving me the greeting that I wished, and if I had held a thought that it might more fitly have been accorded me at the front door the first look at him dispelled any sense of his inhospitality.

He was not the same. Hardly past middle age, he had gone grey and had acquired a pronounced stoop. His figure was thin and angular, his face deeply lined, his complexion dead-white, without a touch of colour. His eyes, unnaturally large, glowed with a fire that was almost uncanny.

He seated me, proffered a cigar, and with grave and obvious sincerity assured me of the pleasure that it gave him to meet me. Some unimportant conversation followed, but all the while I was dominated by a melancholy sense of the great change in him. This he must have perceived, for he suddenly said with a bright enough smile, 'You are disappointed in me – *non sum qualis eram.*'

I hardly knew what to reply, but managed to say: 'Why, really, I don't know: your Latin is about the same.'

He brightened again. 'No,' he said, 'being a dead language, it grows in appropriateness. But please have the patience to wait: where I am going there is perhaps a better tongue. Will you care to have a message in it?'

The smile faded as he spoke, and as he concluded he was looking into my eyes with a gravity that distressed me. Yet I would not surrender myself to his mood, nor permit him to see how deeply his prescience of death affected me.

'I fancy that it will be long,' I said, 'before human speech will cease to serve our need; and then the need, with its possibilities of service, will have passed.'

He made no reply, and I too was silent, for the talk had taken a dispiriting turn, yet I knew not how to give it a more agreeable character. Suddenly, in a pause of the storm, when the dead silence was almost startling by contrast with the previous uproar, I heard a gentle tapping, which appeared to come from the wall behind my chair. The sound was such as might have been made by a human hand, not as upon a door by one asking admittance, but rather, I thought, as an agreed signal, an assurance of someone's presence in an adjoining room; most of us, I fancy, have had more experience of such communications than we should care to relate. I glanced at Dampier. If possibly there was something of amusement in the look he did not observe it. He appeared to have forgotten my presence, and was staring at the wall behind me with an expression in his eyes that I am unable to name, although my memory of it is as vivid today as was my sense of it then. The situation was embarrassing; I rose to take my leave. At this he seemed to recover himself.

'Please be seated,' he said; 'it is nothing – no-one is there.'

But the tapping was repeated, and with the same gentle, slow insistence as before.

'Pardon me,' I said, 'it is late. May I call tomorrow?'

He smiled – a little mechanically, I thought. 'It is very delicate of you,' said he, 'but quite needless. Really, this is the only room in the tower, and no-one is there. At least – ' He left the sentence incomplete, rose, and threw up a window, the only opening in the wall from which the sound seemed to come. 'See.'

Not clearly knowing what else to do I followed him to the window and looked out. A street-lamp some little distance away gave enough light through the murk of the rain that was again falling in torrents to make it entirely plain that 'no-one was there'. In truth there was nothing but the sheer blank wall of the tower.

Dampier closed the window and signing me to my seat resumed his own.

The incident was not in itself particularly mysterious; any one of a dozen explanations was possible (though none has occurred to me), yet it impressed me strangely, the more, perhaps, from my friend's effort to reassure me, which seemed to dignify it with a certain significance and importance. He had proved that no-one was there, but in that fact lay all the interest; and he proffered no explanation. His silence was irritating and made me resentful.

'My good friend,' I said, somewhat ironically, I fear, 'I am not disposed to question your right to harbour as many spooks as you find agreeable to your taste and consistent with your notions of companionship; that is no business of mine. But being just a plain man of affairs, mostly of this world, I find spooks needless to my peace and comfort. I am going to my hotel, where my fellow-guests are still in the flesh.'

It was not a very civil speech, but he manifested no feeling about it. 'Kindly remain,' he said. 'I am grateful for your presence here. What you have heard tonight I believe myself to have heard twice before. Now I *know* it was no illusion. That is much to me – more than you know. Have a fresh cigar and a good stock of patience while I tell you the story.'

The rain was now falling more steadily, with a low, monotonous susurration, interrupted at long intervals by the sudden slashing of the boughs of the trees as the wind rose and failed. The night was well advanced, but both sympathy and curiosity held me a willing listener to my friend's monologue, which I did not interrupt by a single word from beginning to end.

'Ten years ago,' he said, 'I occupied a ground-floor apartment in one of a row of houses, all alike, away at the other end of the town, on what we call Rincon Hill. This had been the best quarter of San Francisco, but had fallen into neglect and decay, partly because the primitive character of its domestic architecture no longer suited the maturing tastes of our wealthy citizens, partly because certain public improvements had made a wreck of it. The row of dwellings in one of which I lived stood a little way back from the street, each having a miniature garden, separated from its neighbours by low iron fences and bisected with mathematical precision by a box-bordered gravel walk from gate to door.

'One morning as I was leaving my lodging I observed a young girl entering the adjoining garden on the left. It was a warm day in June, and she was lightly gowned in white. From her shoulders hung a broad straw hat profusely decorated with flowers and wonderfully beribboned in the fashion of the time. My attention was not long held by the exquisite simplicity of her costume, for no-one could look at her face and think of anything earthly. Do not fear; I shall not profane it by description; it was beautiful exceedingly. All that I had ever seen or dreamed of loveliness was in that matchless living picture by the hand of the Divine Artist. So deeply did it move me that, without a thought of the impropriety of the act, I

unconsciously bared my head, as a devout Catholic or well-bred
Protestant uncovers before an image of the Blessed Virgin. The
maiden showed no displeasure; she merely turned her glorious dark
eyes upon me with a look that made me catch my breath, and
without other recognition of my act passed into the house. For a
moment I stood motionless, hat in hand, painfully conscious of my
rudeness, yet so dominated by the emotion inspired by that vision
of incomparable beauty that my penitence was less poignant than
it should have been. Then I went my way, leaving my heart behind.
In the natural course of things I should probably have remained
away until nightfall, but by the middle of the afternoon I was
back in the little garden, affecting an interest in the few foolish
flowers that I had never before observed. My hope was vain; she
did not appear.

'To a night of unrest succeeded a day of expectation and disappointment, but on the day after, as I wandered aimlessly about
the neighbourhood, I met her. Of course I did not repeat my folly
of uncovering, nor venture by even so much as too long a look to
manifest an interest in her; yet my heart was beating audibly. I
trembled and consciously coloured as she turned her big black
eyes upon me with a look of obvious recognition entirely devoid
of boldness or coquetry.

'I will not weary you with particulars; many times afterward I met
the maiden, yet never either addressed her or sought to fix her
attention. Nor did I take any action toward making her acquaintance. Perhaps my forbearance, requiring so supreme an effort of
self-denial, will not be entirely clear to you. That I was heels over
head in love is true, but who can overcome his habit of thought, or
reconstruct his character?

'I was what some foolish persons are pleased to call, and others,
more foolish, are pleased to be called – an aristocrat; and despite
her beauty, her charms and graces, the girl was not of my class. I
had learned her name – which it is needless to speak – and something of her family. She was an orphan, a dependent niece of the
impossible elderly fat woman in whose lodging-house she lived. My
income was small and I lacked the talent for marrying; it is perhaps
a gift. An alliance with that family would condemn me to its manner
of life, part me from my books and studies, and in a social sense
reduce me to the ranks. It is easy to deprecate such considerations
as these and I have not retained myself for the defence. Let judgment be entered against me, but in strict justice all my ancestors

for generations should be made co-defendants and I be permitted to plead in mitigation of punishment the imperious mandate of heredity. To a *mésalliance* of that kind every globule of my ancestral blood spoke in opposition. In brief, my tastes, habits, instinct, with whatever of reason my love had left me – all fought against it. Moreover, I was an irreclaimable sentimentalist, and found a subtle charm in an impersonal and spiritual relation which acquaintance might vulgarise and marriage would certainly dispel. No woman, I argued, is what this lovely creature seems. Love is a delicious dream; why should I bring about my own awakening?

'The course dictated by all this sense and sentiment was obvious. Honour, pride, prudence, preservation of my ideals – all commanded me to go away, but for that I was too weak. The utmost that I could do by a mighty effort of will was to cease meeting the girl, and that I did. I even avoided the chance encounters of the garden, leaving my lodging only when I knew that she had gone to her music lessons, and returning after nightfall. Yet all the while I was as one in a trance, indulging the most fascinating fancies and ordering my entire intellectual life in accordance with my dream. Ah, my friend, as one whose actions have a traceable relation to reason, you cannot know the fool's paradise in which I lived.

'One evening the devil put it into my head to be an unspeakable idiot. By apparently careless and purposeless questioning I learned from my gossipy landlady that the young woman's bedroom adjoined my own, a party-wall between. Yielding to a sudden and coarse impulse I gently rapped on the wall. There was no response, naturally, but I was in no mood to accept a rebuke. A madness was upon me and I repeated the folly, the offence, but again ineffectually, and I had the decency to desist.

'An hour later, while absorbed in some of my infernal studies, I heard, or thought I heard, my signal answered. Flinging down my books I sprang to the wall and as steadily as my beating heart would permit gave three slow taps upon it. This time the response was distinct, unmistakable: one, two, three – an exact repetition of my signal. That was all I could elicit, but it was enough – too much.

'The next evening, and for many evenings afterward, that folly went on, I always having "the last word". During the whole period I was deliriously happy, but with the perversity of my nature I persevered in my resolution not to see her. Then, as I should have expected, I got no further answers. "She is disgusted," I said to myself, "with what she thinks my timidity in making no more definite advances;" and I resolved to seek her and make her acquaintance and – what? I did not know, nor do I now know, what might have come of it. I know only that I passed days and days trying to meet her, and all in vain; she was invisible as well as inaudible. I haunted the streets where we had met, but she did not come. From my window I watched the garden in front of her house, but she passed neither in nor out. I fell into the deepest dejection, believing that she had gone away, yet took no steps to resolve my doubt by enquiry of my landlady, to whom, indeed, I had taken an unconquerable aversion from her having once spoken of the girl with less of reverence than I thought befitting.

'There came a fateful night. Worn out with emotion, irresolution and despondency, I had retired early and fallen into such sleep as was still possible to me. In the middle of the night something – some malign power bent upon the wrecking of my peace forever – caused me to open my eyes and sit up, wide awake and listening intently for I knew not what. Then I thought I heard a faint tapping on the wall – the mere ghost of the familiar signal. In a few moments it was repeated: one, two, three – no louder than before, but addressing a sense alert and strained to receive it. I was about to reply when the Adversary of Peace again intervened in my affairs with a rascally suggestion of retaliation. She had long and cruelly ignored me; now I would ignore her. Incredible fatuity – may God forgive it! All the rest of the night I lay awake, fortifying my obstinacy with shameless justifications and – listening.

'Late the next morning, as I was leaving the house, I met my landlady, entering.

' "Good-morning, Mr Dampier," she said. "Have you heard the news?"

'I replied in words that I had heard no news; in manner, that I did not care to hear any. The manner escaped her observation.

' "About the sick young lady next door," she babbled on. "What! you did not know? Why, she has been ill for weeks. And now – "

'I almost sprang upon her. "And now," I cried, "now what?"

' "She is dead."

'That is not the whole story. In the middle of the night, as I learned later, the patient, awakening from a long stupor after a week of delirium, had asked – it was her last utterance – that her bed be moved to the opposite side of the room. Those in attendance had thought the request a vagary of her delirium, but had complied. And there the poor passing soul had exerted its failing will to restore a broken connection – a golden thread of sentiment between its innocence and a monstrous baseness owning a blind, brutal allegiance to the Law of Self.

'What reparation could I make? Are there masses that can be said for the repose of souls that are abroad such nights as this – spirits "blown about by the viewless winds" – coming in the storm and darkness with signs and portents, hints of memory and presages of doom?

'This is the third visitation. On the first occasion I was too sceptical to do more than verify by natural methods the character of the incident; on the second, I responded to the signal after it had been several times repeated, but without result. Tonight's recurrence completes the "fatal triad" expounded by Parapelius Necromantius. There is no more to tell.'

When Dampier had finished his story I could think of nothing relevant that I cared to say, and to question him would have been a hideous impertinence. I rose and bade him good-night in a way to convey to him a sense of my sympathy, which he silently acknowledged by a pressure of the hand. That night, alone with his sorrow and remorse, he passed into the Unknown.

John Bartine's Watch

A story by a physician

'The exact time? Good God! my friend, why do you insist? One would think – but what does it matter; it is easily bedtime – isn't that near enough? But, here, if you must set your watch, take mine and see for yourself.'

With that he detached his watch – a tremendously heavy, old-fashioned one – from the chain, and handed it to me; then turned away, and walking across the room to a shelf of books, began an examination of their backs. His agitation and evident distress surprised me; they appeared reasonless. Having set my watch by his, I stepped over to where he stood and said, 'Thank you.'

As he took his timepiece and reattached it to the guard I observed that his hands were unsteady. With a tact upon which I greatly prided myself, I sauntered carelessly to the sideboard and took some brandy and water; then, begging his pardon for my thoughtlessness, asked him to have some and went back to my seat by the fire, leaving him to help himself, as was our custom. He did so and presently joined me at the hearth, as tranquil as ever.

This odd little incident occurred in my apartment, where John Bartine was passing an evening. We had dined together at the club, had come home in a cab and – in short, everything had been done in the most prosaic way; and why John Bartine should break in upon the natural and established order of things to make himself spectacular with a display of emotion, apparently for his own entertainment, I could nowise understand. The more I thought of it, while his brilliant conversational gifts were commending themselves to my inattention, the more curious I grew, and of course had no difficulty in persuading myself that my curiosity was friendly solicitude. That is the disguise that curiosity usually assumes to evade resentment. So I ruined one of the finest sentences of his disregarded monologue by cutting it short without ceremony.

'John Bartine,' I said, 'you must try to forgive me if I am wrong, but with the light that I have at present I cannot concede your right to go all to pieces when asked the time o' night. I cannot admit that it is proper to experience a mysterious reluctance to look your own watch in the face and to cherish in my presence, without explanation, painful emotions which are denied to me, and which are none of my business.'

To this ridiculous speech Bartine made no immediate reply, but sat looking gravely into the fire. Fearing that I had offended I was about to apologise and beg him to think no more about the matter, when looking me calmly in the eyes he said: 'My dear fellow, the levity of your manner does not at all disguise the hideous impudence of your demand; but happily I had already decided to tell you what you wish to know, and no manifestation of your unworthiness to hear it shall alter my decision. Be good enough to give me your attention and you shall hear all about the matter.

'This watch,' he said, 'had been in my family for three generations before it fell to me. Its original owner, for whom it was made, was my great-grandfather, Bramwell Olcott Bartine, a wealthy planter of Colonial Virginia, and as staunch a Tory as ever lay awake nights contriving new kinds of maledictions for the head of Mr Washington, and new methods of aiding and abetting good King George. One day this worthy gentleman had the deep misfortune to perform for his cause a service of capital importance which was not recognised as legitimate by those who suffered its disadvantages. It does not matter what it was, but among its minor consequences was my excellent ancestor's arrest one night in his own house by a party of Mr Washington's rebels. He was permitted to say farewell to his weeping family, and was then marched away into the darkness which swallowed him up forever. Not the slenderest clue to his fate was ever found. After the war the most diligent enquiry and the offer of large rewards failed to turn up any of his captors or any fact concerning his disappearance. He had disappeared, and that was all.'

Something in Bartine's manner that was not in his words – I hardly knew what it was – prompted me to ask: 'What is your view of the matter – of the justice of it?'

'My view of it,' he flamed out, bringing his clenched hand down upon the table as if he had been in a public house dicing with blackguards – 'my view of it is that it was a characteristically dastardly assassination by that damned traitor, Washington, and his ragamuffin rebels!'

For some minutes nothing was said: Bartine was recovering his temper, and I waited. Then I said: 'Was that all?'

'No – there was something else. A few weeks after my great-grandfather's arrest his watch was found lying on the porch at the front door of his dwelling. It was wrapped in a sheet of letter paper bearing the name of Rupert Bartine, his only son, my grandfather. I am wearing that watch.'

Bartine paused. His usually restless black eyes were staring fixedly into the grate, a point of red light in each, reflected from the glowing coals. He seemed to have forgotten me. A sudden threshing of the branches of a tree outside one of the windows, and almost at the same instant a rattle of rain against the glass, recalled him to a sense of his surroundings. A storm had risen, heralded by a single gust of wind, and in a few moments the steady plash of the water on the pavement was distinctly heard. I hardly know why I relate this incident; it seemed somehow to have a certain significance and relevancy which I am unable now to discern. It at least added an element of seriousness, almost solemnity. Bartine resumed: 'I have a singular feeling toward this watch – a kind of affection for it; I like to have it about me, though partly from its weight, and partly for a reason I shall now explain, I seldom carry it. The reason is this: every evening when I have it with me I feel an unaccountable desire to open and consult it, even if I can think of no reason for wishing to know the time. But if I yield to it, the moment my eyes rest upon the dial I am filled with a mysterious apprehension – a sense of imminent calamity. And this is the more insupportable the nearer it is to eleven o'clock – by this watch, no matter what the actual hour may be. After the hands have registered eleven the desire to look is gone; I am entirely indifferent. Then I can consult the thing as often as I like, with no more emotion than you feel in looking at your own. Naturally I have trained myself not to look at that watch in the evening before eleven; nothing could induce me. Your insistence this evening upset me a trifle. I felt very much as I suppose an opium-eater might feel if his yearning for his special and particular kind of hell were re-enforced by opportunity and advice.

'Now that is my story, and I have told it in the interest of your trumpery science; but if on any evening hereafter you observe me wearing this damnable watch, and you have the thoughtfulness to ask me the hour, I shall beg leave to put you to the inconvenience of being knocked down.'

His humour did not amuse me. I could see that in relating his delusion he was again somewhat disturbed. His concluding smile was positively ghastly, and his eyes had resumed something more than their old restlessness; they shifted hither and thither about the room with apparent aimlessness and I fancied had taken on a wild expression, such as is sometimes observed in cases of dementia. Perhaps this was my own imagination, but at any rate I was now persuaded that my friend was afflicted with a most singular and interesting monomania. Without, I trust, any abatement of my affectionate solicitude for him as a friend, I began to regard him as a patient, rich in possibilities of profitable study. Why not? Had he not described his delusion in the interest of science? Ah, poor fellow, he was doing more for science than he knew: not only his story but himself was in evidence. I should cure him if I could, of course, but first I should make a little experiment in psychology – nay, the experiment itself might be a step in his restoration.

'That is very frank and friendly of you, Bartine,' I said cordially, 'and I'm rather proud of your confidence. It is all very odd, certainly. Do you mind showing me the watch?'

He detached it from his waistcoat, chain and all, and passed it to me without a word. The case was of gold, very thick and strong, and singularly engraved. After closely examining the dial and observing that it was nearly twelve o'clock, I opened it at the back and was interested to observe an inner case of ivory, upon which was painted a miniature portrait in that exquisite and delicate manner which was in vogue during the eighteenth century.

'Why, bless my soul!' I exclaimed, feeling a sharp artistic delight – 'how under the sun did you get that done? I thought miniature painting on ivory was a lost art.'

'That,' he replied, gravely smiling, 'is not I; it is my excellent great-grandfather, the late Bramwell Olcott Bartine, Esquire, of Virginia. He was younger then than later – about my age, in fact. It is said to resemble me; do you think so?'

'Resemble you? I should say so! Barring the costume, which I supposed you to have assumed out of compliment to the art – or for *vraisemblance*, so to say – and the no mustache, that portrait is you in every feature, line, and expression.'

No more was said at that time. Bartine took a book from the table and began reading. I heard outside the incessant plash of the rain in the street. There were occasional hurried footfalls on the sidewalks; and once a slower, heavier tread seemed to cease at my door – a policeman, I thought, seeking shelter in the doorway. The boughs of the trees tapped significantly on the window panes, as if asking for admittance. I remember it all through these years and years of a wiser, graver life.

Seeing myself unobserved, I took the old-fashioned key that dangled from the chain and quickly turned back the hands of the watch a full hour; then, closing the case, I handed Bartine his property and saw him replace it on his person.

'I think you said,' I began, with assumed carelessness, 'that after eleven the sight of the dial no longer affects you. As it is now nearly twelve' – looking at my own timepiece – 'perhaps, if you don't resent my pursuit of proof, you will look at it now.'

He smiled good-humouredly, pulled out the watch again, opened it, and instantly sprang to his feet with a cry that Heaven has not had the mercy to permit me to forget! His eyes, their blackness strikingly intensified by the pallor of his face, were fixed upon the watch, which he clutched in both hands. For some time he remained in that attitude without uttering another sound; then, in a voice that I should not have recognised as his, he said: 'Damn you! it is two minutes to eleven!'

I was not unprepared for some such outbreak, and without rising replied, calmly enough: 'I beg your pardon; I must have misread your watch in setting my own by it.'

He shut the case with a sharp snap and put the watch in his pocket. He looked at me and made an attempt to smile, but his lower lip quivered and he seemed unable to close his mouth. His hands, also, were shaking, and he thrust them, clenched, into the pockets of his sack-coat. The courageous spirit was manifestly endeavouring to subdue the coward body. The effort was too great; he began to sway from side to side, as from vertigo, and before I could spring from my chair to support him his knees gave way and he pitched awkwardly forward and fell upon his face. I sprang to assist him to rise; but when John Bartine rises we shall all rise.

The post-mortem examination disclosed nothing; every organ was normal and sound. But when the body had been prepared for burial a faint dark circle was seen to have developed around the neck; at least I was so assured by several persons who said they saw it, but of my own knowledge I cannot say if that was true.

Nor can I set limitations to the law of heredity. I do not know that in the spiritual world a sentiment or emotion may not survive the heart that held it, and seek expression in a kindred life, ages removed.

Surely, if I were to guess at the fate of Bramwell Olcott Bartine, I should guess that he was hanged at eleven o'clock in the evening, and that he had been allowed several hours in which to prepare for the change.

As to John Bartine, my friend, my patient for five minutes, and – Heaven forgive me! – my victim for eternity, there is no more to say. He is buried, and his watch with him – I saw to that. May God rest his soul in Paradise, and the soul of his Virginian ancestor, if, indeed, they are two souls.

The Man out of the Nose

At the intersection of two certain streets in that part of San Francisco known by the rather loosely applied name of North Beach, is a vacant lot, which is rather more nearly level than is usually the case with lots, vacant or otherwise, in that region. Immediately at the back of it, to the south, however, the ground slopes steeply upward, the acclivity broken by three terraces cut into the soft rock. It is a place for goats and poor persons, several families of each class having occupied it jointly and amicably 'from the foundation of the city'. One of the humble habitations of the lowest terrace is noticeable for its rude resemblance to the human face, or rather to such a simulacrum of it as a boy might cut out of a hollowed pumpkin, meaning no offence to his race. The eyes are two circular windows, the nose is a door, the mouth an aperture caused by removal of a board below. There are no doorsteps. As a face, this house is too large; as a dwelling, too small. The blank, unmeaning stare of its lidless and browless eyes is uncanny.

Sometimes a man steps out of the nose, turns, passes the place where the right ear should be and making his way through the throng of children and goats obstructing the narrow walk between his neighbours' doors and the edge of the terrace gains the street by descending a flight of rickety stairs. Here he pauses to consult his watch and the stranger who happens to pass wonders why such a man as that can care what is the hour. Longer observations would show that the time of day is an important element in the man's movements, for it is at precisely two o'clock in the afternoon that he comes forth 365 times in every year.

Having satisfied himself that he has made no mistake in the hour he replaces the watch and walks rapidly southward up the street two squares, turns to the right and as he approaches the next corner fixes his eyes on an upper window in a three-storey building across the way. This is a somewhat dingy structure, originally of red brick and now grey. It shows the touch of age and dust. Built for a dwelling, it is now a factory. I do not know what is made there; the things that are commonly made in a factory, I suppose. I only know that at two o'clock in the afternoon of every day but Sunday it is full of activity and clatter; pulsations of some great engine shake it, and there are recurrent screams of wood tormented by the saw. At the window on which the man fixes an intensely expectant gaze nothing ever appears; the glass, in truth, has such a coating of dust that it has long ceased to be transparent. The man looks at it without stopping; he merely keeps turning his head more and more backward as he leaves the building behind. Passing along to the next corner, he turns to the left, goes round the block, and comes back till he reaches the point diagonally across the street from the factory – point on his former course, which he then retraces, looking frequently backward over his right shoulder at the window while it is in sight. For many years he has not been known to vary his route nor to introduce a single innovation into his action. In a quarter of an hour he is again at the mouth of his dwelling, and a woman, who has for some time been standing in the nose, assists him to enter. He is seen no more until two o'clock the next day. The woman is his wife. She supports herself and him by washing for the poor people among whom they live, at rates which destroy Chinese and domestic competition.

This man is about fifty-seven years of age, though he looks greatly older. His hair is dead white. He wears no beard, and is always newly shaven. His hands are clean, his nails well kept. In the matter of dress he is distinctly superior to his position, as indicated by his surroundings and the business of his wife. He is, indeed, very neatly, if not quite fashionably, clad. His silk hat has a date no earlier than the year before the last, and his boots, scrupulously polished, are innocent of patches. I am told that the suit which he wears during his daily excursions of fifteen minutes is not the one that he wears at home. Like everything else that he has, this is provided and kept in repair by the wife, and is renewed as frequently as her scanty means permit.

Thirty years ago John Hardshaw and his wife lived on Rincon Hill in one of the finest residences of that once aristocratic quarter. He had once been a physician, but having inherited a considerable estate from his father concerned himself no more about the ailments of his fellow-creatures and found as much work as he cared for in managing his own affairs. Both he and his wife were highly cultivated persons, and their house was frequented by a small set of such men and women as persons of their tastes would think worth knowing. So far as these knew, Mr and Mrs Hardshaw lived happily together;

certainly the wife was devoted to her handsome and accomplished husband and exceedingly proud of him.

Among their acquaintances were the Barwells – man, wife and two young children – of Sacramento. Mr Barwell was a civil and mining engineer, whose duties took him much from home and frequently to San Francisco. On these occasions his wife commonly accompanied him and passed much of her time at the house of her friend, Mrs Hardshaw, always with her two children, of whom Mrs Hardshaw, childless herself, grew fond. Unluckily, her husband grew equally fond of their mother – a good deal fonder. Still more unluckily, that attractive lady was less wise than weak.

At about three o'clock one autumn morning Officer No. 13 of the Sacramento police saw a man stealthily leaving the rear entrance of a gentleman's residence and promptly arrested him. The man – who wore a slouch hat and shaggy overcoat – offered the policeman one hundred, then five hundred, then one thousand dollars to be released. As he had less than the first mentioned sum on his person the officer treated his proposal with virtuous contempt. Before reaching the station the prisoner agreed to give him a check for ten thousand dollars and remain ironed in the willows along the river bank until it should be paid. As this only provoked new derision he would say no more, merely giving an obviously fictitious name. When he was searched at the station nothing of value was found on him but a miniature portrait of Mrs Barwell – the lady of the house at which he was caught. The case was set with costly diamonds; and something in the quality of the man's linen sent a pang of unavailing regret through the severely incorruptible bosom of Officer No. 13. There was nothing about the prisoner's clothing nor person to identify him and he was booked for burglary under the name that he had given, the honourable name of John K. Smith. The K. was an inspiration upon which, doubtless, he greatly prided himself.

In the meantime the mysterious disappearance of John Hardshaw was agitating the gossips of Rincon Hill in San Francisco, and was even mentioned in one of the newspapers. It did not occur to the lady whom that journal considerately described as his 'widow', to look for him in the city prison at Sacramento – a town which he was not known ever to have visited. As John K. Smith he was arraigned and, waiving examination, committed for trial.

About two weeks before the trial, Mrs Hardshaw, accidentally learning that her husband was held in Sacramento under an assumed name on a charge of burglary, hastened to that city without daring to mention the matter to anyone and presented herself at the prison, asking for an interview with her husband, John K. Smith. Haggard and ill with anxiety, wearing a plain travelling wrap which covered her from neck to foot, and in which she had passed the night on the steamboat, too anxious to sleep, she hardly showed for what she was, but her manner pleaded for her more strongly than anything that she chose to say in evidence of her right to admittance. She was permitted to see him alone.

What occurred during that distressing interview has never transpired; but later events prove that Hardshaw had found means to subdue her will to his own. She left the prison a broken-hearted woman, refusing to answer a single question, and returning to her desolate home renewed, in a half-hearted way, her enquiries for her missing husband. A week later she was herself missing: she had 'gone back to the States' – nobody knew any more than that.

On his trial the prisoner pleaded guilty – 'by advice of his counsel', so his counsel said. Nevertheless, the judge, in whose mind several unusual circumstances had created a doubt, insisted on the district attorney placing Officer No. 13 on the stand, and the deposition of Mrs Barwell, who was too ill to attend, was read to the jury. It was very brief: she knew nothing of the matter except that the likeness of herself was her property, and had, she thought, been left on the parlour table when she had retired on the night of the arrest. She had intended it as a present to her husband, then and still absent in Europe on business for a mining company.

This witness's manner when making the deposition at her residence was afterward described by the district attorney as most extraordinary. Twice she had refused to testify, and once, when the deposition lacked nothing but her signature, she had caught it from the clerk's hands and torn it in pieces. She had called her children to the bedside and embraced them with streaming eyes, then suddenly sending them from the room, she verified her statement by oath and signature, and fainted – 'slick away', said the district attorney. It was at that time that her physician, arriving upon the scene, took in the situation at a glance and grasping the representative of the law by the collar chucked him into the street and kicked his assistant after him. The insulted majesty of the law was not vindicated; the victim of the indignity did not even mention anything of all this in court. He was ambitious to win his case, and the circumstances of the taking of that deposition were not such as would give it weight if related; and after all, the man on trial had committed an offence against the law's majesty only less heinous than that of the irascible physician.

By suggestion of the judge the jury rendered a verdict of guilty; there was nothing else to do, and the prisoner was sentenced to the penitentiary for three years. His counsel, who had objected to nothing and had made no plea for lenity – had, in fact, hardly said a word – wrung his client's hand and left the room. It was obvious to the whole bar that he had been engaged only to prevent the court from appointing counsel who might possibly insist on making a defence.

John Hardshaw served out his term at San Quentin, and when discharged was met at the prison gates by his wife, who had returned from 'the States' to receive him. It is thought they went straight to Europe; anyhow, a general power-of-attorney to a lawyer still living among us – from whom I have many of the facts of this simple history – was executed in Paris. This lawyer in a short time sold everything that Hardshaw owned in California, and for years nothing was heard of the unfortunate couple, though many to whose ears had come vague and inaccurate intimations of their strange story, and who had known them, recalled their personality with tenderness and their misfortunes with compassion.

Some years later they returned, both broken in fortune and spirits and he in health. The purpose of their return I have not been able to ascertain. For some time they lived, under the name of Johnson, in a respectable enough quarter south of Market Street, pretty well put, and were never seen away from the vicinity of their dwelling. They must have had a little money left, for it is not known that the man had any occupation, the state of his health probably not permitting. The woman's devotion to her invalid husband was matter of remark among their neighbours; she seemed never absent from his side and always supporting and cheering him. They would sit for hours on one of the benches in a little public park, she reading to him, his hand in hers, her light touch occasionally visiting his pale brow, her still beautiful eyes frequently lifted from the book to look into his as she made some comment on the text, or closed the volume to beguile his mood with talk of – what? Nobody ever overheard a conversation between these two. The reader who has had the patience to follow their history to this point may possibly find a pleasure in conjecture: there was probably something to be avoided. The bearing of the man was one of profound dejection; indeed, the unsympathetic youth of the neighbourhood, with that keen sense for visible characteristics which ever distinguishes the young male of our species, sometimes mentioned him among themselves by the name of Spoony Glum.

It occurred one day that John Hardshaw was possessed by the spirit of unrest. God knows what led him whither he went, but he crossed Market Street and held his way northward over the hills, and downward into the region known as North Beach. Turning aimlessly to the left he followed his toes along an unfamiliar street until he was opposite what for that period was a rather grand dwelling, and for this is a rather shabby factory. Casting his eyes casually upward he saw at an open window what it had been better that he had not seen – the face and figure of Elvira Barwell. Their eyes met. With a sharp exclamation, like the cry of a startled bird, the lady sprang to her feet and thrust her body half out of the window, clutching the casing on each side. Arrested by the cry, the people in the street below looked up. Hardshaw stood motionless, speechless, his eyes two flames. 'Take care!' shouted someone in the crowd, as the woman strained further and further forward, defying the silent, implacable law of gravitation, as once she had defied that other law which God thundered from Sinai. The sudden-ness of her movements had tumbled a torrent of dark hair down her shoulders, and now it was blown about her cheeks, almost concealing her face. A moment so, and then – ! a fearful cry rang through the street, as, losing her balance, she pitched headlong from the window, a confused and whirling mass of skirts, limbs, hair, and white face, and struck the pavement with a horrible sound and a force of impact that was felt a hundred feet away. For a moment all eyes refused their office and turned from the sickening spectacle on the sidewalk. Drawn again to that horror, they saw it strangely augmented. A man, hatless, seated flat upon the paving stones, held the broken, bleeding body against his breast, kissing the mangled cheeks and streaming mouth through tangles of wet hair, his own features indistinguishably crimson with the blood that half-strangled him and ran in rills from his soaken beard.

The reporter's task is nearly finished. The Barwells had that very morning returned from a two years' absence in Peru. A week later the widower, now doubly desolate, since there could be no missing the significance of Hardshaw's horrible demonstration, had sailed for I know not what distant port; he has never come back to stay. Hard-shaw – as Johnson no longer – passed a year in the Stockton asylum for the insane, where also, through the influence of pitying friends, his wife was admitted to care for him. When he was discharged, not cured but harmless, they returned to the city; it would seem ever to have had some dreadful fascination for them. For a time they lived near the Mission Dolores, in poverty only less abject than that which is their present lot; but it was too far away from the objective point of the man's daily pilgrimage. They could not afford car fare. So that poor devil of an angel from Heaven – wife to this convict and lunatic – obtained, at a fair enough rental, the blank-faced shanty on the lower terrace of Goat Hill. Thence to the structure that was a dwelling and is a factory the distance is not so great; it is, in fact, an agreeable walk, judging from the man's eager and cheerful look as he takes it. The return journey appears to be a trifle wearisome.

An Adventure at Brownville[1]

I taught a little country school near Brownville, which, as everyone knows who has had the good luck to live there, is the capital of a considerable expanse of the finest scenery in California. The town is somewhat frequented in summer by a class of persons whom it is the habit of the local journal to call 'pleasure seekers', but who by a juster classification would be known as 'the sick and those in adversity.' Brownville itself might rightly enough be described, indeed, as a summer place of last resort. It is fairly well endowed with boarding-houses, at the least pernicious of which I performed twice a day (lunching at the schoolhouse) the humble rite of cementing the alliance between soul and body. From this 'hostelry' (as the local journal preferred to call it when it did not call it a 'caravanserai') to the schoolhouse the distance by the wagon road was about a mile and a half; but there was a trail, very little used, which led over an intervening range of low, heavily-wooded hills, considerably shortening the distance. By this trail I was returning one evening later than usual. It was the last day of the term and I had been detained at the schoolhouse until almost dark, preparing an account of my stewardship for the trustees – two of whom, I proudly reflected, would be able to read it, and the third (an instance of the dominion of mind over matter) would be overruled in his customary antagonism to the schoolmaster of his own creation.

I had gone not more than a quarter of the way when, finding an interest in the antics of a family of lizards which dwelt thereabout and seemed full of reptilian joy for their immunity from the ills incident to life at the Brownville House, I sat upon a fallen tree to observe them. As I leaned wearily against a branch of the gnarled old trunk the twilight deepened in the sombre woods and the faint new moon began casting visible shadows and gilding the leaves of the trees with a tender but ghostly light.

[1] This story was written in collaboration with Miss Ina Lillian Peterson, to whom is rightly due the credit for whatever merit it may have.

I heard the sound of voices – a woman's, angry, impetuous, rising against deep masculine tones, rich and musical. I strained my eyes, peering through the dusky shadows of the wood, hoping to get a view of the intruders on my solitude, but could see no-one. For some yards in each direction I had an uninterrupted view of the trail, and knowing of no other within a half-mile thought the persons heard must be approaching from the wood at one side. There was no sound but that of the voices, which were now so distinct that I could catch the words. That of the man gave me an impression of anger, abundantly confirmed by the matter spoken.

'I will have no threats; you are powerless, as you very well know. Let things remain as they are or, by God! you shall both suffer for it.'

'What do you mean?' – this was the voice of the woman, a cultivated voice, the voice of a lady. 'You would not – murder us.'

There was no reply, at least none that was audible to me. During the silence I peered into the wood in hope to get a glimpse of the speakers, for I felt sure that this was an affair of gravity in which ordinary scruples ought not to count. It seemed to me that the woman was in peril; at any rate the man had not disavowed a willingness to murder. When a man is enacting the role of potential assassin he has not the right to choose his audience.

After some little time I saw them, indistinct in the moonlight among the trees. The man, tall and slender, seemed clothed in black; the woman wore, as nearly as I could make out, a gown of grey stuff. Evidently they were still unaware of my presence in the shadow, though for some reason when they renewed their conversation they spoke in lower tones and I could no longer understand. As I looked the woman seemed to sink to the ground and raise her hands in supplication, as is frequently done on the stage and never, so far as I knew, anywhere else, and I am now not altogether sure that it was done in this instance. The man fixed his eyes upon her; they seemed to glitter bleakly in the moonlight with an expression that made me apprehensive that he would turn them upon me. I do not know by what impulse I was moved, but I sprang to my feet out of the shadow. At that instant the figures vanished. I peered in vain through the spaces among the trees and clumps of undergrowth. The night wind rustled the leaves; the lizards had retired early, reptiles of exemplary habits. The little moon was already slipping behind a black hill in the west.

I went home, somewhat disturbed in mind, half doubting that I had heard or seen any living thing excepting the lizards. It all seemed a trifle odd and uncanny. It was as if among the several phenomena, objective and subjective, that made the sum total of the incident there had been an uncertain element which had diffused its dubious character over all – had leavened the whole mass with unreality. I did not like it.

At the breakfast table the next morning there was a new face; opposite me sat a young woman at whom I merely glanced as I took my seat. In speaking to the high and mighty female personage who condescended to seem to wait upon us, this girl soon invited my attention by the sound of her voice, which was like, yet not altogether like, the one still murmuring in my memory of the previous evening's adventure. A moment later another girl, a few years older, entered the room and sat at the left of the other, speaking to her a gentle 'good-morning'. By *her* voice I was startled: it was without doubt the one of which the first girl's had reminded me. Here was the lady of the sylvan incident sitting bodily before me, 'in her habit as she lived'.

Evidently enough the two were sisters.

With a nebulous kind of apprehension that I might be recognised as the mute inglorious hero of an adventure which had in my consciousness and conscience something of the character of eaves-dropping, I allowed myself only a hasty cup of the lukewarm coffee thoughtfully provided by the prescient waitress for the emergency, and left the table. As I passed out of the house into the grounds I heard a rich, strong male voice singing an aria from *Rigoletto*. I am bound to say that it was exquisitely sung, too, but there was some-thing in the performance that displeased me, I could say neither what nor why, and I walked rapidly away.

Returning later in the day I saw the elder of the two young women standing on the porch and near her a tall man in black clothing – the man whom I had expected to see. All day the desire to know something of these persons had been uppermost in my mind and I now resolved to learn what I could of them in any way that was neither dishonourable nor low.

The man was talking easily and affably to his companion, but at the sound of my footsteps on the gravel walk he ceased, and turning about looked me full in the face. He was apparently of middle age, dark and uncommonly handsome. His attire was faultless, his bearing easy and graceful, the look which he turned upon me open, free, and devoid of any suggestion of rudeness. Nevertheless it affected me with a distinct emotion which on subsequent analysis in

memory appeared to be compounded of hatred and dread – I am
unwilling to call it fear. A second later the man and woman had
disappeared. They seemed to have a trick of disappearing. On entering the house, however, I saw them through the open doorway of
the parlour as I passed; they had merely stepped through a window
which opened down to the floor.

Cautiously 'approached' on the subject of her new guests my
landlady proved not ungracious. Restated with, I hope, some small
reverence for English grammar the facts were these: the two girls
were Pauline and Eva Maynard of San Francisco; the elder was
Pauline. The man was Richard Benning, their guardian, who had
been the most intimate friend of their father, now deceased. Mr
Benning had brought them to Brownville in the hope that the
mountain climate might benefit Eva, who was thought to be in
danger of consumption.

Upon these short and simple annals the landlady wrought an
embroidery of eulogium which abundantly attested her faith in
Mr Benning's will and ability to pay for the best that her house
afforded. That he had a good heart was evident to her from his
devotion to his two beautiful wards and his really touching solicitude for their comfort. The evidence impressed me as insufficient
and I silently found the Scotch verdict, 'Not proven'.

Certainly Mr Benning was most attentive to his wards. In my strolls
about the country I frequently encountered them – sometimes in
company with other guests of the hotel – exploring the gulches,
fishing, rifle shooting, and otherwise wiling away the monotony of
country life; and although I watched them as closely as good manners
would permit I saw nothing that would in any way explain the strange
words that I had overheard in the wood. I had grown tolerably well
acquainted with the young ladies and could exchange looks and even
greetings with their guardian without actual repugnance.

A month went by and I had almost ceased to interest myself in
their affairs when one night our entire little community was thrown
into excitement by an event which vividly recalled my experience in
the forest.

This was the death of the elder girl, Pauline.

The sisters had occupied the same bedroom on the third floor of
the house. Waking in the grey of the morning Eva had found
Pauline dead beside her. Later, when the poor girl was weeping
beside the body amid a throng of sympathetic if not very considerate persons, Mr Benning entered the room and appeared to

be about to take her hand. She drew away from the side of the dead and moved slowly toward the door.

'It is you,' she said – 'you who have done this. You – you – you!'

'She is raving,' he said in a low voice. He followed her, step by step, as she retreated, his eyes fixed upon hers with a steady gaze in which there was nothing of tenderness nor of compassion. She stopped; the hand that she had raised in accusation fell to her side, her dilated eyes contracted visibly, the lids slowly dropped over them, veiling their strange wild beauty, and she stood motionless and almost as white as the dead girl lying near. The man took her hand and put his arm gently about her shoulders, as if to support her. Suddenly she burst into a passion of tears and clung to him as a child to its mother. He smiled with a smile that affected me most disagreeably – perhaps any kind of smile would have done so – and led her silently out of the room.

There was an inquest – and the customary verdict: the deceased, it appeared, came to her death through 'heart disease'. It was before the invention of heart *failure*, though the heart of poor Pauline had indubitably failed. The body was embalmed and taken to San Francisco by someone summoned thence for the purpose, neither Eva nor Benning accompanying it. Some of the hotel gossips ventured to think that very strange, and a few hardy spirits went so far as to think it very strange indeed; but the good landlady generously threw herself into the breach, saying it was owing to the precarious nature of the girl's health. It is not of record that either of the two persons most affected and apparently least concerned made any explanation.

One evening about a week after the death I went out upon the veranda of the hotel to get a book that I had left there. Under some vines shutting out the moonlight from a part of the space I saw Richard Benning, for whose apparition I was prepared by having previously heard the low, sweet voice of Eva Maynard, whom also I now discerned, standing before him with one hand raised to his shoulder and her eyes, as nearly as I could judge, gazing upward into his. He held her disengaged hand and his head was bent with a singular dignity and grace. Their attitude was that of lovers, and as I stood in deep shadow to observe I felt even guiltier than on that memorable night in the wood. I was about to retire, when the girl spoke, and the contrast between her words and her attitude was so surprising that I remained, because I had merely forgotten to go away.

'You will take my life,' she said, 'as you did Pauline's. I know your intention as well as I know your power, and I ask nothing, only that you finish your work without needless delay and let me be at peace.'

He made no reply – merely let go the hand that he was holding, removed the other from his shoulder, and turning away descended the steps leading to the garden and disappeared in the shrubbery. But a moment later I heard, seemingly from a great distance, his fine clear voice in a barbaric chant, which as I listened brought before some inner spiritual sense a consciousness of some far, strange land peopled with beings having forbidden powers. The song held me in a kind of spell, but when it had died away I recovered and instantly perceived what I thought an opportunity. I walked out of my shadow to where the girl stood. She turned and stared at me with something of the look, it seemed to me, of a hunted hare. Possibly my intrusion had frightened her.

'Miss Maynard,' I said, 'I beg you to tell me who that man is and the nature of his power over you. Perhaps this is rude in me, but it is not a matter for idle civilities. When a woman is in danger any man has a right to act.'

She listened without visible emotion – almost I thought without interest, and when I had finished she closed her big blue eyes as if unspeakably weary.

'You can do nothing,' she said.

I took hold of her arm, gently shaking her as one shakes a person falling into a dangerous sleep.

'You must rouse yourself,' I said; 'something must be done and you must give me leave to act. You have said that that man killed your sister, and I believe it – that he will kill you, and I believe that.'

She merely raised her eyes to mine.

'Will you not tell me all?' I added.

'There is nothing to be done, I tell you – nothing. And if I could do anything I would not. It does not matter in the least. We shall be here only two days more; we go away then, oh, so far! If you have observed anything, I beg you to be silent.'

'But this is madness, girl.' I was trying by rough speech to break the deadly repose of her manner. 'You have accused him of murder. Unless you explain these things to me I shall lay the matter before the authorities.'

This roused her, but in a way that I did not like. She lifted her head proudly and said: 'Do not meddle, sir, in what does not concern you. This is my affair, Mr Moran, not yours.'

'It concerns every person in the country – in the world,' I answered, with equal coldness. 'If you had no love for your sister I, at least, am concerned for you.'

'Listen,' she interrupted, leaning toward me. 'I loved her, yes, God knows! But more than that – beyond all, beyond expression, I love *him*. You have overheard a secret, but you shall not make use of it to harm him. I shall deny all. Your word against mine – it will be that. Do you think your "authorities" will believe you?'

She was now smiling like an angel and, God help me! I was heels over head in love with her! Did she, by some of the many methods of divination known to her sex, read my feelings? Her whole manner had altered.

'Come,' she said, almost coaxingly, 'promise that you will not be impolite again.' She took my arm in the most friendly way. 'Come, I will walk with you. He will not know – he will remain away all night.'

Up and down the veranda we paced in the moonlight, she seemingly forgetting her recent bereavement, cooing and murmuring girl-wise of every kind of nothing in all Brownville; I silent, consciously awkward and with something of the feeling of being concerned in an intrigue. It was a revelation – this most charming and apparently blameless creature coolly and confessedly deceiving the man for whom a moment before she had acknowledged and shown the supreme love which finds even death an acceptable endearment.

'Truly,' I thought in my inexperience, 'here is something new under the moon.'

And the moon must have smiled.

Before we parted I had exacted a promise that she would walk with me the next afternoon – before going away forever – to the Old Mill, one of Brownville's revered antiquities, erected in 1860.

'If he is not about,' she added gravely, as I let go the hand she had given me at parting, and of which, may the good saints forgive me, I strove vainly to repossess myself when she had said it – so charming, as the wise Frenchman has pointed out, do we find woman's infidelity when we are its objects, not its victims. In apportioning his benefactions that night the Angel of Sleep overlooked me.

The Brownville House dined early, and after dinner the next day Miss Maynard, who had not been at table, came to me on the veranda, attired in the demurest of walking costumes, saying not a word. 'He' was evidently 'not about'. We went slowly up the road that led to the Old Mill. She was apparently not strong and at times took my arm, relinquishing it and taking it again rather capriciously, I thought. Her mood, or rather her succession of moods, was as mutable as skylight in a rippling sea. She jested as if she had never heard of such a thing as death, and laughed on the lightest incitement, and directly afterward would sing a few bars of some grave melody with such tenderness of expression that I had to turn away my eyes lest she should see the evidence of her success in art, if art it was, not artlessness, as then I was compelled to think it. And she said the oddest things in the most unconventional way, skirting sometimes unfathomable abysms of thought, where I had hardly the courage to set foot. In short, she was fascinating in a thousand and fifty different ways, and at every step I executed a new and profounder emotional folly, a hardier spiritual indiscretion, incurring fresh liability to arrest by the constabulary of conscience for infractions of my own peace.

Arriving at the mill, she made no pretence of stopping, but turned into a trail leading through a field of stubble toward a creek. Crossing by a rustic bridge we continued on the trail, which now led uphill to one of the most picturesque spots in the country. The Eagle's Nest, it was called – the summit of a cliff that rose sheer into the air to a height of hundreds of feet above the forest at its base. From this elevated point we had a noble view of another valley and of the opposite hills flushed with the last rays of the setting sun.

As we watched the light escaping to higher and higher planes from the encroaching flood of shadow filling the valley we heard footsteps, and in another moment were joined by Richard Benning.

'I saw you from the road,' he said carelessly; 'so I came up.'

Being a fool, I neglected to take him by the throat and pitch him into the treetops below, but muttered some polite lie instead. On the girl the effect of his coming was immediate and unmistakable. Her face was suffused with the glory of love's transfiguration: the red light of the sunset had not been more obvious in her eyes than was now the lovelight that replaced it.

'I am so glad you came!' she said, giving him both her hands; and, God help me! it was manifestly true.

Seating himself upon the ground he began a lively dissertation upon the wild flowers of the region, a number of which he had with him. In the middle of a facetious sentence he suddenly ceased speaking and fixed his eyes upon Eva, who leaned against the stump of a tree, absently plaiting grasses. She lifted her eyes in a startled way to his, as if she had *felt* his look. She then rose, cast away her grasses, and moved slowly away from him. He also rose, continuing to look at her. He had still in his hand the bunch of flowers. The girl turned, as if to speak, but said nothing. I recall clearly now something of which I was but half-conscious then – the dreadful contrast between the smile upon her lips and the terrified expression in her eyes as she met his steady and imperative gaze. I know nothing of how it happened, nor how it was that I did not sooner understand; I only know that with the smile of an angel upon her lips and that look of terror in her beautiful eyes Eva Maynard sprang from the cliff and shot crashing into the tops of the pines below!

How and how long afterward I reached the place I cannot say, but Richard Benning was already there, kneeling beside the dreadful thing that had been a woman.

'She is dead – quite dead,' he said coldly. 'I will go to town for assistance. Please do me the favour to remain.'

He rose to his feet and moved away, but in a moment had stopped and turned about.

'You have doubtless observed, my friend,' he said, 'that this was entirely her own act. I did not rise in time to prevent it, and you, not knowing her mental condition – you could not, of course, have suspected.'

His manner maddened me.

'You are as much her assassin,' I said, 'as if your damnable hands had cut her throat.' He shrugged his shoulders without reply and, turning, walked away. A moment later I heard, through the deepening shadows of the wood into which he had disappeared, a rich, strong, baritone voice singing 'La donna e mobile', from *Rigoletto*.

The Mocking-Bird

The time, a pleasant Sunday afternoon in the early autumn of 1861.
The place, a forest's heart in the mountain region of south-western
Virginia. Private Grayrock of the Federal Army is discovered seated
comfortably at the root of a great pine tree, against which he leans,
his legs extended straight along the ground, his rifle lying across
his thighs, his hands (clasped in order that they may not fall away to
his sides) resting upon the barrel of the weapon. The contact of
the back of his head with the tree has pushed his cap downward
over his eyes, almost concealing them; one seeing him would say
that he slept.

Private Grayrock did not sleep; to have done so would have
imperilled the interests of the United States, for he was a long way
outside the lines and subject to capture or death at the hands of the
enemy. Moreover, he was in a frame of mind unfavourable to
repose. The cause of his perturbation of spirit was this: during the
previous night he had served on the picket-guard, and had been
posted as a sentinel in this very forest. The night was clear, though
moonless, but in the gloom of the wood the darkness was deep.
Grayrock's post was at a considerable distance from those to right
and left, for the pickets had been thrown out a needless distance
from the camp, making the line too long for the force detailed to
occupy it. The war was young, and military camps entertained the
error that while sleeping they were better protected by thin lines
a long way out toward the enemy than by thicker ones close in.
And surely they needed as long notice as possible of an enemy's
approach, for they were at that time addicted to the practice of
undressing – than which nothing could be more unsoldierly. On
the morning of the memorable 6th of April, at Shiloh, many of
Grant's men when spitted on Confederate bayonets were as naked
as civilians; but it should be allowed that this was not because of any
defect in their picket line. Their error was of another sort: they had
no pickets. This is perhaps a vain digression. I should not care to

undertake to interest the reader in the fate of an army; what we have here to consider is that of Private Grayrock.

For two hours after he had been left at his lonely post that Saturday night he stood stock-still, leaning against the trunk of a large tree, staring into the darkness in his front and trying to recognise known objects; for he had been posted at the same spot during the day. But all was now different; he saw nothing in detail, but only groups of things, whose shapes, not observed when there was something more of them to observe, were now unfamiliar. They seemed not to have been there before. A landscape that is all trees and undergrowth, moreover, lacks definition, is confused and without accentuated points upon which attention can gain a foothold. Add the gloom of a moonless night, and something more than great natural intelligence and a city education is required to preserve one's knowledge of direction. And that is how it occurred that Private Grayrock, after vigilantly watching the spaces in his front and then imprudently executing a circumspection of his whole dimly visible environment (silently walking around his tree to accomplish it) lost his bearings and seriously impaired his usefulness as a sentinel. Lost at his post – unable to say in which direction to look for an enemy's approach, and in which lay the sleeping camp for whose security he was accountable with his life – conscious, too, of many another awkward feature of the situation and of considerations affecting his own safety, Private Grayrock was profoundly disquieted. Nor was he given time to recover his tranquillity, for almost at the moment that he realised his awkward predicament he heard a stir of leaves and a snap of fallen twigs, and turning with a stilled heart in the direction whence it came, saw in the gloom the indistinct outlines of a human figure.

'Halt!' shouted Private Grayrock, peremptorily as in duty bound, backing up the command with the sharp metallic snap of his cocking rifle – 'who goes there?'

There was no answer; at least there was an instant's hesitation, and the answer, if it came, was lost in the report of the sentinel's rifle. In the silence of the night and the forest the sound was deafening, and hardly had it died away when it was repeated by the pieces of the pickets to right and left, a sympathetic fusillade. For two hours every unconverted civilian of them had been evolving enemies from his imagination, and peopling the woods in his front with them, and Grayrock's shot had started the whole encroaching host into visible existence. Having fired, all retreated, breathless, to the reserves – all but Grayrock, who did not know in what direction to retreat. When, no enemy appearing, the roused camp two miles away had undressed and got itself into bed again, and the picket line was cautiously re-established, he was discovered bravely holding his ground, and was complimented by the officer of the guard as the one soldier of that devoted band who could rightly be considered the moral equivalent of that uncommon unit of value, 'a whoop in hell.'

In the meantime, however, Grayrock had made a close but un-availing search for the mortal part of the intruder at whom he had fired, and whom he had a marksman's intuitive sense of having hit; for he was one of those born experts who shoot without aim by an instinctive sense of direction, and are nearly as dangerous by night as by day. During a full half of his twenty-four years he had been a terror to the targets of all the shooting-galleries in three cities. Unable now to produce his dead game he had the discretion to hold his tongue, and was glad to observe in his officer and comrades the natural assumption that not having run away he had seen nothing hostile. His 'honourable mention' had been earned by not running away anyhow.

Nevertheless, Private Grayrock was far from satisfied with the night's adventure, and when the next day he made some fair enough pretext to apply for a pass to go outside the lines, and the general commanding promptly granted it in recognition of his bravery the night before, he passed out at the point where that had been dis-played. Telling the sentinel then on duty there that he had lost something – which was true enough – he renewed the search for the person whom he supposed himself to have shot, and whom if only wounded he hoped to trail by the blood. He was no more successful by daylight than he had been in the darkness, and after covering a wide area and boldly penetrating a long distance into 'the Confederacy' he gave up the search, somewhat fatigued, seated himself at the root of the great pine tree, where we have seen him, and indulged his disappointment.

It is not to be inferred that Grayrock's was the chagrin of a cruel nature balked of its bloody deed. In the clear large eyes, finely wrought lips, and broad forehead of that young man one could read quite another story, and in point of fact his character was a singularly felicitous compound of boldness and sensibility, courage and conscience.

'I find myself disappointed,' he said to himself, sitting there at the bottom of the golden haze submerging the forest like a subtler sea – 'disappointed in failing to discover a fellow-man dead by my hand!

Do I then really wish that I had taken life in the performance of a duty as well performed without? What more could I wish? If any danger threatened, my shot averted it; that is what I was there to do. No, I am glad indeed if no human life was needlessly extinguished by me. But I am in a false position. I have suffered myself to be complimented by my officers and envied by my comrades. The camp is ringing with praise of my courage. That is not just; I know myself courageous, but this praise is for specific acts which I did not perform, or performed – otherwise. It is believed that I remained at my post bravely, without firing, whereas it was I who began the fusillade, and I did not retreat in the general alarm because bewildered. What, then, shall I do? Explain that I saw an enemy and fired? They have all said that of themselves, yet none believes it. Shall I tell a truth which, discrediting my courage, will have the effect of a lie? Ugh! it is an ugly business altogether. I wish to God I could find my man!'

And so wishing, Private Grayrock, overcome at last by the languor of the afternoon and lulled by the stilly sounds of insects droning and prosing in certain fragrant shrubs, so far forgot the interests of the United States as to fall asleep and expose himself to capture. And sleeping he dreamed.

He thought himself a boy, living in a far, fair land by the border of a great river upon which the tall steamboats moved grandly up and down beneath their towering evolutions of black smoke, which announced them long before they had rounded the bends and marked their movements when miles out of sight. With him always, at his side as he watched them, was one to whom he gave his heart and soul in love – a twin brother. Together they strolled along the banks of the stream; together explored the fields lying farther away from it, and gathered pungent mints and sticks of fragrant sassafras in the hills overlooking all – beyond which lay the Realm of Conjecture, and from which, looking southward across the great river, they caught glimpses of the Enchanted Land. Hand in hand and heart in heart they two, the only children of a widowed mother, walked in paths of light through valleys of peace, seeing new things under a new sun. And through all the golden days floated one unceasing sound – the rich, thrilling melody of a mocking-bird in a cage by the cottage door. It pervaded and possessed all the spiritual intervals of the dream, like a musical benediction. The joyous bird was always in song; its infinitely various notes seemed to flow from its throat, effortless, in bubbles and rills at each heart-beat, like the waters of a pulsing spring. That fresh, clear melody seemed, indeed, the spirit of the scene, the meaning and interpretation to sense of the mysteries of life and love.

But there came a time when the days of the dream grew dark with sorrow in a rain of tears. The good mother was dead, the meadow-side home by the great river was broken up, and the brothers were parted between two of their kinsmen. William (the dreamer) went to live in a populous city in the Realm of Conjecture, and John, crossing the river into the Enchanted Land, was taken to a distant region whose people in their lives and ways were said to be strange and wicked. To him, in the distribution of the dead mother's estate, had fallen all that they deemed of value – the mocking-bird. They could be divided, but it could not, so it was carried away into the strange country, and the world of William knew it no more forever. Yet still through the aftertime of his loneliness its song filled all the dream, and seemed always sounding in his ear and in his heart.

The kinsmen who had adopted the boys were enemies, holding no communication. For a time letters full of boyish bravado and boastful narratives of the new and larger experience – grotesque descriptions of their widening lives and the new worlds they had conquered – passed between them; but these gradually became less frequent, and with William's removal to another and greater city ceased altogether. But ever through it all ran the song of the mocking-bird, and when the dreamer opened his eyes and stared through the vistas of the pine forest the cessation of its music first apprised him that he was awake.

The sun was low and red in the west; the level rays projected from the trunk of each giant pine a wall of shadow traversing the golden haze to eastward until light and shade were blended in undisting-uishable blue.

Private Grayrock rose to his feet, looked cautiously about him, shouldered his rifle and set off toward camp. He had gone perhaps a half-mile, and was passing a thicket of laurel, when a bird rose from the midst of it and perching on the branch of a tree above, poured from its joyous breast so inexhaustible floods of song as but one of all God's creatures can utter in His praise. There was little in that – it was only to open the bill and breathe; yet the man stopped as if struck – stopped and let fall his rifle, looked upward at the bird, covered his eyes with his hands and wept like a child! For the moment he was, indeed, a child, in spirit and in memory, dwelling again by the great river, over against the Enchanted Land! Then with an effort of the will he pulled himself together, picked up his weapon and audibly damning himself for an idiot strode on. Passing an opening that reached into the heart of the little thicket he looked in, and there, supine upon the earth, its arms all abroad, its grey uniform stained with a single spot of blood upon the breast, its white face turned sharply upward and backward, lay the image of himself! – the body of John Grayrock, dead of a gunshot wound, and still warm! He had found his man.

As the unfortunate soldier knelt beside that masterwork of civil war the shrilling bird upon the bough overhead stilled her song and, flushed with sunset's crimson glory, glided silently away through the solemn spaces of the wood. At roll-call that evening in the Federal camp the name William Grayrock brought no response, nor ever again thereafter.

The Suitable Surroundings

The night

One midsummer night a farmer's boy living about ten miles from the city of Cincinnati was following a bridle-path through a dense and dark forest. He had lost himself while searching for some missing cows, and near midnight was a long way from home, in a part of the country with which he was unfamiliar. But he was a stout-hearted lad, and knowing his general direction from his home, he plunged into the forest without hesitation, guided by the stars. Coming into the bridle-path, and observing that it ran in the right direction, he followed it.

The night was clear, but in the woods it was exceedingly dark. It was more by the sense of touch than by that of sight that the lad kept the path. He could not, indeed, very easily go astray; the undergrowth on both sides was so thick as to be almost impenetrable. He had gone into the forest a mile or more when he was surprised to see a feeble gleam of light shining through the foliage skirting the path on his left. The sight of it startled him and set his heart beating audibly.

'The old Breede house is somewhere about here,' he said to himself. 'This must be the other end of the path which we reach it by from our side. Ugh! what should a light be doing there?'

Nevertheless, he pushed on. A moment later he had emerged from the forest into a small, open space, mostly upgrown to brambles. There were remnants of a rotting fence. A few yards from the trail, in the middle of the 'clearing,' was the house from which the light came, through an unglazed window. The window had once contained glass, but that and its supporting frame had long ago yielded to missiles flung by hands of venturesome boys to attest alike their courage and their hostility to the supernatural; for the Breede house bore the evil reputation of being haunted. Possibly it was not, but even the hardiest sceptic could not deny that it was deserted – which in rural regions is much the same thing.

Looking at the mysterious dim light shining from the ruined window the boy remembered with apprehension that his own hand had assisted at the destruction. His penitence was of course poignant in proportion to its tardiness and inefficacy. He half-expected to be set upon by all the unworldly and bodiless malevolences whom he had outraged by assisting to break alike their windows and their peace. Yet this stubborn lad, shaking in every limb, would not retreat. The blood in his veins was strong and rich with the iron of the frontiersman. He was but two removes from the generation that had subdued the Indian. He started to pass the house.

As he was going by he looked in at the blank window space and saw a strange and terrifying sight – the figure of a man seated in the centre of the room, at a table upon which lay some loose sheets of paper. The elbows rested on the table, the hands supporting the head, which was uncovered. On each side the fingers were pushed into the hair. The face showed dead-yellow in the light of a single candle a little to one side. The flame illuminated that side of the face, the other was in deep shadow. The man's eyes were fixed upon the blank window space with a stare in which an older and cooler observer might have discerned something of apprehension, but which seemed to the lad altogether soulless. He believed the man to be dead.

The situation was horrible, but not without its fascination. The boy stopped to note it all. He was weak, faint and trembling; he could feel the blood forsaking his face. Nevertheless, he set his teeth and resolutely advanced to the house. He had no conscious intention – it was the mere courage of terror. He thrust his white face forward into the illuminated opening. At that instant a strange, harsh cry, a shriek, broke upon the silence of the night – the note of a screech-owl. The man sprang to his feet, overturning the table and extinguishing the candle. The boy took to his heels.

The day before

'Good-morning, Colston. I am in luck, it seems. You have often said that my commendation of your literary work was mere civility, and here you find me absorbed – actually merged – in your latest story in the *Messenger*. Nothing less shocking than your touch upon my shoulder would have roused me to consciousness.'

'The proof is stronger than you seem to know,' replied the man addressed: 'so keen is your eagerness to read my story that you are

willing to renounce selfish considerations and forego all the pleasure
that you could get from it.'

'I don't understand you,' said the other, folding the newspaper that
he held and putting it into his pocket. 'You writers are a queer lot,
anyhow. Come, tell me what I have done or omitted in this matter.
In what way does the pleasure that I get, or might get, from your
work depend on me?'

'In many ways. Let me ask you how you would enjoy your breakfast if you took it in this streetcar. Suppose the phonograph so
perfected as to be able to give you an entire opera – singing,
orchestration, and all; do you think you would get much pleasure
out of it if you turned it on at your office during business hours?
Do you really care for a serenade by Schubert when you hear it
fiddled by an untimely Italian on a morning ferryboat? Are you
always cocked and primed for enjoyment? Do you keep every
mood on tap, ready to any demand? Let me remind you, sir, that
the story which you have done me the honour to begin as a means
of becoming oblivious to the discomfort of this car is a ghost story!'

'Well?'

'Well! Has the reader no duties corresponding to his privileges?
You have paid five cents for that newspaper. It is yours. You have the
right to read it when and where you will. Much of what is in it is
neither helped nor harmed by time and place and mood; some of it
actually requires to be read at once – while it is fizzing. But my story
is not of that character. It is not "the very latest advices" from
Ghostland. You are not expected to keep yourself *au courant* with
what is going on in the realm of spooks. The stuff will keep until you
have leisure to put yourself into the frame of mind appropriate to the
sentiment of the piece – which I respectfully submit that you cannot
do in a streetcar, even if you are the only passenger. The solitude is
not of the right sort. An author has rights which the reader is bound
to respect.'

'For specific example?'

'The right to the reader's undivided attention. To deny him this
is immoral. To make him share your attention with the rattle of a
streetcar, the moving panorama of the crowds on the sidewalks,
and the buildings beyond – with any of the thousands of distractions
which make our customary environment – is to treat him with gross
injustice. By God, it is infamous!'

The speaker had risen to his feet and was steadying himself by
one of the straps hanging from the roof of the car. The other

man looked up at him in sudden astonishment, wondering how so trivial a grievance could seem to justify so strong language. He saw that his friend's face was uncommonly pale and that his eyes glowed like living coals.

'You know what I mean,' continued the writer, impetuously crowding his words – 'you know what I mean, Marsh. My stuff in this morning's *Messenger* is plainly sub-headed "A Ghost Story". That is ample notice to all. Every honourable reader will understand it as prescribing by implication the conditions under which the work is to be read.'

The man addressed as Marsh winced a trifle, then asked with a smile: 'What conditions? You know that I am only a plain businessman who cannot be supposed to understand such things. How, when, where should I read your ghost story?'

'In solitude – at night – by the light of a candle. There are certain emotions which a writer can easily enough excite – such as compassion or merriment. I can move you to tears or laughter under almost any circumstances. But for my ghost story to be effective you must be made to feel fear – at least a strong sense of the supernatural – and that is a difficult matter. I have a right to expect that if you read me at all you will give me a chance; that you will make yourself accessible to the emotion that I try to inspire.'

The car had now arrived at its terminus and stopped. The trip just completed was its first for the day and the conversation of the two early passengers had not been interrupted. The streets were yet silent and desolate; the housetops were just touched by the rising sun. As they stepped from the car and walked away together Marsh narrowly eyed his companion, who was reported, like most men of uncommon literary ability, to be addicted to various destructive vices. That is the revenge which dull minds take upon bright ones in resentment of their superiority. Mr Colston was known as a man of genius. There are honest souls who believe that genius is a mode of excess. It was known that Colston did not drink liquor, but many said that he ate opium. Something in his appearance that morning – a certain wildness of the eyes, an unusual pallor, a thickness and rapidity of speech – were taken by Mr Marsh to confirm the report. Nevertheless, he had not the self-denial to abandon a subject which he found interesting, however it might excite his friend.

'Do you mean to say,' he began, 'that if I take the trouble to observe your directions – place myself in the conditions that you demand:

solitude, night and a tallow candle – you can with your ghostly work give me an uncomfortable sense of the supernatural, as you call it? Can you accelerate my pulse, make me start at sudden noises, send a nervous chill along my spine and cause my hair to rise?'

Colston turned suddenly and looked him squarely in the eyes as they walked. 'You would not dare – you have not the courage,' he said. He emphasised the words with a contemptuous gesture. 'You are brave enough to read me in a street car, but – in a deserted house – alone – in the forest – at night! Bah! I have a manuscript in my pocket that would kill you.'

Marsh was angry. He knew himself courageous, and the words stung him. 'If you know such a place,' he said, 'take me there tonight and leave me your story and a candle. Call for me when I've had time enough to read it and I'll tell you the entire plot and – kick you out of the place.'

That is how it occurred that the farmer's boy, looking in at an unglazed window of the Breede house, saw a man sitting in the light of a candle.

The day after

Late in the afternoon of the next day three men and a boy approached the Breede house from that point of the compass toward which the boy had fled the preceding night. The men were in high spirits; they talked very loudly and laughed. They made facetious and good-humoured ironical remarks to the boy about his adventure, which evidently they did not believe in. The boy accepted their raillery with seriousness, making no reply. He had a sense of the fitness of things and knew that one who professes to have seen a dead man rise from his seat and blow out a candle is not a credible witness.

Arriving at the house and finding the door unlocked, the party of investigators entered without ceremony. Leading out of the passage into which this door opened was another on the right and one on the left. They entered the room on the left – the one which had the blank front window. Here was the dead body of a man.

It lay partly on one side, with the forearm beneath it, the cheek on the floor. The eyes were wide open; the stare was not an agreeable thing to encounter. The lower jaw had fallen; a little pool of saliva had collected beneath the mouth. An overthrown table, a partly burned candle, a chair and some paper with writing on it were all else that the room contained. The men looked at the body, touching the face in turn. The boy gravely stood at the head, assuming a look of ownership. It was the proudest moment of his life. One of the men said to him, 'You're a good 'un' – a remark which was received by the two others with nods of acquiescence. It was Scepticism apologising to Truth. Then one of the men took from the floor the sheet of manuscript and stepped to the window, for already the evening shadows were glooming the forest. The song of the whip-poor-will was heard in the distance and a monstrous beetle sped by the window on roaring wings and thundered away out of hearing. The man read.

The manuscript

Before committing the act which, rightly or wrongly, I have resolved on and appearing before my Maker for judgment, I, James R. Colston, deem it my duty as a journalist to make a statement to the public. My name is, I believe, tolerably well known to the people as a writer of tragic tales, but the sombrest imagination never conceived anything so tragic as my own life and history. Not in incident: my life has been destitute of adventure and action. But my mental career has been lurid with experiences such as kill and damn. I shall not recount them here – some of them are written and ready for publication elsewhere. The object of these lines is to explain to whomsoever may be interested that my death is voluntary – my own act. I shall die at twelve o'clock on the night of the 15th of July – a significant anniversary to me, for it was on that day, and at that hour, that my friend in time and eternity, Charles Breede, performed his vow to me by the same act which his fidelity to our pledge now entails upon me. He took his life in his little house in the Copeton woods. There was the customary verdict of 'temporary insanity'. Had I testified at that inquest – had I told all I knew, they would have called *me* mad!'

Here followed an evidently long passage which the man reading read to himself only. The rest he read aloud.

I have still a week of life in which to arrange my worldly affairs and prepare for the great change. It is enough, for I have but few affairs and it is now four years since death became an imperative obligation.

I shall bear this writing on my body; the finder will please hand it to the coroner.

James R. Colston

P.S. – Willard Marsh, on this the fatal fifteenth day of July I hand you this manuscript, to be opened and read under the conditions agreed upon, and at the place which I designated. I forego my intention to keep it on my body to explain the manner of my death, which is not important. It will serve to explain the manner of yours. I am to call for you during the night to receive assurance that you have read the manuscript. You know me well enough to expect me. But, my friend, it *will be after twelve o'clock*. May God have mercy on our souls!

J.R.C.

Before the man who was reading this manuscript had finished, the candle had been picked up and lighted. When the reader had done, he quietly thrust the paper against the flame and despite the protestations of the others held it until it was burnt to ashes. The man who did this, and who afterward placidly endured a severe reprimand from the coroner, was a son-in-law of the late Charles Breede. At the inquest nothing could elicit an intelligent account of what the paper had contained.

From The Times

'Yesterday the Commissioners of Lunacy committed to the asylum Mr James R. Colston, a writer of some local reputation, connected with the *Messenger*. It will be remembered that on the evening of the 15th inst. Mr Colston was given into custody by one of his fellow-lodgers in the Baine House, who had observed him acting very suspiciously, baring his throat and whetting a razor – occasionally trying its edge by actually cutting through the skin of his arm, etc. On being handed over to the police, the unfortunate man made a desperate resistance, and has ever since been so violent that it has been necessary to keep him in a straitjacket. Most of our esteemed contemporary's other writers are still at large.'

The Boarded Window

In 1830, only a few miles away from what is now the great city of Cincinnati, lay an immense and almost unbroken forest. The whole region was sparsely settled by people of the frontier – restless souls who no sooner had hewn fairly habitable homes out of the wilderness and attained to that degree of prosperity which today we should call indigence than impelled by some mysterious impulse of their nature they abandoned all and pushed farther westward, to encounter new perils and privations in the effort to regain the meagre comforts which they had voluntarily renounced. Many of them had already forsaken that region for the remoter settlements, but among those remaining was one who had been of those first arriving. He lived alone in a house of logs surrounded on all sides by the great forest, of whose gloom and silence he seemed a part, for no-one had ever known him to smile nor speak a needless word. His simple wants were supplied by the sale or barter of skins of wild animals in the river town, for not a thing did he grow upon the land which, if needful, he might have claimed by right of undisturbed possession. There were evidences of 'improvement' – a few acres of ground immediately about the house had once been cleared of its trees, the decayed stumps of which were half concealed by the new growth that had been suffered to repair the ravage wrought by the axe. Apparently the man's zeal for agriculture had burned with a failing flame, expiring in penitential ashes.

The little log house, with its chimney of sticks, its roof of warping clapboards weighted with traversing poles and its 'chinking' of clay, had a single door and, directly opposite, a window. The latter, however, was boarded up – nobody could remember a time when it was not. And none knew why it was so closed; certainly not because of the occupant's dislike of light and air, for on those rare occasions when a hunter had passed that lonely spot the recluse had commonly been seen sunning himself on his doorstep if heaven had provided sunshine for his need. I fancy there are few persons living today who ever knew the secret of that window, but I am one, as you shall see.

The man's name was said to be Murlock. He was apparently seventy years old, actually about fifty. Something besides years had had a hand in his aging. His hair and long, full beard were white, his grey, lustreless eyes sunken, his face singularly seamed with wrinkles which appeared to belong to two intersecting systems. In figure he was tall and spare, with a stoop of the shoulders – a burden bearer. I never saw him; these particulars I learned from my grandfather, from whom also I got the man's story when I was a lad. He had known him when living nearby in that early day.

One day Murlock was found in his cabin, dead. It was not a time and place for coroners and newspapers, and I suppose it was agreed that he had died from natural causes or I should have been told, and should remember. I know only that with what was probably a sense of the fitness of things the body was buried near the cabin, alongside the grave of his wife, who had preceded him by so many years that local tradition had retained hardly a hint of her existence. That closes the final chapter of this true story – excepting, indeed, the circumstance that many years afterward, in company with an equally intrepid spirit, I penetrated to the place and ventured near enough to the ruined cabin to throw a stone against it, and ran away to avoid the ghost which every well-informed boy thereabout knew haunted the spot. But there is an earlier chapter – that supplied by my grandfather.

When Murlock built his cabin and began laying sturdily about with his axe to hew out a farm – the rifle, meanwhile, his means of support – he was young, strong and full of hope. In that eastern country whence he came he had married, as was the fashion, a young woman in all ways worthy of his honest devotion, who shared the dangers and privations of his lot with a willing spirit and light heart. There is no known record of her name; of her charms of mind and person tradition is silent and the doubter is at liberty to entertain his doubt; but God forbid that I should share it! Of their affection and happiness there is abundant assurance in every added day of the man's widowed life; for what but the magnetism of a blessed memory could have chained that venturesome spirit to a lot like that?

One day Murlock returned from gunning in a distant part of the forest to find his wife prostrate with fever, and delirious. There was no physician within miles, no neighbour; nor was she in a condition to be left, to summon help. So he set about the task of nursing her back to health, but at the end of the third day she fell into unconsciousness and so passed away, apparently, with never a gleam of returning reason.

From what we know of a nature like his we may venture to sketch in some of the details of the outline picture drawn by my grandfather. When convinced that she was dead, Murlock had sense enough to remember that the dead must be prepared for burial. In performance of this sacred duty he blundered now and again, did certain things incorrectly, and others which he did correctly were done over and over. His occasional failures to accomplish some simple and ordinary act filled him with astonishment, like that of a drunken man who wonders at the suspension of familiar natural laws. He was surprised, too, that he did not weep – surprised and a little ashamed; surely it is unkind not to weep for the dead. 'Tomorrow,' he said aloud, 'I shall have to make the coffin and dig the grave; and then I shall miss her, when she is no longer in sight; but now – she is dead, of course, but it is all right – it *must* be all right, somehow. Things cannot be so bad as they seem.'

He stood over the body in the fading light, adjusting the hair and putting the finishing touches to the simple toilet, doing all mechanically, with soulless care. And still through his consciousness ran an undersense of conviction that all was right – that he should have her again as before, and everything explained. He had had no experience in grief; his capacity had not been enlarged by use. His heart could not contain it all, nor his imagination rightly conceive it. He did not know he was so hard struck; *that* knowledge would come later, and never go. Grief is an artist of powers as various as the instruments upon which he plays his dirges for the dead, evoking from some the sharpest, shrillest notes, from others the low, grave chords that throb recurrent like the slow beating of a distant drum. Some natures it startles; some it stupefies. To one it comes like the stroke of an arrow, stinging all the sensibilities to a keener life; to another as the blow of a bludgeon, which in crushing benumbs. We may conceive Murlock to have been that way affected, for (and here we are upon surer ground than that of conjecture) no sooner had he finished his pious work than, sinking into a chair by the side of the table upon which the body lay, and noting how white the profile showed in the deepening gloom, he laid his arms upon the table's edge, and dropped his face into them, tearless yet and unutterably weary. At that moment came in through the open window a long, wailing sound like the cry of a lost child in the far deeps of the darkening wood! But the man did not move. Again, and nearer than before, sounded that unearthly cry upon his failing sense. Perhaps it was a wild beast; perhaps it was a dream. For Murlock was asleep.

Some hours later, as it afterward appeared, this unfaithful watcher awoke and lifting his head from his arms intently listened – he knew not why. There in the black darkness by the side of the dead, recalling all without a shock, he strained his eyes to see – he knew not what. His senses were all alert, his breath was suspended, his blood had stilled its tides as if to assist the silence. Who – what had waked him, and where was it?

Suddenly the table shook beneath his arms, and at the same moment he heard, or fancied that he heard, a light, soft step – another – sounds as of bare feet upon the floor!

He was terrified beyond the power to cry out or move. Perforce he waited – waited there in the darkness through seeming centuries of such dread as one may know, yet live to tell. He tried vainly to speak the dead woman's name, vainly to stretch forth his hand across the table to learn if she were there. His throat was powerless, his arms and hands were like lead. Then occurred something most frightful. Some heavy body seemed hurled against the table with an impetus that pushed it against his breast so sharply as nearly to overthrow him, and at the same instant he heard and felt the fall of something upon the floor with so violent a thump that the whole house was shaken by the impact. A scuffling ensued, and a confusion of sounds impossible to describe. Murlock had risen to his feet. Fear had by excess forfeited control of his faculties. He flung his hands upon the table. Nothing was there!

There is a point at which terror may turn to madness; and madness incites to action. With no definite intent, from no motive but the wayward impulse of a madman, Murlock sprang to the wall, with a little groping seized his loaded rifle, and without aim discharged it. By the flash which lit up the room with a vivid illumination, he saw an enormous panther dragging the dead woman toward the window, its teeth fixed in her throat! Then there were darkness blacker than before, and silence; and when he returned to consciousness the sun was high and the wood vocal with songs of birds.

The body lay near the window, where the beast had left it when frightened away by the flash and report of the rifle. The clothing was deranged, the long hair in disorder, the limbs lay anyhow. From the throat, dreadfully lacerated, had issued a pool of blood not yet entirely coagulated. The ribbon with which he had bound the wrists was broken; the hands were tightly clenched. Between the teeth was a fragment of the animal's ear.

A Lady from Redhorse

Coronado, June 20

I find myself more and more interested in him. It is not, I am sure, his – do you know any noun corresponding to the adjective 'handsome'? One does not like to say 'beauty' when speaking of a man. He is handsome enough, heaven knows; I should not even care to trust you with him – faithful of all possible wives that you are – when he looks his best, as he always does. Nor do I think the fascination of his manner has much to do with it. You recollect that the charm of art inheres in that which is undefinable, and to you and me, my dear Irene, I fancy there is rather less of that in the branch of art under consideration than to girls in their first season. I fancy I know how my fine gentleman produces many of his effects, and could, perhaps, give him a pointer on heightening them. Nevertheless, his manner is something truly delightful. I suppose what interests me chiefly is the man's brains. His conversation is the best I have ever heard, and altogether unlike anyone's else. He seems to know everything, as, indeed, he ought, for he has been everywhere, read everything, seen all there is to see – sometimes I think rather more than is good for him – and had acquaintance with the *queerest* people. And then his voice – Irene, when I hear it I actually feel as if I ought to have *paid at the door*, though, of course, it is my own door.

July 3

I fear my remarks about Dr Barritz must have been, being thoughtless, very silly, or you would not have written of him with such levity, not to say disrespect. Believe me, dearest, he has more dignity and seriousness (of the kind, I mean, which is not inconsistent with a manner sometimes playful and always charming) than any of the men that you and I ever met. And young Raynor – you knew Raynor at Monterey – tells me that the men all like him, and that he is treated with something like deference everywhere. There is a mystery, too – something about his connection with the Blavatsky people in Northern India. Raynor either would not or could not tell me the particulars. I infer that Dr Barritz is thought – don't you dare to laugh at me – a magician! Could anything be finer than that? An ordinary mystery is not, of course, as good as a scandal, but when it relates to dark and dreadful practices – to the exercise of unearthly powers – could anything be more piquant? It explains, too, the singular influence the man has upon me. It is the undefinable in his art – black art. Seriously, dear, I quite tremble when he looks me full in the eyes with those unfathomable orbs of his, which I have already vainly attempted to describe to you. How dreadful if we have the power to make one fall in love! Do you know if the Blavatsky crowd have that power – outside of Sepoy?

July 1

The strangest thing! Last evening while Auntie was attending one of the hotel hops (I hate them) Dr Barritz called. It was scandalously late – I actually believe he had talked with Auntie in the ballroom, and learned from her that I was alone. I had been all the evening contriving how to worm out of him the truth about his connection with the Thugs in Sepoy, and all of that black business, but the moment he fixed his eyes on me (for I admitted him, I'm ashamed to say) I was helpless, I trembled, I blushed, I – O Irene, Irene, I love the man beyond expression, and you know how it is yourself!

Fancy! I, an ugly duckling from Redhorse – daughter (they say) of old Calamity Jim – certainly his heiress, with no living relation but an absurd old aunt, who spoils me a thousand and fifty ways – absolutely destitute of everything but a million dollars and a hope in Paris – I daring to love a god like him! My dear, if I had you here, I could tear your hair out with mortification.

I am convinced that he is aware of my feeling, for he stayed but a few moments, said nothing but what another man might have said half as well, and pretending that he had an engagement went away. I learned today (a little bird told me – the bell bird) that he went straight to bed. How does that strike you as evidence of exemplary habits?

July 17

That little wretch, Raynor, called yesterday, and his babble set me almost wild. He never runs down – that is to say, when he extermin- ates a score of reputations, more or less, he does not pause between one reputation and the next. (By the way, he enquired about you,

and his manifestations of interest in you had, I confess, a good deal
of *vraisemblance*.)

Mr Raynor observes no game laws; like Death (which he would
inflict if slander were fatal) he has all seasons for his own. But I like
him, for we knew one another at Redhorse when we were young and
true-hearted and barefooted. He was known in those far fair days as
'Giggles', and I – O Irene, can you ever forgive me? – I was called
'Gunny'. God knows why; perhaps in allusion to the material of my
pinafores; perhaps because the name is in alliteration with 'Giggles',
for Gig and I were inseparable playmates, and the miners may have
thought it a delicate compliment to recognise some kind of relation-
ship between us.

Later, we took in a third – another of Adversity's brood, who, like
Garrick between Tragedy and Comedy, had a chronic inability to
adjudicate the rival claims (to himself) of Frost and Famine. Between
him and the grave there was seldom anything more than a single
suspender and the hope of a meal which would at the same time
support life and make it insupportable. He literally picked up a
precarious living for himself and an aged mother by 'chloriding the
dumps', that is to say, the miners permitted him to search the heaps
of waste rock for such pieces of 'pay ore' as had been overlooked;
and these he sacked up and sold at the Syndicate Mill. He became a
member of our firm – 'Gunny, Giggles, and Dumps' thenceforth –
through my favour; for I could not then, nor can I now, be indifferent to his courage and prowess in defending against Giggles the
immemorial right of his sex to insult a strange and unprotected
female – myself. After old Jim struck it in the Calamity, and I began
to wear shoes and go to school, and in emulation Giggles took to
washing his face, and became Jack Raynor, of Wells, Fargo & Co.,
and old Mrs Barts was herself chlorided to her fathers, Dumps
drifted over to San Juan Smith and turned stage driver, and was
killed by road agents, and so forth.

Why do I tell you all this, dear? Because it is heavy on my heart.
Because I walk the Valley of Humility. Because I am subduing myself
to permanent consciousness of my unworthiness to unloose the
latchet of Dr Barritz's shoe. Because – oh, dear, oh, dear – there's a
cousin of Dumps at this hotel! I haven't spoken to him. I never had
any acquaintance with him, but – do you suppose he has recognised
me? Do, please, give me in your next your candid, sure-enough
opinion about it, and say you don't think so. Do you think He knows
about me already and that is why He left me last evening when He

saw that I blushed and trembled like a fool under His eyes? You know I can't bribe *all* the newspapers, and I can't go back on anybody who was good to Gunny at Redhorse – not if I'm pitched out of society into the sea. So the skeleton sometimes rattles behind the door. I never cared much before, as you know, but now – *now* it is not the same. Jack Raynor I am sure of – he will not tell him. He seems, indeed, to hold him in such respect as hardly to dare speak to him at all, and I'm a good deal that way myself. Dear, dear! I wish I had something besides a million dollars! If Jack were three inches taller I'd marry him alive and go back to Redhorse and wear sackcloth again to the end of my miserable days.

July 25

We had a perfectly splendid sunset last evening, and I must tell you all about it. I ran away from Auntie and everybody, and was walking alone on the beach. I expect you to believe, you infidel! that I had not looked out of my window on the seaward side of the hotel and seen him walking alone on the beach. If you are not lost to every feeling of womanly delicacy you will accept my statement without question. I soon established myself under my sunshade and had for some time been gazing out dreamily over the sea, when he approached, walking close to the edge of the water – it was ebb tide. I assure you the wet sand actually brightened about his feet! As he approached me, he lifted his hat, saying: 'Miss Dement, may I sit with you? – or will you walk with me?'

The possibility that neither might be agreeable seems not to have occurred to him. Did you ever know such assurance? Assurance? My dear, it was gall, downright *gall*! Well, I didn't find it wormwood, and replied, with my untutored Redhorse heart in my throat: 'I – I shall be pleased to do *anything*.' Could words have been more stupid? There are depths of fatuity in me, friend o' my soul, which are simply bottomless!

He extended his hand, smiling, and I delivered mine into it without a moment's hesitation, and when his fingers closed about it to assist me to my feet, the consciousness that it trembled made me blush worse than the red west. I got up, however, and after a while, observing that he had not let go my hand, I pulled on it a little, but unsuccessfully. He simply held on, saying nothing, but looking down into my face with some kind of a smile – I didn't know – how could I? – whether it was affectionate, derisive, or what, for I did not look at him. How beautiful he was! – with the red fires of the sunset burning in the depths of his eyes. Do you know, dear, if the Thugs and Experts of the Blavatsky region have any special kind of eyes? Ah, you should have seen his superb attitude, the godlike inclination of his head as he stood over me after I had got upon my feet! It was a noble picture, but I soon destroyed it, for I began at once to sink again to the earth. There was only one thing for him to do, and he did it; he supported me with an arm about my waist.

'Miss Dement, are you ill?' he said.

It was not an exclamation; there was neither alarm nor solicitude in it. If he had added: 'I suppose that is about what I am expected to say,' he would hardly have expressed his sense of the situation more clearly. His manner filled me with shame and indignation, for I was suffering acutely. I wrenched my hand out of his, grasped the arm supporting me, and, pushing myself free, fell plump into the sand and sat helpless. My hat had fallen off in the struggle, and my hair tumbled about my face and shoulders in the most mortifying way.

'Go away from me,' I cried, half-choking. 'Oh, *please* go away, you – you Thug! How dare you think *that* when my leg is asleep?'

I actually said those identical words! And then I broke down and sobbed. Irene, I *blubbered*!

His manner altered in an instant – I could see that much through my fingers and hair. He dropped on one knee beside me, parted the tangle of hair, and said, in the tenderest way: 'My poor girl, God knows I have not intended to pain you. How should I? – I who love you – I who have loved you for – for years and years!'

He had pulled my wet hands away from my face and was covering them with kisses. My cheeks were like two coals, my whole face was flaming and, I think, steaming. What could I do? I hid it on his shoulder – there was no other place. And, oh, my dear friend, how my leg tingled and thrilled, and how I wanted to kick!

We sat so for a long time. He had released one of my hands to pass his arm about me again, and I possessed myself of my handkerchief and was drying my eyes and my nose. I would not look up until that was done; he tried in vain to push me a little away and gaze into my eyes. Presently, when it was all right, and it had grown a bit dark, I lifted my head, looked him straight in the eyes, and smiled my best – my level best, dear.

'What do you mean,' I said, 'by "years and years"?'

'Dearest,' he replied, very gravely, very earnestly, 'in the absence of the sunken cheeks, the hollow eyes, the lank hair, the slouching gait, the rags, dirt, and youth, can you not – will you not understand? Gunny, I'm Dumps!'

In a moment I was upon my feet and he upon his. I seized him by the lapels of his coat and peered into his handsome face in the deepening darkness. I was breathless with excitement.

'And you are not dead?' I asked, hardly knowing what I said.

'Only dead in love, dear. I recovered from the road agent's bullet, but this, I fear, is fatal.'

'But about Jack – Mr Raynor? Don't you know – '

'I am ashamed to say, darling, that it was through that unworthy person's invitation that I came here from Vienna.'

Irene, they have played it upon your affectionate friend,

MARY JANE DEMENT

P.S. – The worst of it is that there is no mystery. That was an invention of Jack to arouse my curiosity and interest. James is not a Thug. He solemnly assures me that in all his wanderings he has never set foot in Sepoy.

The Famous Gilson Bequest

It was rough on Gilson. Such was the terse, cold, but not altogether unsympathetic judgement of the better public opinion at Mammon Hill – the dictum of respectability. The verdict of the opposite, or rather the opposing, element – the element that lurked red-eyed and restless about Moll Gurney's 'deadfall', while respectability took it with sugar at Mr Jo. Bentley's gorgeous 'saloon' – was to pretty much the same general effect, though somewhat more ornately expressed by the use of picturesque expletives, which it is needless to quote. Virtually, Mammon Hill was a unit on the Gilson question. And it must be confessed that in a merely temporal sense all was not well with Mr Gilson. He had that morning been led into town by Mr Brentshaw and publicly charged with horse stealing; the sheriff meantime busying himself about The Tree with a new manila rope and Carpenter Pete being actively employed between drinks upon a pine box about the length and breadth of Mr Gilson. Society having rendered its verdict, there remained between Gilson and eternity only the decent formality of a trial.

These are the short and simple annals of the prisoner: he had recently been a resident of New Jerusalem, on the north fork of the Little Stony, but had come to the newly discovered placers of Mammon Hill immediately before the 'rush' by which the former place was depopulated. The discovery of the new diggings had occurred opportunely for Mr Gilson, for it had only just before been intimated to him by a New Jerusalem vigilance committee that it would better his prospects in, and for, life to go somewhere; and the list of places to which he could safely go did not include any of the older camps; so he naturally established himself at Mammon Hill. Being eventually followed thither by all his judges, he ordered his conduct with considerable circumspection, but as he had never been known to do an honest day's work at any industry sanctioned by the stern local code of morality except draw poker he was still an object of suspicion. Indeed, it was conjectured that he was the author of the many daring depredations that had recently been committed with pan and brush on the sluice boxes.

Prominent among those in whom this suspicion had ripened into a steadfast conviction was Mr Brentshaw. At all seasonable and un-seasonable times Mr Brentshaw avowed his belief in Mr Gilson's connection with these unholy midnight enterprises, and his own willingness to prepare a way for the solar beams through the body of anyone who might think it expedient to utter a different opinion – which, in his presence, no-one was more careful not to do than the peace-loving person most concerned. Whatever may have been the truth of the matter, it is certain that Gilson frequently lost more 'clean dust' at Jo. Bentley's faro table than it was recorded in local history that he had ever honestly earned at draw poker in all the days of the camp's existence. But at last Mr Bentley – fearing, it may be, to lose the more profitable patronage of Mr Brentshaw – peremptorily refused to let Gilson copper the queen, intimating at the same time, in his frank, forthright way, that the privilege of losing money at 'this bank' was a blessing appertaining to, proceeding logically from, and coterminous with, a condition of notorious commercial righteousness and social good repute.

The Hill thought it high time to look after a person whom its most honoured citizen had felt it his duty to rebuke at a considerable personal sacrifice. The New Jerusalem contingent, particularly, began to abate something of the toleration begotten of amusement at their own blunder in exiling an objectionable neighbour from the place which they had left to the place whither they had come. Mammon Hill was at last of one mind. Not much was said, but that Gilson must hang was 'in the air'. But at this critical juncture in his affairs he showed signs of an altered life if not a changed heart. Perhaps it was only that 'the bank' being closed against him he had no further use for gold dust. Anyhow the sluice boxes were molested no more forever. But it was impossible to repress the abounding energies of such a nature as his, and he continued, possibly from habit, the tortuous courses which he had pursued for profit of Mr Bentley. After a few tentative and resultless undertakings in the way of high-way robbery – if one may venture to designate road-agency by so harsh a name – he made one or two modest essays in horse-herding, and it was in the midst of a promising enterprise of this character, and just as he had taken the tide in his affairs at its flood, that he made shipwreck. For on a misty, moonlight night Mr Brentshaw rode up alongside a person who was evidently leaving that part of the country, laid a hand upon the halter connecting Mr Gilson's wrist with Mr Harper's bay mare, tapped him familiarly on the cheek with the barrel of a navy revolver and requested the pleasure of his company in a direction opposite to that in which he was travelling.

It was indeed rough on Gilson.

On the morning after his arrest he was tried, convicted, and sentenced. It only remains, so far as concerns his earthly career, to hang him, reserving for more particular mention his last will and testament, which, with great labour, he contrived in prison, and in which, probably from some confused and imperfect notion of the rights of captors, he bequeathed everything he owned to his 'lawfle execketer', Mr Brentshaw. The bequest, however, was made conditional on the legatee taking the testator's body from The Tree and 'planting it white'.

So Mr Gilson was – I was about to say 'swung off', but I fear there has been already something too much of slang in this straightforward statement of facts; besides, the manner in which the law took its course is more accurately described in the terms employed by the judge in passing sentence: Mr Gilson was 'strung up'.

In due season Mr Brentshaw, somewhat touched, it may well be, by the empty compliment of the bequest, repaired to The Tree to pluck the fruit thereof. When taken down the body was found to have in its waistcoat pocket a duly attested codicil to the will already noted. The nature of its provisions accounted for the manner in which it had been withheld, for had Mr Brentshaw previously been made aware of the conditions under which he was to succeed to the Gilson estate he would indubitably have declined the responsibility. Briefly stated, the purport of the codicil was as follows:

Whereas, at divers times and in sundry places, certain persons had asserted that during his life the testator had robbed their sluice boxes; therefore, if during the five years next succeeding the date of this instrument anyone should make proof of such assertion before a court of law, such person was to receive as reparation the entire personal and real estate of which the testator died seized and possessed, minus the expenses of court and a stated compensation to the executor, Henry Clay Brentshaw; provided, that if more than one person made such proof the estate was to be equally divided between or among them. But in case none should succeed in so establishing the testator's guilt, then the whole property, minus court expenses, as aforesaid, should go to the said Henry Clay Brentshaw for his own use, as stated in the will.

The syntax of this remarkable document was perhaps open to critical objection, but that was clearly enough the meaning of it. The orthography conformed to no recognised system, but being mainly phonetic it was not ambiguous. As the probate judge remarked, it would take five aces to beat it. Mr Brentshaw smiled good-humouredly, and after performing the last sad rites with amusing ostentation, had himself duly sworn as executor and conditional legatee under the provisions of a law hastily passed (at the instance of the member from the Mammon Hill district) by a facetious legislature; which law was afterward discovered to have created also three or four lucrative offices and authorised the expenditure of a considerable sum of public money for the construction of a certain railway bridge that with greater advantage might perhaps have been erected on the line of some actual railway.

Of course Mr Brentshaw expected neither profit from the will nor litigation in consequence of its unusual provisions; Gilson, although frequently 'flush', had been a man whom assessors and tax collectors were well satisfied to lose no money by. But a careless and merely formal search among his papers revealed title deeds to valuable estates in the East and certificates of deposit for incredible sums in banks less severely scrupulous than that of Mr Jo. Bentley.

The astounding news got abroad directly, throwing the Hill into a fever of excitement. The Mammon Hill *Patriot*, whose editor had been a leading spirit in the proceedings that resulted in Gilson's departure from New Jerusalem, published a most complimentary obituary notice of the deceased, and was good enough to call attention to the fact that his degraded contemporary, the Squaw Gulch *Clarion*, was bringing virtue into contempt by beslavering with flattery the memory of one who in life had spurned the vile sheet as a nuisance from his door. Undeterred by the press, however, claimants under the will were not slow in presenting themselves with their evidence; and great as was the Gilson estate it appeared conspicuously paltry considering the vast number of sluice boxes from which it was averred to have been obtained. The country rose as one man!

Mr Brentshaw was equal to the emergency. With a shrewd application of humble auxiliary devices, he at once erected above the bones of his benefactor a costly monument, overtopping every rough head-board in the cemetery, and on this he judiciously caused to be in-scribed an epitaph of his own composing, eulogising the honesty, public spirit and cognate virtues of him who slept beneath, 'a victim to the unjust aspersions of Slander's viper brood'.

Moreover, he employed the best legal talent in the Territory to defend the memory of his departed friend, and for five long years the Territorial courts were occupied with litigation growing out of the Gilson bequest. To fine forensic abilities Mr Brentshaw opposed abilities more finely forensic; in bidding for purchasable favours he offered prices which utterly deranged the market; the judges found at his hospitable board entertainment for man and beast, the like of which had never been spread in the Territory; with mendacious witnesses he confronted witnesses of superior mendacity.

Nor was the battle confined to the temple of the blind goddess – it invaded the press, the pulpit, the drawing-room. It raged in the mart, the exchange, the school; in the gulches, and on the street corners. And upon the last day of the memorable period to which legal action under the Gilson will was limited, the sun went down upon a region in which the moral sense was dead, the social con-science callous, the intellectual capacity dwarfed, enfeebled, and confused! But Mr Brentshaw was victorious all along the line.

On that night it so happened that the cemetery in one corner of which lay the now honoured ashes of the late Milton Gilson, Esq., was partly under water. Swollen by incessant rains, Cat Creek had spilled over its banks an angry flood which, after scooping out unsightly hollows wherever the soil had been disturbed, had partly subsided, as if ashamed of the sacrilege, leaving exposed much that had been piously concealed. Even the famous Gilson monument, the pride and glory of Mammon Hill, was no longer a standing rebuke to the 'viper brood'; succumbing to the sapping current it had toppled prone to earth. The ghoulish flood had exhumed the poor, decayed pine coffin, which now lay half-exposed, in pitiful contrast to the pompous monolith which, like a giant note of admiration, emphas-ised the disclosure.

To this depressing spot, drawn by some subtle influence he had sought neither to resist nor analyze, came Mr Brentshaw. An altered man was Mr Brentshaw. Five years of toil, anxiety, and wakefulness had dashed his black locks with streaks and patches of grey, bowed his fine figure, drawn sharp and angular his face, and debased his walk to a doddering shuffle. Nor had this lustrum of fierce contention wrought less upon his heart and intellect. The careless good humour that had prompted him to accept the trust of the dead man had given place to a fixed habit of melancholy. The firm, vigorous intellect had overripened into the mental mellowness of second childhood. His broad understanding had narrowed to the accommodation of a single idea; and in place of the quiet, cynical incredulity of former days, there was in him a haunting faith in the supernatural, that flitted and fluttered about his soul, shadowy, batlike, ominous of insanity. Unsettled in all else, his understanding clung to one conviction with the tenacity of a wrecked intellect. That was an unshaken belief in the entire blamelessness of the dead Gilson. He had so often sworn to this in court and asserted it in private conversation – had so frequently and so triumphantly established it by testimony that had come expensive to him (for that very day he had paid the last dollar of the Gilson estate to Mr Jo. Bentley, the last witness to the Gilson good character) – that it had become to him a sort of religious faith. It seemed to him the one great central and basic truth of life – the sole serene verity in a world of lies.

On that night, as he seated himself pensively upon the prostrate monument, trying by the uncertain moonlight to spell out the epitaph which five years before he had composed with a chuckle that memory had not recorded, tears of remorse came into his eyes as he remembered that he had been mainly instrumental in compassing by a false accusation this good man's death; for during some of the legal proceedings, Mr Harper, for a consideration (forgotten) had come forward and sworn that in the little transaction with his bay mare the deceased had acted in strict accordance with the Harperian wishes, confidentially communicated to the deceased and by him faithfully concealed at the cost of his life. All that Mr Brentshaw had since done for the dead man's memory seemed pitifully inadequate – most mean, paltry, and debased with selfishness!

As he sat there, torturing himself with futile regrets, a faint shadow fell across his eyes. Looking toward the moon, hanging low in the west, he saw what seemed a vague, watery cloud obscuring her; but as it moved so that her beams lit up one side of it he perceived the clear, sharp outline of a human figure. The apparition became momentarily more distinct, and grew, visibly; it was drawing near. Dazed as were his senses, half locked up with terror and confounded with dreadful imaginings, Mr Brentshaw yet could but perceive, or think he perceived, in this unearthly shape a strange similitude to the mortal part of the late Milton Gilson, as that person had looked when taken from The Tree five years before. The likeness was indeed complete, even to the full, stony eyes, and a certain shadowy circle about the neck. It was without coat or hat, precisely as Gilson had been when laid in his poor, cheap casket by the not ungentle hands of Carpenter Pete – for whom someone had long since performed the same neighbourly office. The spectre, if such it was, seemed to bear something in its hands which Mr Brentshaw could not clearly make out. It drew nearer, and paused at last beside the coffin containing the ashes of the late Mr Gilson, the lid of which was awry, half-disclosing the uncertain interior. Bending over this, the phantom seemed to shake into it from a basin some dark substance of dubious consistency, then glided stealthily back to the lowest part of the cemetery. Here the retiring flood had stranded a number of open coffins, about and among which it gurgled with low sobbings and stilly whispers. Stooping over one of these, the apparition carefully brushed its contents into the basin, then returning to its own casket, emptied the vessel into that, as before. This mysterious operation was repeated at every exposed coffin, the ghost sometimes dipping its laden basin into the running water, and gently agitating it to free it of the baser clay, always hoarding the residuum in its own private box. In short, the immortal part of the late Milton Gilson was cleaning up the dust of its neighbours and providently adding the same to its own.

Perhaps it was a phantasm of a disordered mind in a fevered body. Perhaps it was a solemn farce enacted by pranking existences that throng the shadows lying along the border of another world. God knows; to us is permitted only the knowledge that when the sun of another day touched with a grace of gold the ruined cemetery of Mammon Hill his kindliest beam fell upon the white, still face of Henry Brentshaw, dead among the dead.

A Holy Terror

There was an entire lack of interest in the latest arrival at Hurdy-Gurdy. He was not even christened with the picturesquely descriptive nick-name which is so frequently a mining camp's word of welcome to the newcomer. In almost any other camp thereabout this circumstance would of itself have secured him some such appellation as 'The White-headed Conundrum,' or 'No Sarvey' – an expression naively supposed to suggest to quick intelligences the Spanish *quien sabe*. He came without provoking a ripple of concern upon the social surface of Hurdy-Gurdy – a place which to the general Californian contempt of men's personal history superadded a local indifference of its own. The time was long past when it was of any importance who came there, or if anybody came. No-one was living at Hurdy-Gurdy.

Two years before, the camp had boasted a stirring population of two or three thousand males and not fewer than a dozen females. A majority of the former had done a few weeks' earnest work in demonstrating, to the disgust of the latter, the singularly mendacious character of the person whose ingenious tales of rich gold deposits had lured them thither – work, by the way, in which there was as little mental satisfaction as pecuniary profit; for a bullet from the pistol of a public-spirited citizen had put that imaginative gentleman beyond the reach of aspersion on the third day of the camp's existence. Still, his fiction had a certain foundation in fact, and many had lingered a considerable time in and about Hurdy-Gurdy, though now all had been long gone.

But they had left ample evidence of their sojourn. From the point where Injun Creek falls into the Rio San Juan Smith, up along both banks of the former into the canyon whence it emerges, extended a double row of forlorn shanties that seemed about to fall upon one another's neck to bewail their desolation; while about an equal number appeared to have straggled up the slope on either hand

and perched themselves upon commanding eminences, whence they craned forward to get a good view of the affecting scene. Most of these habitations were emaciated as by famine to the condition of mere skeletons, about which clung unlovely tatters of what might have been skin, but was really canvas. The little valley itself, torn and gashed by pick and shovel, was unhandsome with long, bending lines of decaying flume resting here and there upon the summits of sharp ridges, and stilting awkwardly across the intervals upon un-hewn poles. The whole place presented that raw and forbidding aspect of arrested development which is a new country's substitute for the solemn grace of ruin wrought by time. Wherever there remained a patch of the original soil a rank overgrowth of weeds and brambles had spread upon the scene, and from its dank, unwholesome shades the visitor curious in such matters might have obtained numberless souvenirs of the camp's former glory – fellowless boots mantled with green mould and plethoric of rotting leaves; an occasional old felt hat; desultory remnants of a flannel shirt; sardine boxes inhumanly mutilated and a surprising profusion of black bottles distributed with a truly catholic impartiality, everywhere.

2

The man who had now rediscovered Hurdy-Gurdy was evidently not curious as to its archaeology. Nor, as he looked about him upon the dismal evidences of wasted work and broken hopes, their dis-piriting significance accentuated by the ironical pomp of a cheap gilding by the rising sun, did he supplement his sigh of weariness by one of sensibility. He simply removed from the back of his tired burro a miner's outfit a trifle larger than the animal itself, picketed that creature, and selecting a hatchet from his kit moved off at once across the dry bed of Injun Creek to the top of a low, gravelly hill beyond.

Stepping across a prostrate fence of brush and boards he picked up one of the latter, split it into five parts and sharpened them at one end. He then began a kind of search, occasionally stooping to examine something with close attention. At last his patient scrutiny appeared to be rewarded with success, for he suddenly erected his figure to its full height, made a gesture of satisfaction, pronounced the word 'Scarry' and at once strode away with long, equal steps, which he counted. Then he stopped and drove one of his stakes into the earth. He then looked carefully about him, measured off a number of paces over a singularly uneven ground and hammered in another. Pacing off twice the distance at a right angle to his former course he drove down a third, and repeating the process sank home the fourth, and then a fifth. This he split at the top and in the cleft inserted an old letter envelope covered with an intricate system of pencil tracks. In short, he staked off a hill-claim in strict accordance with the local mining laws of Hurdy-Gurdy and put up the customary notice.

It is necessary to explain that one of the adjuncts to Hurdy-Gurdy – one to which that metropolis became afterward itself an adjunct – was a cemetery. In the first week of the camp's existence this had been thoughtfully laid out by a committee of citizens. The day after had been signalised by a debate between two members of the committee, with reference to a more eligible site, and on the third day the necropolis was inaugurated by a double funeral. As the camp had waned the cemetery had waxed; and long before the ultimate inhabitant, victorious alike over the insidious malaria and the forthright revolver, had turned the tail of his pack-ass upon Injun Creek the outlying settlement had become a populous if not popular suburb. And now, when the town was fallen into the sere and yellow leaf of an unlovely senility, the graveyard – though somewhat marred by time and circumstance, and not altogether exempt from innovations in grammar and experiments in orthography, to say nothing of the devastating coyote – answered the humble needs of its denizens with reasonable completeness. It comprised a generous two acres of ground, which with commendable thrift but needless care had been selected for its mineral unworth, contained two or three skeleton trees (one of which had a stout lateral branch from which a weather-wasted rope still significantly dangled), half a hundred gravelly mounds, a score of rude headboards displaying the literary peculiarities above mentioned and a struggling colony of prickly pears. Altogether, God's Location, as with characteristic reverence it had been called, could justly boast of an indubitably superior quality of desolation. It was in the most thickly settled part of this interesting demesne that Mr Jefferson Doman staked off his claim. If in the prosecution of his design he should deem it expedient to remove any of the dead they would have the right to be suitably reinterred.

3

This Mr Jefferson Doman was from Elizabethtown, New Jersey, where six years before he had left his heart in the keeping of a golden-haired, demure-mannered young woman named Mary Matthews, as collateral security for his return to claim her hand.

'I just *know* you'll never get back alive – you never do succeed in anything,' was the remark which illustrated Miss Matthews's notion of what constituted success and, inferentially, her view of the nature of encouragement. She added: 'If you don't I'll go to California too. I can put the coins in little bags as you dig them out.'

This characteristically feminine theory of auriferous deposits did not commend itself to the masculine intelligence: it was Mr Doman's belief that gold was found in a liquid state. He deprecated her intent with considerable enthusiasm, suppressed her sobs with a light hand upon her mouth, laughed in her eyes as he kissed away her tears, and with a cheerful 'Ta-ta' went to California to labour for her through the long, loveless years, with a strong heart, an alert hope and a steadfast fidelity that never for a moment forgot what it was about. In the meantime, Miss Matthews had granted a monopoly of her humble talent for sacking up coins to Mr Jo. Seeman, of New York, gambler, by whom it was better appreciated than her commanding genius for unsacking and bestowing them upon his local rivals. Of this latter aptitude, indeed, he manifested his disapproval by an act which secured him the position of clerk of the laundry in the State prison, and for her the sobriquet of 'Split-faced Moll'. At about this time she wrote to Mr Doman a touching letter of renunciation, enclosing her photograph to prove that she had no longer had a right to indulge the dream of becoming Mrs Doman, and recounting so graphically her fall from a horse that the staid 'plug' upon which Mr Doman had ridden into Red Dog to get the letter made vicarious atonement under the spur all the way back to camp. The letter failed in a signal way to accomplish its object; the fidelity which had before been to Mr Doman a matter of love and duty was thenceforth a matter of honour also; and the photograph, showing the once pretty face sadly disfigured as by the slash of a knife, was duly instated in his affections and its more comely predecessor treated with contumelious neglect. On being informed of this, Miss Matthews, it is only fair to say, appeared less surprised than from the apparently low estimate of Mr Doman's generosity which the tone of her former letter attested one would naturally have expected her to be. Soon after, however, her letters grew infrequent, and then ceased altogether.

But Mr Doman had another correspondent, Mr Barney Bree, of Hurdy-Gurdy, formerly of Red Dog. This gentleman, although a notable figure among miners, was not a miner. His knowledge of mining consisted mainly in a marvellous command of its slang, to which he made copious contributions, enriching its vocabulary with a wealth of uncommon phrases more remarkable for their aptness than their refinement, and which impressed the unlearned 'tenderfoot' with a lively sense of the profundity of their inventor's acquirements. When not entertaining a circle of admiring auditors from San Francisco or the East he could commonly be found pursuing the comparatively obscure industry of sweeping out the various dance houses and purifying the cuspidors.

Barney had apparently but two passions in life – love of Jefferson Doman, who had once been of some service to him, and love of whisky, which certainly had not. He had been among the first in the rush to Hurdy-Gurdy, but had not prospered, and had sunk by degrees to the position of grave-digger. This was not a vocation, but Barney in a desultory way turned his trembling hand to it whenever some local misunderstanding at the card table and his own partial recovery from a prolonged debauch occurred coincidently in point of time. One day Mr Doman received, at Red Dog, a letter with the simple postmark, 'Hurdy, Cal.', and being occupied with another matter, carelessly thrust it into a chink of his cabin for future perusal. Some two years later it was accidentally dislodged and he read it. It ran as follows:

Hurdy, June 6

FRIEND JEFF: I've hit her hard in the boneyard. She's blind and lousy. I'm on the divvy – that's me, and mum's my lay till you toot.

Yours, BARNEY

P.S. – I've clayed her with Scarry.

With some knowledge of the general mining camp argot and of Mr Bree's private system for the communication of ideas Mr Doman had no difficulty in understanding by this uncommon epistle that Barney while performing his duty as grave digger had uncovered a quartz ledge with no outcroppings; that it was visibly rich in free gold; that, moved by considerations of friendship, he was willing to accept Mr Doman as a partner and awaiting that gentleman's declaration of his will in the matter would discreetly keep the discovery a secret. From the postscript it was plainly inferable that in order to conceal the treasure he had buried above it the mortal part of a person named Scarry.

From subsequent events, as related to Mr Doman at Red Dog, it would appear that before taking this precaution Mr Bree must have had the thrift to remove a modest competency of the gold; at any rate, it was at about that time that he entered upon that memorable series of potations and treatings which is still one of the cherished traditions of the San Juan Smith country, and is spoken of with respect as far away as Ghost Rock and Lone Hand. At its conclusion some former citizens of Hurdy-Gurdy, for whom he had performed the last kindly office at the cemetery, made room for him among them, and he rested well.

4

Having finished staking off his claim Mr Doman walked back to the centre of it and stood again at the spot where his search among the graves had expired in the exclamation, 'Scarry'. He bent again over the headboard that bore that name and as if to reinforce the senses of sight and hearing ran his forefinger along the rudely carved letters. Re-erecting himself he appended orally to the simple inscription the shockingly forthright epitaph, 'She was a holy terror!'

Had Mr Doman been required to make these words good with proof – as, considering their somewhat censorious character, he doubtless should have been – he would have found himself embarrassed by the absence of reputable witnesses, and hearsay evidence would have been the best he could command. At the time when Scarry had been prevalent in the mining camps thereabout – when, as the editor of the *Hurdy Herald* would have phrased it, she was 'in the plenitude of her power' – Mr Doman's fortunes had been at a low ebb, and he had led the vagrantly laborious life of a prospector. His time had been mostly spent in the mountains, now with one companion, now with another. It was from the admiring recitals of these casual partners, fresh from the various camps, that his judgement of Scarry had been made up; he himself had never had the doubtful advantage of her acquaintance and the precarious distinction of her favour. And when, finally, on the termination of her perverse career at Hurdy-Gurdy he had read in a chance copy of the *Herald* her column-long obituary (written by the local

humorist of that lively sheet in the highest style of his art) Doman
had paid to her memory and to her historiographer's genius the
tribute of a smile and chivalrously forgotten her. Standing now at
the graveside of this mountain Messalina he recalled the leading
events of her turbulent career, as he had heard them celebrated at
his several campfires, and perhaps with an unconscious attempt at
self-justification repeated that she was a holy terror, and sank his
pick into her grave up to the handle. At that moment a raven, which
had silently settled upon a branch of the blasted tree above his head,
solemnly snapped its beak and uttered its mind about the matter
with an approving croak.

Pursuing his discovery of free gold with great zeal, which he
probably credited to his conscience as a grave-digger, Mr Barney
Bree had made an unusually deep sepulchre, and it was near sunset
before Mr Doman, labouring with the leisurely deliberation of one
who has 'a dead sure thing' and no fear of an adverse claimant's
enforcement of a prior right, reached the coffin and uncovered it.
When he had done so he was confronted by a difficulty for which he
had made no provision; the coffin – a mere flat shell of not very well-
preserved redwood boards, apparently – had no handles, and it filled
the entire bottom of the excavation. The best he could do without
violating the decent sanctities of the situation was to make the
excavation sufficiently longer to enable him to stand at the head of
the casket and getting his powerful hands underneath erect it upon
its narrower end; and this he proceeded to do. The approach of night
quickened his efforts. He had no thought of abandoning his task at
this stage to resume it on the morrow under more advantageous
conditions. The feverish stimulation of cupidity and the fascination
of terror held him to his dismal work with an iron authority. He no
longer idled, but wrought with a terrible zeal. His head uncovered,
his outer garments discarded, his shirt opened at the neck and
thrown back from his breast, down which ran sinuous rills of per-
spiration, this hardy and impenitent gold-getter and grave-robber
toiled with a giant energy that almost dignified the character of his
horrible purpose; and when the sun fringes had burned themselves
out along the crest line of the western hills, and the full moon had
climbed out of the shadows that lay along the purple plain, he had
erected the coffin upon its foot, where it stood propped against the
end of the open grave. Then, standing up to his neck in the earth at
the opposite extreme of the excavation, as he looked at the coffin
upon which the moonlight now fell with a full illumination, he was

thrilled with a sudden terror to observe upon it the startling apparition of a dark human head – the shadow of his own. For a moment
this simple and natural circumstance unnerved him. The noise of his
laboured breathing frightened him, and he tried to still it, but his
bursting lungs would not be denied. Then, laughing half-audibly
and wholly without spirit, he began making movements of his head
from side to side, in order to compel the apparition to repeat them.
He found a comforting reassurance in asserting his command over
his own shadow. He was temporising, making, with unconscious
prudence, a dilatory opposition to an impending catastrophe. He felt
that invisible forces of evil were closing in upon him, and he parleyed
for time with the Inevitable.

He now observed in succession several unusual circumstances.
The surface of the coffin upon which his eyes were fastened was not
flat; it presented two distinct ridges, one longitudinal and the other
transverse. Where these intersected at the widest part there was a
corroded metallic plate that reflected the moonlight with a dismal
lustre. Along the outer edges of the coffin, at long intervals, were
rust-eaten heads of nails. This frail product of the carpenter's art had
been put into the grave the wrong side up!

Perhaps it was one of the humours of the camp – a practical
manifestation of the facetious spirit that had found literary expression
in the topsy-turvy obituary notice from the pen of Hurdy-Gurdy's
great humorist. Perhaps it had some occult personal signification
impenetrable to understandings uninstructed in local traditions. A
more charitable hypothesis is that it was owing to a misadventure on
the part of Mr Barney Bree, who, making the interment unassisted
(either by choice for the conservation of his golden secret, or through
public apathy), had committed a blunder which he was afterward
unable or unconcerned to rectify. However it had come about, poor
Scarry had indubitably been put into the earth face downward.

When terror and absurdity make alliance, the effect is frightful. This strong-hearted and daring man, this hardy night worker
among the dead, this defiant antagonist of darkness and desolation,
succumbed to a ridiculous surprise. He was smitten with a thrilling
chill – shivered, and shook his massive shoulders as if to throw off
an icy hand. He no longer breathed, and the blood in his veins,
unable to abate its impetus, surged hotly beneath his cold skin.
Unleavened with oxygen, it mounted to his head and congested his
brain. His physical functions had gone over to the enemy; his very
heart was arrayed against him. He did not move; he could not have

cried out. He needed but a coffin to be dead – as dead as the death
that confronted him with only the length of an open grave and the
thickness of a rotting plank between.

Then, one by one, his senses returned; the tide of terror that had
overwhelmed his faculties began to recede. But with the return of his
senses he became singularly unconscious of the object of his fear. He
saw the moonlight gilding the coffin, but no longer the coffin that it
gilded. Raising his eyes and turning his head, he noted, curiously and
with surprise, the black branches of the dead tree, and tried to
estimate the length of the weather-worn rope that dangled from its
ghostly hand. The monotonous barking of distant coyotes affected
him as something he had heard years ago in a dream. An owl flapped
awkwardly above him on noiseless wings, and he tried to forecast the
direction of its flight when it should encounter the cliff that reared
its illuminated front a mile away. His hearing took account of a
gopher's stealthy tread in the shadow of the cactus. He was intensely
observant; his senses were all alert; but he saw not the coffin. As
one can gaze at the sun until it looks black and then vanishes, so his
mind, having exhausted its capacities of dread, was no longer conscious of the separate existence of anything dreadful. The Assassin
was cloaking the sword.

It was during this lull in the battle that he became sensible of a
faint, sickening odour. At first he thought it was that of a rattle-
snake, and involuntarily tried to look about his feet. They were
nearly invisible in the gloom of the grave. A hoarse, gurgling sound,
like the death-rattle in a human throat, seemed to come out of the
sky, and a moment later a great, black, angular shadow, like the same
sound made visible, dropped curving from the topmost branch of
the spectral tree, fluttered for an instant before his face and sailed
fiercely away into the mist along the creek.

It was the raven. The incident recalled him to a sense of the
situation, and again his eyes sought the upright coffin, now illuminated by the moon for half its length. He saw the gleam of the metallic
plate and tried without moving to decipher the inscription. Then he
fell to speculating upon what was behind it. His creative imagination
presented him a vivid picture. The planks no longer seemed an
obstacle to his vision and he saw the livid corpse of the dead woman,
standing in grave-clothes, and staring vacantly at him, with lidless,
shrunken eyes. The lower jaw was fallen, the upper lip drawn away
from the uncovered teeth. He could make out a mottled pattern on
the hollow cheeks – the maculations of decay. By some mysterious

process his mind reverted for the first time that day to the photograph of Mary Matthews. He contrasted its blonde beauty with the forbidding aspect of this dead face – the most beloved object that he knew with the most hideous that he could conceive.

The Assassin now advanced and displaying the blade laid it against the victim's throat. That is to say, the man became at first dimly, then definitely, aware of an impressive coincidence – a relation – a parallel between the face on the card and the name on the headboard. The one was disfigured, the other described a disfiguration. The thought took hold of him and shook him. It transformed the face that his imagination had created behind the coffin lid; the contrast became a resemblance; the resemblance grew to identity. Remembering the many descriptions of Scarry's personal appearance that he had heard from the gossips of his camp-fire he tried with imperfect success to recall the exact nature of the disfiguration that had given the woman her ugly name; and what was lacking in his memory fancy supplied, stamping it with the validity of conviction. In the maddening attempt to recall such scraps of the woman's history as he had heard, the muscles of his arms and hands were strained to a painful tension, as by an effort to lift a great weight. His body writhed and twisted with the exertion. The tendons of his neck stood out as tense as whip-cords, and his breath came in short, sharp gasps. The catastrophe could not be much longer delayed, or the agony of anticipation would leave nothing to be done by the *coup de grâce* of verification. The scarred face behind the lid would slay him through the wood.

A movement of the coffin diverted his thought. It came forward to within a foot of his face, growing visibly larger as it approached. The rusted metallic plate, with an inscription illegible in the moonlight, looked him steadily in the eye. Determined not to shrink, he tried to brace his shoulders more firmly against the end of the excavation, and nearly fell backward in the attempt. There was nothing to support him; he had unconsciously moved upon his enemy, clutching the heavy knife that he had drawn from his belt. The coffin had not advanced and he smiled to think it could not retreat. Lifting his knife he struck the heavy hilt against the metal plate with all his power. There was a sharp, ringing percussion, and with a dull clatter the whole decayed coffin lid broke in pieces and came away, falling about his feet. The quick and the dead were face to face – the frenzied, shrieking man – the woman standing tranquil in her silences. She was a holy terror!

5

Some months later a party of men and women belonging to the highest social circles of San Francisco passed through Hurdy-Gurdy on their way to the Yosemite Valley by a new trail. They halted for dinner and during its preparation explored the desolate camp. One of the party had been at Hurdy-Gurdy in the days of its glory. He had, indeed, been one of its prominent citizens; and it used to be said that more money passed over his faro table in any one night than over those of all his competitors in a week; but being now a millionaire engaged in greater enterprises, he did not deem these early successes of sufficient importance to merit the distinction of remark. His invalid wife, a lady famous in San Francisco for the costly nature of her entertainments and her exacting rigour with regard to the social position and 'antecedents' of those who attended them, accompanied the expedition. During a stroll among the shanties of the abandoned camp Mr Porfer directed the attention of his wife and friends to a dead tree on a low hill beyond Injun Creek.

'As I told you,' he said, 'I passed through this camp in 1852, and was told that no fewer than five men had been hanged here by vigilantes at different times, and all on that tree. If I am not mistaken, a rope is dangling from it yet. Let us go over and see the place.'

Mr Porfer did not add that the rope in question was perhaps the very one from whose fatal embrace his own neck had once had an escape so narrow that an hour's delay in taking himself out of that region would have spanned it.

Proceeding leisurely down the creek to a convenient crossing, the party came upon the cleanly picked skeleton of an animal which Mr Porfer after due examination pronounced to be that of an ass. The distinguishing ears were gone, but much of the inedible head had been spared by the beasts and birds, and the stout bridle of horsehair was intact, as was the riata, of similar material, connecting it with a picket pin still firmly sunken in the earth. The wooden and metallic elements of a miner's kit lay nearby. The customary remarks were made, cynical on the part of the men, sentimental and refined by the lady. A little later they stood by the tree in the cemetery and Mr Porfer sufficiently unbent from his dignity to place himself beneath the rotten rope and confidently lay a coil of it about his neck, somewhat, it appeared, to his own satisfaction, but greatly to the horror of his wife, to whose sensibilities the performance gave a smart shock.

An exclamation from one of the party gathered them all about an open grave, at the bottom of which they saw a confused mass of human bones and the broken remnants of a coffin. Coyotes and buzzards had performed the last sad rites for pretty much all else. Two skulls were visible and in order to investigate this somewhat unusual redundancy one of the younger men had the hardihood to spring into the grave and hand them up to another before Mrs Porfer could indicate her marked disapproval of so shocking an act, which, nevertheless, she did with considerable feeling and in very choice words. Pursuing his search among the dismal debris at the bottom of the grave the young man next handed up a rusted coffin plate, with a rudely cut inscription, which with difficulty Mr Porfer deciphered and read aloud with an earnest and not altogether unsuccessful attempt at the dramatic effect which he deemed befitting to the occasion and his rhetorical abilities:

MANUELITA MURPHY
Born at the Mission San Pedro
Died in Hurdy-Gurdy, Aged 47
Hell's full of such

In deference to the piety of the reader and the nerves of Mrs Porfer's fastidious sisterhood of both sexes let us not touch upon the painful impression produced by this uncommon inscription, further than to say that the elocutionary powers of Mr Porfer had never before met with so spontaneous and overwhelming recognition.

The next morsel that rewarded the ghoul in the grave was a long tangle of black hair defiled with clay: but this was such an anticlimax that it received little attention. Suddenly, with a short exclamation and a gesture of excitement, the young man unearthed a fragment of greyish rock, and after a hurried inspection handed it up to Mr Porfer. As the sunlight fell upon it it glittered with a yellow lustre – it was thickly studded with gleaming points. Mr Porfer snatched it, bent his head over it a moment and threw it lightly away with the simple remark: 'Iron pyrites – fool's gold.'

The young man in the discovery shaft was a trifle disconcerted, apparently.

Meanwhile, Mrs Porfer, unable longer to endure the disagreeable business, had walked back to the tree and seated herself at its root. While rearranging a tress of golden hair which had slipped from its confinement she was attracted by what appeared to be and really was the fragment of an old coat. Looking about to assure herself that so unladylike an act was not observed, she thrust her jewelled hand into the exposed breast pocket and drew out a mouldy pocket-book. Its contents were as follows:

One bundle of letters, postmarked 'Elizabethtown, New Jersey'.

One circle of blonde hair tied with a ribbon.

One photograph of a beautiful girl.

One ditto of same, singularly disfigured.

One name on back of photograph – 'Jefferson Doman'.

A few moments later a group of anxious gentlemen surrounded Mrs Porfer as she sat motionless at the foot of the tree, her head dropped forward, her fingers clutching a crushed photograph. Her husband raised her head, exposing a face ghastly white, except the long, deforming cicatrice, familiar to all her friends, which no art could ever hide, and which now traversed the pallor of her countenance like a visible curse.

Mary Matthews Porfer had the bad luck to be dead.

A Diagnosis of Death

'I am not so superstitious as some of your physicians – men of science, as you are pleased to be called,' said Hawver, replying to an accusation that had not been made. 'Some of you – only a few, I confess – believe in the immortality of the soul, and in apparitions which you have not the honesty to call ghosts. I go no further than a conviction that the living are sometimes seen where they are not, but have been – where they have lived so long, perhaps so intensely, as to have left their impress on everything about them. I know, indeed, that one's environment may be so affected by one's personality as to yield, long afterward, an image of one's self to the eyes of another. Doubtless the impressing personality has to be the right kind of personality as the perceiving eyes have to be the right kind of eyes – mine, for example.'

'Yes, the right kind of eyes, conveying sensations to the wrong kind of brain,' said Dr Frayley, smiling.

'Thank you; one likes to have an expectation gratified; that is about the reply that I supposed you would have the civility to make.'

'Pardon me. But you say that you know. That is a good deal to say, don't you think? Perhaps you will not mind the trouble of saying how you learned.'

'You will call it an hallucination,' Hawver said, 'but that does not matter.' And he told the story.

'Last summer I went, as you know, to pass the hot weather term in the town of Meridian. The relative at whose house I had intended to stay was ill, so I sought other quarters. After some difficulty I succeeded in renting a vacant dwelling that had been occupied by an eccentric doctor of the name of Mannering, who had gone away years before, no-one knew where, not even his agent. He had built the house himself and had lived in it with an old servant for about ten years. His practice, never very extensive, had after a few years been given up entirely. Not only so, but he had withdrawn himself almost altogether from social life and become a recluse. I was told by the village doctor, about the only person with whom he held any relations, that during his retirement he had devoted himself to a single line of study, the result of which he had expounded in a book that did not commend itself to the approval of his professional brethren, who, indeed, considered him not entirely sane. I have not seen the book and cannot now recall the title of it, but I am told that it expounded a rather startling theory. He held that it was possible in the case of many a person in good health to forecast his death with precision, several months in advance of the event. The limit, I think, was eighteen months. There were local tales of his having exerted his powers of prognosis, or perhaps you would say diagnosis; and it was said that in every instance the person whose friends he had warned had died suddenly at the appointed time, and from no assignable cause. All this, however, has nothing to do with what I have to tell; I thought it might amuse a physician.

'The house was furnished, just as he had lived in it. It was a rather gloomy dwelling for one who was neither a recluse nor a student, and I think it gave something of its character to me – perhaps some of its former occupant's character; for always I felt in it a certain melancholy that was not in my natural disposition, nor, I think, due to loneliness. I had no servants that slept in the house, but I have always been, as you know, rather fond of my own society, being much addicted to reading, though little to study. Whatever was the cause, the effect was dejection and a sense of impending evil; this was especially so in Dr Mannering's study, although that room was the lightest and most airy in the house. The doctor's life-size portrait in oil hung in that room, and seemed completely to dominate it. There was nothing unusual in the picture; the man was evidently rather good looking, about fifty years old, with iron-grey hair, a smooth-shaven face and dark, serious eyes. Something in the picture always drew and held my attention. The man's appearance became familiar to me, and rather "haunted" me.

'One evening I was passing through this room to my bedroom, with a lamp – there is no gas in Meridian. I stopped as usual before the portrait, which seemed in the lamplight to have a new expression, not easily named, but distinctly uncanny. It interested but did not disturb me. I moved the lamp from one side to the other and observed the effects of the altered light. While so engaged I felt an impulse to turn round. As I did so I saw a man moving across the room directly toward me! As soon as he came near enough for the lamplight to illuminate the face I saw that it was Dr Mannering himself; it was as if the portrait were walking!

' "I beg your pardon," I said, somewhat coldly, "but if you knocked I did not hear."

'He passed me, within an arm's length, lifted his right forefinger, as in warning, and without a word went on out of the room, though I observed his exit no more than I had observed his entrance.

'Of course, I need not tell you that this was what you will call an hallucination and I call an apparition. That room had only two doors, of which one was locked; the other led into a bedroom, from which there was no exit. My feeling on realising this is not an important part of the incident.

'Doubtless this seems to you a very commonplace "ghost story" – one constructed on the regular lines laid down by the old masters of the art. If that were so I should not have related it, even if it were true. The man was not dead; I met him today in Union Street. He passed me in a crowd.'

Hawver had finished his story and both men were silent. Dr Frayley absently drummed on the table with his fingers.

'Did he say anything today?' he asked – 'anything from which you inferred that he was not dead?'

Hawver stared and did not reply.

'Perhaps,' continued Frayley, 'he made a sign, a gesture – lifted a finger, as in warning. It's a trick he had – a habit when saying something serious – announcing the result of a diagnosis, for example.'

'Yes, he did – just as his apparition had done. But, good God! did you ever know him?'

Hawver was apparently growing nervous.

'I knew him. I have read his book, as will every physician some day. It is one of the most striking and important of the century's contributions to medical science. Yes, I knew him; I attended him in an illness three years ago. He died.'

Hawver sprang from his chair, manifestly disturbed. He strode forward and back across the room; then approached his friend, and in a voice not altogether steady, said: 'Doctor, have you anything to say to me – as a physician?'

'No, Hawver; you are the healthiest man I ever knew. As a friend I advise you to go to your room. You play the violin like an angel. Play it; play something light and lively. Get this cursed bad business off your mind.'

The next day Hawver was found dead in his room, the violin at his neck, the bow upon the strings, his music open before him at Chopin's funeral march.